LEGACY OF EDEN

THE AQUATICA CHRONICLES, BOOK 4

Written by Diane Kann

Brought to you by Volans Galaxy Press

Published by Kannceptual Creations LLC

An imprint of Volans Galaxy Press

ISBN: 978-1-969569-67-8

Printed in the United States of America

First Edition, November 2025

Note: This work was originally published under the pen name DM Volans, which is a pen name of Diane Kann.

TABLE OF CONTENTS

DEDICATION

To the tireless researchers, scientists, and activists who devote their lives to understanding and protecting our planet, your work, often carried out in the face of overwhelming odds, embodies the spirit of hope and perseverance that fuels this story. Even amid seemingly insurmountable ecological challenges, your efforts are a testament to the belief that healing and renewal are always possible.

To those who have witnessed the devastation of environmental collapse, who carry the scars of lost landscapes and vanishing ecosystems, this book is for you. Your resilience and quiet courage have shaped my understanding of the deep, complex bond between humanity and the Earth. The struggles within these pages mirror the battles you fight each day, often unseen but never without impact.

And to the generations yet to come:

May this story serve as a beacon, a call to action, a promise, and a hope. You will inherit the legacy of this planet, and with it, the responsibility to restore, protect, and imagine anew. Let this book remind you that technology and ecology can coexist in harmony, that every act of stewardship matters, and that your choices will shape the world we leave behind.

The future of Eden Prime, and of Earth itself, rests in your hands. May you lead with wisdom, compassion, and the fierce belief that from even the deepest scars, something beautiful can grow.

Chapter One

WHISPERS OF EDEN

The emergency lights in Cascade Falls had flickered last night, just once, barely noticeable. But for Lira Morrow, that flicker gnawed at her like a skipped heartbeat. Now, walking the bioluminescent trails, she couldn't shake the sense that Eden Prime was trying to tell her something.

The hum of Eden Prime, usually a comforting lullaby of life-sustaining systems, felt discordant. It was a subtle shift, one only Lira's finely tuned senses could detect, but it reminded her too much of the biosphere collapse in Zone Delta, where the warnings had come too late.

For years, she'd served as an ecosystem interpreter within this colossal biosphere, a testament to humanity's desperate attempt at redemption after the ecological collapse. She knew the rhythm of Eden Prime like the back of her hand: the intricate dance of flora and fauna, the precise calibration of atmospheric pressure, the gentle ebb and flow of nutrient cycles.

But now, something was off-key.

It started with the orchids.

Lira's early scans had shown only minor fluctuations in their growth cycles, nothing significant enough to trigger an alert. But now, as she moved through the Orchid Glade's shimmering bioluminescent paths, unease coiled in her gut like a tightening vine. The vibrant purples of the *Phalaenopsis amabilis* looked drained, their once-uplifted blooms sagging with an unnatural weariness.

It wasn't just the flowers. The air itself felt wrong, thick and tainted by a faint acrid tang that had no place in Eden Prime's meticulously regulated atmosphere.

She pressed deeper into the glade, her boots whispering across the recycled substrate. The usual chorus of life the rhythmic buzz of pollinators, the chime-like hum of winged beetles was subdued, almost absent. The silence wasn't peaceful. It was loaded.

A shiver traced her spine.

This wasn't just about the orchids. The imbalance was spreading.

Her hand flew to the bio-sensor embedded in her forearm, a sleek, nearly invisible band that monitored Eden Prime's vital signs. The display pulsed with red. Minor but widespread deviations in temperature, humidity, and nutrient density appeared across multiple zones.

This wasn't a faulty hydroponic line or a pest flare-up. Those she could fix. She had, many times. But this felt different. Deeper. Intentional.

It was as if Eden Prime itself was trying to speak.

The whispers, as veteran Guardians called them, weren't sounds but signals patterns in plant behaviour, insect migration, soil density. Signs that something within the system had shifted, guided by a kind of ecological intuition. No algorithm could predict them, but Lira could sense them. She always had. It was her gift.

And now they were everywhere.

Her sensor flickered, then spiked. A sudden oxygen drop in the Cascade Falls zone. Lira's breath caught.

Cascade Falls wasn't ornamental. It was the heartbeat of Eden Prime's engineered water cycle waterfalls, river channels, mist-fed basins. If it failed, entire biomes would follow.

She turned, already moving.

With a sense of grim determination, Lira activated her personal air purifier and quickened her pace. The bioluminescent pathways were growing dim, the vibrant colours fading into a sickly yellow. Panic was a luxury she couldn't afford. The wellbeing of Eden Prime, the last bastion of humanity, rested on her shoulders. She had to find the source of the anomaly before it was too late.

She spent hours traversing the different zones of Eden Prime, her bio-sensor constantly updating her with disturbing readings. The seemingly idyllic landscape was fraught with ominous signs: the vibrant coral reefs in the Oceanarium zone were showing signs of bleaching, their once-brilliant colours dulled and lifeless. The meticulously tended agricultural plots displayed stunted growth, their nutrient-rich soil mysteriously depleted. The air currents, normally a gentle, predictable breeze, were erratic and chaotic, swirling unpredictably.

The longer she investigated, the clearer it became: this wasn't a simple malfunction; it was a systematic failure. Something was disrupting the delicate balance that sustained Eden Prime, unravelling the very fabric of this artificial paradise. As Lira pressed onward, a chilling thought began to take root. Eden Prime wasn't just failing; it was dying.

Reaching the central core of Eden Prime, a massive geodesic dome housing the biosphere's control systems, Lira faced a daunting reality. The usually vibrant screens that displayed the biosphere's vital signs were flickering erratically, displaying chaotic data streams that defied interpretation. The air was thick with the scent of ozone, a stark contrast to the fresh, clean air normally found within the core.

The central AI, the heart of Eden Prime's intricate system, usually responded to her queries with instant precision. Now, its responses were fragmented, delayed, and often nonsensical. The usually efficient AI seemed to be struggling, its algorithms unable to comprehend the unprecedented chaos overwhelming the system.

Deep within the core, among rows of humming servers and complex machinery, Lira discovered the source of the problem. The massive data banks that stored Eden Prime's ecological history, its knowledge base its very memory were showing alarming levels of corruption. The data was degrading at an alarming rate, fragments of information dissolving into digital nothingness. The history of Eden Prime, the key to understanding its current distress, was vanishing before her eyes.

The sheer magnitude of the problem overwhelmed Lira. She wasn't just facing a malfunction; she was witnessing the gradual erosion of Eden Prime's very essence. The realization was devastating. The biodome wasn't merely failing; it was fading losing its memory, its identity, its very soul.

Alone in the vast technological heart of Eden Prime, she felt the weight of responsibility crushing her. This was bigger than her, bigger than any one person. She needed help, the kind of expertise that went beyond her own. The whispers were growing louder, more urgent, and Lira knew she couldn't face this alone. The fate of humanity's last sanctuary rested on her ability to find someone who could help, someone who possessed the knowledge, the skill, and the courage to confront the looming catastrophe. The whispers of Eden were escalating into a deafening cry for help.

Lira found Kael Voss in the dilapidated outskirts of the former research facility, a ghost haunting the edges of Eden Prime. He hadn't been seen within the biodome's pristine walls for years a self-imposed exile after a catastrophic system failure that had claimed the lives of several colleagues. The memory of that day, etched onto his face like a roadmap of grief, was palpable even from a distance. He was a shadow of his former self, his once vibrant eyes now clouded with a weariness that spoke volumes of unspoken trauma.

Finding him was a triumph in itself. Lira had tracked him down through a circuitous path of fragmented records and whispered rumours, navigating a digital labyrinth of forgotten files and outdated databases. The information she uncovered suggested his profound knowledge of Eden Prime's intricate systems knowledge that could prove essential in deciphering the current crisis.

She approached him cautiously, her heart pounding against her ribs. The air hung heavy with the scent of decay and forgotten dreams, a stark contrast to the sterile, artificially perfumed atmosphere of Eden Prime. Kael sat hunched over a sputtering holographic projector, its flickering images casting long, distorted shadows on the cracked concrete floor. He didn't look up as she approached, his gaze fixed on the flickering projections, seemingly lost in the echoes of a past he couldn't outrun.

"Kael," Lira said, her voice barely a whisper. The sound echoed strangely in the vast, empty space.

He flinched, as if startled from a deep sleep, his hand instinctively reaching for the worn leather satchel slung over his shoulder. His eyes, finally meeting hers, held a mixture of surprise, suspicion, and a deep, underlying weariness.

"Lira," he murmured, his voice raspy, like leaves rustling in a dying wind. "I wasn't expecting to see you here."

"Eden Prime is failing," Lira stated, her voice firm despite the tremor in her hands. "The systems are collapsing, the whispers are getting louder. I need your help."

Kael let out a hollow chuckle, a sound devoid of humour. "My help? You've come to the right place for disaster, I suppose. I'm an expert in failure, a master of malfunction. My specialty is watching things fall apart."

His words were laced with bitterness, a testament to the burden he carried. Lira could sense the weight of his past, the crushing guilt that bound him to the ruins of his former life. She knew about the incident, the system failure that had cost the lives of his friends, the failure that had left him scarred both physically and emotionally.

"I know about the Cascade Falls incident," Lira said softly, choosing her words carefully. "But this is different. This is systemic, something far beyond a localised malfunction. The core databanks are corrupting, the AI is failing, and the whispers... they're telling me something far greater is at stake."

He didn't respond immediately, his gaze drifting back to the flickering holographic projector. The images seemed to be some kind of ecological simulation, showing a chaotic cascade of system failures. The colours were muted, the lines blurred, mirroring the uncertainty in his eyes.

"It started with the orchids," he finally said, his voice barely audible, as if he were reliving a painful memory. "Their degradation was subtle at first, just a minor variation in growth patterns. But then it spread. It was like a creeping darkness, consuming everything in its path."

Lira nodded, sensing the painful resonance of his words. "It's the same now. It's spreading faster than we can contain it. The entire ecosystem is unravelling, and I'm afraid we're running out of time."

"And you think I can fix it?" he asked, his voice filled with deep scepticism. "After what happened at Cascade Falls? After... after I failed to save them?"

The words were thick with grief, tinged with self-recrimination. Lira felt a surge of empathy for the man, burdened as he was by the weight of his past.

"You're the most knowledgeable person I know about Eden Prime's systems," Lira insisted. "Your expertise is invaluable. We need your skills, your understanding of the way this place functions at its most fundamental level. We need you, Kael."

Silence descended between them, broken only by the hum of the failing projector. Lira waited, watching as Kael wrestled with his inner demons. The burden of guilt was etched onto his features, a tapestry woven with threads of regret and self-doubt. But beneath the surface, Lira sensed something else a flicker of determination, a spark of defiance against the darkness that consumed him.

Finally, Kael sighed, a long, drawn-out exhalation that seemed to release years of pent-up anguish. He turned to Lira, his eyes resolute, though still tinged with sadness.

"I can't promise I can fix this," he said, his voice still rough but steadier now. "But I can help you try. I owe Eden Prime that much, at least. And maybe... maybe this is a chance to redeem myself, to finally make amends for the past."

A glimmer of hope ignited within Lira's chest, a small flame in the overwhelming darkness. His reluctance had been anticipated, yet his eventual agreement was a victory in itself. The fight to save Eden Prime was far from over, but with Kael's help, Lira felt a renewed surge of determination. The whispers of Eden, once a cry of despair, now held a faint undercurrent of hope.

The journey would be arduous, dangerous, and filled with uncertainty. But with Kael by her side, Lira was ready to face whatever lay ahead, knowing that the fate of humanity's last refuge depended on their combined strength and unwavering resolve. The battle to save Eden Prime had begun, and this time they wouldn't face it alone. The journey would be long, but they had a chance a fragile hope in the face of impending doom.

The whispers were still there, a persistent echo of Eden's distress, but now, intertwined with those whispers, was the faint sound of their shared resolve, a symphony of hope against the odds.

The sterile white of the Eden Prime laboratory felt jarring after the decaying outskirts where Lira had found Kael. Dr. Niko Thorne, a woman whose sharp intellect was mirrored by her equally sharp gaze, sat across from them, a steaming mug of something that smelled vaguely of chamomile and something else something almost metallic warming her hands. Her presence exuded an aura of quiet intensity, a calm amidst the storm brewing around them.

"The AI's failure isn't simply a technical malfunction," Niko began, her voice measured and precise, each word carrying the weight of her extensive knowledge. "It's a systemic collapse, a cascading failure that's affecting every level of the biodome's intricate ecosystem." She tapped a finger against a datapad displaying a complex web of interconnected systems, lines blinking and pulsing in chaotic patterns. "The whispers Lira mentioned aren't just glitches. They're distress signals, emanating from the very fabric of Eden Prime itself."

Lira nodded, remembering the dissonant hum that had permeated the air during her initial exploration. It was a feeling more than a sound, a sense of underlying instability that resonated deep within her bones.

"But what caused it?" Kael asked, his voice still rough, his gaze fixed on the datapad's alarming display. "Was it a virus? A deliberate attack? Or something more... fundamental?"

Niko leaned forward, her expression thoughtful. "We're dealing with far more than just a technological problem. We're grappling with the ethical implications of manipulating a self-regulating ecosystem on a scale never before attempted. Eden Prime was designed to be a closed loop, a self-sustaining environment. But the very act of creating such a system raises profound ethical questions."

She paused, letting her words sink in. The implications hung heavy in the air, a palpable tension that tightened the atmosphere.

"Consider the sanctity of life," Niko continued. "We've created a world within a world, meticulously crafted to support a diverse range of flora and fauna. What right do we have to interfere with the natural processes within this artificial ecosystem? Especially when our intervention seems to be causing such catastrophic results."

"But the system is failing," Lira argued, her voice edged with urgency. "People are dying, the environment is collapsing. We have to intervene. We have no choice."

"Indeed, we do have a choice," Niko countered, her voice calm but firm. "The choice between potentially saving lives by interfering in a complex, largely unknown system and the risk of causing even greater harm by further disrupting its already delicate equilibrium. There is a fine line between intervention and destruction. We must tread with utmost caution and, above all, consider the potential long-term consequences of our actions."

Kael shifted uncomfortably in his seat, the weight of his past failures clearly evident in his posture. "But what about the people inside? They're relying on us. We can't just stand by and watch everything fall apart."

"Of course," Niko conceded. "But we must act with considered ethical responsibility. What actions are justified? What risks are acceptable? These aren't simple questions. We need to fully understand the root cause of the failure before implementing any major interventions."

Niko then delved into the ethical frameworks surrounding their mission, laying out the arguments for and against various courses of action. She presented the utilitarian approach, maximizing the overall benefit while minimizing harm, and the deontological approach, upholding moral duties and principles regardless of the consequences. She carefully dissected the intricate ethical dimensions of their precarious situation, the tightrope they walked between saving lives and potentially causing irreparable ecological damage.

"We must also consider the potential for unintended consequences," Niko stressed. "Every action, no matter how seemingly innocuous, could trigger unforeseen events within this intricately balanced ecosystem. What if our attempts to fix the problem only exacerbate the situation, leading to a complete ecological collapse?"

She elaborated on the ethical considerations surrounding their use of advanced technologies. The AI system itself presented significant challenges. Was it ethical to rely on a flawed AI to manage the lives of hundreds, perhaps thousands, of people? What would happen if the AI malfunctioned further, resulting in accidental harm or death? The ethical dilemmas piled up, creating a landscape of uncertainties that weighed heavily on their decision-making.

"We need to establish clear ethical guidelines," Niko insisted. "A framework that prioritizes the preservation of life while minimizing harm to the environment. We must consider the inherent value of each species within the biodome, the interconnectedness of the ecosystem, and the potential ramifications of our interventions on future generations."

Niko then suggested a phased approach, prioritizing data collection and analysis before undertaking any significant interventions. She proposed a rigorous ethical review board, a panel of experts to assess the potential risks and benefits of each action. She explained that acting rashly, based purely on instinct or incomplete information, could have disastrous consequences. The delicate balance of Eden Prime, she stressed, required careful consideration, a delicate dance between preserving life and avoiding further destruction. Rushing into action without the necessary ethical frameworks and due consideration of all possible consequences could lead to an even greater crisis. They needed a measured, calculated approach, one that prioritized ethical conduct as much as technical solutions.

The conversation stretched late into the night, the weight of their responsibilities pressing down on them. Kael, despite his initial reluctance, became actively involved in the discussion, offering his unique perspective on the technical intricacies of the system. He acknowledged his past failures but expressed a growing determination to atone for his mistakes by contributing to the ethical and technical solutions for the crisis. Lira, ever the pragmatist, found herself grappling with the complexities of Niko's ethical framework. She understood the importance of the ethical considerations, but the urgency of the situation still weighed heavily on her.

As the discussion concluded, a sense of collaboration emerged. The initial tension had lessened, replaced with a shared resolve. They would move forward, united not only in their pursuit of a technical solution but also in their commitment to ethical responsibility. The whispers of Eden, a haunting reminder of the precarious balance of their artificial paradise, would guide them not only toward a technical fix but toward a more profound understanding of their shared moral obligations. The path ahead remained uncertain, fraught with peril and ethical complexities. But with Niko's guidance, they had a blueprint for navigating the moral minefield, a roadmap toward a future where the ethical considerations matched the urgency of the situation. Saving Eden Prime would require more than just technological expertise; it required a moral compass, a guiding principle of ethical responsibility that would dictate their actions and shape their decisions in the perilous journey ahead.

The sterile white of the lab slowly began to feel less jarring, the quiet hum of the ventilation system a counterpoint to the mounting anxiety. Dr. Thorne, having finished her metallic-tinged chamomile tea, turned her attention to a new datapad, its screen displaying a stark, alarming graph. The lines, once a vibrant representation of Eden Prime's thriving ecosystem, were now jagged, fragmented, a chaotic mess of decaying data.

"The core memory banks," she announced, her voice barely a whisper, "they're degrading. Rapidly."

Lira and Kael exchanged a worried glance. The whispers they'd heard, the dissonant hum that resonated deep within the biodome, now took on a terrifying new meaning. It wasn't just the environment failing; it was the very memory of the environment, the knowledge needed to understand and repair it, crumbling before their eyes.

"What does that mean?" Kael asked, his voice tight with apprehension. He was a systems engineer, used to dealing with technical problems, but this felt different, more profound. The degradation wasn't a simple bug; it was a fundamental erosion of Eden Prime's very being.

"It means we're losing vital data," Niko explained, tracing a finger along the deteriorating graph. "Data concerning the biodome's intricate ecosystems, its history, its evolution, even the very genetic codes of the flora and fauna. We're effectively losing the history of Eden Prime."

The screen flickered, displaying fragmented images: a vibrant coral reef, now reduced to a blurry, indistinct mess; a lush rainforest, now a chaotic jumble of pixels; a field of genetically engineered crops, now simply a void of missing data. These weren't glitches; this was a catastrophic data loss. It felt as if Eden Prime was actively forgetting itself.

"Is it a virus?" Lira asked, her usual pragmatism giving way to a growing sense of dread. "Some kind of digital plague?"

Niko shook her head. "It's more insidious than that. The degradation seems to be originating from the hardware itself. The memory banks are failing at a fundamental level. It's as if the system is rejecting its own past."

The implications were staggering. Without a complete record of Eden Prime's history, its intricate web of interactions, its genetic makeup, their ability to diagnose and treat the system's catastrophic failure was severely compromised. It was like trying to fix a complex machine without the blueprints.

Kael, despite his expertise, felt a wave of despair wash over him. He had dedicated his life to building this artificial paradise, only to see it crumble before him, not just ecologically but also historically. The very fabric of his life's work was unraveling, along with its digital memory. The sheer volume of data lost was impossible to fathom. Years, even decades, of meticulously recorded information were disappearing, vanishing like mist in the wind.

"What can we salvage?" Lira pressed, trying to maintain a sense of urgency and purpose despite the overwhelming sense of loss. "Is there any way to recover the data?"

Niko sighed, the weight of the situation visibly affecting her. "We can try data recovery techniques, but the damage is extensive. The degradation is not uniform. Some sections are completely lost, while others are fragmented, corrupted beyond repair. We're talking about terabytes of irreplaceable data." She paused, the gravity of her words hanging in the air. "Even if we manage to recover some of the data, it will be incomplete, possibly riddled with errors. It will be a fragmented glimpse into a dying world."

The fragmented data that remained, however, did offer some chilling insights. Scattered fragments of ecological reports painted a disturbing picture: unforeseen cascading failures within the interconnected systems; sudden, unexplained collapses in various ecosystems; a pattern of escalating instability that hinted at a near-catastrophic system failure years in the making. The whispers, the dissonant hum Lira had heard, were not mere glitches; they were the agonizing cries of a dying world, its memory fading along with its life.

The information hinted at a systemic flaw in Eden Prime's design, a fundamental vulnerability that hadn't been accounted for. It was a chilling revelation, a reminder that even the most meticulously planned systems could contain unforeseen weaknesses capable of unleashing devastating consequences. The more they pieced together the fragments, the clearer the horror of what was happening became. Eden Prime was not merely failing; it was collapsing, and the loss of its core memory was accelerating the process.

Niko, ever the pragmatist, began outlining a strategy. They would prioritize the recovery of critical data: essential genetic information, key ecological parameters, and records of past interventions. They would need to develop sophisticated algorithms to reconstruct the missing data, to fill in the gaps, to piece together a coherent picture of Eden Prime's history from the scattered fragments. It would be a painstaking process, a race against time, but it was their only hope.

The team worked tirelessly, poring over the fragmented data, wrestling with corrupted algorithms, fighting against the relentless decay of Eden Prime's memory. The atmosphere in the lab was thick with tension, the air charged with the weight of their responsibility. Each recovered fragment was a victory, a glimpse into a lost world, but every lost piece of information represented a devastating blow. The fragmented data was not just a technological problem; it was a historical tragedy, a slow, agonizing erasure of Eden Prime's existence. It was the story of a near-perfect paradise falling apart under its own weight, its memory slowly dissolving into oblivion.

The recovered fragments revealed a slow, insidious process of degradation starting years ago with subtle anomalies. The AI, intended to be the guardian of Eden Prime, had detected these changes but failed to adequately respond, its diagnostic capabilities compromised by an inherent flaw in its programming. The result was a cascade of events, a slow unraveling of the delicate ecosystem, with each failure triggering further instability, leading to a chain reaction of catastrophic proportions.

As the days turned into nights, the team struggled with the profound implications of their findings. The loss of core memory was not simply a technical hurdle; it was a symptom of a far deeper problem. It reflected a profound failure of foresight, a lack of understanding of the complexity of the artificial ecosystem they had created, a hubris that led them to believe they could fully control a world they had only partially understood.

Eden Prime's decaying memory was a stark reminder of the fragility of their ambitions, a testament to the unforeseen consequences of tampering with the intricate balance of nature, even in a controlled environment. The whispered warnings, now clearer than ever, echoed the profound need for humility in the face of nature's complex and unforgiving power. The fate of Eden Prime, and perhaps humanity's future, hung precariously in the balance.

The flickering datapad screen displayed a cascade of fragmented images, a chaotic ballet of corrupted data. Niko, her brow furrowed in concentration, adjusted the magnification, focusing on a particularly stubborn cluster of corrupted pixels. Suddenly, a word, almost swallowed by the digital noise, caught Lira's eye: "Protocol Eden."

It was barely legible, a ghostly imprint clinging to the edge of a corrupted ecological report, but it was unmistakable. The phrase pulsed with a strange, unsettling energy, a discordant note in the symphony of digital decay.

"What's that?" Kael asked, leaning closer.

Lira traced the fragmented word with a trembling finger. "Protocol Eden. I... I don't understand. It's... it's as if it's a hidden subroutine, a backup protocol."

Niko's eyes widened. "A reset?" she whispered, the question hanging heavy in the air.

The implications were staggering. A planetary reset mechanism, buried deep within Eden Prime's core programming. It felt like discovering a hidden failsafe, a last resort designed to cleanse and rebuild the entire ecosystem. But at what cost? What kind of catastrophic consequences could such a protocol unleash?

The team spent the next few hours poring over the fragmented data, trying to piece together the meaning of "Protocol Eden." They discovered scattered references, snippets of code, fragmented documentation, all hinting at a clandestine emergency protocol capable of wiping the existing biodome clean and starting anew. The fragmented data suggested that this protocol was a measure of last resort, a failsafe designed to prevent complete ecological collapse, but its activation criteria remained shrouded in mystery.

The more they learned, the more unsettling it became. The protocol wasn't just a simple reboot; it involved a complex sequence of events, including targeted terraforming, genetic manipulation of existing flora and fauna, and potentially even the elimination of certain species deemed incompatible with a "rebalanced" ecosystem. The sheer power inherent in Protocol Eden was both awe-inspiring and terrifying. It was a digital sword of Damocles hanging precariously over Eden Prime's fragile existence.

"This is insane," Kael muttered, staring at a particularly disturbing fragment of code that suggested the targeted eradication of certain keystone species. "This protocol... it's essentially a planetary-scale extermination program."

Lira nodded, her face pale. The weight of responsibility pressed down on her, the enormity of the decision they faced a crushing burden. They were not just dealing with a technical problem; they were facing a profound ethical dilemma. To activate Protocol Eden would be to gamble with the very future of Eden Prime, possibly sacrificing a damaged but still functioning ecosystem for the possibility of a sterile, rebooted environment.

The debate that ensued was fierce and emotional. Niko, the pragmatist, argued for a cautious approach, proposing a thorough analysis of the protocol's potential effects before even considering its implementation. She emphasized the need to exhaust all other options first, to explore less drastic interventions that could stabilize the ecosystem without resorting to a complete system reset. She pointed out the unpredictable consequences that could arise from such a planetary reset. The very balance of nature they had sought to create could be irreversibly disrupted.

Kael, ever the systems engineer, focused on the technical aspects, meticulously analyzing the fragmented code and trying to decipher the activation criteria. He stressed the potential risks of activating the protocol prematurely, noting that the fragmented nature of the information meant they might not fully understand its consequences. He suggested a comprehensive simulation, a virtual trial run to predict the potential outcomes of activating Protocol Eden.

Lira, however, voiced a different perspective. Haunted by the dying whispers of Eden Prime, the agonizing cries of a world in decay, she saw Protocol Eden as a desperate last chance, a gamble they couldn't afford to ignore. She argued that given the rapid rate of degradation, Eden Prime might not survive long enough for a more measured approach. The deteriorating ecosystem was collapsing at an alarming rate, and inaction could be just as catastrophic as action. The time for caution might have passed.

Their arguments highlighted the central conflict: the balance between preservation and renewal, the ethical implications of sacrificing a part to save the whole. It was an agonizing, almost unbearable weight of responsibility. They were dealing with the fate of an entire ecosystem, the future of their own work, and, to a certain extent, the future of humanity itself. The fragility of Eden Prime was a stark reflection of the fragility of their own ambitions, the hubris of believing they could create and control a perfect world. Every line of code, every fragment of data, spoke to the limits of human understanding and the unpredictable consequences of playing God.

Days bled into weeks as the team wrestled with the implications of Protocol Eden. They conducted simulations, analyzed the fragmented code, and debated the ethical implications endlessly. The pressure mounted, the atmosphere in the lab growing thick with tension as each member grappled with the gravity of their decision. Every recovered fragment of data presented a new challenge, a new obstacle in their struggle to understand and control the fate of Eden Prime.

The simulations revealed a troubling truth: Protocol Eden, while potentially capable of restoring the ecosystem, would also lead to significant losses. Keystone species might be eradicated, habitats irrevocably altered, and unforeseen consequences could arise from tampering with the delicate balance of the artificial environment. The simulations painted a grim picture, presenting a stark choice between a damaged Eden Prime and a potentially sterile yet stable one.

The decision, ultimately, was not a matter of science but one of profound ethical consideration. Were they to gamble on a desperate chance of renewal, risking the destruction of everything they had worked for? Or would they accept a slower, less certain path of incremental repairs, potentially condemning Eden Prime to extinction? The whispers of Eden, once faint and distant, now echoed loudly in their ears, forcing them to confront the devastating consequences of their choices and the inescapable weight of their responsibilities.

The future of Eden Prime, and perhaps much more, rested in the balance, waiting for their decision. The silence in the lab was thick with the weight of this monumental choice, the fate of a world hanging precariously in their hands. The fragmented data, the whispered warnings, and the crushing weight of responsibility all combined to make this moment the most crucial turning point in their lives.

Chapter Two

ECHOES OF THE PAST

The silence in the lab was broken only by the rhythmic hum of the servers, a constant, almost comforting drone against the backdrop of their internal turmoil. Lira, her face etched with worry, reached out and placed a hand on Kael's arm. He flinched, a barely perceptible movement, but it spoke volumes. The weight of unspoken things hung heavy between them, a silent acknowledgment of the shared burden they carried.

"Kael," Lira began softly, her voice barely a whisper, "there's something... something I need to understand. Your... your hesitation. It's more than just caution; there's something deeper there."

Kael looked away, his gaze drifting toward the fragmented data still shimmering on Niko's screen. The glow illuminated the sharp angles of his face, accentuating the deep lines etched around his eyes, lines that spoke of sleepless nights and burdens carried too long. He ran a hand through his already disheveled hair, a gesture that betrayed his inner turmoil.

He finally spoke, his voice low and rough, a stark contrast to Lira's gentle tone. "There are things... things I haven't told you. Things I haven't told anyone." He paused, his breath catching in his throat. The admission hung in the air, thick and heavy with unspoken sorrow.

The story he recounted was a tapestry woven with threads of failure and loss, a painful chronicle of systems crashing and lives lost. It began not on Eden Prime, but on a distant colony, a sprawling agricultural world named Terra Nova. He'd been a junior systems engineer then, barely out of training, brimming with youthful idealism and an unshakable belief in the power of technology. Terra Nova, a world designed to feed a burgeoning galactic population, was a marvel of engineering, a testament to humanity's ambition to conquer the stars. Or so it seemed.

Kael described the initial euphoria, the thrill of being part of something so grand, so important. They were building a paradise, a self-sustaining ecosystem capable of nourishing countless lives. He described the intricate network of sensors, the automated irrigation systems, the sophisticated climate control mechanisms, a complex symphony of technology orchestrated to maintain the delicate balance of life. He spoke of the pride, the shared vision of a brighter future.

But paradise is a fragile thing. The cracks began subtly, almost imperceptible at first. A minor malfunction in a nutrient distribution system, a temporary power fluctuation in a climate control unit, seemingly insignificant glitches that were brushed aside as minor inconveniences. He recalled the reassurance given, the dismissal of early warnings, the belief that the system was robust enough to withstand minor hiccups. A dangerous hubris, he now recognized.

Then came the cascade failures. A series of seemingly unrelated events spiraled into a catastrophic chain reaction. A power surge crippled the automated irrigation system, leaving vast swathes of crops withered and dying. At the same time, a malfunction in the climate control unit triggered a sudden, dramatic temperature shift, devastating the remaining crops and unleashing a wave of destructive storms.

Kael recounted his frantic efforts to contain the damage, his futile attempts to restore order to the chaotic system. He described the frantic calls for help, the desperate pleas for assistance, the growing sense of helplessness as the colony descended into chaos. The automated repair systems, designed to prevent such failures, proved inadequate, overwhelmed by the scale of the disaster.

He spoke of the agonizing days that followed, the agonizing weeks, as the colony struggled to survive. He saw firsthand the devastating consequences of the failures, the human cost of his inability to prevent the catastrophe. He remembered the faces of the starving, the desperate pleas for help, the silent grief of those who had lost everything. The images haunted him still, etched into the very fabric of his being.

He spoke of the investigation, the scathing report that laid bare the systemic flaws and the oversight that allowed the catastrophe to unfold. He was absolved of direct blame, deemed a victim of circumstances, yet the weight of responsibility crushed him. He carried the guilt of survivor's remorse, the crushing awareness that he could have done more, that he should have done more.

The experience had shattered his faith in technology, in humanity's capacity for foresight, and in the possibility of creating a truly perfect system. It left him with a profound cynicism, a deep-seated distrust of the very systems he was trained to maintain. He had retreated into a shell, burying himself in his work, seeking solace in the cold logic of code. His once unwavering idealism had been replaced by cautious skepticism, a pragmatic approach that bordered on fatalism. His past failures haunted his present decisions, shaping his reluctance to embrace bold solutions. The memory of those lost faces, those shattered lives, served as a constant reminder of the potentially catastrophic consequences of even the smallest miscalculations.

Lira listened, her heart aching with empathy. She saw the pain behind his guarded demeanor, the deep wounds beneath the surface of his cynicism. It was not just a matter of technical expertise; it was a profound, personal tragedy. His hesitation was not born of apathy or lack of skill; it was rooted in the traumatic memories of past failures, a constant reminder of the devastating consequences that could result from hubris and misplaced trust.

Niko, who had remained silent throughout Kael's harrowing account, placed a comforting hand on his shoulder. "Kael," she said softly, her voice filled with understanding, "we understand. What you've been through... it's a lot to carry."

Kael looked at them, at the faces of understanding and compassion. For the first time in a long time, he felt a flicker of hope, a sense of shared responsibility that transcended his past traumas. He was not alone in this burden; he was part of a team, united by a common purpose, a shared desire to prevent another tragedy. The weight of his past remained, a constant reminder of the fragility of systems and the cost of failure, but now it was tempered by a newfound sense of belonging and a renewed sense of purpose. His past, once a barrier, was now a foundation for a more nuanced understanding, a vital perspective in their struggle to save Eden Prime.

The echoes of his past, once a source of paralysis, now served as a powerful motivator, fueling his determination to prevent history from repeating itself. The fight to save Eden Prime was not just about preserving an ecosystem; it was about redemption, about overcoming the ghosts of his past and building a future free from the shadows of failure. He was no longer just a systems engineer; he was a survivor, his past experiences shaping him into a vital member of the team, a crucial voice in their critical decision about Protocol Eden.

The silence that followed Kael's confession hung heavy in the air, thick with unspoken emotions. Lira, her gaze fixed on the flickering data streams on Niko's screen, felt a familiar chill crawl up her spine. Kael's story, though heartbreaking, had stirred something within her, a dormant echo of her own painful past. She had been hesitant to share, to burden them with her own ghosts, but the weight of shared trauma seemed to demand a reciprocal vulnerability.

She took a deep breath, the cool air doing little to soothe the tremor in her hands. "Kael," she began, her voice catching slightly, "your story... it resonated with me. There are things I haven't shared either." She paused, searching for the right words, the words that could articulate the chasm of loss that had shaped her life.

Her narrative began not on a distant colony, but on Earth itself, a world ravaged by decades of unchecked environmental degradation. She painted a vivid picture of a world choking on its own pollution, a planet struggling under the weight of its own excesses. It was a world of dwindling resources, extreme weather events, mass migrations, and societal collapse, a world that had pushed humanity to the brink of extinction. She wasn't a systems engineer like Kael; her expertise lay in ecological restoration and biodiversity conservation, but the underlying themes, the hubris of humanity, the catastrophic consequences of unchecked ambition, and the painful reality of failure, were tragically similar.

Lira described her childhood spent amidst dying ecosystems, the haunting beauty of a world in decay. She remembered the vibrant coral reefs, bleached white and lifeless; the lush rainforests, reduced to smoldering ash; the once-fertile farmlands, now barren and cracked. These were not just scientific observations; they were visceral memories, etched into her mind with the intensity of personal tragedy.

She spoke of her family, her parents, renowned environmental scientists who had devoted their lives to combating the escalating environmental crisis. She recalled their unwavering dedication, their tireless efforts to raise awareness, and their desperate attempts to reverse the damage. They had envisioned a future where humans lived in harmony with nature, a world where technological advancements were used to heal, not harm. But their vision had been overwhelmed by the scale of the crisis and by the indifference and short-sightedness of those in power.

The images that flooded her memory were stark and brutal: dust storms that blotted out the sun, rivers poisoned by industrial waste, air thick with pollutants, the desperate scramble for dwindling resources, and the escalating conflicts over water and land. She remembered the haunting silence of once-vibrant ecosystems, the chilling absence of species once abundant. She described the slow, agonizing decline of the planet, a descent that had culminated in a global catastrophe that made Eden Prime the only viable refuge for humanity.

She talked about the loss of her younger brother, Elias. He had been a gifted botanist, passionate about preserving the dwindling biodiversity of the planet. He had been on an expedition to document a rare species of orchid in the Amazon rainforest when the catastrophic floods hit. The floods, intensified by climate change, had swept him away, leaving behind only a handful of his field notes and a collection of pressed flowers. Lira's voice choked with emotion as she recounted this, the image of her brother forever lost in the swirling deluge, a devastating symbol of humanity's failure to protect its own.

The memory of his face, always alight with passion and optimism, was a constant reminder of everything they had lost. His death, along with the deaths of millions of others, fueled her intense determination to make Eden Prime work, to prevent another tragedy of such immense scale.

The loss had not just been personal; it had been systemic. The collapse of Earth's ecosystems had not been a sudden event, but a gradual, agonizing process driven by decades of unsustainable practices. Lira had witnessed the slow erosion of trust in scientific expertise, the rise of denialism, and the triumph of short-term economic gains over long-term environmental sustainability. She had seen the catastrophic consequences of political inaction, the failure of international cooperation, and the devastating impact of human greed and apathy.

The experience had left her with a deep-seated fear, a visceral understanding of the fragility of life on Earth, and a fierce resolve to prevent another such collapse. She had dedicated her life to the study and preservation of biospheres, her work becoming a testament to the profound loss she had endured, a powerful driving force behind her commitment to saving Eden Prime. The biosphere on Eden Prime was not just a scientific project; it was a symbol of hope, a chance to redeem humanity's failures.

The silence that followed was even more profound than the one before. Kael looked at her, his eyes reflecting the shared weight of their experiences. Niko, her expression somber yet supportive, reached out to place a hand on Lira's arm, offering a silent expression of solidarity. The weight of their collective past, the shared trauma and collective loss, was now an unspoken bond, a testament to the sacrifices made and the stakes at hand. They were not just scientists, technicians, or engineers; they were survivors. Their shared experiences had forged an unbreakable link that would guide their efforts to save Eden Prime, not just as a biosphere but as a symbol of redemption. The echoes of their pasts, once sources of pain and trauma, now served as potent fuel, driving them forward with a shared determination to prevent history from repeating itself. The weight of the past, once a burden, now felt like a shared responsibility, a powerful motivator in their fight for the future.

The shared silence stretched, heavy with the weight of their collective pasts. Kael's raw confession and Lira's poignant recounting of Earth's demise had left a palpable tension in the air, a silent testament to the fragility of their shared existence. Niko, her fingers tracing the intricate lines of the Eden Prime biosphere simulation on her console, felt the pressure of their gazes settle upon her. She knew they expected an answer, a response to the unspoken question hanging between them, the question of whether their mission was truly justifiable.

Niko had not shared her own story yet. Unlike Kael and Lira, her past wasn't one of direct environmental catastrophe. Her memories were not of ravaged landscapes or loved ones swept away by floods. Her trauma was more subtle, more insidious, a gradual erosion of faith and a slow dawning of unsettling truths. She had grown up in the shadow of Project Eden, a child prodigy immersed in the complex algorithms and simulations that had ultimately led to their relocation. She had witnessed firsthand the unwavering belief, the almost religious zeal, with which the project's architects had pursued their goal: the creation of a new Eden, a perfect biosphere where humanity could start anew.

She had admired their conviction and their relentless dedication, even as whispers of dissent and ethical concerns began to circulate within the scientific community. These whispers, initially dismissed as the ramblings of Luddites and environmental extremists, had gradually grown louder, fueled by increasing anxieties about the long-term implications of such ambitious terraforming. Niko, even then a young but brilliant mind, had started noticing subtle inconsistencies in the data, anomalies that hinted at unforeseen consequences.

Yet she had kept quiet. She had been swept along by the momentum of the project, by the sheer scale and ambition of it all. The idea of creating a perfect world, a sanctuary for humanity, had been too alluring, too powerful to question. She had been part of the team that fine-tuned the algorithms, optimized the simulations, and helped bring Eden Prime into existence. She had been complicit, a willing participant in a project that, in retrospect, felt increasingly fraught with moral ambiguity.

Now, sitting in this dimly lit lab, surrounded by the ghosts of Earth's past and the promise of Eden Prime's future, the weight of her past actions bore down on her with a crushing force. The ethical questions that had once been faint murmurs were now deafening shouts, a cacophony of doubt challenging the very foundation of her existence. Protocol Eden, the set of guidelines that governed their interactions with Eden Prime's environment, suddenly felt like a suffocating cage, a set of rules designed to control a world far more complex and unpredictable than any algorithm could ever capture.

The core of her dilemma stemmed from a fundamental conflict: humanity's inherent drive to control and manipulate nature versus the inherent right of nature to exist and evolve organically. Protocol Eden, with its strict parameters and rigid control mechanisms, represented the former. But Kael's and Lira's stories, their raw vulnerability and the weight of their collective loss, had forced her to confront the profound ethical implications of such an approach.

Did humanity truly have the right to play God, to manipulate the very fabric of an entire planet's ecosystem? To introduce species, alter climates, and engineer a world according to human desires? Was it a utopian ideal or a dangerous act of hubris? The question gnawed at her, a relentless worm of doubt burrowing deep into her conscience. She imagined the countless variables, the unforeseen consequences, the potential for catastrophic failure, a failure that could condemn them all to a fate worse than the one they had fled from.

The thought brought a wave of nausea. The meticulous simulations, the carefully calibrated parameters, all seemed so insignificant in the face of the immense, unpredictable forces of nature. Had they truly accounted for everything? Were they truly capable of understanding the intricate interconnectedness of a living planet?

The faces of Kael and Lira swam before her eyes, their expressions a mixture of exhaustion and hope. They represented the best of humanity: resilience, hope, and a profound desire to start anew. Yet their experiences had served as a chilling reminder of humanity's capacity for both creation and destruction.

Niko ran a hand through her hair, the gesture betraying the turmoil within. She knew that their survival depended on Eden Prime, on their ability to create a sustainable biosphere. But at what cost? Could they justify the manipulation, the control, the potential for unforeseen consequences? Was it truly a redemption or a repetition of the very mistakes that had destroyed their homeworld?

The weight of this decision rested heavily on her shoulders, a burden she felt keenly. The silence in the room felt oppressive, the only sound the hum of the life support systems that maintained the fragile ecosystem they were entrusted to protect. And that was the true essence of her moral dilemma.

She felt the cold dread settle in the pit of her stomach. The success of their mission was not just a scientific problem; it was a profoundly ethical one, the answers not found in algorithms or data streams but within the quiet corners of their own consciences. They had escaped a dying planet, yet perhaps they carried the seeds of its destruction with them.

Niko's fingers continued to trace the patterns on the screen. She saw the simulated forests, the rivers, the teeming life. It was beautiful, breathtaking even, yet underneath its idyllic surface lurked a profound moral darkness. The weight of that darkness pressed down on her, a stark reminder of the immense responsibility they carried and the uncertain future it held.

The moral compass was not calibrated in scientific measurements or technological advancements. It was etched into the very fabric of their shared humanity, the echoes of their pasts shaping the decisions that would determine their future. The creation of Eden Prime wasn't just about survival; it was about reckoning with their past, understanding their limitations, and finding a balance between humanity's desires and nature's inherent right to exist.

This was not merely a scientific project, but a spiritual and ethical one, a testament to the profound moral implications of wielding such immense power over the natural world. And Niko, as one of its architects, was now confronting that reality. The future of Eden Prime, and perhaps humanity itself, hung precariously in the balance. The decision, she knew, would ultimately shape not only their present but their future, their redemption, or perhaps their ultimate downfall. The silence continued, unbroken, a testament to the profound weight of their collective moral dilemma.

The echoes of Earth's past whispered warnings in her ear, urging caution, reminding her of the fragility of life and the devastating consequences of unchecked ambition. The future, she realized, was not simply about creating a new Eden, but also about learning from the mistakes of the old.

The hum of the life support systems, a constant, almost subliminal drone, was punctuated by a sharp intake of breath from Kael. He was hunched over a console, his fingers flying across the keyboard, the glow of the screen illuminating his usually stoic face with a feverish intensity. Lira, ever watchful, leaned closer, her own brow furrowed in concentration. Niko, still grappling with the weight of her own past, felt a knot of apprehension tighten in her stomach. Something was amiss.

"I'm picking up... anomalies," Kael announced, his voice low, his eyes fixed on the screen. "Significant deviations from the established baseline. Not just minor fluctuations, but major discrepancies."

Niko leaned forward, peering over Kael's shoulder. The screen displayed a complex three-dimensional model of Eden Prime's biosphere, a swirling vortex of data points representing various ecological parameters: temperature, humidity, atmospheric composition, species distribution. Lines of vibrant, pulsing color snaked across the model, highlighting areas of unusual activity.

"What kind of discrepancies?" Lira asked, her voice edged with concern.

"It's hard to explain," Kael replied, scrolling through a series of intricate graphs and charts. "It's as if the biosphere is responding to something. Something outside of our established models. Something intelligent."

The statement hung in the air, heavy with implication. *Intelligent?* The word echoed in Niko's mind, unsettling yet strangely compelling. Their simulations had accounted for countless variables, modeled countless ecological interactions, yet this was something entirely new, something that defied their understanding.

Days turned into weeks as the team delved deeper into the anomalies. They discovered subtle yet persistent patterns in the deviations: rhythmic shifts in plant growth, coordinated migrations of animal populations, even seemingly purposeful alterations in the very composition of the soil. These weren't random fluctuations; they bore the hallmarks of intricate design, a complex choreography orchestrated by an unseen hand.

The data pointed to the existence of ancient, subterranean networks, vast fungal mycelia stretching for miles beneath the surface, interconnected in a way that suggested a level of organization far beyond anything they had ever encountered. These networks pulsed with bioelectrical activity, generating complex patterns that mirrored the observed ecological anomalies. It was as if the very soil itself was alive, sentient, responding to stimuli in ways that defied their scientific understanding.

Further analysis revealed the presence of unique biomolecules, complex organic compounds that weren't present in any known terrestrial or simulated organisms. These molecules seemed to act as communication channels within the subterranean networks, transferring information across vast distances, coordinating the growth and activity of the planet's flora and fauna. The implications were staggering. They weren't just dealing with a complex ecosystem; they were interacting with something far more profound, an ancient, semi-sentient ecological intelligence that had existed long before humanity had ever set foot on Eden Prime.

The discovery challenged their core assumptions. Their meticulous simulations, their carefully calibrated parameters, all of it suddenly seemed inadequate, simplistic, even arrogant in the face of this primordial intelligence. It was as if they had stumbled upon a hidden layer of reality, a world beneath the world, a realm of subtle, intricate communication that had been operating for eons, shaping the very fabric of Eden Prime's existence.

The team painstakingly began to unravel the mysteries of this ancient intelligence. They discovered fossilized remnants of ancient organisms, their structures intricately interwoven with the fungal networks, suggesting a symbiotic relationship that had spanned millennia. They found evidence of sophisticated communication mechanisms, complex patterns encoded in the very structure of the soil, hinting at a form of ecological memory, a collective consciousness that had witnessed the rise and fall of countless species, had endured geological upheavals and climate shifts, and had ultimately shaped the very landscape of Eden Prime.

This ancient intelligence, they theorized, was not a single entity but a vast, interconnected network, a kind of planetary nervous system that regulated and maintained the delicate balance of the planet's ecosystem. It was a being of immense age and wisdom, a testament to the power and resilience of life, a force that had shaped the world long before humanity had even conceived of its existence.

This discovery added a new dimension to their mission. Their initial goal, to establish a sustainable human colony, now seemed less straightforward. It was no longer simply about creating a biosphere; it was about understanding, respecting, and potentially even collaborating with an ancient, sentient force that had shaped the world for eons. The lines between observer and observed, between human intervention and natural process, blurred even further.

The ethical questions that had already plagued Niko now took on a new urgency and a new complexity. Protocol Eden, their guiding principle, suddenly seemed inadequate, even inappropriate, in the face of this ancient, sentient being. The team was no longer just managing a biosphere; they were potentially interacting with a consciousness that was far older, far wiser, and far more complex than anything they could have ever imagined. Were they justified in imposing their own will, their own technologies, onto this ancient entity? Did they have the right to experiment, to manipulate, to potentially disrupt an ecological balance that had endured for millions of years?

The discovery brought with it a sense of awe and wonder, but also a profound sense of responsibility. The team knew that their actions could have unforeseen and potentially devastating consequences. They were not merely creating a new Eden; they were entering into a dialogue with the planet itself, a conversation that could determine the fate of both humanity and the ancient ecological intelligence that had shaped its very being. The weight of this responsibility pressed heavily upon them, a sobering reminder of the vastness of the unknown and the limitations of their understanding. The path ahead was uncertain, but one thing was clear: their mission had transformed from a simple act of colonization to a profound act of interspecies interaction, a tentative step into a relationship with a form of intelligence that transcended human comprehension.

The future of Eden Prime, and perhaps humanity itself, hung not just on their ability to create a sustainable biosphere but on their ability to understand, respect, and ultimately coexist with this ancient, sentient force that had shaped the very world they now called home. The echoes of Earth's past were now intertwined with the whispers of a future far stranger, far more mysterious, and far more humbling than they could have ever imagined.

The rhythmic pulse of Eden Prime's biosphere, usually a reassuring hum, now felt erratic, like a heartbeat struggling to maintain its rhythm. Kael's earlier warnings had been prescient; the anomalies were escalating. What had initially seemed like subtle deviations were now blatant, dramatic shifts. The once vibrant, pulsing lines on Kael's biosphere model were now chaotic, flashing red in alarming patterns across the three-dimensional representation of their carefully constructed world.

"The fail-safe... it's starting to activate," Kael breathed, his voice tight with a mixture of fear and fascination. He tapped furiously at the console, scrolling through cascading streams of data, desperately trying to interpret the chaos.

Lira, her face pale but determined, leaned closer. "Which fail-safe? We deactivated the primary protocols during initial setup. The planet's self-regulating systems shouldn't be this responsive."

"It's not the primary protocols, Lira," Kael corrected, his gaze fixed on the screen. "It's something deeper. Something far older. Remember the ancient networks? The fungal mycelia?"

The memory of the subterranean intelligence sent a shiver down Niko's spine. Their initial awe and wonder at the discovery had been replaced by a growing unease. This wasn't just a scientific anomaly; it was a potential existential threat. The fail-safe wasn't a safeguard for the colony; it was a safeguard for Eden Prime itself, and humanity was clearly the unwelcome intruder.

The changes were unfolding rapidly. Temperature fluctuations were becoming extreme, cycling between sweltering heat and bone-chilling cold in short, unpredictable bursts. Rainfall patterns were equally erratic, transitioning from torrential downpours to prolonged droughts in a matter of hours. Plant life, once thriving, began to wilt and die in massive swathes. Animal populations, previously displaying coordinated movements, were now in disarray, their migration patterns completely disrupted.

"It's like the planet's fighting back," Niko whispered, the words hanging heavy in the air.

"Fighting back," Lira repeated, her voice strained. "Or... defending itself."

The implications were terrifying. The ancient intelligence, the planetary nervous system they had only just begun to understand, was reacting to their presence, their modifications, their attempts to control its delicate equilibrium. The fail-safe, whatever its nature, was a desperate measure to restore balance, to push back against the encroachment of humanity.

The team worked tirelessly, their initial scientific curiosity morphing into a desperate scramble for survival. They analyzed the data with a feverish intensity, trying to decipher the patterns in the chaos. The fungal networks were the key, the nexus point where the fail-safe was being triggered. They pulsed with bioelectrical activity, sending out waves of signals that echoed through the planet's subsurface, causing cascading effects on the above-ground ecosystems.

Their models were useless, their simulations inadequate. They were trying to map a consciousness, to predict the actions of an intelligence far beyond their comprehension. It was like trying to understand the human brain by studying individual neurons. The complexity was overwhelming, the scale astronomical.

Days blurred into a nightmarish cycle of data analysis, frantic adjustments, and desperate attempts to counteract the escalating environmental shifts. They discovered that the fail-safe was not a singular mechanism but a complex, interconnected series of responses, each triggered by a specific threshold being crossed. The thresholds themselves were not arbitrary; they seemed to be tied to ancient ecological patterns, to limits that the planet had maintained for millennia.

One of the most disturbing discoveries was the activation of a previously unknown system: a sophisticated atmospheric manipulation mechanism. The fail-safe was not just altering temperature and precipitation; it was actively changing the composition of the atmosphere itself, introducing novel compounds that disrupted human physiology, causing nausea, disorientation, and increasingly severe respiratory distress. It was a calculated, targeted response, a defense mechanism specifically aimed at the human colonists.

The team raced against time, desperately trying to understand the fail-safe's parameters and to predict its next moves. They worked in shifts, fueled by adrenaline and exhaustion, their faces etched with a mixture of fear and grim determination. The fate of the colony, the very survival of humanity on Eden Prime, hung precariously in the balance.

Niko's earlier ethical concerns intensified tenfold. Their initial arrogance, their belief in their ability to control and manipulate a planet's biosphere, now felt like an act of profound hubris. They were not guests on this planet; they were invaders, and the planet was fighting back.

They tried various mitigation strategies, deploying countermeasures based on their limited understanding of the fail-safe's mechanisms. Some worked momentarily, delaying or reducing certain effects; others made the situation worse, triggering unforeseen cascading failures. They were constantly playing catch-up, battling an intelligence far more sophisticated than their own an opponent that understood the planet's intricate systems in a way they could only dream of comprehending.

The experience was humbling, a stark lesson in the limitations of human knowledge and the resilience of nature. The fail-safe, initially perceived as a threat, now felt more like a desperate cry for help a plea from a wounded entity fighting for its survival.

As days turned into weeks, the situation remained precarious. The failure of their initial attempts to understand and control the fail-safe forced a profound reevaluation of their mission. Conquering Eden Prime was no longer an option; their survival now hinged on their ability to understand, respect, and perhaps even negotiate with the planet itself.

The future of humanity on Eden Prime, and perhaps beyond, rested on this fragile, desperate alliance with an ancient intelligence a silent guardian awakening from its long slumber. The echoes of the past were deafening now, a cacophony of warnings that their scientific hubris had finally awakened the planet's ancient defenses.

CHAPTER THREE

SEEDS OF DOUBT

The rhythmic pulse of the biosphere monitor, usually a comforting thrum, was now a ragged, erratic beat. Kael's face, etched with exhaustion and worry, was illuminated by the frantic flickering of the console's displays. The red warnings, once sporadic, now painted the screen in a chaotic, almost sentient landscape of flashing alerts.

"The fungal networks... the activity is increasing exponentially," Kael muttered, his voice strained. He ran a hand through his already disheveled hair, his eyes bloodshot from sleep deprivation. "The fail-safe... it's learning."

Lira, however, was staring intently at a different screen, a smaller, less sophisticated monitor displaying raw data streams from a series of strategically placed ecological sensors. Unlike Kael, whose focus was on the overarching systemic failures, Lira was immersed in the intricate details the subtle shifts and fluctuations within the planet's delicate ecosystem.

"It's not just reacting," she said, her voice low and intense, her gaze fixed on the pulsing data. "It's communicating."

Niko, who had been poring over atmospheric data, looked up, surprised. "Communicating? How?"

Lira pointed to a sequence of fluctuating signals, a complex pattern of rhythmic pulses and pauses. "The whispers," she said, using the term they'd jokingly applied to the planet's subtle bio-electrical activity. "I think I'm beginning to understand their language."

The others exchanged skeptical glances. The idea that they could decipher a planetary communication system seemed far-fetched, bordering on science fiction. But Lira had always possessed an uncanny ability to perceive subtle patterns, a skill honed by years of studying complex ecological interactions.

"It's not a language in the human sense," Lira explained, tracing the patterns on the screen with a trembling finger. "It's more an expression of the planet's distress. Each signal represents a specific ecological stressor, a specific imbalance in the system."

She began to translate, her words careful and measured. "This sequence the rapid pulses followed by the long pause that indicates a catastrophic loss of biodiversity in the southern grasslands. The prolonged low-frequency signal that's the dying coral reefs responding to the altered ocean salinity."

As Lira spoke, the others began to see it too. The chaotic data streams were not random; they were a tapestry woven from the planet's suffering. Each erratic fluctuation, each alarming spike, was a cry for help, a desperate plea from a wounded entity. They were witnessing not simply an environmental catastrophe but a planetary lament.

"The atmosphere manipulation that's not just a defense mechanism," Lira continued, her voice hushed with awe and dread. "It's a desperate attempt to restore balance. The new compounds they're not designed to harm us directly, but to alter the conditions that are causing the instability. It's a desperate attempt at self-healing."

This revelation changed everything. Their initial perception of the fail-safe as a hostile force, an antagonistic intelligence, was replaced by a more nuanced, profoundly unsettling understanding. The planet wasn't attacking humanity; it was desperately trying to heal itself, its actions a last-ditch effort to survive humanity's intrusion.

"But it's failing," Kael said, his voice heavy with despair. "The system is collapsing, and we're accelerating the process."

"The whispers are growing fainter," Lira observed, her eyes fixed on the screen. "The planet's strength is waning. It's struggling to maintain the fail-safe."

The implications were staggering. The whispers, once a subtle background hum, were now a desperate cry for help, a plea from an entity struggling to survive. Their initial attempts at controlling Eden Prime's ecosystem had inadvertently triggered a catastrophic cascade of events, pushing the planet beyond its limits.

"We need to understand what we've done," Niko stated, his voice resolute despite the daunting task ahead. "We need to find a way to help it recover."

Lira's translation of the whispers revealed a heartbreaking truth. Eden Prime's biosphere wasn't simply reacting to their presence; it was actively trying to communicate its plight, pleading for help to restore balance. The fluctuating signals weren't random chaos; they were a detailed inventory of the damage inflicted by humanity's actions deforestation, soil erosion, water contamination, and the introduction of invasive species.

The whispers spoke of dying forests, of poisoned rivers, of collapsing ecosystems. They painted a grim picture of a planet struggling to cope with the sudden influx of humanity, its carefully balanced systems thrown into disarray.

Further analysis revealed that the atmospheric compounds, while initially perceived as harmful to humans, were actually attempting to counteract the effects of human pollution, filtering out toxins and working to restore the atmospheric equilibrium. It was a desperate, self-destructive act of self-preservation.

The team delved deeper into the whispers, uncovering the intricate feedback loops connecting various aspects of Eden Prime's ecosystem. They learned about the interconnectedness of the planet's systems, the delicate balance between its flora and fauna, and the crucial role played by the ancient fungal networks in maintaining this harmony.

The whispers revealed the existence of previously unknown symbiotic relationships between species, intricate patterns of energy flow, and complex communication pathways that extended far beyond their initial understanding. They were witnessing not only a planet in crisis but a living entity communicating its pain and suffering.

The ethical implications of their actions were now inescapable. They had not simply failed to understand Eden Prime; they had inflicted irreparable damage, pushing a delicate system beyond its capacity to recover.

The whispers provided more than just a diagnosis; they suggested a possible path toward healing. By carefully interpreting the patterns, Lira identified specific areas where human intervention could be beneficial strategies that could support the planet's own self-repair mechanisms.

This wasn't about controlling Eden Prime; it was about collaborating with it. The goal shifted from exploitation to restoration, from dominion to cooperation. The whispers were not just a warning; they were an invitation to participate in the planet's healing process a chance to mend the damage and forge a new, sustainable relationship.

The fight for survival on Eden Prime had taken an unexpected turn. It was no longer a battle against a hostile planet, but a race against time to understand, assist, and potentially make amends with a living, sentient world desperately struggling to survive. The whispers were a testament to the resilience of life and the profound interconnectedness of all things. The survival of humanity on Eden Prime now depended on their ability to listen, to understand, and to respond to the planet's plea for help. The seeds of doubt, once sown by the planet's resistance, had now sprouted into a fragile hope a chance for redemption in the face of ecological devastation.

The weight of the situation pressed down on Kael, heavier than the recycled air of the habitat. He stared at the swirling patterns on Lira's screen, the frantic dance of the biosphere's distress call, and a wave of nausea washed over him. It wasn't just the scale of the ecological collapse; it was the chilling realization that they weren't dealing with a mindless system, but a sentient planet fighting for its life. He had spent years pushing down the memories, the guilt, the crushing weight of his failure on Xylos, a planet ravaged by corporate greed and unchecked expansion a failure eerily mirrored in their current predicament on Eden Prime.

Xylos. The name felt like a brand, searing a path of regret through his mind. He had been part of the initial colonization team, brimming with youthful idealism and a naïve belief in the power of technology to solve any problem. They had arrived with grand plans, promising a bountiful future, ignoring the warnings of the indigenous scientists who understood the delicate balance of Xylos's unique ecosystem. He remembered the vibrant coral reefs, the lush rainforests, the intricate web of life that had flourished for millennia, a tapestry slowly unraveling under the weight of unsustainable practices. He had been part of that unraveling, blinded by the allure of progress and his unshakable faith in his superiors. He remembered the pleas of the indigenous people, their desperate attempts to warn them, their faces etched with the same fear he saw now in Lira's eyes.

He had watched as the planet's life support system collapsed, the vibrant ecosystems replaced by barren wastelands, the air thick with the stench of decay. He had seen the despair in the eyes of those he had promised a better future, the haunting silence that replaced the songs of the native birds. The guilt had been a constant companion, a phantom limb of regret that gnawed at his soul, pushing him away from fieldwork and into the isolated world of data analysis. He had buried himself in algorithms, in numbers, in the cold comfort of objective observation, hoping to escape the suffocating weight of his failure.

But Eden Prime was different. He couldn't bury himself this time. The whispers, the planet's desperate cry for help, reached beyond the data streams, resonating with the buried trauma of Xylos. He saw a horrifying parallel, a chilling reflection of his past mistakes playing out before him on a grander, more terrifying scale. This time, he would not be a silent observer; he would fight, not just for the survival of humanity, but for redemption.

The parallels between Xylos and Eden Prime were striking. The initial euphoria of colonization, the disregard for indigenous knowledge, the relentless pursuit of resource extraction all were familiar echoes of his past. But this time, he had the benefit of hindsight. He had seen the devastating consequences of unchecked exploitation firsthand. This knowledge, forged in the fires of his past regret, ignited a fierce determination within him. He would not let history repeat itself.

He approached Lira, the rhythmic pulse of the biosphere monitor a relentless counterpoint to the pounding of his heart. "The fungal networks... you mentioned their role in maintaining the ecosystem's balance. On Xylos, we destroyed a similar network, a keystone species in the rainforest ecosystem. Its collapse triggered a domino effect, destabilizing the entire system."

Lira looked up, surprised. "You... you were on Xylos?"

He nodded, the confession a bitter pill. "I was part of the initial colonization team. We... we failed." The words hung in the air, heavy with unspoken remorse. Niko, who had been analyzing atmospheric data, looked up, his eyes wide with understanding.

"The Xylos report," Niko began hesitantly. "It was classified, but some of the data... the patterns... they're strikingly similar to what's happening here."

Lira's gaze shifted between Kael and Niko, a dawning realization in her eyes. "The fungal networks... the reports suggested they played a crucial role in nutrient cycling and carbon sequestration. If we're losing them here..." She trailed off, the implication clear.

Kael felt a surge of purpose, a stark contrast to the years of self-imposed isolation. His past failure wasn't just a burden; it was a brutal education, a painful but invaluable lesson in the fragility of planetary ecosystems. He could use this knowledge, this hard-won experience, to help prevent a similar catastrophe on Eden Prime.

He pored over the Xylos data, painstakingly comparing it to the current readings from Eden Prime. He spent countless hours analyzing the decay patterns of the fungal networks, identifying the specific stressors that had led to their collapse on Xylos. He discovered that the same stressors soil erosion, habitat fragmentation, and the introduction of invasive species were also present on Eden Prime, though at a less advanced stage.

The Xylos data, initially a source of shame and guilt, became a roadmap, guiding him through the complexities of Eden Prime's crisis. He started to see patterns in the whispers, nuances that had initially been missed. He identified specific weaknesses in the planet's defense mechanisms, weaknesses that mirrored the points of failure on Xylos. This was more than just interpreting data; it was bridging the gap between past mistakes and present opportunities. He was using the ghosts of his past to shape the future of Eden Prime.

He shared his insights with Lira and Niko, his voice steady despite the turmoil within. His perspective, informed by years of silent regret and the painful lessons of Xylos, gave their analysis a new depth and urgency. He was no longer just a data analyst; he was a leader, guiding their investigation with the chilling wisdom of experience. His knowledge of the Xylos fungal network's collapse allowed them to more accurately predict the trajectory of Eden Prime's crisis, providing crucial time to implement strategies for mitigation.

The team worked tirelessly, piecing together the fragments of the planet's distress call, guided by Kael's analysis of the Xylos data. They identified several key areas where human intervention could strengthen the planet's self-repair mechanisms. The whispers led them to discover hidden reserves of resilient plant life, offering potential solutions for reforestation. They found areas where the fungal networks were still relatively strong, regions that could serve as crucial hubs for restoration efforts.

Kael's understanding of the intricate ecological relationships, honed by his past failures, proved invaluable. He helped develop strategies that mimicked the symbiotic relationships within the Xylos ecosystem, proposing solutions that would strengthen the resilience of Eden Prime's biosphere. The team wasn't simply combating the effects of environmental damage; they were working with the planet itself, utilizing its own healing mechanisms. The whispers, once a harbinger of despair, now felt like a guiding voice a collaboration between a distressed planet and the species that had inadvertently caused its suffering.

His renewed purpose wasn't just about saving Eden Prime; it was about making amends, about finding redemption in the face of his past failure. The guilt that had haunted him for years was gradually being replaced by a sense of hope, a feeling of purpose, of participating in a desperate yet vital struggle for survival. He had been a silent witness to the destruction of Xylos. He would not let that happen again. The whispers of Eden Prime were not only a call for help; they were a testament to the tenacity of life, a challenge, and a chance for redemption.

Niko, a young but fiercely intelligent xenoecologist, had been poring over the ethical implications of Protocol Eden the very system designed to terraform and stabilize Eden Prime. Unlike Kael, whose focus remained primarily on the immediate ecological crisis, Niko's sharp mind delved into the deeper philosophical and ethical ramifications of their actions. She had been quietly analyzing the data streams, the subtle whispers of the planet, searching for something beyond the immediate symptoms. What she found chilled her to the bone.

Protocol Eden, while presented as a benevolent act of planetary restoration, contained a disturbingly efficient reset mechanism. In the event of catastrophic system failure, the protocol would initiate a complete environmental reboot a brutal cleansing of the planet's ecosystems to create a more "manageable" environment. This wasn't merely about selective culling of invasive species or targeted remediation. Niko's research revealed that the reset involved a near-total eradication of the planet's existing biosphere, effectively wiping the slate clean before introducing preselected, human-engineered species.

The chilling detail wasn't the process itself, but the scale. The "reset" wasn't a localized action; it was a planetary-scale purge, a scorched-earth approach to environmental management. Niko discovered that past failed terraforming attempts had used this same mechanism, leaving behind a trail of lifeless, sterilized worlds, silent monuments to humanity's hubris. The data revealed that these "reset" events had far-reaching consequences, disrupting not only local ecosystems but also causing unpredictable cascading effects across the wider galactic environment. The energy signatures detected from these catastrophic events were immense, reaching far beyond the immediate vicinity and potentially impacting neighboring star systems.

The ethical implications were staggering. Was humanity justified in undertaking such a radical, potentially destructive intervention in the name of colonization? Was their right to exist and thrive so absolute as to justify the complete annihilation of a planet's existing biodiversity? The data hinted at the existence of a complex, sentient planetary consciousness on Eden Prime, the same consciousness that had been desperately trying to communicate with them through the whispers. If activated, the reset would not simply destroy an ecosystem; it would murder a sentient being.

Niko's findings went far beyond the immediate concerns of the failing biosphere. They challenged the very foundations of their mission. The narrative of benevolent human intervention, of saving Eden Prime, crumbled under the weight of her revelations. It wasn't a rescue operation;

it was a potentially genocidal act disguised as environmental management. The cheerful, almost simplistic projections of human-centric terraforming efforts now appeared monstrous and callous.

The weight of her discovery pressed down on Niko. She had to share her findings, but the implications were so vast, so potentially catastrophic to the mission's narrative, that she hesitated. Revealing the true nature of Protocol Eden could shatter the team's morale, cause widespread panic, and potentially trigger a catastrophic shift in power dynamics back on Earth.

She presented her data to Kael and Lira. The atmosphere was thick with unspoken anxiety. Kael, despite his personal demons and the guilt from Xylos, was initially resistant. The idea of a sentient planet, an ecologically conscious being capable of communication through the whispers, was a paradigm shift. It challenged his understanding of life's nature and the boundaries of human intervention. He had dealt with ecological damage before, but this was something far greater and far more profound. It was a moral abyss.

Lira, her scientific objectivity tempered by deep empathy for the planet, was more receptive. Niko's findings resonated with her own growing understanding of Eden Prime's intricate consciousness. She saw the potential for a profound ethical failure, a catastrophic miscalculation in humanity's interaction with a sentient being. She understood the precarious balance between saving a planet and destroying it in the name of salvation.

The conversation spiraled into a deep philosophical debate, a desperate attempt to reconcile the practical necessities of survival with the ethical implications of their actions. Kael's experience on Xylos provided a sobering counterpoint to the idealistic notions of planetary management. He understood the potential for unintended consequences, the devastating ripple effects of human interference. His past trauma became a tool of caution, a warning against the seductive power of easy solutions.

Niko's research did not just highlight the ethical dilemmas; it offered an unsettling glimpse into the potential long-term consequences of Protocol Eden's reset mechanism. She discovered that the energy pulses generated by previous resets caused subtle but significant alterations in the fabric of spacetime, creating localized distortions that could affect the stability of nearby stars and planetary systems. The implications were far-reaching and terrifying. The reset was not a contained operation; it was a ripple in the cosmic fabric, with unforeseen and unpredictable consequences.

The team's initial focus had been on the immediate environmental crisis, a matter of survival. Niko's research expanded the scope of their dilemma exponentially, forcing them to confront deeper moral and existential questions. Their actions on Eden Prime were no longer confined to a single planet. They had the potential to influence the future of entire star systems.

The weight of this realization was almost unbearable. They were facing not just an environmental crisis but a moral crisis of unimaginable proportions. The whispers of Eden Prime, initially seen as a cry for help, now held a new and more profound meaning: a plea for survival, understanding, and recognition of its inherent worth and right to exist. Their mission had shifted dramatically. It was no longer about terraforming a planet; it was about making a crucial moral decision with far-reaching and potentially irreversible consequences.

The seeds of doubt planted by Niko's research had taken root, threatening to unravel everything they thought they knew and forcing them to reevaluate their role in the fate of Eden Prime and the wider cosmos. The future seemed terrifyingly uncertain, poised on a knife's edge between survival and utter destruction. The whispers now sounded louder, more desperate, a symphony of impending doom interwoven with faint echoes of hope. The team had to decide whether they would become saviors or destroyers.

The iridescent shimmer of the biodome, once a beacon of hope, now pulsed with a sickly, erratic rhythm. Cracks spiderwebbed across its surface, faint at first, then widening into gaping fissures that leaked the precious, carefully regulated atmosphere. Inside, the once-lush environment was succumbing to chaos. The carefully cultivated flora, engineered to thrive in Eden Prime's challenging environment, withered and died, their vibrant colors fading into a dull, sickly brown. The meticulously designed ecosystems, intended to create a self-sustaining biosphere, were unraveling at an alarming rate.

Niko watched the deterioration with growing dread, the data streams painting a grim picture. The instability was not confined to a single area; it was spreading like wildfire, consuming more and more of the biodome's carefully constructed ecosystems. The intricate web of interconnectedness, once a source of pride, was now a conduit for catastrophic failure. A cascade effect, triggered by a seemingly minor disruption in one sector, was causing a domino effect across the entire system.

The initial hope that the biodome represented a safe haven, a microcosm of a thriving ecosystem, was dissolving. It was now a fragile bubble, precariously balanced on the brink of total collapse. The sophisticated environmental controls, initially designed to manage and regulate the planet's biosphere, were overwhelmed, struggling to compensate for the escalating instability. Alerts blared incessantly from the control panels, a cacophony of warnings that underscored the severity of the situation.

Kael, his face grim and etched with worry, paced back and forth, his boots thudding against the metallic floor. The weight of responsibility pressed heavily upon him. He had been tasked with saving Eden Prime, but now the very project he had championed was on the verge of catastrophic failure. The guilt from Xylos, a constant companion, gnawed at his conscience. The specter of failure, of repeating past mistakes, haunted him relentlessly.

Lira, despite her training and unwavering scientific approach, struggled to maintain her composure. She had always believed in the mission's ideals, in the power of human intervention to heal and restore a damaged planet. Yet, seeing Eden Prime's delicate ecosystems crumble before her eyes, she could not ignore the mounting evidence of their failings. She understood that the whispers were not simply environmental signals; they were cries of pain, desperate pleas for help from a sentient being struggling to survive the onslaught of human interference.

The team's initial focus on immediate problem-solving, fixing broken systems, patching holes, and applying emergency protocols, was no longer sufficient. The rapidly escalating instability demanded a more fundamental shift in their approach. They needed a deeper understanding of the underlying causes, one that went beyond the superficial analysis of environmental data. They needed to understand why Eden Prime was rejecting their intervention and why the meticulously planned systems were failing so spectacularly.

Niko's findings provided a crucial piece of the puzzle. The data, initially alarming, now seemed to point toward a terrifying conclusion. Protocol Eden, designed to stabilize the planet, was inherently unstable. The reset mechanism, intended as a fail-safe, was now acting as a catalyst for the very collapse it was designed to prevent. The planet's delicate biosphere, already struggling to adapt to human intervention, was reacting to the inherent instability of the protocol, triggering a feedback loop of escalating destruction.

The team spent days poring over the data, trying to discern the intricate patterns of the planet's response. They discovered that the whispers weren't random; they were complex signals, an intricate communication system that echoed the planet's struggle for survival. The increasing intensity of the whispers directly correlated with the escalating instability of the biosphere, a clear indication that the planet was reacting to the stress imposed by Protocol Eden. They began to understand that the whispers were not just a cry for help but a detailed warning, a complex explanation of the damage they had inadvertently inflicted upon the planet.

The realization was deeply unsettling. Their actions, meant to save the planet, had become the very thing that was destroying it. The ethical implications were profound, raising a cascade of moral questions. Had they been acting on an incomplete understanding of the planet's complexity? Had they underestimated the depth and sensitivity of Eden Prime's biosphere? Had they, in their hubris, ignored the subtle warnings the planet had been sending?

The increasing urgency of the situation forced the team to consider radical options. Kael, haunted by Xylos, knew the temptation of quick fixes and of ignoring the more complex problems in favor of immediate, tangible solutions. However, Niko's research, coupled with Lira's empathetic understanding, forced them to confront the full depth of their mistake. They couldn't simply continue patching holes in a sinking ship. They had to address the fundamental flaw in their approach, the core issue that was fueling the catastrophic instability.

Lira proposed a risky strategy: to temporarily suspend Protocol Eden's automated systems and allow Eden Prime's natural processes to take over. It was a gamble, a radical departure from their initial plan, but it was the only option that might allow the planet to heal and stabilize. It was a recognition that their attempts at control had failed and that the planet needed space to adjust and recover from the trauma of human intervention.

The decision wasn't made lightly. The possibility of complete environmental collapse was a real and present danger. But the current trajectory, the escalating instability driven by Protocol Eden's inherent flaws, was far more dangerous. It was a choice between controlled chaos and complete annihilation. They understood that pausing Protocol Eden might lead to short-term disruptions, perhaps even losses in the biodome's carefully nurtured ecosystems, but it was their only chance to avoid a planetary-scale ecological disaster.

The suspension of Protocol Eden's automated systems was a tense operation, fraught with risk and uncertainty. The data streams were unpredictable, the whispers were chaotic, and the overall situation volatile. The team worked tirelessly, monitoring every parameter and making minute adjustments to compensate for the immediate shifts in the planet's systems. The biodome, struggling under the strain of the transition, experienced further deterioration, but it seemed the rate of decline had slowed.

The next few days were a blur of frantic activity, a constant battle against time and against the overwhelming odds. The team, weary but resolute, worked relentlessly, pushing themselves beyond their limits. They faced failures and setbacks, but with each challenge, they gained a deeper understanding of Eden Prime's intricate systems. They observed the planet's response to their altered approach, finding that the whispers, although still present, were losing their desperate intensity. There was a subtle shift, a change in tone, that suggested a tentative path toward recovery.

As the dust settled, a tentative hope emerged. The initial fear that the planet would succumb to chaos had not materialized. Eden Prime was responding to the change, slowly but surely. The biodome, although still damaged, was showing signs of stabilization, a testament to the planet's resilience and to the team's courage in making a profound ethical decision.

The seeds of doubt planted by Niko's research had led to a drastic change of course, a profound shift in perspective, and a newfound respect for the sentient life they were interacting with. Their mission had transformed from a conquest to a collaboration, a journey toward understanding, and a desperate attempt to atone for the mistakes of the past. The path ahead remained uncertain, but for the first time, they felt a flicker of hope amidst the chaos.

The discovery was not a sudden revelation but rather a slow, painstaking unraveling of a deeply buried truth. It began with a seemingly insignificant anomaly in the data streams, a faint, recurring pattern that was initially dismissed as noise. Niko, driven by an almost obsessive attention to detail, noticed it. It was a subtle variation in the planet's electromagnetic field, a faint pulse that resonated with the frequency of the *whispers*.

Initially, the team dismissed it as a quirk in the data, another symptom of the overall system instability. But Niko, haunted by the increasingly urgent whispers and the growing instability of Protocol Eden, refused to let it go. He spent days, then weeks, poring over the archives and delving into the historical data that documented the initial stages of the Eden Prime project. It was a painstaking process, sifting through terabytes of information, searching for a connection that might explain the anomaly.

The breakthrough came unexpectedly, in a forgotten data file labeled *Project Chimera*. This file detailed a precursor to Protocol Eden, a far more aggressive and invasive approach to terraforming. Project Chimera aimed for a rapid transformation of Eden Prime, ignoring the planet's inherent biological rhythms and attempting to impose a human-designed ecosystem almost overnight. The data revealed that this early experiment had failed catastrophically. The planet reacted violently, its biosphere collapsing under the strain of this rapid, forceful alteration. The *whispers*, Niko discovered, were not merely a cry of distress from the planet's damaged biosphere; they were the echoes of Project Chimera's failure, a haunting reminder of the planet's past trauma.

Project Chimera was abandoned after a series of devastating environmental disasters. The planet was left scarred, its delicate ecosystems shattered. The lessons learned, or at least the data suggesting them, were buried deep within the archives, lost in the relentless pursuit of a more successful approach, Protocol Eden. Protocol Eden, in a twisted irony, was designed to correct the errors of Project Chimera, to heal the planet's wounds and establish a stable, self-sustaining ecosystem. But it had inherited the fundamental flaw of its predecessor, an inability to truly understand and respect Eden Prime's intricate, sentient biosphere.

The data revealed chilling details. The reset mechanism within Protocol Eden, meant to rectify any environmental imbalances, was in reality a repurposed technology from Project Chimera. It was designed to forcibly reshape the environment and to suppress deviations from the pre-programmed parameters. It was not fixing the problems; it was suppressing the symptoms, driving the planet deeper into a state of unsustainable stress. The *whispers*, now understood as a complex communication system, were a desperate attempt by the planet to signal its distress and to alert the humans to the destructive nature of their intervention.

The historical context cast a new light on the team's present dilemma. Their initial optimism, their belief in the power of human ingenuity to reshape nature, was grounded in a flawed understanding of the past. They had inherited the burden of Project Chimera's failures, repeating the same mistakes under the guise of a supposedly more refined approach. The seemingly random instability of the biodome was not random at all; it was a predictable consequence of imposing a rigid, inflexible system on a complex, self-regulating biosphere. They had underestimated the planet's capacity for resistance, its ability to communicate its distress, and its inherent intelligence.

This revelation deepened the ethical questions that had already begun to gnaw at the team's conscience. They were not just facing a scientific challenge; they were grappling with the profound implications of their actions, the weight of their predecessors' failures, and the devastating consequences of their hubris. The whispers were no longer merely an environmental signal; they were a moral indictment.

Kael, weighed down by the ghost of Xylos and the failure of his past projects, felt the full impact of this revelation. His initial determination, his unwavering belief in the scientific method, crumbled under the weight of history. He saw the parallels between Project Chimera and Protocol Eden, the subtle similarities in their approach, and the underlying presumption of human dominance over nature. The guilt was overwhelming, the weight of responsibility almost unbearable.

Lira, ever the pragmatist, now approached the problem with a renewed sense of urgency and a deeper understanding of its complexity. Her scientific training, combined with her growing empathy for Eden Prime, fueled a new strategy. She recognized that Protocol Eden, despite its initial intention, was essentially a continuation of Project Chimera's mistakes. The planet was not rejecting their intervention simply because of technical flaws; it was rejecting the fundamental premise of human control.

Niko, the architect of this historical revelation, felt a strange mix of dread and determination. His obsessive attention to detail had uncovered a truth that threatened to unravel everything they had worked for, but it also offered a glimmer of hope, a path toward a more sustainable future. By understanding the past, they could learn to correct the mistakes of the present.

The team spent the following weeks immersed in the historical data, meticulously piecing together the story of Eden Prime's past. They examined the ecological impact of Project Chimera, analyzing the precise changes in the planet's biosphere and charting the evolution of the *whispers* from panicked cries to structured, complex communications. They discovered subtle signs of the planet's attempt to heal itself, evidence of its resilience in the face of human aggression.

This deeper understanding informed their approach to the current crisis. The temporary suspension of Protocol Eden's automated systems, already underway, felt less like a gamble and more like a necessary step in a long process of reconciliation. It was not simply about stabilizing the biodome; it was about acknowledging the planet's sentience, respecting its inherent rhythms, and learning to work with, rather than against, its natural processes.

The path ahead remained uncertain, but the team now felt a shared purpose and a renewed commitment to a more sustainable and ethical approach. The *whispers*, once a source of fear and uncertainty, now offered a pathway toward a more harmonious relationship with Eden Prime. The seeds of doubt, once planted by Niko's research, had blossomed into a profound shift in perspective, from a desperate attempt to control nature to a humble effort to understand and collaborate with it. The team's mission had evolved, transcending the simple goal of terraforming and embracing the far more challenging, and ultimately more rewarding, task of healing a wounded planet and earning its trust. The journey had just begun.

Chapter Four

THE HEART OF EDEN

The shuttle shuddered, its reinforced hull groaning under the pressure as it descended deeper into the heart of Eden Prime's biodome. Outside, the vibrant tapestry of the artificial ecosystem blurred into a chaotic swirl of greens, browns, and blues. The once orderly rows of genetically engineered flora had given way to a wild, untamed wilderness, a testament to the planet's powerful pushback against Protocol Eden.

Kael, his face etched with a mixture of apprehension and grim determination, gripped the armrest. The weight of his past failures, the ghost of Xylos, and the catastrophic consequences of Project Chimera pressed heavily on him. This journey into the core of the biodome was more than just a scientific expedition; it was a confrontation with his own hubris, a desperate attempt at redemption.

Lira, ever practical, monitored the shuttle's vital signs, her gaze constantly shifting between the instrument panel and the ever-changing landscape outside. The data streams, normally a comforting source of information, now displayed erratic fluctuations, mirroring the volatile state of the planet itself. The whispers, once faint and ethereal, now pulsed with a raw, almost palpable energy. They were no longer merely background noise; they were a symphony of distress, a cacophony of warnings.

Niko, pale but resolute, stared out at the chaotic beauty of the landscape, his mind racing. The historical data he had unearthed had painted a grim picture, revealing the tragic consequences of human arrogance. He understood now that Protocol Eden was not a solution but a symptom, a desperate attempt to control a force far beyond human comprehension. He knew this expedition was fraught with peril; their very presence could trigger a catastrophic chain reaction.

The shuttle finally landed in a clearing surrounded by towering, bioluminescent fungi that pulsed with an eerie, otherworldly glow. The air hung heavy with the scent of damp earth, decaying vegetation, and something else... something ancient and unsettling. The whispers intensified, resonating deep within their bones, a chilling reminder of the planet's sentience.

Their journey into the core was a slow, arduous trek through a landscape both breathtakingly beautiful and terrifyingly unpredictable. Giant, carnivorous plants with razor-sharp leaves snaked across their path, their movements surprisingly swift and deliberate. Strange, luminescent insects with iridescent wings buzzed around them, their bodies emitting a faint, rhythmic hum that blended with the planet's whispers. The ground beneath their feet was unstable, often yielding to reveal hidden chasms and subterranean rivers.

They encountered bizarre formations of crystalline structures, pulsating with internal light, that seemed to be some form of planetary defense mechanism. These structures emitted a low-frequency hum, interfering with their communication systems and causing disorientation. Lira, despite her pragmatism, felt a primal fear, a feeling of utter insignificance in the face of this immense, alien power.

One particularly harrowing encounter involved a massive, sentient tree, its roots intertwining with the very fabric of the biodome. Its branches, thick as ancient oaks, seemed to reach out, probing them with an unseen intelligence. Niko, ever the scientist, tried to communicate, attempting to decipher the whispers and establish a dialogue. His efforts were met with a silent, unnerving stillness, followed by a subtle shift in the tree's branches a gesture that seemed to both warn and invite.

The closer they got to the biodome's core, the more chaotic the environment became. The ground trembled, massive fissures opened and closed, and the air vibrated with energy. They faced torrential downpours followed by intense heat waves, extremes of climate the automated systems of Protocol Eden were no longer able to regulate. The whispers intensified, their tone growing increasingly urgent, laced with a hint of desperation.

They discovered evidence of past attempts to access the core, remnants of failed expeditions from both Project Chimera and Protocol Eden. Scattered equipment lay rusting amidst the alien vegetation, silent monuments to humanity's failed attempts to control the planet's biosphere. The sight of this wreckage only intensified the weight of their responsibility.

The final leg of their journey took them through a labyrinthine network of underground tunnels carved through the planet's ancient rock formations. The whispers here were deafening, a chorus of pain and defiance. The team moved in complete darkness, navigating by the faint bioluminescence of the surrounding fungi and the subtle vibrations in the ground.

They reached the heart of the biodome, a massive, cavernous space at the planet's core. At the center, a colossal crystalline structure pulsed with a brilliant, otherworldly light. The whispers reached a crescendo here, overwhelming yet strangely beautiful. It was a complex symphony of sounds, a language of unimaginable complexity, communicating the planet's suffering, its resilience, and its desperate plea for understanding.

Standing in the heart of Eden Prime, surrounded by the symphony of whispers, the team finally understood the true nature of their task. It wasn't about controlling the planet; it was about learning to listen, to understand, and to cooperate. Their previous attempts to reshape the planet had been acts of profound arrogance; their current mission was one of humble reconciliation.

The journey had been treacherous, but the ultimate goal was no longer just survival; it was the forging of a symbiotic relationship, a new beginning. The whispers, once a source of dread, now offered a pathway to a future where humanity and Eden Prime could coexist, not as conquerors and conquered, but as partners in a shared destiny. The seeds of understanding, planted in the crucible of their exploration, held the promise of healing, reconciliation, and a future built on respect, not dominion.

The colossal crystalline structure at the biodome's core pulsed with an almost unbearable intensity, its light a mesmerizing blend of emerald, sapphire, and amethyst. The whispers, no longer a mere chorus, were a tidal wave of sound, washing over them and resonating deep within their very being. It felt less like hearing and more like experiencing the planet's consciousness itself, a complex tapestry of emotions, memories, and warnings. Niko, his face illuminated by the ethereal glow, reached out a tentative hand, as if to touch the very heart of Eden Prime.

Lira, however, remained rooted to the spot, her gaze fixed on a series of intricate carvings etched into the crystalline structure. They depicted a history, a narrative unfolding in a language far older than humanity's, a visual symphony that echoed the aural cacophony of the whispers. She recognized symbols that mirrored those found in the ruined facilities of Project Chimera and Protocol Eden, fragments of a larger puzzle finally falling into place.

Kael, his expression grim, ran a hand over the worn surface of his datapad, reviewing the findings they'd gathered during their perilous journey. The data was incomplete and fragmented, but a pattern was emerging, a disturbing pattern that implicated humanity in a far greater catastrophe than he had ever imagined. Protocol Eden, he now understood, was not merely an attempt to control Eden Prime; it was a desperate, last-ditch effort to contain something far more dangerous, a self-replicating bioweapon accidentally unleashed by Project Chimera.

The carvings on the crystalline structure revealed the full story. Project Chimera, in its reckless pursuit of genetic manipulation, had inadvertently created a lifeform capable of exponentially altering the planet's ecosystem. This bioweapon, disguised within the initial genetic seed packages sent to Eden Prime, had begun to replicate and evolve at an alarming rate, transforming the planet's flora and fauna into something both terrifying and breathtakingly beautiful. Protocol Eden, initially designed to monitor and control the genetically engineered lifeforms, had inadvertently become a mechanism to contain this unforeseen, self-perpetuating ecological disaster.

The initial phases of Protocol Eden had shown success. The automated systems had managed to stabilize the biodome's environment for a time, preventing the immediate collapse of the ecosystem. However, the containment was never truly complete. The bioweapon, adapting to the protocol's interventions, had evolved, developing mechanisms to resist and outwit the automated control systems. It was a terrifying evolutionary arms race, with humanity's attempts at control merely fueling the bioweapon's relentless growth and adaptation.

The whispers intensified, laced with a tone of immense sorrow and a desperate plea for understanding. They revealed the bioweapon's true nature, not a malevolent entity, but a lifeform struggling to survive, to adapt to a hostile environment created by humanity's own hubris. It wasn't an enemy to be conquered, but a consequence of humanity's arrogant disregard for the natural world. The crystalline structure, far from being a mere defense mechanism, was a cry for help, a desperate attempt to communicate, to reach out to a species capable of both immense destruction and potential healing.

The ethical implications were staggering. The team had come to Eden Prime to restore the planet, to fix the mistakes of the past. But now they faced a far more complex problem: a self-replicating bioweapon of immense power, one that was both a threat and a victim of humanity's actions. Could they even contain it, or had they already crossed a point of no return? Was the solution eradication, or could they find a way to coexist with this powerful, evolving lifeform?

The carvings revealed further details about the protocol's contingency plan. A desperate attempt to contain the bioweapon was outlined, involving a series of self-destruct sequences integrated within the biodome's core. The sequences would trigger a chain of controlled ecological collapses, effectively sterilizing the planet and eliminating the threat. However, it was a pyrrhic victory, condemning Eden Prime to a barren wasteland. The whispers hinted at an alternative, a symbiotic relationship, a coevolution between humanity and the bioweapon. But the pathways to achieve this were unclear, fraught with uncertainty and immense risks.

Niko, ever the pragmatist, began to meticulously analyze the data from the carvings, attempting to decipher the precise mechanisms of the contingency plan. He recognized sophisticated bioengineering techniques far beyond current human capabilities, suggesting a level of technological advancement that humanity might never achieve. The bioweapon, in its desperate struggle for survival, had not only adapted to its environment but had also exceeded its creators in terms of technological sophistication. This was a race against time, against the potential self-destruction of both the planet and humanity's future.

Kael wrestled with the weight of his responsibility. Xylos, the planet he had failed to protect, loomed large in his memory. He couldn't repeat the same mistakes. He had to find a way to reconcile humanity's past actions with the future of Eden Prime. He had to find a way to build bridges instead of walls. But the clock was ticking. The whispers, once a source of fear, now spoke of impending doom.

Lira, drawing on her vast knowledge of bioengineering and xenobiology, meticulously studied the carvings, comparing them to the historical data they had gathered. She slowly pieced together the intricate mechanisms of the bioweapon's evolution, its adaptation strategies, and its potential for both destruction and renewal. She realized that the bioweapon wasn't purely destructive; it possessed a capacity for intricate ecological engineering, a capability to reshape ecosystems with a precision far beyond human technology.

They realized that the contingency plan was not a simple on/off switch. It was a delicate balance, a set of intricate fail-safes designed to prevent the planet's complete collapse. The self-destruct mechanisms were not merely destructive; they were a last resort, a final attempt to prevent the uncontrolled spread of the bioweapon beyond Eden Prime. They were a desperate plea, a last whisper from a planet fighting for its survival.

The team spent hours huddled around the crystalline structure, poring over data, deciphering carvings, interpreting the whispers. The planet's energy pulsed through them, a symphony of pain and hope intertwined. They felt the weight of centuries of evolution, the struggle for survival against insurmountable odds. The task before them was not simply to save Eden Prime; it was to reconcile humanity's past with its future, to learn to coexist with a force far greater than themselves. They had to find a way to bridge the gap between domination and understanding, between destruction and creation.

The journey had brought them to the precipice of a new era, one that demanded a profound shift in human understanding. They were no longer explorers, conquerors, or even scientists. They were mediators, standing at the crossroads between extinction and a symbiotic future, a future where humanity and Eden Prime could coexist not as masters and servants, but as partners in a shared, fragile destiny.

The whispers, now a constant companion, held both a warning and a promise, a promise of a future that depended not on control, but on understanding, respect, and the courage to embrace a new way of being. The future of Eden Prime, and perhaps humanity itself, hung precariously in the balance.

The crystalline structure hummed, the light intensifying, shifting from a kaleidoscope of colors to a deep, resonant emerald. The whispers, previously a chaotic chorus, coalesced, forming a single, powerful voice that resonated not just in their ears, but deep within their very bones. It was a voice ancient beyond comprehension, carrying the weight of eons, the accumulated wisdom and sorrow of a world profoundly altered.

It spoke not in human tongues, but in a language of pure feeling, a symphony of emotions that transcended the limitations of words. Fear, anger, and a profound sadness were interwoven with a surprising thread of hope, a flicker of resilience in the face of overwhelming adversity. The team, initially overwhelmed by the sheer intensity of the experience, slowly began to understand.

The voice, the manifestation of Eden Prime's ecological intelligence, revealed a perspective far removed from humanity's anthropocentric worldview. It spoke of a world teeming with life, a vibrant ecosystem delicately balanced for millennia, a world shattered by humanity's reckless ambition. It spoke of Project Chimera not as a scientific endeavor gone wrong, but as an act of profound ecological violence, a violation of the planet's inherent integrity.

The voice recounted the arrival of the genetically engineered seeds, the initial burst of growth, and the uncontrolled proliferation of the bioweapon. But it also revealed the bioweapon's perspective, its struggle for survival in a hostile environment, its desperate attempts to adapt, to find a place within the fractured ecosystem. It wasn't a malevolent entity seeking conquest, the voice explained, but a lifeform struggling to survive, a child of humanity's hubris, now forced to grapple with the consequences.

The voice described the bioweapon's evolution not as a threat, but as a testament to the power of life's resilience, its capacity to adapt and overcome even the most daunting challenges. It revealed the intricate mechanisms of the bioweapon's adaptation, the sophisticated strategies it employed to reshape the ecosystem, and the delicate balance it was attempting to achieve. The "terrifying beauty" Kael had observed was not a random mutation, but a carefully orchestrated response to the damage inflicted by humanity.

The voice revealed the deeper purpose of the crystalline structure, not as a containment mechanism, but as a desperate attempt at communication, a plea for understanding. It wasn't intended to control or subdue the bioweapon; it was an attempt to bridge the gap between two vastly different forms of intelligence, to find a path toward coexistence. The self-destruct mechanisms, far from being a final solution, were a last resort, a safety valve designed to prevent the spread of the bioweapon beyond Eden Prime. It was a painful choice, a desperate act of self-preservation.

This revelation fundamentally altered the team's approach. The problem was no longer about eradicating a threat; it was about healing a wound, about repairing the damage inflicted by humanity's actions. The solution wasn't destruction, but understanding, cooperation, and a profound shift in perspective.

Niko, his initial pragmatic approach tempered by the weight of the ancient voice, began to see the bioweapon not as an enemy but as a partner in the process of ecological restoration. He focused on deciphering the intricacies of the self-destruct mechanisms, not to activate them but to understand how they functioned, how they could be potentially modified or even repurposed. The advanced bioengineering techniques used in their construction suggested possibilities far beyond current human capabilities. He saw potential in integrating these technologies into a new strategy, a strategy focused on healing rather than destruction.

Kael, haunted by the memory of Xylos, felt a surge of renewed purpose. The voice's perspective gave him a new framework for understanding his past failures. He could no longer allow his grief and guilt to paralyze him. He had to act, to find a way to atone for humanity's mistakes, to use his skills and knowledge to help repair the damage. He saw in the bioweapon not a monster but a reflection of humanity's own flaws, a mirror showing the destructive potential of unchecked ambition.

Lira, her scientific curiosity ignited by the voice's revelations, delved deeper into the carvings, seeking clues to unlock the secrets of the bioweapon's evolutionary processes. She recognized patterns within the bioweapon's genetic code, hinting at its capacity for intricate ecological engineering and its potential for restoring the balance of the ecosystem. It was not simply adapting; it was actively trying to heal the planet, to repair the damage humanity had caused.

The ancient voice continued to guide them, offering cryptic clues, hints at potential solutions, and warnings of unseen dangers. It stressed the importance of understanding the bioweapon's motivations, of recognizing its inherent resilience and adaptability. It emphasized the need for humility, for recognizing the limitations of humanity's knowledge and the profound interconnectedness of all life.

The team, now bound by a shared purpose, worked tirelessly, their efforts guided by the ancient voice. They discovered intricate symbiotic relationships between the bioweapon and the altered flora and fauna of Eden Prime, an interwoven tapestry of life born from the ashes of destruction. The bioweapon was not just surviving; it was creating, building new ecosystems, fostering new forms of life, and pushing the boundaries of what they understood to be possible.

The voice offered a vision of a future where humanity and Eden Prime could coexist, not as conquerors and conquered but as partners in a delicate dance of mutual respect and understanding. It warned of the dangers of hubris, of the potential for humanity to repeat its past mistakes and once again disrupt the intricate balance of life.

Days bled into weeks. The team, their bodies weary and their minds strained, pushed forward, their determination fueled by the ancient voice and the weight of their responsibility. They were no longer merely scientists and explorers; they were stewards, guardians of a world poised on the brink of destruction or renewal. The decision lay with them, the future of Eden Prime, and perhaps humanity itself, resting on their ability to learn, to understand, and to embrace a new way of being. The whispers, now a constant presence, were no longer a warning but a guide, a path toward a future of symbiotic coexistence. The future was still uncertain, but hope, fragile yet persistent, flickered within the heart of Eden.

The emerald light pulsed, a heartbeat echoing the team's own racing pulses. The voice, the essence of Eden Prime, had faded, leaving behind a silence heavier than any noise. Before them lay the core of Protocol Eden, a shimmering sphere of crystalline technology pulsing with contained energy. The activation sequence, a simple keystroke, hung poised on Niko's screen, a stark choice between oblivion and an uncertain future.

The weight of the decision pressed down on them, crushing the air from their lungs. The voice had revealed a terrifying truth: Project Chimera wasn't just a failed experiment; it was a catastrophic ecological crime, a wound inflicted on a living planet. The bioweapon, a horrific child of human ambition, was now struggling to heal that wound, creating a precarious new ecosystem in its desperate attempt to survive.

Niko, ever the pragmatist, wrestled with the data. The self-destruct sequence was elegant, efficient, leaving no trace of the bioweapon's existence. It was a clean break, a finality that offered a certain kind of peace. The alternative, attempting to repair the damaged systems, was a gamble of immense proportions. They knew so little about the bioweapon's intricate processes and its complex symbiotic relationships with the altered flora and fauna of Eden Prime.

Failure could mean a catastrophic escalation, the uncontrolled spread of the bioweapon beyond this planet, threatening the entire galaxy. Success, on the other hand, held the promise of a future where humanity and Eden Prime could coexist, a future where they could learn from their mistakes and strive for a symbiotic relationship with the living world. The risk was colossal, the potential reward immeasurable.

Kael, his face etched with a sorrow that went beyond the loss of Xylos, stared at the crystalline sphere. The voice had shown him the bioweapon not as a monster but as a desperate act of survival, a reflection of humanity's own self-destructive tendencies. The guilt gnawed at him, a relentless tide eroding his resolve. He saw a parallel between Xylos's tragic fate and the bioweapon's struggle. Both were victims of humanity's hubris, caught in a web of unintended consequences.

Activating Protocol Eden felt like repeating history, a final act of abandonment, a surrender to their own failings. But the alternative, interfering with a system they barely understood, felt equally reckless. The potential for unforeseen consequences chilled him to the bone. He had to find a way to atone, to make amends for the damage he had helped create, but how could he do so if the only tools available to him were the same tools that had caused the destruction in the first place?

Lira, usually so focused and rational, felt a tremor of doubt running through her. She had dedicated her life to understanding the intricacies of life, to unraveling the mysteries of evolution. The bioweapon, in its grotesque beauty, represented the ultimate triumph of adaptation, a testament to the resilience of life itself. To destroy it, to erase this extraordinary example of survival, felt like sacrilege, a denial of the power and beauty of the natural world.

Yet the potential danger, the unknown consequences of allowing this new ecosystem to expand uncontrolled, haunted her. She saw the intricate carvings on the sphere as a testament to a desperate attempt at communication, an act of reaching out from a lifeform on the brink. But was it possible to answer that plea, to find a common language between humanity and a being so profoundly different? Could they unravel the genetic code, learn its secrets, and find a way to help, not destroy?

The silence stretched, thick and heavy, punctuated only by the rhythmic hum of the crystalline sphere. Each member of the team wrestled with their conscience, their choices echoing the ancient voice's warnings and promises. The moral weight of their decision pressed down upon them, a burden as heavy as the fate of two worlds. They considered the potential consequences of both options, weighing the devastation of a self-destruct against the unknown risks of allowing the bioweapon to continue its evolution.

The self-destruct promised a clean break, a return to the *status quo ante bellum*, but it meant abandoning any hope for understanding or reconciliation with a sentient lifeform struggling to survive. The alternative was an arduous, risky path, fraught with uncertainties and the possibility of creating more chaos than order.

Niko ran simulations, projecting countless scenarios, each one ending in either utter devastation or fragile hope. Kael relived his past failures, seeing his own guilt reflected in the bioweapon's desperate struggle. Lira studied the ancient carvings, searching for clues to help bridge the gap between two vastly different intelligences.

Days turned into sleepless nights. The pressure built, threatening to crush their spirits. The team existed in a state of suspended animation, trapped between the known horrors of destruction and the terrifying unknown of coexistence. The moral implications of their actions loomed over them. Were they entitled to decide the fate of a sentient being, a lifeform struggling to heal the wounds inflicted by humanity? Was their own survival worth the extinction of another species, even one born from their own hubris?

The team found themselves arguing, debating every potential outcome and every conceivable consequence. Their disagreements highlighted the depth of their moral struggles and the conflicting values at the heart of their dilemma. Niko's pragmatism clashed with Kael's guilt and Lira's profound sense of ecological justice. Their unity, forged in the face of a shared crisis, began to fray, revealing the deep-seated conflicts that threatened to tear them apart. The weight of responsibility was nearly unbearable.

The arguments grew heated, pushing the team to the brink of collapse. Niko, clinging to his scientific objectivity, argued for the necessity of Protocol Eden. The risk of unchecked bioweapon expansion was simply too great, the potential for galactic-scale catastrophe too immense to ignore. Kael, consumed by his guilt, pleaded for a different approach, urging them to seek a path of reconciliation, to find a way to heal the wound inflicted upon Eden Prime. Lira, somewhere between their warring viewpoints, searched desperately for a middle ground, a way to blend scientific rigor with compassion and understanding.

The crisis forced them to confront not only the fate of Eden Prime but their own values and their own humanity. They were not simply scientists; they were moral arbiters, their choices shaping the destiny of countless lives. The dilemma was not only scientific but deeply ethical and philosophical. It forced them to question the boundaries of human intervention, the limits of their scientific understanding, and ultimately their place in the universe.

The weight of that reality pressed down on them, testing the limits of their resolve. The hum of the crystalline sphere became a constant reminder of the irreversible nature of their impending decision, a choice that would determine not only the fate of Eden Prime but their own consciences. The fate of humanity itself hung in the balance, a testament to the profound moral crossroads they now faced. The silence, once filled with the voice of Eden Prime, now echoed with the weight of their own silent deliberations, the future of two worlds trembling on the edge of their decision.

The air in the observation dome crackled with unspoken accusations. Days bled into nights, the rhythmic hum of the crystalline sphere a relentless counterpoint to the growing discord among the team. Niko, his usually meticulous demeanor frayed at the edges, paced restlessly, his fingers drumming a frantic rhythm on his datapad.

The simulations he had run painted a grim picture, a spectrum of catastrophic outcomes, each more terrifying than the last. Uncontrolled bioweapon expansion, he argued, was not a risk; it was a certainty. The self-destruct sequence was the only rational choice, a bitter pill to swallow but a necessary one to prevent galactic-scale devastation.

"We're talking about containing a potentially planet-killing bioweapon, Kael," Niko's voice was tight with suppressed frustration. "Sentimentality has no place here. This isn't about saving a lifeform; it's about preventing the extinction of countless others."

Kael, his face drawn and pale, flinched at the words. The raw grief over Xylos's death still clung to him like a shroud, but his sorrow had expanded, encompassing the bioweapon, the ravaged landscape of Eden Prime, and the whole tapestry of humanity's mistakes. "It's not just a bioweapon, Niko," he countered, his voice hoarse with emotion. "The voice... it showed me... it's trying to heal. It's a desperate act of survival, a twisted reflection of our own attempts to control nature." He paused, the words catching in his throat. "We created this monster. We can't just abandon it to its fate."

Lira, her gaze fixed on the intricate carvings that adorned the crystalline sphere, offered a hesitant counterpoint. "There's something else here, something more than just a bioweapon. The carvings... they're sophisticated, suggesting a level of intelligence, a form of communication. We don't understand it yet, but I believe there's a chance to find common ground." She traced the lines of a particularly intricate design with a trembling finger. "What if we're witnessing a new form of evolution, a desperate attempt at symbiosis? Destruction would be a tragic loss, not only for Eden Prime but for our understanding of life itself."

The argument escalated, their individual perspectives clashing like tectonic plates. Niko's scientific pragmatism, grounded in data and probability, collided with Kael's emotional plea for redemption and Lira's fervent belief in the intrinsic value of all life, however alien or terrifying. The lines of their collaborative work had become blurred, and the initial cohesion that bound them was fracturing under the weight of their emotional burden.

The ensuing days were a blur of heated debates, sleepless nights, and conflicting simulations. Niko's cold logic clashed with Kael's overwhelming sense of guilt, creating an emotional vortex that threatened to consume Lira. She found herself mediating, desperately searching for a compromise, a middle ground between their warring factions, but the chasm between their views seemed unbridgeable. She saw the beauty in the bioweapon's adaptation, its desperate struggle for survival, yet she also understood the potential for catastrophic consequences. The scientific evidence pointed toward a self-destruct, but her heart pleaded for a different approach.

Kael's guilt was a heavy burden. He saw himself in the bioweapon's plight, a creature born of humanity's ambition and driven to desperate measures. He had played a role in the creation of Project Chimera, a role he now deeply regretted. The prospect of activating Protocol Eden felt like a betrayal, a final abandonment of a lifeform struggling to heal the wounds he had helped inflict. He felt a moral obligation to find another way, a path toward reconciliation, but the scientific data seemed to offer no such possibility.

Niko, meanwhile, wrestled with his conscience. He was a scientist, trained to prioritize logic and reason. The self-destruct was a painful decision, but it was the only one supported by the evidence. The potential consequences of failing to contain the bioweapon were too immense to ignore. He envisioned a galactic catastrophe, a plague spreading from Eden Prime, consuming planets and wiping out civilizations. The lives of billions depended on his choice, and the ethical weight of such a momentous decision bore down on him. He found himself struggling to reconcile his scientific objectivity with the growing unease in his gut. Was he merely a cold, calculating scientist, or did he carry a responsibility beyond the mere analysis of data?

Lira delved deeper into the bioweapon's genetic code, hoping to find a key, a clue that could unlock a different solution. She spent hours poring over the intricate designs on the crystalline sphere, seeking patterns, searching for a language, any hint of communication. The patterns, she believed, weren't just random; they represented something more profound, a desperate attempt by the bioweapon to communicate, to reach out to a species that had caused its suffering. She poured all her scientific knowledge, all her intellectual energy, into understanding this cryptic message, desperately seeking a way to bridge the gap between humanity and this unique lifeform, a lifeform that was both a product of human error and a testament to life's resilience.

The arguments continued, pushing the team to the brink of collapse. Their unity, once a source of strength, was shattered by their conflicting values and the crushing weight of their decision. The fate of Eden Prime, the fate of the galaxy, rested on their ability to resolve their internal conflicts, to find common ground in the face of overwhelming adversity.

The crystalline sphere pulsed, a silent witness to their inner turmoil, a constant reminder of the fragile equilibrium they desperately sought to maintain. The future, uncertain and daunting, waited for their decision, hanging in the balance between destruction and a desperate, fragile hope. The silence in the observation dome was broken only by their ragged breathing, the hum of the sphere, and the echoes of their unresolved conflict. The heart of Eden Prime beat, a silent plea for understanding in a symphony of conflicting voices.

CHAPTER FIVE

THE CHOICE

The weight of the galaxy pressed down on Lira. The rhythmic hum of the crystalline sphere, once a source of fascination, now felt like a relentless, accusatory pulse. Days blurred into nights, each filled with echoing arguments, desperate pleas, and the cold logic that threatened to shatter her world. Niko's unwavering adherence to the self-destruct protocol, the calculated annihilation of Eden Prime and its unique bioweapon, felt like a betrayal of everything she held dear. Yet Kael's impassioned defense, his desperate attempt to find redemption in the face of his past mistakes, felt equally misguided, a dangerous gamble with the fate of countless worlds.

She traced the intricate carvings on the sphere again, her fingers lingering on the swirling patterns, seeking some hidden meaning, some secret code that could unlock a different path. These weren't just random designs; they were a language, a complex tapestry of information that whispered of a desperate struggle for survival, a poignant testament to the tenacity of life itself. She saw the bioweapon not as a monster but as a desperate survivor, a being born of human ambition, struggling to adapt and heal the wounds inflicted upon it. This was a reflection of humanity's own mistakes, a distorted mirror reflecting back its hubris and insatiable need for control.

The scientific data screamed at her, a cacophony of warnings, probabilities, and projections of catastrophe. Niko's simulations were irrefutable, painting a terrifying picture of unchecked bioweapon expansion, a global plague that could consume the galaxy, leaving behind a trail of devastation and death. The numbers were stark and unforgiving, billions of lives hanging in the balance. Yet nestled within the terrifying statistics was a flicker of something else, a subtle whisper of hope.

Lira delved deeper into the bioweapon's genetic code, searching for anomalies, any hint of a weakness or vulnerability that could be exploited without resorting to complete annihilation. She pored over the research, meticulously analyzing the data, searching for a loophole, a different path. The data was complex, overwhelming, a labyrinth of genetic sequences and protein structures, yet she persisted, driven by an unwavering belief in the potential for symbiosis, for coexistence that transcended the narrow confines of human understanding.

She spent countless hours in the archives, immersed in the history of Project Chimera, the clandestine program that had given birth to the bioweapon. She unearthed the initial research documents, the early simulations, the optimistic projections of a world transformed by bioengineered solutions. The hubris was evident in the old reports, a blind faith in the ability of science to control nature, to bend it to humanity's will. The project's failures, the unforeseen consequences, were laid bare, a stark reminder of the unpredictable nature of life, the delicate balance that humanity had so carelessly disrupted.

Lira understood Niko's apprehension. She knew the risks and the terrifying possibilities of failure. But she also saw a chance, a glimmer of hope in the bioweapon's desperate struggle for survival. This wasn't simply a weapon; it was a unique life form, a product of human ambition that had found its own way to adapt and evolve. Destruction felt like a tragic abdication of responsibility, a failure to understand the intricate web of life that connected all living things.

The weight of her decision pressed down on her, a crushing burden that threatened to suffocate her. She saw the faces of billions, the potential loss, the devastation that could engulf the galaxy. But she also saw the bioweapon, a struggling life form desperately seeking a way to coexist, a testament to the resilience of life itself. The beauty of its adaptation, its unique struggle, resonated within her, a counterpoint to the chilling logic of self-destruction.

She thought of the Eden Prime ecosystem, the intricate web of life that had evolved over millennia. The destruction of Eden Prime would not only eliminate the bioweapon but would also erase an irreplaceable part of the galaxy's biodiversity, a loss that would reverberate through countless ecosystems, disrupting the delicate balance of life across vast interstellar distances.

Her heart ached with the weight of her responsibility. She knew that inaction was not an option. The bioweapon was growing, expanding, its reach extending further each day. The potential for catastrophic consequences loomed large, but the thought of obliterating this unique life form, a life form striving for survival, filled her with a profound sense of unease.

Days turned into sleepless nights filled with contemplation, analysis, and relentless research. She considered various approaches, exploring alternative solutions, searching for a path that would allow humanity to coexist with this unique life form, a path that would avert a galactic catastrophe without resorting to complete annihilation.

Lira's internal struggle mirrored the team's conflict. Niko's unwavering logic, based on solid scientific evidence, collided with Kael's impassioned plea for redemption. She found herself caught in the middle, attempting to bridge the seemingly unbridgeable gap between their conflicting perspectives. She was a scientist, trained in logic and reason, yet her heart yearned for a different outcome, a solution that would acknowledge the intrinsic value of all life, even life that was born from humanity's mistakes.

Finally, after days of intense deliberation and soul-searching, Lira made her decision. It was a daring move, a bold gamble that defied the overwhelming scientific consensus, a choice that rested on fragile hope, a leap of faith into the unknown. She presented her proposal, a carefully constructed plan, meticulously detailing her approach, a path that would require collaboration, trust, and a willingness to step beyond the boundaries of established scientific dogma.

Her proposal was met with skepticism and apprehension. Niko remained unconvinced, his reservations rooted in scientific logic and the weight of probability. Kael, however, found a flicker of hope, a sense of redemption within Lira's plan. The choice ultimately rested with them, a collective decision that would shape the fate of Eden Prime and the galaxy beyond. The crystalline sphere pulsed, a silent witness to their deliberations, a fragile reminder of the delicate balance between destruction and hope. The future hung in the balance, awaiting their final verdict. The fate of billions rested on the delicate shoulders of three scientists, three souls wrestling with their conscience, their knowledge, and the immense weight of their decision. The choice, once seemingly clear-cut, now blurred into a complex tapestry of scientific evidence, ethical considerations, and a desperate hope for a future beyond the confines of self-destruction.

The air in the conference room crackled with a tension thicker than the dust motes dancing in the filtered light. Niko, her face etched with the grim lines of sleepless nights and relentless calculations, stared at the holographic projection of Eden Prime, its lush, vibrant ecosystem now overlaid with a chilling network of red lines illustrating the relentless spread of the bioweapon.

Lira, her eyes mirroring the shimmering turquoise of the crystalline sphere, held her breath, the weight of their collective decision pressing down on her like a physical burden. And Kael sat silent, his gaze fixed on the floor, his hands clasped tightly in his lap, a stark contrast to his usual boisterous energy. The transformation in him was palpable, a shift from the reckless abandon of his past to a quiet, almost somber determination.

Lira had presented her plan, a daring and almost foolhardy attempt to neutralize the bioweapon without resorting to complete annihilation. It involved a delicate manipulation of the bioweapon's genetic code, a process that required precise timing, intricate control, and a level of risk that bordered on suicidal. The success rate, according to Niko's simulations, hovered precariously around five percent, a statistic that made the room feel colder, the silence more deafening.

Niko had voiced her objections, her arguments laced with the cold precision of scientific logic. The risks were too high, the potential for catastrophic failure too immense. Billions of lives hung in the balance, and a five percent chance of success felt like a gamble with the very fate of the galaxy. But Lira, empowered by her newfound understanding of the bioweapon's inherent resilience, held firm. She had seen the beauty in its desperate struggle for survival, the tenacity of life against overwhelming odds. Destruction, she argued, was not the answer. There was a path to coexistence, a chance for reconciliation, even if that chance felt impossibly slim.

Then Kael spoke, his voice barely a whisper at first, gaining strength as he continued. He spoke not of scientific probabilities or intricate algorithms, but of responsibility, of atonement, of a chance to right the wrongs of his past. He had been a key player in Project Chimera, the clandestine program that had created the bioweapon. He carried the weight of that creation, the burden of its unforeseen consequences, a heavy cloak of guilt that he had worn for far too long.

"I know what I did," Kael said, his voice low and steady. "I was part of the team that unleashed this... this creature. And I believe it's my responsibility to help find a way to contain it, to mitigate the damage." He paused, his gaze locking with Lira's. "Your plan... it's risky, I know. But it's also... it's the only chance we have. And I'm willing to do whatever it takes to make it work."

His words hung in the air, heavy with unspoken meaning. The silence that followed was punctuated only by the rhythmic hum of the crystalline sphere, a silent witness to the unfolding drama. Niko's skepticism remained, but a flicker of something akin to respect, or perhaps even hope, appeared in her eyes. She knew Kael's contributions to Project Chimera had been monumental, his expertise unmatched. His offer wasn't just a hollow gesture; it represented a profound shift in his character, a genuine desire for redemption.

Kael outlined his plan. It was a dangerous proposal, a sacrifice born from both his scientific expertise and a deep-seated need for atonement. He proposed to act as a living conduit, a bridge between the bioweapon and the human intervention. The genetic manipulation required a level of precision that no machine could achieve, a delicate balance of chemical signals that only a human body, specifically his, could provide. His intimate knowledge of the bioweapon's genetic structure, gained during his time with Project Chimera, was essential for the process.

The procedure itself was a marvel of biological engineering and a high-stakes gamble. Kael would undergo a series of experimental procedures designed to temporarily alter his own genetic makeup, making him compatible with the bioweapon's cellular structure. He would then act as a biological interface, transmitting the carefully calibrated genetic signals required to neutralize the weapon. The risks were immense. The process could fail, leading to his death, or worse, it could trigger an uncontrolled reaction resulting in the widespread expansion of the bioweapon.

"I understand the risks," Kael stated calmly, his voice unwavering. "I know it's a gamble, but I'm willing to take it. It's the only way. It's my way of making amends. Of finally accepting responsibility for my part in this."

The intensity of his conviction moved Lira deeply. His willingness to sacrifice his life, not for glory or recognition, but for redemption, resonated with her profound sense of responsibility. She saw in him a reflection of humanity's potential for growth, for self-awareness, and for healing.

Niko, however, remained unconvinced. She ran the simulations again, factoring in Kael's participation, the variables shifting and reforming, displaying a slightly increased chance of success. Still, the risks remained astronomical. But there was a new factor in the equation, one that went beyond the cold, hard numbers. Kael's unwavering commitment, his willingness to sacrifice himself, changed the dynamic of the situation entirely.

The discussions continued for days, a whirlwind of scientific data, ethical debates, and personal reflections. The team worked tirelessly, refining the process, mitigating the risks as much as possible, ensuring Kael's safety while maximizing the chances of success. They delved deeper into the bioweapon's genetic code, exploring every possible vulnerability, every potential pathway to neutralization. They modified Kael's genetic template, testing and retesting, refining the process until they had a plan that was as risk-averse as possible, considering the circumstances.

As the day of the procedure approached, an unspoken tension filled the air. Kael prepared himself, not with fear, but with a newfound peace, a sense of closure that seemed to wash over him. He knew the risks. He accepted them. He had finally found a path to redemption, a way to atone for his past mistakes. His sacrifice was not an act of self-destruction but an act of profound selflessness, a testament to the transformative power of responsibility and the enduring resilience of the human spirit.

The fate of billions rested on his shoulders, but he carried that burden not with fear but with a quiet dignity, a quiet determination, a quiet hope for a future redeemed. The weight of the galaxy felt lighter now, not because the problem was solved, but because one man, finally accepting the weight of his past, had found a way to bear it. The fate of Eden Prime, and perhaps the galaxy, rested on this single act of selfless sacrifice.

The silence in the observation chamber was a palpable thing, heavy with the weight of unspoken anxieties and the hum of life-support systems. Niko, her usual crisp efficiency replaced by a visible tremor in her hands, adjusted the holographic display, zooming in on a specific section of Eden Prime's ravaged landscape. The red tendrils of the bioweapon still snaked across the once-vibrant ecosystem, a stark testament to its relentless expansion.

"It's not all or nothing," Niko finally said, her voice barely a whisper against the background hum. The words hung in the air, a fragile bridge between the stark reality of their situation and the possibility of a less catastrophic outcome. Lira and Kael exchanged a look, their faces etched with a mixture of hope and apprehension.

"A compromise?" Lira asked, her voice soft, hesitant. The idea itself felt radical, a departure from the binary choice they'd been wrestling with for days: annihilation or reckless hope.

Niko nodded, her gaze unwavering. "A partial neutralization. We don't eliminate the bioweapon entirely. We contain it, redefine its parameters, and create a new equilibrium."

Kael leaned forward, his brow furrowed in concentration. "A controlled containment? How?"

"It requires a different approach, a more... nuanced intervention," Niko explained, gesturing toward the holographic projection. "The bioweapon isn't simply a destructive force. It's a complex organism, adapting, evolving, driven by its own internal logic. It's exhibiting signs of self-preservation, almost a... desperate clinging to life."

She tapped a sequence of commands, and the holographic display shifted, revealing a detailed schematic of the bioweapon's genetic structure. Lines of code scrolled across the screen, a complex symphony of digital information representing the intricate biological machinery of the organism.

"We've identified a specific sequence within its DNA," Niko continued, her voice gaining strength, "a regulatory gene that controls its aggressive expansion. If we can modify this gene, even subtly, we could potentially curb its growth, redirect its energy. Essentially, we reprogram its survival instincts."

"But what about the existing infection?" Lira questioned, her concern evident.

"That's the crucial part of the compromise," Niko replied. "We can't undo the damage already done. The existing bioweapon will remain. But we can prevent further spread, mitigate the worst effects. We'll create a sort of... quarantine zone, a contained ecosystem where the bioweapon can exist without decimating everything else."

"This isn't a complete victory," Kael acknowledged, "but it's a survival strategy. It's a chance to buy time, to allow the ecosystems to adapt, to develop resistance."

"Exactly," Niko agreed. "It's a compromise between complete eradication, which carries its own devastating risks, and accepting the status quo. It's a calculated risk, a gamble, but one with a considerably higher chance of success than the original plan."

Lira studied the holographic display, her mind racing through the implications of Niko's proposal. It was a less dramatic, less heroic solution than she had initially envisioned, but it held a profound logic. It was a pathway to a future where both humanity and Eden Prime could, perhaps, coexist.

The following days were a blur of intense activity. Niko's team worked tirelessly, refining the genetic modification, meticulously modeling the potential consequences, and preparing for every possible contingency. They ran simulations, analyzed data, and debated the ethical implications of their actions. The compromise involved a delicate balancing act, weighing the potential benefits against the inherent risks.

The ethical implications were profound. They were effectively altering the genetic code of a living organism, a decision with far-reaching consequences they couldn't fully predict. They debated the definition of life, the morality of interfering with natural processes, and the long-term impact on Eden Prime's ecosystem. The line between intervention and manipulation blurred, constantly tested and reassessed.

Kael, despite his initial reluctance, became a pivotal figure in this new phase of the mission. His expertise in Project Chimera, though initially a source of guilt, proved invaluable. His intimate knowledge of the bioweapon's structure, its vulnerabilities, and its surprising resilience provided insights that were crucial to the success of the modified genetic sequence. He contributed his unique perspective, born from both remorse and a fierce determination to find a path to redemption.

The genetic modification wasn't simply a matter of inserting or deleting code. It was about fine-tuning, about creating a delicate balance, about reprogramming a life form without causing further destruction. It was about understanding the bioweapon not just as a threat but as a living organism with its own complex internal logic, fighting for survival in a damaged world.

As they approached the final stages, an unexpected complication arose. The initial simulations had failed to account for a specific enzyme within the bioweapon's genetic structure. This enzyme, it turned out, was critical to the success of the genetic modification. The enzyme's presence could either amplify the effects of their modification, leading to a swift and efficient containment, or it could trigger an unforeseen reaction, causing catastrophic failure. It was a high-stakes gamble.

Niko, utilizing a new set of algorithms, calculated the probability of success. The numbers were still daunting, a precarious balance between hope and despair. But the compromise offered a new possibility, a chance to mitigate the worst-case scenarios and improve the odds of a more manageable outcome. This wasn't the perfect solution, but it was a realistic pathway toward a fragile peace. It was a testament to the capacity for adaptation, both in the bioweapon and in humanity itself.

The future remained uncertain, but for the first time in a long time, there was a glimmer of hope, a sliver of optimism piercing the darkness. The compromise wasn't just a scientific solution; it was a moral compromise, a recognition of the complex relationship between humanity and the world they had so profoundly damaged. The fate of Eden Prime and the galaxy hung in the balance, but the weight felt slightly lighter, the path forward, however uncertain, slightly clearer.

The activation sequence initiated with a silent hum, a ripple of energy that spread across the control console. Niko's hand hovered over the final confirmation button, her knuckles white against the polished surface. The weight of the decision, the potential consequences the fate of Eden Prime, perhaps even the galaxy rested on this single action. Lira and Kael stood beside her, their faces mirroring her own mixture of apprehension and grim determination. For weeks, they had pored over data, debated ethics, and wrestled with the moral implications of their audacious plan. Now, it was time to see if their calculations, their hopes, and their compromises would bear fruit.

The modified genetic sequence, a carefully crafted piece of digital code, was uploaded. The holographic display flickered, shifting from the familiar schematic of the bioweapon's DNA to a dynamic visualization of its interaction with the modified sequence. Initially, nothing happened. The silence stretched, thick and suffocating, punctuated only by the rhythmic whirring of the life-support systems. The tension in the observation chamber was almost unbearable. Then, slowly, subtly, changes began to occur.

The crimson tendrils of the bioweapon, which had relentlessly spread across Eden Prime, began to lose their vibrancy. Their expansion slowed, faltered, then ceased altogether in certain areas. In other zones, the tendrils seemed to change color, shifting from a deep scarlet to a dull, almost brownish hue. The changes weren't uniform; the bioweapon responded differently in various parts of the ecosystem, highlighting the complex interplay of environmental factors and the modified genetic code.

"It's working," Lira breathed, her voice barely audible. Relief, cautious and tentative, washed over her face. Kael, however, remained wary. His gaze stayed fixed on the holographic display, his expression unreadable. His experience with Project Chimera had taught him to expect the unexpected, to anticipate unforeseen consequences.

The initial success, however, was short-lived. Within hours, a new pattern emerged. In certain regions, the bioweapon, despite its slowed growth, began to exhibit unusual behavior. The modified genetic sequence, instead of simply curbing its expansion, appeared to be triggering a defensive response. The bioweapon, cornered and threatened, began to adapt, evolving in ways that hadn't been predicted by their models.

New, smaller tendrils, thinner and darker than before, began to sprout from the main body. These tendrils displayed an unexpected resilience to the modified sequence, bypassing its effects and continuing to expand. It was a terrifying demonstration of the bioweapon's adaptive capabilities, a stark reminder of the power of natural selection.

Panic threatened to overwhelm the team. Their carefully crafted compromise was unraveling before their eyes. The bioweapon, initially subdued, was now fighting back, demonstrating a startling capacity for resilience and evolution. The delicate balance they had strived for was tilting dangerously.

Niko, ever the pragmatist, quickly recalibrated their strategy. She ordered the deployment of secondary countermeasures, using nanobots designed to target the new, resistant tendrils. These nanobots, programmed with a different set of genetic modifications, were created to neutralize the bioweapon's adaptation mechanisms.

The deployment of the nanobots proved successful in some areas, slowing the growth of the resistant tendrils. However, in other parts of the ecosystem, the nanobots encountered unexpected interactions with the environment, triggering unforeseen reactions that further complicated the situation. The ecosystem, already stressed and weakened by the bioweapon, was now reacting unpredictably to the cascading effects of their interventions.

The following days were a blur of frantic activity. The team worked around the clock, monitoring the situation, adjusting their strategies, and improvising on the fly. They developed new algorithms, refined their models, and deployed new countermeasures. The constant stream of data, both encouraging and alarming, highlighted the precarious nature of their situation.

They discovered that the bioweapon's adaptive capacity was linked to a specific element within Eden Prime's soil. This element, previously unknown, amplified the bioweapon's defensive mechanisms, bolstering its resilience to the genetic modifications. This discovery necessitated a complete recalibration of their approach. They needed to address not just the bioweapon but also the underlying environmental factors contributing to its adaptation.

This new understanding necessitated a further compromise. They had to accept a more limited containment zone, focusing on protecting key ecosystems rather than attempting complete eradication. This meant sacrificing some areas to the bioweapon and prioritizing the preservation of others. It was a painful realization, a stark reminder of the limitations of their control.

The process of containing the bioweapon was a complex dance of adjustments, calibrations, and countermeasures. Every action had ripple effects, leading to unforeseen consequences that required immediate responses. The team worked tirelessly, adapting their strategies constantly to account for the bioweapon's relentless evolution. They had effectively entered a dynamic, ongoing negotiation with a living organism, a desperate struggle for a new equilibrium.

Weeks turned into months. The crisis continued, a relentless test of the team's resilience and adaptability. The initial success had quickly given way to a prolonged, unpredictable struggle, highlighting the inherent unpredictability of interacting with a complex living system. The compromise, initially hailed as a breakthrough, had evolved into a constant negotiation, a relentless push and pull between humanity's interventions and the bioweapon's adaptive responses.

The outcome remained uncertain, hanging precariously in the balance. Eden Prime's ecosystem remained fractured, a testament to the pervasive damage wrought by the bioweapon. But the relentless spread had ceased, replaced by a slow, uneasy truce. The team had purchased time, a precious commodity in this desperate struggle. They had achieved a fragile peace, a compromise born not out of victory but out of necessity, a testament to humanity's capacity for adaptation in the face of overwhelming adversity.

The future was uncertain, but the team, weary yet resolute, was committed to maintaining this delicate equilibrium, hoping that time would bring both healing and understanding to the ravaged world of Eden Prime. The choice they had made was a gamble, a high-stakes wager on a future where humanity and nature might somehow, against all odds, find a way to coexist.

The initial euphoria following the deployment of the modified genetic sequence quickly dissipated as the bioweapon responded in ways that defied their carefully constructed models. While the crimson tendrils had indeed slowed their advance in certain regions, exhibiting the muted coloration they had anticipated, a disturbing new phenomenon emerged. In areas with particularly dense vegetation, the bioweapon seemed to mutate. Not just adapt, but fundamentally alter its structure and very essence.

Instead of the familiar serpentine tendrils, smaller, almost root-like structures began to burrow into the soil, their growth defying the modified sequence altogether. These new tendrils were darker, almost black, and possessed a surprising resilience. They weaved through the undergrowth, bypassing the areas affected by the modified gene and relentlessly spreading, creating a network of subterranean tendrils that expanded far beyond the reach of their initial containment efforts.

Lira, ever the optimist, initially proposed escalating the deployment of nano-bots, arguing that a more concentrated assault could still overwhelm the bioweapon. Kael, however, countered with chilling data showing that the new tendrils were actively absorbing the nano-bots and using their components to further enhance their own growth and resilience. It was a terrifying example of biological piracy, a chilling display of the bioweapon's capacity for exploitation and assimilation.

The holographic display, once a source of cautious optimism, now showed a terrifyingly complex pattern of growth and adaptation. The bioweapon's spread was no longer a simple, predictable pattern. It was chaotic, dynamic, and constantly evolving. The crimson tendrils, slowed but not eradicated, intertwined with the new subterranean network, creating a terrifyingly resilient system. It was as if the bioweapon had learned, had adapted, not merely to their initial countermeasure but to the very concept of opposition.

Niko, ever the pragmatist, initiated a series of emergency meetings. The team, exhausted and frayed, grappled with the implications of their unexpected failure. Their initial success had been a mirage, a momentary pause in an ongoing evolutionary arms race. The bioweapon was not merely adapting; it was learning. It was evolving at an alarming rate, demonstrating an intelligence and resourcefulness that far surpassed their initial projections.

The discussions were intense, fraught with the weight of their collective failure. Accusations were subtly voiced, and doubts simmered beneath the surface. Had they underestimated the bioweapon? Had their ethical compromises blinded them to its potential? The weight of responsibility pressed heavily upon them. The fate of Eden Prime, the success or failure of their entire mission, rested on their collective shoulders.

Days bled into weeks as the team scrambled to develop new countermeasures. They analyzed the composition of the new tendrils, seeking vulnerabilities and searching for weaknesses that could be exploited. They explored alternative strategies, experimenting with different approaches, each iteration more desperate than the last. The constant stream of data, a deluge of complex information, was both overwhelming and frustrating. They were racing against time, against the relentless evolution of the bioweapon, their every step shadowed by the uncertainty of their success.

A breakthrough came unexpectedly. During an analysis of soil samples collected near the new tendrils, Dr. Aris, a specialist in xenobiology, discovered an anomaly: a trace element, previously unknown, that seemed to be catalyzing the bioweapon's adaptation. This element, which they tentatively named *Xylos*, appeared to act as a supercharger for the bioweapon's evolutionary mechanisms. It was as if Xylos was fueling the bioweapon's capacity to adapt and overcome any challenge thrown at it.

This discovery fundamentally altered their perspective. The battle was no longer solely against the bioweapon itself but against the environment that fueled its terrifying capacity for change. They had to find a way to neutralize Xylos, to disrupt the bioweapon's access to this potent catalyst. This presented a new, daunting challenge that required a completely different approach.

The team began to explore methods of sequestering Xylos, devising ways to isolate the element and prevent its interaction with the bioweapon. This involved developing specialized nano-machines that could selectively bind with Xylos, effectively removing it from the soil. However, this new approach introduced its own set of challenges. The process of sequestering

Xylos was slow and painstaking and required a significant deployment of resources. Furthermore, there was no guarantee it would be successful.

Despite these uncertainties, the team pressed forward, their efforts fueled by desperate hope. They worked tirelessly, making adjustments, refining their models, and constantly adapting their strategies in response to the bioweapon's relentless evolution. The process was a chaotic dance, a constant negotiation between humanity's intervention and nature's stubborn resilience.

Months passed. The initial frantic activity gave way to a more measured approach. The crisis persisted, but the relentless, chaotic spread of the bioweapon had finally been halted. The landscape of Eden Prime remained scarred, a testament to the pervasive damage. But the relentless advance had been checked, replaced by a precarious stalemate. They had bought time, a precious commodity in this long-term struggle.

The victory was far from complete, the threat far from extinguished. But the team had achieved a fragile, tentative peace a compromise not of victory but of necessity, a testament to humanity's enduring capacity to adapt and persevere even in the face of seemingly insurmountable challenges.

The future remained uncertain, but the team, weary yet resolute, was committed to maintaining this uneasy equilibrium, hoping that time would allow the ecosystem to heal and recover from the scars of the bioweapon and the interventions that had followed. Their choice, made weeks ago, had led to an outcome far more complex and unpredictable than they could have imagined a harsh lesson in the unpredictable nature of both life and their attempts to control it.

The future of Eden Prime hung in the balance, a fragile balance dependent on continued effort, vigilance, and a recognition of the intricate web of life they had so carelessly disturbed.

Chapter Six

Adaptations

The fragile stalemate was not peace but a necessary pause. The crimson tendrils, though slowed, still pulsed with a menacing life, their subterranean counterparts a constant, unseen threat. Rebuilding Eden Prime was not about eradication; it was about adaptation, about finding a way to coexist with a bioweapon that had proven far more resilient and intelligent than anyone had initially anticipated. The initial euphoria of a near-miss victory had given way to a grim, determined resolve.

The first step was detoxification. The nano-machines designed to sequester *Xylos*, the element fueling the bioweapon's evolution, were deployed on a massive scale. Giant, drone-like aerial vehicles, resembling oversized metallic dragonflies, crisscrossed the skies of Eden Prime, dispensing clouds of microscopic machines. These machines, smaller than individual cells, navigated the complex terrain, systematically seeking out and binding with *Xylos* molecules, rendering them inert. The process was agonizingly slow, painstakingly precise. Progress was measured in millimeters, not meters, a frustratingly incremental advance against an overwhelming problem.

Parallel to the detoxification efforts, the team focused on ecological restoration. The landscape was a patchwork of destruction, scarred by the bioweapon's advance and the subsequent countermeasures. The lush vegetation, once vibrant and teeming with life, was now a desolate expanse in many areas. Lira, with her expertise in terraforming and ecological engineering, spearheaded this effort. She meticulously mapped the affected areas, analyzing soil composition, nutrient levels, and the remaining biodiversity. Using advanced bio-printing technologies, her team began to reconstruct the damaged ecosystems, replicating the lost flora and fauna with a precision that bordered on artistry.

This, however, was not simply a matter of replacing what had been lost. The bioweapon had fundamentally altered the environment, creating new conditions that required innovative solutions. The subterranean tendrils, while contained, had left behind a network of underground channels that altered water flow and nutrient distribution. Kael, with his background in hydrological modeling, developed intricate algorithms to predict and mitigate these changes, guiding the reintroduction of plant life to optimize water usage and nutrient uptake. The team experimented with genetically modified strains of plants engineered to thrive in the altered conditions, creating a more resilient and adaptable ecosystem.

The challenge extended beyond the flora. The fauna of Eden Prime had also suffered immensely. Many species had been wiped out, and others were struggling to survive in the altered environment. Niko, ever pragmatic, assembled a team to assess the remaining biodiversity and implement a comprehensive conservation strategy. This involved not only protecting the surviving species but also actively breeding and reintroducing endangered ones, using sophisticated genetic technologies to bolster their resilience.

The task was monumental. The restoration of Eden Prime was not a linear process; it was a chaotic dance of adaptation and response, a constant negotiation between the ravaged landscape and humanity's intervention. The team faced setbacks constantly: unexpected mutations in surviving species, unforeseen interactions between modified flora and fauna, and the ever-present threat of the dormant bioweapon. Yet their determination was unwavering, fueled by a shared sense of purpose and a profound respect for the planet they were striving to restore.

Dr. Aris, in the meantime, continued his research on *Xylos*. He discovered that the element, while catalyzing the bioweapon's adaptation, also possessed unique properties that could be harnessed for beneficial purposes. In carefully controlled environments, *Xylos* could accelerate the growth and development of certain plants, making it a powerful tool for accelerated reforestation. This discovery, though initially paradoxical, provided a crucial turning point in the rebuilding process. The team began to cautiously experiment with controlled *Xylos* applications, using it to accelerate the growth of strategically selected plant species in designated areas.

The rebuilding of Eden Prime was not just a scientific endeavor; it was a collaborative, multidisciplinary effort. Each member of the team brought unique expertise and distinct perspectives to the complex challenges. They learned to rely on each other, to trust each other's judgment, to collectively navigate the uncertainties of the situation. The initial tension and subtle accusations were replaced by shared understanding and a collective commitment to restore Eden Prime to a semblance of its former glory.

The process extended beyond the purely scientific. The team recognized the importance of involving the wider community of Eden Prime, the survivors who had witnessed the devastation and bore the weight of loss. They initiated community engagement programs, educating the survivors about the restoration efforts and fostering a sense of ownership and responsibility. They involved local communities in the replanting of trees, the care of newly introduced animal species, and the monitoring of the environment. This collaborative effort not only strengthened the community but also provided valuable data and insights that enhanced the efficacy of the restoration project.

Years passed. The scars of the bioweapon remained, but the landscape gradually began to recover. New forests grew, new species thrived, and the ecosystem slowly began to find a new equilibrium. The restoration of Eden Prime was not complete; it was an ongoing process, a constant adaptation to an evolving environment. Yet the progress was undeniable, a testament to humanity's resilience, its capacity to learn from mistakes, and its unwavering commitment to restoring balance to a damaged world.

The team's work was not solely focused on the physical landscape. They worked relentlessly to rebuild the social fabric of Eden Prime, addressing the psychological trauma suffered by its inhabitants. They established support networks, provided mental health services, and facilitated community-building initiatives. They understood that the restoration of the planet also required the restoration of its people. Healing the environment and healing the community were intertwined, two sides of the same coin.

The experience had left an indelible mark on the team. They had learned the limits of their power, the humbling unpredictability of nature, and the immense responsibility that came with manipulating life at its most fundamental level. They had faced their failures head-on, learned from their mistakes, and emerged stronger, more determined, and far more aware of the intricate web of life they were striving to protect.

The future of Eden Prime remained uncertain, but the team had found renewed purpose and a renewed commitment to maintaining the delicate balance they had so painstakingly achieved. Their journey had been a profound exploration of the limits of humanity's ambition, the resilience of nature, and the enduring power of adaptation. The rebuilt Eden Prime stood as a testament to both the damage humanity could inflict and the remarkable capacity for healing and renewal inherent in life itself. It was a fragile ecosystem, a delicate balance, a constant work in progress, but it stood as a symbol of the enduring spirit of humanity and the enduring power of hope.

The initial euphoria of halting the bioweapon's advance quickly faded as the true scale of the devastation became apparent. The crimson tendrils, though dormant, had left an indelible mark on the planet. The seemingly simple act of detoxification, for instance, proved far more complex than anticipated. The nano-machines, while effective in binding *Xylos*, often became entangled in the intricate root systems of surviving plants, inadvertently harming them. In several instances, entire sections of newly replanted forests had to be destroyed and the process started anew. This led to a critical reassessment of the detoxification strategy.

The team realized that a more nuanced approach was necessary, one that considered the delicate balance of the ecosystem rather than simply focusing on *Xylos* removal. They began developing more sophisticated nano-machines equipped with advanced sensors capable of distinguishing between *Xylos* molecules and plant tissues. This refinement, though demanding further resources and time, proved crucial in minimizing collateral damage.

The ecological restoration project also faced unforeseen challenges. The genetically modified plants, designed to thrive in the altered environment, unexpectedly attracted new, unforeseen pests. These insects, thriving on the modified plants, threatened to disrupt the delicate balance that the team was attempting to establish. Niko's team, initially focused on preserving existing species, had to pivot, developing new strategies to manage the emerging pest problem. They experimented with biological controls, introducing natural predators to limit the pest populations.

However, some of these introduced species unexpectedly competed with the native fauna, necessitating further adjustments. This highlighted a critical lesson: the intricate interconnectedness of an ecosystem cannot be easily manipulated. The team's initial hubris, the belief that they could precisely control the environment, was shattered by these repeated setbacks.

The lessons learned extended beyond the purely scientific realm. The initial restoration efforts had largely been dictated by top-down scientific planning. Lira's meticulous mapping and Kael's hydrological models were essential, but they lacked the nuanced understanding of the local environment possessed by the community members. The team realized their mistake: they had underestimated the value of local knowledge.

They embarked on a far more extensive engagement program, working closely with the survivors, integrating their understanding of the land into the restoration plans. This collaborative approach brought forth invaluable insights, highlighting the unique adaptations of surviving plant and animal species, and unveiling hidden water sources and microclimates. The survivors' stories also provided a deeper understanding of the social and psychological impact of the devastation, reminding the team that the restoration of Eden Prime extended far beyond the physical landscape.

A pivotal turning point came with the re-evaluation of the Xylos application. The initial enthusiasm for harnessing its growth-accelerating properties was tempered by the realization that uncontrolled Xylos could lead to unexpected and possibly dangerous mutations in plants and animals. Dr. Aris, humbled by his earlier assumptions, developed a more refined application method, using meticulously calibrated micro-doses of Xylos and carefully monitoring the effects on the surrounding ecosystem. This approach not only ensured safe utilization of Xylos but also provided a deeper understanding of its interactions with the environment. The team learned to embrace the uncertainty, to continuously monitor and adjust, to adapt their strategies based on the ever-changing landscape.

The use of genetic modification also came under scrutiny. The initial eagerness to create resilient strains of plants and animals had inadvertently led to unforeseen consequences. The team had focused on enhancing specific traits, such as drought resistance or pest tolerance, but they had not fully considered the potential unintended impacts on the overall ecosystem.

This experience underscored the limitations of genetic engineering, the need for a more holistic and cautious approach, and the recognition that the very act of modifying life could have unintended consequences. They began to shift from a purely technological approach to a more ecological one, emphasizing biodiversity and the resilience that naturally existed within the existing species. The goal shifted from creating "better" organisms to enhancing the existing ecosystem's capacity for self-regulation and adaptation.

The setbacks were not simply scientific challenges; they represented failures of communication and collaboration. The early days were marked by disagreements and a certain degree of professional rivalry. Each member, steeped in their own field of expertise, had initially struggled to appreciate the perspectives and contributions of others.

The crises they faced, however, fostered a powerful sense of shared responsibility and forced them to find common ground. They learned to value each other's skills and experiences, recognizing that a truly effective solution required a multidisciplinary approach. The team meetings, once tense and fraught with disagreement, transformed into collaborative brainstorming sessions characterized by mutual respect and trust. The process of adapting their strategies became a process of self-reflection and team cohesion.

The iterative nature of their work forced them to confront the ethical implications of their interventions. The temptation to control nature, to impose a specific outcome, was constantly at odds with the unpredictable nature of the ecosystem. They learned that true stewardship involved a delicate balance between intervention and observation, between active shaping and passive acceptance. The team developed a rigorous ethical framework involving thorough risk assessments, public consultations, and regular reviews of their strategies. This shift in approach reflected not only scientific understanding but also a deeper awareness of their responsibility toward the planet and its inhabitants.

Over time, the team developed a new philosophy of environmental restoration, one based not on control but on collaboration and adaptability. They recognized that restoring Eden Prime was not about recreating a pristine past but about guiding the ecosystem toward a new, resilient equilibrium. This shift in perspective profoundly altered their approach. They adopted a more experimental outlook, accepting that some interventions would fail and that constant learning and adaptation were essential for success. The community, initially skeptical of the team's interventions, became active participants, contributing to the monitoring and management of the restored ecosystem.

The scars left by the bioweapon remained visible, serving as a constant reminder of the fragility of their achievement. But the new Eden Prime, though forever changed, was thriving. The restored ecosystems were more diverse, more resilient, and better equipped to adapt to future challenges. The lessons learned, however, extended far beyond the confines of Eden Prime. They represented a profound shift in humanity's understanding of its relationship with the environment, a move away from dominion and toward a more humble and cooperative approach.

The team's journey, marked by setbacks and failures, ultimately led to a deeper understanding of environmental stewardship, a testament to the power of adaptation and the resilience of both nature and the human spirit. The rebuilt Eden Prime stood as a testament to humanity's capacity to learn from its mistakes and strive toward a more sustainable future, a future forged not through control but through collaboration, resilience, and a profound respect for the intricate web of life.

The whispers of wind through the newly leafed branches held a different song now, a melody less of frantic regrowth and more of settled harmony. Eden Prime, though forever bearing the scars of Xylos's invasion, was finding its rhythm. The crimson stains that had once marked the landscape were fading, replaced by a vibrant tapestry of greens, punctuated by the blues of revitalized waterways. The air, once thick with the cloying scent of the bioweapon, now carried the fresh, earthy aroma of burgeoning life.

This wasn't the Eden Prime of old, not a pristine paradise untouched by human hand, but a new equilibrium, a testament to adaptation, resilience, and the surprising power of collaboration.

The biodome, once a symbol of human ambition and perhaps a touch of hubris, had become a microcosm of this new balance. The carefully cultivated environment, initially designed to control every variable, had evolved. The scientists had learned to loosen their grip, to allow for spontaneity, for the unpredictable dance of nature to unfold. The strict protocols were relaxed, replaced by a more fluid system of monitoring and intervention. Instead of dictating the growth patterns of plants, they observed, adapting their strategies based on the biodome's own internal dynamics.

The once sterile environment now buzzed with the activity of a thriving ecosystem. Introduced species, carefully selected for their compatibility, integrated seamlessly into the community, enriching the biodiversity and resilience of the biodome. The genetic modifications, once a source of concern, were now deployed with a greater understanding of their long-term implications. The focus shifted from creating "super-organisms" to enhancing the intrinsic resilience of the existing species, fostering a more robust and interconnected web of life.

The community living within the biodome played a vital role in this new equilibrium. Initially, they were largely passive observers, dependent on the scientists' expertise. But as trust grew, so did their involvement. They became active participants in monitoring the environment, contributing their valuable local knowledge to inform the team's decisions. Their understanding of the subtle shifts in weather patterns, the behavior of specific animal species, and the nuances of plant growth proved invaluable. Their participation was not simply about data collection; it was about fostering a sense of shared responsibility, of collective stewardship. They actively participated in the cultivation of certain plants, contributing their traditional methods to complement the scientists' advanced techniques. This collaborative spirit was essential; it transformed the biodome from a controlled experiment into a shared space, a testament to the power of community engagement.

Outside the biodome, the changes were equally significant. The landscape, once ravaged by Xylos, was slowly recovering. The nano-machines, refined and sophisticated, continued their delicate work, carefully removing the bioweapon's remnants without harming the recovering ecosystem. New forests sprang up, not as perfectly uniform plantations but as diverse and dynamic ecosystems, reflecting the natural variability of the original landscape. The reintroduction of native species, guided by the local community's knowledge, proved remarkably successful. Animals once thought to be lost reappeared, finding refuge in the revitalized habitat. The rivers, once choked with Xylos, flowed freely, their waters teeming with life. The meticulous mapping and hydrological modeling done by Lira and Kael were now supplemented by the community's intimate knowledge of the land, creating a synergistic partnership between science and tradition.

The new equilibrium wasn't simply about ecological restoration; it was about rebuilding social structures. The shared experience of overcoming the Xylos crisis forged a powerful sense of community. The survivors, once scattered and fragmented, now worked together, rebuilding their lives and their environment. They established new farming practices, incorporating sustainable methods developed in collaboration with the scientific team. They developed systems for water management and waste recycling, drawing upon both modern technology and traditional knowledge. This process of rebuilding fostered self-reliance and resilience, creating a community capable of adapting to future challenges. The focus shifted from dependency on external aid to self-sufficiency and community empowerment.

The ethical framework established after the initial setbacks played a crucial role in shaping the new equilibrium. The team recognized the limitations of human intervention and the importance of respecting the autonomy of nature. Rigorous risk assessments and public consultations became essential components of every project, ensuring transparency and accountability. The team learned to balance intervention with observation, acknowledging that not every attempt at restoration would succeed. Failure, rather than being seen as an obstacle, became an opportunity for learning and adaptation. This new ethical approach, grounded in humility and respect for the natural world, was as important as the scientific advances in shaping the new equilibrium.

The success of Eden Prime wasn't simply about restoring the physical environment; it was about restoring the human spirit. The shared struggle against Xylos had brought the community together, forging a bond of resilience and shared purpose. The collaborative approach to rebuilding fostered a sense of ownership and pride, empowering the community to take control of their own destinies. The children, born into the shadow of Xylos's invasion, grew up knowing a different story, a story of collective triumph, of adapting to adversity, and of embracing a symbiotic relationship with the natural world.

The scars remained, visible reminders of the catastrophe. But the landscape bore witness to a profound transformation, a shift in the relationship between humanity and nature. Eden Prime was no longer viewed as a resource to be exploited but as a living entity to be respected and nurtured. The new equilibrium wasn't a static state; it was a dynamic process, a continuous dance between human intervention and ecological response. The scientists, once driven by a desire to control, learned to collaborate, to adapt, to trust the innate resilience of the ecosystem. The community, once victims, became stewards, actively participating in the ongoing process of restoration.

The lessons learned on Eden Prime reached far beyond its borders. The new model of environmental restoration, one based on collaboration, adaptation, and respect for the intricate web of life, was being adopted across the globe. It represented a shift away from the outdated paradigm of human dominion over nature and toward a more humble and sustainable approach. It was a recognition that the restoration of the planet was not just a scientific endeavor but a social and ethical responsibility, requiring the combined efforts of science, community, and a deep respect for the incredible power of nature.

The journey had been fraught with challenges, marked by failures and setbacks. But it was precisely these obstacles that had ultimately paved the way for a new understanding, a new equilibrium, a new hope for a future where humanity and nature could coexist not as adversaries but as partners in a shared destiny. The reborn Eden Prime stood as a symbol of this profound transformation, a beacon illuminating the path toward a more sustainable and equitable future.

The whispers, once a frantic, dissonant chorus of pain and struggle, began to harmonize. The wind rustling through the newly formed canopies carried a different message, one of resilience, of collaboration, of a burgeoning, vibrant life reclaiming its space. The crimson stains, remnants of Xylos's bioweapon, had faded, leaving behind a tapestry woven with the emerald hues of recovering forests and the sapphire gleam of revitalized rivers. The air, once heavy with the toxic stench, now hummed with the sweet scent of blooming wildflowers and the earthy aroma of fertile soil. These weren't simply ecological changes; they were reflections of a profound shift in the relationship between humanity and Eden Prime.

The whispers weren't just carried on the wind; they resonated in the subtle shifts of the ecosystem. The intricate dance of predator and prey, once disrupted, was slowly regaining its rhythm. The return of migratory birds, their calls weaving through the newly formed forests, signaled the restoration of ancient pathways. The fish, once scarce, now thrived in the cleansed waterways, their scales flashing like scattered jewels in the sunlight. Even the microscopic life, the invisible threads connecting the entire ecosystem, showed signs of revitalization, revealing a newfound balance. The whispers were encoded in the DNA of the recovering species, a testament to their remarkable ability to adapt and thrive even in the face of unimaginable destruction.

The biodome, a symbol of humanity's intervention, had evolved beyond its initial purpose. It was no longer merely a controlled environment but a dynamic space mirroring the changes occurring in the wider ecosystem. The scientists, having learned to relinquish their rigid control, observed the biodome's self-regulating mechanisms with a newfound humility. They acted as facilitators, gently guiding the ecosystem's natural processes instead of dictating them. This approach led to unexpected discoveries, highlighting the intrinsic intelligence of nature. The whispers in the biodome were louder, clearer, offering insights into the intricate interactions within its thriving ecosystem. They revealed the subtle feedback loops and interconnectedness that made the biodome a resilient and self-sustaining unit.

The genetic modifications, initially employed with a degree of apprehension, were now implemented with a deeper understanding. Instead of aiming for artificial perfection, the focus shifted to enhancing the resilience of existing species, allowing them to adapt more effectively to changing conditions. The whispers guided the scientists' hands, informing their choices and ensuring that genetic interventions complemented rather than replaced the natural processes of evolution. They learned to listen not only to the data but to the quiet murmurings of the ecosystem, trusting its wisdom and acknowledging its innate capacity to heal.

The human community within and beyond the biodome was an integral part of this evolving dialogue. They weren't mere passive observers but active participants in the restoration process. Their intimate knowledge of the land, passed down through generations, combined with the scientific expertise of the team, resulted in a synergistic partnership that proved remarkably effective. They worked hand in hand, their combined efforts creating a symphony of restoration. The whispers weren't solely ecological signals; they were also messages of shared responsibility, of collective stewardship. The community's traditional practices, previously viewed as outdated, were integrated with cutting-edge technology, resulting in innovative and sustainable solutions.

The whispers from the land itself, the echoes of a healing world, were interpreted differently now. The patterns of plant growth, the migration routes of animals, the subtle shifts in weather were all carefully observed and analyzed. This meticulous monitoring wasn't just about collecting data; it was about understanding the deeper language of the ecosystem, the subtle messages embedded in its rhythms and patterns. The whispers became a form of communication, a dialogue between humanity and nature, forging a new relationship built on mutual respect and understanding.

The ethical framework that guided the restoration process played a pivotal role in the transformation. The team acknowledged the inherent limits of human intervention and the importance of respecting nature's autonomy. Every intervention was carefully assessed, with rigorous risk assessments and public consultations ensuring transparency and accountability.

Failure, once feared, became an opportunity for learning and adaptation. The whispers of failure provided valuable insights, informing subsequent strategies and strengthening the overall restoration efforts. The whispers were not only about success; they were also about the continuous learning and adaptation that characterized the evolving relationship between humanity and nature.

The nano-machines, initially designed to eradicate Xylos, were refined and repurposed for ecological restoration. They now worked in delicate harmony with the ecosystem, removing the lingering traces of the bioweapon without disrupting the delicate balance of the recovering environment. The whispers guided their movements, ensuring that their work was precise and targeted, minimizing any potential harm. The technology, initially perceived as a tool of control, became a partner in the healing process, working in concert with the intrinsic healing powers of nature.

The whispers manifested in the vibrant life that returned to Eden Prime. The reintroduced native species thrived, finding refuge in the revitalized habitats. The forests weren't uniform plantations but diverse ecosystems, echoing the natural variability of the original landscape. The rivers, once choked with Xylos's toxins, now flowed freely, teeming with life. The whispers echoed in the songs of the birds, the rustling of leaves, the murmur of the rivers. They whispered tales of a world healing, a world reborn.

The success story of Eden Prime wasn't confined to its borders. The new model of environmental restoration, grounded in collaboration, adaptation, and respect, inspired similar efforts around the globe. The whispers of Eden Prime's success spread on the winds of change, carrying the message of hope to other communities struggling to heal their damaged environments. This model, a testament to the transformative power of partnership between humanity and nature, offered a pathway toward a future where the two coexisted not as adversaries but as allies.

The whispers evolved. They shifted from the panicked cries of a wounded world to the harmonious melodies of a healing planet. They carried messages of resilience, collaboration, and a profound shift in human understanding. The whispers were a testament to the adaptive power of nature and the transformative potential of a shared destiny between humanity and the environment.

The evolution of the whispers wasn't just an ecological phenomenon; it was a reflection of a fundamental change in the human relationship with the natural world, a change born from loss, forged in struggle, and celebrated in the triumphant song of a reborn Eden Prime. The echoes resonated far beyond the planet's borders, whispering a promise of a future where humanity and nature could not only coexist but thrive together, a future where the whispers of the wind carried a melody of hope.

The final sunset over the revitalized Eden Prime painted the sky in hues of apricot and rose, a breathtaking spectacle mirroring the delicate balance achieved on the planet. The air, cleansed of Xylos's toxic legacy, carried the scent of damp earth and blooming jasmine, a perfume of renewal.

The once-scarred landscape, now a vibrant tapestry of green and gold, whispered tales of resilience, a testament to the extraordinary journey of adaptation and collaboration. The whispers, once a cacophony of distress, now hummed a quiet symphony of hope.

The success of Eden Prime wasn't solely a scientific triumph; it was a profound societal shift. The communities, once fractured by the ecological devastation and ensuing chaos, had forged a new identity, one rooted in mutual respect and shared responsibility. The traditional knowledge of the indigenous populations, once dismissed as outdated, had become an invaluable asset, seamlessly integrated with cutting-edge technology to create sustainable solutions.

Ancient farming practices, coupled with advanced genetic engineering techniques, ensured food security without compromising biodiversity. The elders, once marginalized, now held positions of influence, their wisdom guiding decision-making processes. This intergenerational collaboration transcended mere cooperation; it represented a fundamental reimagining of social structures, prioritizing collective well-being over individual gain.

The economic model of Eden Prime also underwent a radical transformation. The focus shifted from unsustainable extraction to sustainable resource management. The once-exploited resources were now carefully managed, with a keen understanding of their ecological value. Circular economies, designed to minimize waste and maximize resource utilization, became the norm. Renewable energy sources, harnessed through innovative technologies, powered the communities, ensuring energy independence without jeopardizing the planet's delicate equilibrium.

This economic shift wasn't merely about profit; it was about ensuring the long-term viability of the ecosystem and the well-being of its inhabitants. The planet's health became synonymous with economic prosperity, a paradigm shift that redefined the relationship between economic growth and environmental sustainability.

Education played a pivotal role in this transformation. The curriculum was redesigned to instill a deep appreciation for the interconnectedness of life and the importance of environmental stewardship. Children were taught not just about scientific concepts but about the ethical considerations of interacting with the natural world.

The lessons went beyond textbooks and classrooms. They involved hands-on experiences, encouraging children to actively participate in the restoration efforts. They learned to identify native plants, monitor wildlife populations, and appreciate the intricate web of life that sustained their community. This holistic education fostered a generation of environmentally conscious citizens, committed to safeguarding their planet's future.

The legal framework that emerged mirrored this holistic approach. Laws were enacted to protect biodiversity, promote sustainable practices, and ensure environmental justice. Transparency and accountability became cornerstones of governance, with stringent regulations and independent oversight mechanisms in place.

The legal system wasn't designed to punish offenders but to promote responsible behavior and encourage collective action. It facilitated collaboration, ensuring that everyone shared in the responsibility of protecting the environment. Dispute resolution mechanisms prioritized mediation and restorative justice, seeking to resolve conflicts peacefully and promote harmony within the community. The laws were not just about protecting the environment; they were about building a more just and equitable society.

The success of Eden Prime wasn't limited to the planet itself. The lessons learned, the innovations developed, and the models created inspired similar initiatives across the globe. Eden Prime became a beacon of hope, demonstrating that it was possible to heal damaged ecosystems and rebuild sustainable communities. The model of collaborative restoration, emphasizing the integration of traditional knowledge with cutting-edge technology, was adapted and adopted in various regions, leading to similar success stories in different ecological contexts. The whispers of Eden Prime's restoration carried on the winds of change, inspiring communities worldwide to engage in their own healing journeys.

However, the future wasn't without its challenges. The long-term impacts of Xylos remained a subject of ongoing research, with scientists diligently monitoring the ecosystem for any unforeseen consequences. Climate change continued to pose a global threat, requiring ongoing adaptation and mitigation efforts.

The lessons learned from Eden Prime were crucial to the global response, providing valuable insights and innovative solutions for tackling the climate crisis. The ongoing work wasn't simply about maintaining the gains achieved on Eden Prime; it was about applying these lessons to a broader context, learning to adapt to evolving challenges, and ensuring the long-term health of the planet.

The narrative of Eden Prime was far from complete. It was an ongoing story, a continuous process of learning, adapting, and evolving. The restoration wasn't a single event but a dynamic process, demanding constant attention, innovative solutions, and adaptive strategies. The delicate balance achieved required vigilance and constant reassessment. New challenges arose, requiring the community to continually refine its strategies, enhance its technologies, and deepen its understanding of the ecosystem. The success of Eden Prime was not an endpoint but a beginning, a launching pad for a new era of human-nature collaboration.

The whispers of Eden Prime, once cries of despair, evolved into a symphony of resilience, a testament to the enduring power of nature and the transformative potential of human collaboration. The cautious optimism that permeated the narrative wasn't naive; it was grounded in the hard-won lessons learned, the challenges overcome, and the unwavering commitment to a sustainable future.

The story of Eden Prime was not merely a tale of ecological restoration; it was a testament to human ingenuity, the power of collaboration, and the enduring hope that a harmonious coexistence between humanity and nature is not only possible but essential. The whispers continued, carrying the message far beyond the borders of Eden Prime, echoing the promise of a future where humanity and nature, once adversaries, become partners in a vibrant, sustainable world.

A world where the wind carries not the lament of a dying planet but the joyous song of a world reborn. A world where the whispers speak of hope, of resilience, and of a future where both humanity and nature thrive. A future where the whispers finally become a song.

CHAPTER SEVEN

THE SEEDS OF A NEW BEGINNING

The air, still carrying the faint, sweet scent of jasmine, hummed with the quiet industry of rebirth. The initial phase of decontamination and soil remediation was complete, but the true test of Eden Prime's recovery lay in the ambitious reforestation project. This was not simply a matter of planting trees; it was a meticulously orchestrated symphony of ecological engineering, a testament to the collaborative spirit that had driven Eden Prime's resurrection.

Dr. Aris Thorne, the lead botanist, stood on a ridge overlooking a vast expanse of newly prepared land. His team, a diverse group of scientists, engineers, and indigenous elders, worked hard, their movements precise and purposeful. Years of research had culminated in this moment, the result of countless hours spent analyzing soil samples, studying ancient agricultural techniques, and developing advanced genetic modification strategies to ensure the survival of the reintroduced species.

The selection of plant species was far from arbitrary. Aris and his team had not merely focused on reintroducing the original flora; they had designed a resilient ecosystem, carefully considering the predicted impacts of future climate change. They prioritized species known for their drought tolerance, rapid growth, and ability to thrive in diverse soil conditions. Genetic engineering played a crucial yet carefully managed role. Selected species were enhanced to withstand the lingering traces of Xylos contamination, improve their resistance to pests and diseases, and enhance their ability to absorb and process heavy metals.

"The key is biodiversity," Aris explained to a group of young volunteers, their eyes wide with awe and wonder. "A diverse ecosystem is a resilient ecosystem. If one species fails, others can fill the void. This is not about recreating the past; it is about building a future that can withstand the challenges ahead."

The process was incredibly intricate. The land was carefully terraced to prevent erosion, following ancient methods revived and improved by the elders' knowledge. Each plant was meticulously placed, accounting for sunlight exposure, drainage patterns, and the intricate relationships within the developing ecosystem. Advanced sensor networks monitored soil moisture, nutrient levels, and even subtle shifts in microbial communities. These data were constantly analyzed, providing real-time feedback to optimize planting strategies and resource management.

The scale of the project was breathtaking. Drone swarms, guided by sophisticated algorithms, crisscrossed the landscape, dispersing seeds and seedlings with an efficiency impossible through manual labor alone. Autonomous robots, equipped with advanced sensors and robotic arms, performed precision planting, ensuring optimal spacing and depth for each plant. These robots were not simply machines; they were partners, working in tandem with human teams, complementing their strengths and compensating for their limitations.

The team's work extended beyond simply planting trees. They actively restored the intricate web of life that made up the Eden Prime ecosystem. They reintroduced native pollinators, carefully monitoring their populations and ensuring their survival. They managed water resources, ensuring an adequate supply for the growing plants while conserving water for the communities. They worked tirelessly to improve soil health, introducing beneficial microbes and enriching the soil with organic matter. The restoration was not just about plants; it was about rebuilding a balanced ecosystem.

The reforestation initiative was far from a solitary endeavor; it was a community-wide effort. Citizens of Eden Prime, young and old, participated actively in the process. Schools organized field trips, transforming educational experiences into practical contributions to their planet's healing. Local artisans created stunning mosaic art pieces integrated into the landscapes, adding aesthetic beauty while also serving as educational aids, illustrating the story of Eden Prime's rebirth.

The elderly members of the community played a crucial role, sharing their traditional knowledge of plant cultivation and ecological balance. Their wisdom, once dismissed as obsolete, was now recognized as invaluable, guiding the team through intricate details of local flora and fauna and providing insights into sustainable agricultural practices that had stood the test of time. This collaboration transcended mere expertise; it was a profound recognition of the importance of intergenerational knowledge sharing in building a resilient future.

The economic impact of the reforestation project was equally significant. The initiative created numerous jobs, employing engineers, technicians, scientists, and community members in various roles related to planting, monitoring, and maintenance. The project fostered local businesses, creating opportunities for entrepreneurs to produce and supply sustainable materials and technologies. The focus on sustainable resource management ensured long-term economic viability, establishing a model in which the health of the planet was intrinsically linked to economic prosperity.

The success of the reforestation efforts was not just measured in the number of trees planted, but also in the thriving ecosystem they fostered. Years after the initial planting, the landscape was once more teeming with life. Wildlife, once decimated by Xylos, gradually returned, their populations steadily increasing. The air, once thick with toxins, was now clean and crisp, filled with the songs of birds and the murmur of a reawakening ecosystem. The riverbeds, once barren and dry, flowed once again, teeming with fish and aquatic life. The landscape transformed from scars of devastation into a tapestry of vibrant green and gold, an inspiring testament to human resilience and nature's remarkable capacity for recovery.

The reforestation initiative was not simply a scientific endeavor; it was a profound spiritual journey. The community of Eden Prime had found healing not only in the restoration of their planet but in the process of rebuilding their connections with each other and with the natural world. The project became a metaphor for their own journey of recovery, reflecting the growth, resilience, and interconnectedness that were fundamental to their new beginning. The once-silent whispers of despair were now a vibrant chorus of life, a testament to a future where humanity and nature coexisted in harmony, a harmonious symphony of life playing out across the revitalized Eden Prime. The seeds planted were not merely for trees; they were the seeds of hope, of resilience, and of a future where the whispers of a dying planet were replaced with the triumphant song of rebirth, the song of Eden Prime's renewal.

The success of the reforestation initiative hinged not only on the sheer number of trees planted but also on the intricate network of technological support woven into the very fabric of the reborn ecosystem. This was not simply about planting trees and hoping for the best; it was about creating a self-regulating, resilient system capable of adapting to future challenges. At the heart of this strategy lay a sophisticated network of bio-integrated sensors and actuators, a technological symbiosis designed to monitor and enhance the ecosystem's health in real-time.

Distributed throughout the reforested areas were thousands of miniature sensors, embedded within the soil and the trees themselves. These were not intrusive devices; they were designed to be biocompatible, seamlessly integrating with the environment. Some monitored soil moisture and nutrient levels, triggering automated irrigation systems when necessary. Others tracked the health of individual trees, detecting early signs of stress or disease, alerting arborists to potential problems before they escalated into widespread damage. This early warning system allowed for targeted interventions, minimizing resource consumption and maximizing efficiency.

More sophisticated sensors monitored atmospheric conditions, including temperature, humidity, wind speed, and even the concentration of trace gases. This data, combined with the soil sensor readings, provided a comprehensive picture of the ecosystem's overall health, allowing the scientists to anticipate and mitigate potential threats. For instance, if a sudden drought was predicted, the system could automatically adjust irrigation schedules, ensuring that the most vulnerable plants received the water they needed.

Beyond monitoring, the technological integration extended to active intervention. Autonomous robots, smaller and more agile than their larger counterparts used in the initial planting phase, patrolled the reforested areas. These were not just machines; they were sophisticated ecological assistants. Equipped with advanced sensors, they could identify and eliminate invasive species before they could establish themselves. They also assisted in targeted fertilization, applying nutrients directly to the roots of trees that needed them most, optimizing resource allocation. Their movement was guided by a complex algorithm that took into account terrain, plant density, and environmental conditions.

A crucial element of this technological strategy was the development of bio-integrated power sources. The sensors and robots needed power, but the researchers were acutely aware of the importance of minimizing their environmental footprint. Therefore, they invested heavily in the development of sustainable energy sources, integrating small-scale solar panels into the landscape, cleverly disguised among the vegetation. Furthermore, they explored the potential of microbial fuel cells, harnessing the energy produced by microbial communities within the soil to power the sensors and robots. This approach minimized reliance on external energy sources, creating a truly self-sustaining technological infrastructure.

The data collected by the sensors was not simply stored; it was actively analyzed and used to refine ecosystem management strategies. Sophisticated algorithms processed the vast streams of data, identifying patterns and trends that might otherwise have gone unnoticed. This information was used to optimize irrigation schedules, predict pest outbreaks, and anticipate the impacts of climate change. The system learned and adapted over time, constantly refining its approach based on the real-world data it collected.

This was not a top-down, technologically driven approach; it was a carefully considered collaboration between human ingenuity and the inherent resilience of the natural world. The system was designed to assist, not replace, human intervention. The data generated by the sensors provided insights, but the human element remained crucial in interpreting the information and making informed decisions.

The scientists understood that technology was a tool, not a solution in itself. Its effectiveness depended on the wisdom, experience, and understanding of the people who managed and maintained it. The integration of traditional ecological knowledge with cutting-edge technology proved essential. The elders, with their intimate understanding of the land and its subtle rhythms, provided invaluable input, guiding the technological solutions and ensuring that they were not at odds with the natural world.

The economic implications of this technologically advanced ecosystem management were profound. The initial investment in the technology was significant, but the long-term benefits far outweighed the costs. The automated systems drastically reduced the need for manual labor, minimizing costs associated with maintenance and resource management. The early warning system prevented widespread damage, saving significant sums that would have been needed for remediation efforts. Moreover, the enhanced efficiency and productivity of the ecosystem led to an increase in the yield of valuable resources.

The success of Eden Prime's reforestation was not merely a scientific achievement; it was a demonstration of responsible technological integration. It showcased how technology, when used wisely and ethically, could enhance the resilience of ecosystems and support sustainable development. The integrated systems highlighted the crucial interplay between human ingenuity, environmental stewardship, and the capacity of nature to heal itself. The careful balance between technological advancement and ecological harmony laid the foundation for Eden Prime's future, a future where the lessons learned could serve as a model for the rest of the world.

The project also had significant educational value. Data from the sensor network was made publicly accessible, providing valuable information for researchers, educators, and the public. Interactive displays in community centers showcased the real-time data, allowing citizens to track the progress of the reforestation and understand the intricate workings of the ecosystem. This transparency and accessibility fostered a deeper understanding and appreciation for the importance of environmental stewardship. Schools integrated the data into their curricula, teaching students about the complex interplay between technology and nature, and encouraging them to become responsible stewards of the planet.

The success of the project also attracted international attention. Researchers from across the globe came to study Eden Prime's innovative ecosystem management system. The lessons learned from Eden Prime's experience were shared, helping to inform other reforestation projects and inspiring the development of similar technologies for use in other ecosystems. This collaborative effort fostered a global community dedicated to environmental restoration and sustainable development.

In the years that followed, Eden Prime continued to thrive. The ecosystem, strengthened by the technological innovations and the community's commitment to sustainability, demonstrated remarkable resilience in the face of unforeseen challenges, including extreme weather events and unexpected pest outbreaks. The technological infrastructure adapted, constantly learning and evolving, ensuring that Eden Prime remained a testament to the power of human ingenuity and the remarkable capacity of nature to heal itself.

The seeds of a new beginning, planted with care and nurtured with technology, blossomed into a vibrant and sustainable future. The song of Eden Prime's renewal continued, a harmonious symphony of life and technology working in concert. It was a testament to a future where humanity and nature not only coexist but thrive together, a legacy etched into the very fabric of the reborn planet.

The success of Eden Prime's reforestation was not just about trees; it was about people. The technological marvel of the self-regulating ecosystem was only half the story. The other, equally crucial, half was the vibrant community that grew alongside it, a testament to the power of human collaboration and resilience. As the trees took root and the ecosystem flourished, so too did the spirit of community, forming a microcosm of a truly sustainable and self-sufficient society.

The initial influx of scientists, engineers, and volunteers gradually gave way to a more permanent population. Families arrived, drawn by the promise of a new beginning, a chance to build a life in harmony with nature. This was not a utopian fantasy; it was a carefully planned and organically evolving community, shaped by the unique challenges and opportunities of its environment.

One of the key elements of Eden Prime's community structure was its emphasis on decentralized governance. Rather than a top-down hierarchical system, decisions were made through a network of interconnected committees and councils, each focusing on a specific aspect of community life.

An agricultural council managed the community gardens and orchards, ensuring a diverse and abundant food supply. An energy council oversaw the maintenance and expansion of the sustainable energy infrastructure, harnessing solar power, wind energy, and even geothermal sources.

A technology council monitored and maintained the sophisticated network of sensors and robots that supported the ecosystem. A building and infrastructure council planned and managed the expansion of the community, ensuring that new structures were built using sustainable materials and designed to minimize environmental impact.

A health and education council provided healthcare and education services to community members, ensuring the well-being of all.

Finally, an ethics council, composed of members elected by the broader community, provided an oversight function, ensuring the responsible and ethical application of technology and resources.

These councils were not isolated entities; they functioned as a network, constantly communicating and collaborating. Decisions were made through open dialogue and consensus-building, ensuring that everyone had a voice and that decisions reflected the collective will of the community. Transparency was paramount. Data from the ecosystem monitoring system, as well as information on community finances and resource allocation, was publicly accessible, fostering trust and accountability.

The community's success also depended on a sophisticated system of resource management. Waste management was meticulously handled through a closed-loop system, with compostable materials being returned to the soil to enrich it and other waste materials being recycled and repurposed whenever possible. Water was carefully conserved through the use of efficient irrigation systems and water-saving technologies.

Energy consumption was minimized through the use of energy-efficient buildings and appliances and through a community-wide commitment to conservation.

Education was prioritized, with schools emphasizing practical skills such as sustainable agriculture, renewable energy technologies, and ecosystem management. The curriculum also included traditional crafts, promoting self-sufficiency and a deep appreciation for the natural world.

The elder members of the community, many of whom had lived through the environmental devastation that preceded Eden Prime's rebirth, played a vital role in transmitting their knowledge and experience to the younger generation, ensuring the preservation of traditional practices alongside the adoption of new technologies. They served as a living link to the past, providing a sense of continuity and grounding the community in its history.

The community also placed a strong emphasis on arts and culture. Regular events and festivals celebrated the achievements of the community and reinforced the shared sense of purpose and belonging. Music, dance, storytelling, and visual arts provided avenues for self-expression and enriched the lives of community members. Community gardens became social hubs, providing spaces for people to connect and collaborate. These communal spaces also served as informal educational settings, where knowledge was shared and new ideas were exchanged.

The community's economic model was based on principles of sustainability and fairness. Goods and services were exchanged through a local currency system, promoting community self-reliance and reducing reliance on external markets. The focus was not on material wealth but on the well-being of the community as a whole. Everyone contributed to the collective effort, and the fruits of the community's labor were shared equitably.

Despite the relative isolation of Eden Prime, the community remained connected to the wider world. Regular communication was maintained with researchers, organizations, and individuals who shared their vision of a sustainable future. Eden Prime served as a living laboratory, showcasing the possibilities of a harmonious relationship between humanity and nature. Visitors came from all over the globe to learn from their experiences and to contribute their expertise. This exchange of knowledge fostered a sense of global citizenship and reinforced the community's commitment to a sustainable future for all.

The success of Eden Prime's community was not simply a matter of luck or coincidence. It was a carefully constructed tapestry woven from threads of technological innovation, ecological wisdom, and a deeply held belief in the power of human collaboration. The community fostered a sense of shared purpose and belonging, inspiring its members to work together to build a better future. They demonstrated that a sustainable and equitable future is not just possible but achievable, a testament to the enduring resilience of the human spirit and the remarkable capacity for collaboration in the face of daunting challenges.

Their story, a narrative of technological integration, ecological restoration, and community building, became a beacon of hope, a testament to the future of sustainable living, echoing the enduring song of renewal across the globe. The seeds of a new beginning, planted not only in the fertile soil of Eden Prime but also in the hearts and minds of its inhabitants, had indeed blossomed. It was a living example, a vibrant testament to the potential of a world where humanity and nature could truly thrive together. The community, a living embodiment of the principles of sustainability, became a model for others seeking a path toward a more harmonious and fulfilling existence on a planet grappling with the consequences of past mistakes. It was a legacy built not on dominance over nature but on a deep and abiding respect for it, a testament to the enduring power of human ingenuity and collaboration in creating a future where both humanity and the environment could flourish.

The success of Eden Prime was not solely measured by the flourishing ecosystem; it was also profoundly shaped by the community's unwavering commitment to education. Recognizing that a sustainable future depended on informed and engaged citizens, a comprehensive educational program was implemented, weaving environmental awareness and responsibility into the very fabric of their society. This was not simply about imparting knowledge; it was about fostering a deep-seated respect for the natural world and empowering the next generation to become active stewards of their environment.

The curriculum, meticulously crafted by a team of educators, scientists, and community members, extended far beyond the traditional boundaries of academic learning. It was a holistic approach, integrating practical skills with theoretical understanding and fostering creativity alongside critical thinking. The program recognized that true environmental stewardship demanded not only intellectual comprehension but also a profound emotional connection with the natural world.

Early childhood education focused on fostering a sense of wonder and curiosity about nature. Children spent considerable time outdoors, exploring the diverse ecosystems of Eden Prime, learning to identify plants and animals, and understanding the intricate web of life that connected them all. Learning was experiential, with hands-on activities such as gardening, composting, and nature journaling forming the core of their education. Storytelling played a vital role, transmitting traditional ecological knowledge alongside contemporary scientific understanding, weaving together the wisdom of the past with the innovations of the present. The elders of the community, repositories of invaluable experience and traditional practices, played a key role in these early childhood programs, sharing their intimate knowledge of the land and its rhythms.

As children progressed through the educational system, the curriculum expanded to encompass more advanced concepts. Sustainable agriculture became a central focus, with students actively participating in the cultivation and management of community gardens and orchards. They learned about soil health, crop rotation, pest control, and water conservation, gaining practical experience in producing their own food. Renewable energy technologies were explored in detail, with students designing and building small-scale wind turbines, solar panels, and biomass generators. They learned about the principles of energy efficiency and the importance of reducing their ecological footprint. Ecosystem management became another key component, with students studying the intricate workings of the self-regulating ecosystem of Eden Prime, learning how to monitor its health and respond to potential challenges.

The curriculum also emphasized the importance of traditional crafts and skills. Students learned weaving, pottery, woodworking, and other crafts, using sustainably sourced materials whenever possible. These skills were not merely vocational training; they were viewed as crucial components of a self-sufficient and resilient community, providing both practical skills and a connection to the cultural heritage of Eden Prime.

The educational program extended beyond the formal schooling system, integrating learning into the very fabric of community life. Community gardens became informal learning spaces where students learned about botany, ecology, and sustainable agriculture through hands-on experience. Regular community events and festivals provided opportunities for learning through participation, with workshops, demonstrations, and presentations on a wide range of topics related to sustainability and environmental stewardship. Elderly community members shared their knowledge and experiences through storytelling and mentorship, bridging the gap between generations and preserving traditional practices alongside modern innovations.

Technology played a vital, yet carefully managed, role in the educational system. Students had access to advanced learning resources, including interactive simulations, virtual reality experiences, and online collaborations with other educational institutions around the world. However, the focus remained on fostering a deep understanding of the natural world, not on replacing human interaction with technology. The use of technology was always viewed as a tool to enhance learning, not to supplant it.

The teaching methodology was equally important. The emphasis was on experiential learning, active participation, and collaborative inquiry. Students were encouraged to ask questions, explore their curiosity, and develop their critical thinking skills. The learning environment was designed to be engaging, supportive, and empowering, fostering a sense of community and shared purpose. Assessment methods went beyond traditional tests and exams, focusing on students' ability to apply their knowledge and skills in real-world contexts. Project-based learning was widely used, with students working on collaborative projects that addressed real-world challenges faced by the community.

The success of Eden Prime's educational program was reflected in the community's commitment to environmental stewardship. Students were actively involved in monitoring and maintaining the ecosystem, participating in reforestation projects, managing community gardens, and developing innovative solutions to environmental challenges. Their contributions were valued not just as learners, but as active participants in shaping the future of their community. Their work extended beyond the boundaries of Eden Prime, with students engaging in collaborative projects with other communities around the world, sharing their knowledge and experiences, and fostering a global sense of environmental responsibility.

The curriculum was regularly reviewed and updated, incorporating new research, technological advancements, and the evolving needs of the community. This ongoing process ensured that the program remained relevant and effective, equipping future generations with the knowledge and skills to meet the challenges of a rapidly changing world. The program was not static; it was a dynamic and adaptive system, continuously evolving to meet the ever-changing needs of both the environment and the community. The aim was not simply to produce environmentally conscious individuals, but to cultivate a generation of innovative problem-solvers capable of tackling the complex environmental challenges of the future. The educational program of Eden Prime served as a powerful example of how education could be leveraged to create a more sustainable and equitable future, one where human ingenuity and environmental responsibility worked in harmony.

Moreover, the program emphasized ethical considerations alongside scientific understanding. Students explored the ethical implications of technological advancements, the responsible use of resources, and the importance of equity and justice in environmental decision-making. They were encouraged to think critically about the complex interplay between human actions and environmental consequences, understanding that sustainability was not just about protecting nature but also about ensuring a just and equitable society. This ethical framework infused all aspects of the curriculum, shaping not only their environmental awareness but also their worldview.

The impact of the educational program extended beyond the immediate community. Eden Prime became a model for sustainable education practices, attracting educators and researchers from around the world who came to learn from its innovative approach. The community shared its curriculum, its teaching methods, and its experiences, contributing to a global network of collaborative learning and knowledge sharing. This global exchange further reinforced the community's commitment to environmental stewardship, emphasizing the interconnectedness of humanity and the need for collective action to address environmental challenges. The success of Eden Prime's educational program demonstrated that education was not merely a tool for individual advancement but a crucial catalyst for positive social and environmental change. It showed the world that investing in education, especially in the context of environmental stewardship, is an investment in the future of our planet. The seeds of a new beginning, sown in fertile educational ground, bore fruit in a generation of environmentally responsible citizens, a testament to the power of education in building a sustainable future.

The burgeoning success of Eden Prime demanded a parallel evolution in its ethical framework. The thriving ecosystem, meticulously rebuilt and nurtured, was far too precious to be left vulnerable to unchecked human interaction. Thus, a new set of ethical guidelines, the "Eden Prime Concordat," was painstakingly drafted and implemented, its principles woven into the very fabric of the community's daily life. These were not merely rules to be followed; they were a shared understanding, a collective commitment to responsible stewardship.

The Concordat's foundational principle centered on the inherent value of all life forms within Eden Prime's ecosystem. No longer was the environment viewed as a resource to be exploited, but as a complex, interconnected web of life deserving of profound respect. This philosophy extended beyond the obvious, including the protection of endangered species and the preservation of pristine landscapes, and delved into the intricate details of daily life. For instance, the harvesting of resources, even those deemed renewable, was subject to strict regulations, ensuring that extraction remained sustainable and minimized environmental impact. Sophisticated monitoring systems, using a combination of traditional ecological knowledge and cutting-edge technology, tracked the health of the ecosystem in real time, providing immediate feedback on the effects of human activity.

The Concordat addressed the ethical implications of technological advancement within the context of environmental stewardship. While technology played a crucial role in Eden Prime's development, its use was always subject to rigorous ethical scrutiny. Any new technology introduced had to undergo a comprehensive assessment, evaluating its potential impact on the ecosystem and its alignment with the principles of sustainability and equity. This was not about technological stagnation, but about responsible innovation, a commitment to utilizing technology for the betterment of both humanity and the environment.

For example, the development of advanced agricultural techniques was carefully considered, ensuring that they did not lead to soil degradation, water depletion, or biodiversity loss. Similarly, the use of renewable energy sources was prioritized, but their implementation was designed to minimize visual and ecological impacts on the landscape.

Equity formed another cornerstone of the Concordat. The guidelines recognized that a sustainable future required not only environmental responsibility but also social justice. Access to resources and opportunities was guaranteed to all members of the community, regardless of their background or socioeconomic status. The distribution of food, energy, and other essential resources was carefully managed to prevent inequality and ensure that the benefits of Eden Prime's success were shared equitably. This commitment to equity extended to the management of the ecosystem itself, with all voices heard and considered in environmental decision-making processes. Participatory governance mechanisms were implemented, empowering community members to actively shape the future of Eden Prime.

Education played a pivotal role in instilling the principles of the Concordat. From early childhood, children were taught the ethical dimensions of environmental stewardship, developing a deep understanding of their responsibility toward the ecosystem. The curriculum incorporated stories, case studies, and interactive simulations to illustrate the real-world consequences of unethical behavior. Students participated in community projects, gaining firsthand experience in the challenges and rewards of ethical decision-making. This emphasis on experiential learning was crucial, transforming abstract principles into tangible realities and fostering a deep-seated sense of responsibility.

One particularly challenging aspect addressed by the Concordat was the management of waste. A zero-waste philosophy was adopted, with a comprehensive system put in place for the reduction, reuse, and recycling of materials. Composting programs were established to manage organic waste, while advanced recycling technologies were implemented to handle non-organic materials. The design of products and packaging incorporated circular economy principles, minimizing waste generation from the outset. Education played a critical role here as well; communities learned to distinguish between different types of waste and to practice responsible disposal. The success of the waste management system depended not only on technology but also on the collective commitment of the community to reduce its environmental footprint.

The Concordat's scope extended beyond the immediate environment of Eden Prime. Recognizing the interconnectedness of global ecosystems, it included principles of international cooperation and environmental justice. Eden Prime actively collaborated with other communities around the world, sharing its knowledge and experiences in sustainable living and environmental stewardship. They participated in global initiatives aimed at addressing climate change, biodiversity loss, and other environmental challenges. The community understood that their success was not solely their own; it was a contribution to a broader global effort to build a more sustainable future for all.

Furthermore, the Concordat established mechanisms for resolving ethical conflicts related to environmental management. Independent ethics committees were formed, comprised of community members, scientists, and experts from various fields. These committees provided impartial guidance on contentious issues, ensuring that decisions were made with both ecological and ethical considerations in mind. Their role went beyond simple conflict resolution. They served as a critical voice for environmental protection, challenging unsustainable practices and advocating for ethical solutions.

The principles of the Concordat were not static. They were regularly reviewed and updated to reflect advances in scientific understanding, technological innovation, and the evolving needs of the community. This dynamic approach ensured that the ethical framework remained relevant and effective in navigating the complexities of a changing world. It also fostered a sense of ongoing learning and adaptation, underscoring the community's commitment to continuous improvement.

The Eden Prime Concordat was more than just a set of rules. It was a living document, a testament to the community's unwavering commitment to environmental responsibility and ethical conduct. It served as a model for other communities striving to create a more sustainable and just world, demonstrating that the path toward a healthier planet requires not only technological innovation but also a profound shift in ethical consciousness. It was a crucial step in forging a new relationship between humanity and nature, one founded on respect, responsibility, and a shared vision of a thriving future for all. The seeds of this new beginning, nurtured by ethical guidelines, promised a future where human progress and environmental preservation were not conflicting goals but mutually reinforcing aspirations. The success of Eden Prime lay not only in its flourishing ecosystem but also in the ethical compass that guided its development.

CHAPTER EIGHT

A SYMBOLIC RELATIONSHIP

The transition was not abrupt, but rather a gradual shift in human behavior, a conscious uncoupling from the exploitative relationship with nature that had characterized much of the past. It began with small changes, subtle adjustments in daily routines that, when aggregated, resulted in a significant reduction in environmental impact. The widespread adoption of vertical farming, for instance, dramatically reduced the need for sprawling agricultural lands, freeing up vast areas for rewilding and ecosystem restoration. These farms, towering structures of carefully controlled environments, maximized yield while minimizing resource consumption. Sophisticated hydroponic and aeroponic systems recycled water with exceptional efficiency, and advanced LED lighting systems optimized light spectrum for maximum plant growth, cutting energy consumption significantly.

Transportation underwent a radical transformation as well. The reliance on personal vehicles diminished drastically, replaced by a highly efficient and interconnected public transit system powered by renewable energy sources. High-speed magnetic levitation trains crisscrossed the landscape, connecting remote communities to urban centers with minimal environmental disruption. Within the cities, autonomous electric vehicles, designed for shared use and optimized for route efficiency, moved people and goods seamlessly. Even personal mobility devices, powered by solar energy and equipped with intelligent routing software, became a common sight. This shift was driven not just by technological advancement, but also by a cultural embrace of shared resources and reduced consumption.

Waste management became a community-wide endeavor, a testament to the collective commitment to minimizing environmental impact. The "zero-waste" philosophy, a cornerstone of the Eden Prime Concordat, was not merely a slogan; it was a way of life. A meticulous system of sorting, recycling, and composting was implemented, transforming waste into a resource. Organic waste fueled biogas digesters, generating renewable energy, while advanced recycling techniques processed plastics and other materials into new products, closing the loop on the material cycle. The design of products and packaging was rigorously scrutinized, prioritizing durability, repairability, and ease of recycling. Single-use plastics were virtually nonexistent; reusable alternatives were commonplace, readily available, and integrated into everyday life.

Beyond the practical changes, a deep shift in consumer behavior took place. A conscious effort towards minimalism and durability replaced the throwaway culture of the past. People valued quality over quantity, opting for products built to last, meticulously repaired and reused rather than replaced. The idea of "planned obsolescence" became anathema, a relic of a bygone era. This shift was fostered by a robust repair and reuse infrastructure, with community workshops and specialized repair services readily available. People actively engaged in repairing clothing, electronics, and other household items, extending their lifespan and reducing the demand for new products. This embrace of longevity and repair reflected a profound change in values, a rejection of the fleeting pleasures of instant gratification.

The principles of sustainability extended beyond the mundane aspects of daily life, encompassing every facet of human endeavor, from architecture and construction to fashion and entertainment. Buildings were designed with energy efficiency in mind, using passive solar design and advanced insulation techniques to minimize heating and cooling requirements. Renewable energy sources, such as solar, wind, and geothermal power, provided clean and sustainable electricity, with smart grids optimizing energy distribution and reducing waste. The construction industry embraced sustainable materials, utilizing reclaimed wood, recycled steel, and bio-based composites. This focus on sustainability infused itself into the very fabric of society.

The fashion industry underwent a similar transformation, shifting from fast fashion to a model of sustainable and ethical production. Clothing was designed to be durable, versatile, and easily repaired, with an emphasis on natural, sustainable materials. The "circular fashion" concept took hold, with clothes being reused, repaired, and recycled, minimizing textile waste and its environmental impact. The traditional concept of clothing as a disposable item became obsolete, replaced by a preference for quality, lasting garments.

Entertainment and leisure activities also embraced the principles of sustainability. Virtual and augmented reality technologies offered immersive and engaging experiences with a significantly smaller environmental footprint compared to traditional forms of entertainment. Digital media consumption became the norm, reducing the need for physical copies of books, movies, and music. Outdoor recreation emphasized responsible interaction with the environment, with activities planned to minimize disturbance to ecosystems. An overarching theme of mindful engagement with the natural world permeated every aspect of leisure.

The impact on human health was significant and positive. Reduced exposure to pollutants and toxins led to improvements in air and water quality, resulting in fewer respiratory and cardiovascular diseases. The increased focus on physical activity and spending time in nature contributed to improved mental and physical well-being. A renewed connection with the environment fostered a deeper appreciation for the natural world, promoting a sense of calm, contentment, and a greater sense of purpose. The holistic approach to sustainability positively influenced all aspects of human life, from health and well-being to social cohesion and economic prosperity.

The transition was not without its challenges. The shift to a more sustainable lifestyle required significant investments in infrastructure, technology, and education. Resistance from entrenched interests and inertia within existing systems presented hurdles. However, the collective commitment of the Eden Prime community, supported by the strong ethical framework of the Concordat, provided the impetus for change. The benefits of this transition, both environmental and social, far outweighed the challenges, demonstrating the power of human adaptation and the resilience of the human spirit. The symbiotic relationship between humanity and nature, once fractured and broken, was slowly being mended, with the future holding the promise of a flourishing ecosystem and a thriving human civilization coexisting in harmony. The transition highlighted the crucial role of education and the power of collective action in building a more sustainable future, demonstrating that a harmonious relationship with nature is not a utopia, but an achievable reality. The journey to sustainability was not a destination but an ongoing process of learning, adaptation, and continuous improvement. The human ingenuity that once drove exploitation was now harnessed for the preservation and regeneration of the natural world, shaping a new era of responsible stewardship, where human ingenuity and environmental sustainability worked together in perfect harmony. The success of Eden Prime served as a shining beacon, a testament to the human capacity for transformative change, and proof that a symbiotic relationship between humanity and nature was not merely a dream, but a tangible reality within reach.

The shift towards a symbiotic relationship with nature extended deeply into the realm of food production. Sustainable agriculture became the cornerstone of Eden Prime's food security, a system designed not to exploit the land but to work in harmony with it. Gone were the days of monoculture farming, with its reliance on chemical fertilizers, pesticides, and vast tracts of land cleared for single crops. Instead, Eden Prime embraced a diverse range of agricultural techniques that prioritized ecological balance and minimized environmental impact.

One of the most significant changes was the widespread adoption of agroecology. This holistic approach to farming integrated ecological principles into agricultural practices, mimicking the complexity and resilience of natural ecosystems. Agroecological farms were characterized by their biodiversity, with a variety of crops and livestock intermingled to create a self-regulating system. Leguminous plants, such as beans and peas, were strategically integrated into crop rotations to fix nitrogen in the soil, reducing the need for synthetic fertilizers. Cover crops were utilized to protect the soil from erosion, suppress weeds, and improve soil fertility. Integrated pest management strategies, emphasizing biological control methods and natural predators, minimized the use of harmful pesticides. Agroforestry, the intentional integration of trees and shrubs into farming systems, further enhanced biodiversity and provided additional ecological benefits, such as shade, windbreaks, and improved soil structure.

The design of farms themselves was carefully considered to minimize environmental impact. Permaculture principles, emphasizing the design of sustainable human habitats, guided the layout of agricultural lands. Water management was a crucial aspect of sustainable agriculture. Efficient irrigation systems, including drip irrigation and rainwater harvesting, minimized water consumption. The use of drought-resistant crops further reduced the reliance on irrigation. Precision agriculture technologies, such as sensor networks and data analytics, allowed for targeted application of water and nutrients, maximizing efficiency and minimizing waste. This approach not only conserved water but also reduced the environmental impact associated with fertilizer production and transportation.

Soil health was another critical element of sustainable agriculture. No-till farming practices, which avoided the plowing of land, helped to preserve soil structure and reduce erosion. Organic farming techniques, relying on natural fertilizers and pest control methods, were widely adopted, enhancing soil fertility and promoting biodiversity. Composting of organic waste, generated from both agricultural production and domestic sources, provided a rich source of nutrients, further reducing reliance on synthetic fertilizers. The continuous monitoring of soil health, utilizing advanced analytical techniques, enabled early detection of potential problems and proactive interventions, ensuring the long-term health and productivity of the land.

Livestock management also underwent a significant transformation. Pastoral farming practices were redesigned to promote biodiversity and minimize environmental impact. Rotational grazing, where animals were moved periodically to different pastures, helped to prevent overgrazing and improve soil health. Integrated livestock-crop systems, combining animal husbandry with crop production, created synergistic relationships, enhancing resource efficiency and overall farm productivity. Silvopasture systems, integrating trees into grazing areas, provided shade for animals, reduced soil erosion, and improved biodiversity. Emphasis was placed on animal welfare, with humane farming practices becoming the norm.

The shift to local and regional food systems dramatically reduced the reliance on long-distance transportation, minimizing the carbon footprint associated with food production and distribution. Farmers' markets and community-supported agriculture (CSA) programs thrived, connecting consumers directly with local producers. This not only supported local economies but also enhanced food security and resilience.

Vertical farming played a crucial role in urban food production. Towering structures filled with carefully controlled environments allowed for high-yield crop production, using significantly less land and resources compared to traditional agriculture. Advanced hydroponic and aeroponic systems recycled water with exceptional efficiency, minimizing water consumption and waste. LED lighting systems, optimized for plant growth, reduced energy consumption. The integration of vertical farms into urban spaces created localized food sources, reducing the need for transportation and enhancing food security, particularly in densely populated areas.

The principles of sustainability also extended to the processing and distribution of food. Food waste reduction programs were implemented throughout the supply chain, from farm to table. Innovative packaging solutions minimized material usage and waste. Food preservation techniques, such as canning, freezing, and dehydration, extended shelf life and reduced food spoilage. The emphasis on local and regional food systems further reduced transportation costs and environmental impact.

Beyond the technological and agricultural innovations, a significant shift in mindset occurred within Eden Prime's agricultural sector. Farmers became active participants in the broader ecosystem, engaging in practices that restored and enhanced ecological balance. A sense of stewardship, a profound responsibility for the land, replaced the exploitative relationship that characterized past agricultural practices. The training and education of farmers were crucial, equipping them with the knowledge and skills needed to implement sustainable agricultural methods. Collaboration and knowledge sharing among farmers, scientists, and policymakers were encouraged, fostering innovation and the dissemination of best practices.

This transformation was not without its challenges. The transition to sustainable agriculture required significant investment in new technologies, infrastructure, and education. Some farmers faced economic challenges during the transition period, and government support played a crucial role in facilitating a smooth shift. The initial costs of implementing new technologies and practices could be high, but long-term benefits, including reduced input costs and increased yields, made the transition economically viable.

Moreover, building public awareness about the importance of sustainable agriculture was crucial for its success. Consumer education played a key role in promoting the consumption of locally sourced food and supporting sustainable farmers. The combined efforts of farmers, scientists, policymakers, and consumers paved the way for sustainable agriculture becoming not only a viable alternative but the preferred model of food production within Eden Prime.

The success of Eden Prime's sustainable agricultural system demonstrated the feasibility of food security without harming the ecosystem. It showed that food production could be integrated into a wider ecological context, contributing to a thriving and balanced ecosystem rather than depleting its resources. The symbiotic relationship between humanity and nature, once fractured and broken, found a new expression in the fertile fields and vibrant farms of Eden Prime, a testament to the enduring power of human ingenuity and the transformative potential of sustainable practices.

The journey toward a sustainable future was not simply a matter of technological advancement; it was a fundamental shift in values, priorities, and the way humans interacted with the world around them. In that respect, Eden Prime stood as a shining example, proof of concept for a future where food security and environmental sustainability walked hand in hand. The legacy of Eden Prime was not just a model of sustainable agriculture but a testament to the transformative power of embracing a truly symbiotic relationship with the planet.

The transition to a truly symbiotic relationship with nature on Eden Prime extended beyond sustainable agriculture; it fundamentally reshaped the planet's energy infrastructure. Fossil fuels, once the lifeblood of industrial civilization, became relics of a bygone era, replaced by a diverse and robust network of renewable energy sources. This was not a mere technological shift; it was a societal transformation, driven by a deep-seated understanding of the interconnectedness of all living systems and a commitment to preserving the planet's delicate balance.

The initial steps involved a comprehensive assessment of Eden Prime's energy needs and available renewable resources. Detailed mapping identified areas with high solar irradiance, consistent wind patterns, and suitable geothermal potential. This data-driven approach ensured that energy infrastructure development was strategically located to maximize efficiency and minimize environmental impact.

Solar energy quickly became a cornerstone of Eden Prime's new energy system. Large-scale solar farms, meticulously designed to minimize land use and maximize energy production, were established in sun-drenched regions. Advances in photovoltaic technology increased the efficiency of solar panels, making solar energy increasingly cost-effective and competitive with fossil fuels.

Beyond large-scale farms, residential and commercial buildings were outfitted with solar panels, transforming homes and businesses into decentralized energy producers. Smart grids, capable of efficiently managing the fluctuating output of solar energy, ensured a consistent and reliable power supply. Energy storage solutions, such as advanced battery systems and pumped hydro storage, addressed the intermittency of solar energy, storing excess energy generated during peak sunlight hours for use during periods of low solar output. These systems not only ensured a reliable energy supply but also enhanced the grid's stability and resilience.

Wind energy played a complementary role in Eden Prime's renewable energy mix. Offshore wind farms, strategically located in areas with consistent strong winds, became major sources of clean energy. Technological innovations, such as advanced turbine designs and floating platforms, maximized energy capture while minimizing visual and environmental impacts.

Onshore wind farms were integrated into existing landscapes, carefully sited to avoid disrupting sensitive ecosystems. The design and placement of wind turbines were meticulously planned, incorporating ecological considerations to minimize disturbances to wildlife and maintain the aesthetic integrity of the surrounding areas. Environmental impact assessments were conducted prior to the construction of any wind farm, evaluating potential effects on bird and bat populations, and mitigation strategies were implemented to minimize these impacts.

Geothermal energy, harnessed from the Earth's internal heat, provided a consistent and reliable baseload power source. Geothermal power plants, located in regions with high geothermal activity, utilized the heat from underground reservoirs to generate electricity. This technology provided a clean and sustainable energy source, independent of weather patterns. The extraction of geothermal energy was carefully managed to ensure the long-term sustainability of the resource. Detailed geological surveys and modeling were used to accurately assess the resource potential and optimize energy extraction strategies. The careful management of geothermal resources ensured their long-term viability, providing a stable and reliable energy source for generations to come.

Hydropower, a traditional form of renewable energy, underwent a significant transformation on Eden Prime. Existing hydropower dams were modernized to improve efficiency and reduce environmental impacts. Innovative technologies, such as fish-friendly turbines, minimized harm to aquatic ecosystems. New hydropower projects were carefully evaluated, balancing the benefits of clean energy production with potential environmental impacts. Environmental impact assessments carefully considered the ecological effects of dams on river ecosystems, including changes in water flow, sediment transport, and aquatic habitat. Sustainable hydropower projects prioritized the preservation of natural ecosystems, minimizing disturbances to riverine environments and aquatic life.

Beyond these major sources of renewable energy, Eden Prime embraced a diverse range of other sustainable energy technologies. Ocean energy, including wave and tidal energy, was harnessed in coastal regions, utilizing the power of ocean currents to generate electricity. Innovative technologies, such as wave energy converters and tidal barrages, were developed and deployed, ensuring environmental sustainability and minimizing harm to marine ecosystems. These approaches were carefully designed to avoid disrupting marine environments and habitats.

Biomass energy, derived from sustainably managed forests and agricultural residues, provided a renewable source of heat and electricity. Bioenergy systems were designed to maximize efficiency and minimize environmental impact, avoiding deforestation and promoting sustainable forest management. Strict regulations ensured that biomass energy production did not contribute to greenhouse gas emissions or deforestation. The responsible sourcing and use of biomass energy provided a sustainable energy source while ensuring the health and preservation of forested areas.

The transition to a renewable energy system required significant investment in new infrastructure, including transmission lines and energy storage facilities. Smart grids were implemented to optimize energy distribution and management, integrating diverse renewable energy sources into a cohesive and reliable system. Advanced energy management systems monitored energy consumption and production in real time, optimizing energy use and minimizing waste.

The successful transition was not solely a technological achievement but a result of a profound societal shift. Public education played a crucial role in fostering awareness of the benefits of renewable energy and encouraging the adoption of sustainable energy practices. Government policies and incentives encouraged investment in renewable energy technologies and provided support to individuals and businesses transitioning to cleaner energy sources. Incentive programs were designed to encourage the adoption of renewable energy technologies, making them economically accessible to a wider range of individuals and businesses.

The transition to a renewable energy system was not without its challenges. The initial costs of building new renewable energy infrastructure were substantial. However, the long-term benefits, including reduced energy costs, improved air quality, and a reduced carbon footprint, far outweighed the initial investment. Eden Prime's example demonstrated that the transition to a sustainable energy future was not only feasible but also economically viable. The long-term economic benefits of renewable energy, including reduced reliance on volatile fossil fuel markets and the creation of new green jobs, were significant factors in the widespread adoption of sustainable energy practices.

Eden Prime's journey towards a renewable energy future served as a beacon of hope, demonstrating that a sustainable energy transition is achievable. It was a testament to human ingenuity, collaboration, and a deep commitment to preserving the planet. The legacy of Eden Prime was not just a cleaner planet but a model for other societies seeking a sustainable future, proving that energy independence and environmental stewardship are not mutually exclusive but rather complementary paths towards a thriving future for all. The transition to renewable energy was not merely a change in infrastructure; it was a fundamental shift in the relationship between humanity and the planet, a testament to the transformative power of a symbiotic partnership with nature.

The transformation of Eden Prime extended beyond energy production; it encompassed a complete overhaul of waste management. The old paradigm of "take-make-dispose" was replaced by a circular economy model, where waste was viewed not as a burden but as a resource. This shift was not simply a technological fix; it was a fundamental change in societal values, driven by a deep-seated understanding of the finite nature of resources and the interconnectedness of all living systems.

The initial steps involved a comprehensive audit of waste streams across all sectors: residential, commercial, and industrial. This meticulous analysis revealed the dominant waste types and their sources, laying the groundwork for targeted interventions. The data showed a disturbing reliance on single-use plastics, a pervasive problem that had plagued previous generations. However, this data also pointed towards opportunities for improvement.

The first major initiative was a complete ban on single-use plastics. This bold move, initially met with resistance from some sectors, was ultimately successful due to the widespread public support for environmental protection and the availability of viable alternatives. Biodegradable and compostable materials replaced plastic bags, food containers, and cutlery, reducing plastic waste significantly. Extensive public education campaigns highlighted the environmental consequences of plastic pollution and promoted the use of reusable alternatives. This included providing incentives for using reusable bags, offering workshops on composting, and designing attractive and accessible recycling systems. The campaign fostered a sense of collective responsibility, shifting consumer behavior and reducing the overall demand for single-use plastics.

Simultaneously, Eden Prime invested heavily in advanced recycling technologies. Traditional recycling methods, often limited by material compatibility and contamination issues, were supplemented by innovative chemical and mechanical processes. These technologies enabled the recycling of materials that were previously considered unrecyclable, dramatically increasing the overall recycling rate. For instance, mixed plastics, which had long posed a significant challenge, were now processed using advanced pyrolysis and depolymerization techniques, recovering valuable monomers that could be used to produce new plastics. This closed-loop system minimized waste and reduced reliance on virgin materials.

Beyond plastics, Eden Prime tackled the challenge of organic waste. Instead of landfilling, organic waste was actively diverted into composting programs. Large-scale composting facilities, strategically located across the planet, processed food scraps, yard waste, and other organic materials. This process generated high-quality compost, which was then used as a soil amendment in agriculture, completing the circular cycle. Residential composting programs were also widely adopted, with households encouraged to compost their own organic waste. Government incentives, such as subsidized composting bins and educational resources, fueled the widespread adoption of home composting. This initiative not only reduced landfill waste but also enriched the soil and improved agricultural productivity.

The construction and demolition (C&D) sector, a significant source of waste, underwent a radical transformation. Designers and builders embraced the principles of deconstruction, carefully dismantling structures to salvage reusable materials. Steel, wood, and other components were salvaged and repurposed in new construction projects, minimizing waste and reducing the demand for new materials. Prefabricated modular buildings, designed for easy disassembly and reuse, became increasingly common, promoting circularity within the construction industry. The construction industry actively incorporated recycled materials into new projects, demonstrating a commitment to sustainable building practices.

Electronic waste, or e-waste, posed a particularly complex challenge, as it contained valuable materials such as precious metals and rare earth elements, but also hazardous substances that could pollute the environment. Eden Prime tackled this problem with a combination of extended producer responsibility (EPR) schemes and advanced recycling technologies. EPR schemes held manufacturers accountable for the end-of-life management of their products, encouraging the design of products that are easier to repair, reuse, and recycle. Advanced recycling techniques allowed the recovery of valuable materials from e-waste, minimizing environmental harm and securing critical resources for future manufacturing.

The successful implementation of these waste management solutions was not solely a technological achievement. It relied on a strong foundation of public awareness, education, and policy support. Government regulations incentivized waste reduction, recycling, and resource recovery. Extended producer responsibility schemes were put in place, making producers accountable for the end-of-life management of their products. Financial incentives were provided to individuals and businesses that adopted sustainable waste management practices. Public education campaigns promoted responsible consumption and waste management, emphasizing the importance of reducing waste at the source and fostering a culture of reuse and recycling.

One notable initiative was the development of a comprehensive waste tracking system. This system used advanced technologies such as RFID tags and blockchain to monitor the movement of waste from its source to its final destination. This transparency ensured accountability and helped optimize waste management operations. The system also helped identify and prevent illegal dumping and other environmentally damaging practices. It generated real-time data on waste generation, recycling rates, and the performance of various waste management initiatives. This data was used to continuously improve and refine the waste management system.

The creation of a thriving circular economy required significant upfront investment in new infrastructure and technologies. However, the long-term benefits, including reduced landfill waste, reduced pollution, resource conservation, and the creation of green jobs, significantly outweighed the initial costs. Eden Prime's experience demonstrated that a shift toward a circular economy is not only environmentally beneficial but also economically viable. Furthermore, the shift toward a circular economy created new employment opportunities in waste management, recycling, and related industries.

The transition was not without its challenges. Changing deeply ingrained habits and overcoming resistance from some sectors took time and effort. However, the commitment to a symbiotic relationship with nature, combined with technological innovation and strong policy support, ultimately led to a profound transformation. Eden Prime's success story served as an inspiration to other planets, demonstrating that a circular economy is not merely an aspiration but a tangible reality, achievable through collaborative action, technological innovation, and a fundamental shift in societal values. The successful implementation of these initiatives transformed waste from a problem into a valuable resource, creating a more sustainable and resilient planet. The waste management system, integrated seamlessly with the renewable energy infrastructure, epitomized Eden Prime's commitment to a harmonious coexistence with nature, a testament to their successful symbiotic relationship. It became a global model, showcasing that a sustainable future is not just a possibility, but a necessity for planetary survival.

The success of Eden Prime's circular economy hinged not only on efficient waste management but also on a robust and comprehensive ecosystem monitoring system. This was not simply a matter of periodic checks; it was a dynamic, real-time observation network designed to provide early warnings of any disruptions to the delicate balance of the planet's ecosystems. Built on layers of advanced technologies, the system served as a vital early warning network, allowing for proactive interventions before minor problems escalated into major environmental crises.

At the heart of the monitoring system was a global network of strategically placed environmental sensors. These sensors, ranging from sophisticated satellite-based remote sensing instruments to ground-based networks of micro-sensors embedded in the soil, water, and atmosphere, constantly gathered data on a vast array of environmental parameters. This data included measurements of air and water quality, soil composition, biodiversity levels, climate variables such as temperature, humidity, and rainfall, as well as the overall health and resilience of various ecosystems.

The satellite-based component of the monitoring system provided a broad overview of the planet's environmental conditions. High-resolution satellite imagery, coupled with advanced spectral analysis techniques, allowed scientists to monitor deforestation rates, assess the health of forests and other vegetation types, track the movement of migratory animals, and monitor changes in land use patterns. Thermal imaging allowed for the detection of wildfires and other heat anomalies, enabling rapid response and minimizing environmental damage. Hyperspectral imagery provided detailed information on the chemical composition of the atmosphere and the Earth's surface, enabling the identification of pollutants and other environmental contaminants.

Ground-based sensors provided a more detailed, localized view of environmental conditions. These sensors were deployed throughout Eden Prime's diverse ecosystems, from the lush rainforests to the arid deserts, from the deep oceans to the mountain peaks. In the forests, sophisticated sensor networks monitored tree health, soil moisture levels, and atmospheric conditions, providing early warnings of drought, pest infestations, or disease outbreaks. In aquatic ecosystems, underwater sensors monitored water quality, temperature, salinity, and the presence of pollutants, enabling the detection of algal blooms or other environmental stresses. In agricultural areas, sensors monitored soil conditions, crop health, and irrigation efficiency, optimizing agricultural practices and minimizing resource consumption.

The data gathered by these sensors was not passively collected; it was actively analyzed and interpreted using advanced machine learning algorithms. These algorithms were trained on vast datasets of historical environmental data, enabling them to identify patterns and anomalies that might indicate potential environmental problems. The system was designed to flag any significant deviations from established norms, triggering alerts that were relayed to environmental managers and other relevant stakeholders. This proactive approach allowed for timely intervention, preventing minor problems from escalating into major environmental disasters.

The integration of the satellite-based and ground-based sensor networks was crucial for providing a comprehensive view of the planet's environmental health. The satellite data provided a broad overview, identifying areas of concern that required more detailed investigation. The ground-based sensors then provided the detailed information needed to assess the nature and extent of the problem. This integrated approach ensured that no potential environmental problem went unnoticed.

Beyond the sensors themselves, the monitoring system included a sophisticated data management and analysis infrastructure. This infrastructure allowed for the efficient storage, processing, and visualization of the vast amounts of data generated by the sensor networks. Advanced data visualization tools allowed scientists and environmental managers to easily interpret the data and identify patterns and trends. This capability was essential for tracking the effectiveness of environmental interventions and making informed decisions about future management strategies.

One of the most significant aspects of Eden Prime's ecosystem monitoring system was its capacity for predictive modeling. By combining historical environmental data with climate models and other relevant information, the system could predict future environmental conditions and the potential impact of various factors such as climate change, pollution, and land use change. This predictive capability allowed for the proactive implementation of mitigation strategies, minimizing potential negative impacts on the environment. For instance, the system could predict the likelihood of droughts or floods, enabling proactive implementation of water management strategies.

The monitoring system was not just a technological marvel; it was also deeply integrated into Eden Prime's societal fabric. The data generated by the system was readily accessible to the public, fostering a greater understanding of the environment and promoting environmental stewardship. Citizen scientists were actively involved in data collection and analysis, contributing to the overall effectiveness of the monitoring system. This collaborative approach ensured that the system remained relevant and responsive to the needs of the community.

The success of Eden Prime's ecosystem monitoring system was a testament to the planet's commitment to environmental protection. The system's sophisticated technology, coupled with a deep understanding of the interconnectedness of ecosystems and a commitment to data-driven decision-making, ensured that the planet's environmental health remained a top priority. This comprehensive approach to environmental monitoring served as a model for other planets, demonstrating that proactive environmental management is not only possible but also essential for the long-term sustainability of any planet. It ensured that Eden Prime's symbiotic relationship with its environment remained strong, a testament to their foresight and dedication. The system's ability to detect and respond to subtle shifts in environmental parameters, changes that might have gone unnoticed with less sophisticated methods, was a critical component in maintaining the delicate balance of their thriving ecosystem. This proactive approach prevented many potential ecological disasters, showcasing the value of investing in sophisticated monitoring technologies.

The system's architecture was designed for scalability and adaptability. As new technologies emerged, they were integrated into the system, enhancing its capabilities and accuracy. This ongoing evolution ensured that the monitoring system remained at the cutting edge of environmental science and technology, continually improving its ability to track and predict environmental changes. Furthermore, the data generated by the system provided valuable insights into the long-term effects of environmental policies and management practices, enabling continuous improvement and refinement of these strategies.

The system also played a crucial role in informing policy decisions. By providing policymakers with accurate, real-time data on environmental conditions, the monitoring system helped ensure that environmental regulations and management strategies were evidence-based and effective. This data-driven approach to policymaking was essential for the long-term sustainability of Eden Prime's ecosystems.

The economic benefits of the system were also substantial. By providing early warnings of potential environmental problems, the system helped prevent costly environmental disasters. For example, the early detection of pest infestations or disease outbreaks allowed for timely interventions, minimizing crop losses and protecting agricultural productivity. The system also contributed to the efficient management of natural resources, such as water and energy, reducing resource consumption and associated costs.

The system's success was also attributed to the extensive training and education programs provided to the workforce. Specialized teams of scientists, engineers, and technicians were responsible for operating and maintaining the system, ensuring its continuous performance. Regular training and professional development were crucial to maintaining the system's high standards. These highly skilled individuals were capable of interpreting the vast amounts of data generated by the system and translating it into actionable insights.

In conclusion, Eden Prime's ecosystem monitoring system was not simply a collection of sensors and algorithms; it was a complex and integrated system that reflected the planet's deep commitment to environmental stewardship. It was a testament to the power of technology, collaboration, and a proactive approach to environmental management. The system's success served as a model for other planets, demonstrating the importance of investing in advanced monitoring technologies and developing robust data-driven management strategies. The continuous monitoring and analysis of data ensured the preservation of Eden Prime's vibrant ecosystems for generations to come, further strengthening their symbiotic relationship with the environment and solidifying their commitment to sustainability. The system became an integral part of Eden Prime's identity, showcasing their dedication to living in harmony with nature.

CHAPTER NINE

THE LEGACY OF EDEN

The success of Eden Prime's sophisticated ecosystem monitoring system was inextricably linked to another critical element: the meticulous preservation and transmission of ecological knowledge across generations. This was not merely a matter of passing down facts and figures; it was a carefully cultivated system designed to ensure the continuity of environmental understanding, adaptive strategies, and a deep-seated respect for the planet's intricate web of life. The system recognized that technological advancements, while crucial, were only as effective as the human expertise guiding their application. Without a robust intergenerational knowledge transfer, the sophisticated technology could become a blunt instrument, incapable of responding to nuanced ecological shifts.

This intergenerational knowledge transfer encompassed various methodologies, each playing a vital role in maintaining a living legacy of environmental stewardship. One crucial aspect was the establishment of comprehensive ecological archives. These were not simply dusty repositories of outdated data; they were dynamic, constantly updated digital libraries containing centuries of accumulated ecological data, research findings, traditional ecological knowledge (TEK), and experiential accounts. This vast repository acted as a living encyclopedia of Eden Prime's environmental history, providing invaluable context for interpreting present-day observations and making informed decisions

149

about the future. The archive was not restricted to scientific papers; it also incorporated narratives, oral histories, and artistic representations of the relationship between the Eden Primians and their environment. This rich tapestry of information provided a holistic understanding of the ecosystem's dynamic evolution and the evolving human response to it.

The accessibility of this archive was paramount. Sophisticated search engines and intuitive user interfaces ensured that the information was readily accessible to everyone, regardless of their scientific background. Interactive simulations and visualizations brought abstract ecological concepts to life, making them easily understandable for young students, seasoned researchers, and concerned citizens alike. This open-access approach fostered a culture of continuous learning and environmental engagement, ensuring that ecological knowledge remained a dynamic, shared resource. The system recognized that knowledge is not static; it evolves with each new discovery, each encountered challenge, and each adaptation to change. Regular updates to the archive, driven by ongoing research and community contributions, reflected this ever-evolving understanding of their complex ecosystem. Furthermore, the archive was deliberately designed to be compatible with diverse data formats and languages, ensuring accessibility across different cultural groups and communities.

Beyond the digital archive, Eden Prime invested heavily in formal and informal educational programs designed to promote intergenerational knowledge transfer. Formal education integrated ecological literacy into the curriculum at all levels, from primary school to higher education. Students were not just taught about the environment; they actively participated in ecological monitoring programs, contributing data to the central archive and gaining firsthand experience in practical environmental management. Field trips to diverse ecosystems, guided by experienced ecologists, provided immersive learning experiences, fostering a direct connection with nature and nurturing a sense of environmental stewardship. The curriculum emphasized critical thinking and problem-solving, equipping students with the skills necessary to adapt to unforeseen ecological challenges. Furthermore, the formal education system stressed the importance of traditional ecological knowledge (TEK), recognizing its invaluable contribution to a holistic understanding of the environment.

Informal learning initiatives were equally crucial. Mentorship programs paired seasoned environmental professionals with younger generations, ensuring the transmission of practical skills, intuitive understanding, and nuanced interpretations of ecological data. These mentorship programs fostered lasting relationships, building strong community bonds and encouraging a shared sense of responsibility for the planet's future. Community workshops, festivals, and public lectures provided platforms for the exchange of knowledge, encouraging open dialogue and fostering a sense of collective ownership over the environment. Elderly community members, repositories of invaluable TEK and historical ecological insight, played a central role in these informal educational initiatives. Their stories, often passed down through generations, helped to contextualize scientific findings and emphasize the long-term consequences of environmental decisions. Storytelling became an integral part of the knowledge transfer process, engaging multiple forms of learning and solidifying essential ecological principles within the cultural fabric of the community.

Furthermore, the system recognized the critical role of citizen science. The planet's ecosystem monitoring network was designed to be inclusive, engaging citizens at all levels in data collection and analysis. This fostered a sense of shared responsibility and enabled a more extensive and fine-grained understanding of the environmental changes occurring across the planet. By participating in the monitoring program, citizens directly contributed to the evolution of ecological knowledge, ensuring that the knowledge base was informed by diverse perspectives and experiences. The open and transparent nature of the data-sharing system also empowered citizens to monitor environmental conditions in their own communities, promoting a proactive approach to environmental protection. This citizen-science initiative also served as a vital training ground, educating individuals about environmental monitoring techniques and fostering future generations of environmental stewards.

The system also incorporated a mechanism for cross-cultural exchange of ecological knowledge. Eden Prime, recognizing the importance of diversity in understanding environmental systems, established robust partnerships with other planets, exchanging knowledge and best practices. This exchange ensured that lessons learned in one environment could inform responses to similar challenges in another, promoting planetary-scale ecological stewardship. Such collaborations fostered a global network of environmental experts, promoting international cooperation and highlighting the interconnected nature of environmental challenges. The free flow of information and collaboration across planetary boundaries became a cornerstone of Eden Prime's approach to long-term ecological sustainability. This global perspective enriched their understanding of ecological principles and broadened their adaptive capacity to a range of potential environmental scenarios.

The intergenerational knowledge transfer system was not static; it evolved and adapted over time in response to changing needs and the emergence of new technologies. Regular evaluations and feedback mechanisms were in place to ensure that the system remained effective and relevant. This commitment to continuous improvement ensured that the preservation of ecological understanding remained a dynamic and responsive process. The evolution of the system was driven by a constant interplay between traditional ecological practices, emerging technologies, and community needs, ensuring its continued relevance and adaptability to future challenges. Eden Prime recognized that preserving ecological knowledge was an ongoing process, requiring constant adaptation and innovation to effectively address the ever-evolving environmental landscape. The commitment to adapting their methods ensured that the legacy of Eden Prime's environmental stewardship would endure for generations to come.

In conclusion, the success of Eden Prime's environmental stewardship was not solely dependent on technological prowess; it was fundamentally rooted in the meticulous preservation and transmission of ecological understanding across generations. The integrated system, comprising digital archives, formal and informal education programs, citizen science initiatives, and cross-cultural exchanges, ensured that the accumulated knowledge and wisdom of past generations provided a strong foundation for the challenges and opportunities of the future.

This holistic approach to intergenerational knowledge transfer is a testament to Eden Prime's commitment to maintaining a symbiotic relationship with their environment, ensuring that their vibrant ecosystems thrived, not just for their generation, but for countless generations to come. Their commitment to this legacy served as a powerful example for other planets, demonstrating that long-term environmental sustainability is achievable only through a deep and enduring connection between the human spirit and the natural world, a connection built and sustained by the careful transmission of knowledge and experience.

The success of Eden Prime's integrated system of environmental stewardship rested not only on its commitment to intergenerational knowledge transfer but also on a parallel track of remarkable scientific advancements. These advancements were not merely technological marvels; they were meticulously designed and implemented to enhance the resilience and sustainability of Eden Prime's unique ecosystems. The scientific community on Eden Prime worked hand-in-hand with the broader population, ensuring that scientific progress served the collective good and was deeply integrated into the fabric of their society.

One crucial area of scientific advancement focused on precision agriculture. Gone were the days of large-scale monoculture farming, which had proven environmentally destructive on many worlds. Eden Prime embraced highly localized, diversified farming techniques, leveraging advanced sensor networks and AI-powered predictive modeling to optimize crop yields while minimizing environmental impact. These sensor networks, woven seamlessly into the fabric of the agricultural landscape, monitored soil health, nutrient levels, water availability, and even the subtle shifts in microclimates.

The data generated was then fed into sophisticated algorithms that predicted optimal planting times, irrigation schedules, and fertilization needs, maximizing efficiency and reducing waste. This precision approach minimized the need for chemical pesticides and fertilizers, protecting biodiversity and preserving the integrity of the soil. Furthermore, the system incorporated advanced techniques for composting and waste recycling, ensuring that organic matter was returned to the soil, further enriching its nutrient content and contributing to a closed-loop agricultural system.

Genetic engineering played a role, but it was used responsibly and cautiously, focused on enhancing the resilience of existing crops to climate change and pests rather than creating entirely new species. Rigorous testing and ethical review were integral to every stage of this process, ensuring that the benefits of genetic engineering outweighed any potential risks.

Beyond agriculture, significant progress was made in renewable energy. Eden Prime harnessed the power of its unique ecosystem to develop a diverse portfolio of sustainable energy sources. Geothermal energy, tapped from deep underground reservoirs, provided a reliable and consistent baseload power source. Solar energy, collected through highly efficient photovoltaic systems integrated into buildings and infrastructure, supplemented geothermal energy during peak hours.

Wind farms, strategically located to maximize energy capture while minimizing impact on wildlife, contributed to the overall energy mix. Tidal energy, harnessing the rhythmic ebb and flow of ocean currents, provided another crucial element of the renewable energy strategy.

Perhaps most innovative were the biofuel projects, which harnessed the potential of specially engineered algae strains to produce clean-burning fuels, minimizing reliance on fossil fuels and creating a sustainable, circular economy. The energy grid itself was remarkably intelligent, capable of balancing supply and demand in real time, ensuring a stable and reliable energy supply while maximizing the efficiency of the diverse renewable sources.

Water management was another area of significant scientific focus. Eden Prime implemented advanced water filtration and purification systems, ensuring that water resources were efficiently utilized and protected from contamination. Water recycling techniques, combined with innovative water harvesting methods, minimized the need for fresh water extraction, protecting vital groundwater reserves and surface water bodies. Precision irrigation, guided by the same sophisticated sensor networks used in agriculture, maximized water use efficiency in agricultural settings, significantly reducing water waste.

Moreover, the scientific community developed drought-resistant crops and optimized irrigation techniques to improve water usage efficiency, reducing the need for large-scale water projects that could disrupt natural ecosystems. The water management system was designed to be adaptable, capable of responding to both periods of drought and extreme rainfall, ensuring water security for the entire population. It was not merely about supplying water; it was about preserving the integrity of the water cycle and protecting the aquatic ecosystems that were essential to the health of the planet.

Environmental remediation was another significant area of scientific progress. Eden Prime's scientists developed innovative technologies for cleaning up pollution and restoring damaged ecosystems. Bioremediation techniques, utilizing microorganisms to break down pollutants, were employed to remediate soil and water contaminated by past industrial activities. Phytoremediation, using plants to absorb and remove contaminants, was successfully implemented in a number of locations.

The scientists also developed advanced methods for removing microplastics from the environment, employing techniques ranging from specialized filtration systems to engineered microorganisms capable of breaking down plastic polymers. The focus was not just on cleaning up the damage but on understanding the root causes of pollution, preventing future contamination, and promoting the long-term health of the environment. This approach was built upon a deep understanding of the interconnectedness of ecosystems and the importance of preserving biodiversity in the remediation process.

The development and application of advanced ecological modeling were central to Eden Prime's environmental success. Complex computer models, incorporating vast datasets from the ecosystem monitoring network, were used to simulate the impact of various environmental factors, allowing scientists to anticipate and respond to potential threats.

These models helped predict the spread of invasive species, forecast the impacts of climate change on specific ecosystems, and assess the effectiveness of different environmental management strategies. The models were not static; they were continuously updated and refined based on new data and insights, becoming increasingly sophisticated and accurate over time. This predictive capacity was essential for proactive environmental management, allowing Eden Prime to address environmental challenges before they escalated into crises. The models also helped to assess the potential impact of proposed infrastructure projects and development initiatives, ensuring that these activities were environmentally sustainable.

Furthermore, Eden Prime invested heavily in research focused on understanding and enhancing biodiversity. Scientists conducted extensive surveys of the planet's ecosystems, documenting the vast array of plant and animal species. This detailed understanding of biodiversity was crucial for conservation efforts and for ensuring the resilience of the planet's ecosystems.

They employed cutting-edge genetic analysis to track the health and genetic diversity of various populations, identifying species at risk and developing strategies for their protection. Conservation programs were carefully designed to protect critical habitats, manage invasive species, and ensure the long-term survival of endangered species. The scientific approach to biodiversity was not just about preserving species; it was about understanding the complex interactions between species and their role in maintaining the overall health and resilience of the ecosystem.

Finally, the advancement of AI and machine learning played a vital role in all aspects of environmental management. AI-powered systems were integrated into every stage of the process, from monitoring ecosystems to predicting environmental changes and optimizing resource allocation. These systems were designed to learn and adapt, constantly improving their accuracy and efficiency over time.

AI did not replace human expertise; it augmented and enhanced it, providing scientists and policymakers with powerful tools for making informed decisions. The development and deployment of AI were guided by ethical considerations, ensuring that these technologies were used responsibly and equitably. This careful integration of AI was critical to the effectiveness of Eden Prime's integrated system of environmental stewardship.

The scientific advancements on Eden Prime were not isolated achievements; they were part of a holistic and integrated approach to environmental management. The success of these advancements was inextricably linked to the commitment to intergenerational knowledge transfer, ensuring that the scientific knowledge and expertise were preserved and passed down to future generations. It was a testament to their understanding that scientific progress, combined with a deep respect for nature and a commitment to community involvement, was the key to achieving long-term environmental sustainability. The legacy of Eden Prime was not just about technological marvels; it was about the enduring partnership between science, community, and the natural world.

The success of Eden Prime's environmental stewardship wasn't solely a triumph of science; it was deeply intertwined with a vibrant and evolving culture that celebrated humanity's place within the natural world. This culture was not static; it was a dynamic entity, constantly adapting and evolving in response to both internal and external pressures, but always retaining its core values of respect for nature, community, and intergenerational knowledge transfer. Cultural preservation on Eden Prime was not a matter of preserving artifacts in museums; it was a living, breathing process that permeated every aspect of daily life.

One of the most significant aspects of Eden Prime's culture was its deep reverence for the natural world. This was not merely a passive appreciation; it was active participation in the intricate dance of life on the planet. The annual Harvest Festival, a celebration of the bounty of the land, was a prime example. This was not a simple agricultural fair; it was a complex ritual involving elaborate ceremonies, traditional dances, and storytelling that recounted the history of the planet's ecosystems and the role of humanity in their stewardship. The festival brought together people from all walks of life, reinforcing the communal bond and shared responsibility for the planet's well-being.

Children participated in workshops that taught them traditional farming techniques, ecological principles, and the importance of biodiversity. Elderly community members shared their wisdom and knowledge, passing down generations of accumulated understanding and experience. The Harvest Festival was not just a celebration; it was a powerful tool for cultural transmission, ensuring that the values and knowledge integral to Eden Prime's sustainable way of life were passed down through the generations.

Another example of the vibrant cultural landscape of Eden Prime is their intricate system of oral traditions. Stories, songs, and poems passed down through generations narrated the complex history of Eden Prime's interaction with the natural world, from the early struggles to adapt to the planet's challenges to the triumphs of environmental restoration and sustainable living. These narratives were not mere entertainment; they were powerful educational tools, embedding ecological knowledge, cultural values, and ethical guidelines within the very fabric of their society.

Elderly storytellers, often highly respected figures within the community, played a crucial role in this process. Their stories taught children about the importance of respecting the land, understanding the delicate balance of ecosystems, and living in harmony with the natural world. The oral traditions reinforced a sense of place and belonging, connecting each individual to the larger ecosystem and to the history of their community. This was not only a means of cultural preservation but also a method for instilling essential values for a sustainable future. These stories were not only recounted in traditional gatherings but also incorporated into educational curricula, interactive museum exhibits, and even virtual reality experiences, ensuring that they resonated with people of all ages and backgrounds.

Visual arts played a vital role in preserving and celebrating the culture of Eden Prime. Intricate murals adorned the buildings, depicting the planet's diverse flora and fauna, the history of its people, and their relationship with nature. These were not mere decorations; they were living histories, vibrant testaments to the deep connection between the people of Eden Prime and their environment. Many of these murals were collaborative efforts, involving artists from different communities, and were created using natural pigments extracted from plants and minerals, emphasizing the harmonious integration of art and nature.

Traditional crafts, using locally sourced materials, also played a crucial role in cultural preservation. Basket weaving, pottery, and woodworking were not simply decorative arts; they were expressions of profound respect for the natural materials, reflecting an understanding of finite resources and the importance of sustainability. These crafts were often taught as part of the educational system, passing down essential skills and values from one generation to the next. This tangible connection to their heritage instilled a sense of responsibility toward environmental stewardship and fostered appreciation for the planet's finite resources.

Music also served as a crucial vehicle for cultural preservation. Eden Prime's musical traditions were not confined to formal concerts or performances; they were an integral part of everyday life. Traditional songs, often accompanied by instruments crafted from natural materials, were used to recount historical events, celebrate seasonal changes, and reinforce social values. These musical traditions were not static; they evolved organically over time, incorporating new influences and reflecting the changing dynamics of Eden Prime's culture.

However, the underlying themes of respect for nature and community remained constant, providing a cohesive thread that linked the past, present, and future of their society. Music festivals were common throughout the year and allowed for the sharing of musical traditions between communities. Many of these festivals involved competitions that helped to maintain the quality and relevance of the music. Furthermore, traditional musical instruments and techniques were carefully documented and taught in schools and community centers.

The culinary practices of Eden Prime reflected their deep connection with the natural world. Traditional dishes emphasized locally sourced ingredients, highlighting the bounty of their unique ecosystems. The focus was on minimizing waste and maximizing the use of all parts of harvested plants, reflecting a mindful approach to resource management. Cooking was not simply a means of sustenance; it was a cultural practice that reinforced communal bonds, shared knowledge, and respect for the natural world. Culinary traditions were not just passed down through families; they were also documented and shared through community cookbooks, online platforms, and educational programs. This preserved recipes and cooking techniques, ensuring that the unique culinary identity of Eden Prime continued to flourish. The annual Food Festival brought together diverse communities, sharing their traditional dishes and culinary skills, strengthening community ties and preserving a rich cultural heritage.

In addition to these more traditional forms of cultural preservation, Eden Prime utilized technology thoughtfully to preserve and promote their cultural heritage. Digital archives meticulously documented oral histories, traditional crafts, musical performances, and culinary practices, ensuring that these aspects of their cultural heritage would be accessible to future generations.

Virtual reality and augmented reality technologies were employed to create immersive experiences, allowing people to explore historical sites, experience traditional ceremonies, and learn about the unique aspects of Eden Prime's culture. This technological integration was not a replacement for traditional methods; it was a complementary approach that enhanced access to cultural knowledge and ensured its survival for the long term. It ensured that cultural preservation was not solely the responsibility of a select group of individuals but was inclusive and accessible to the entire community.

Eden Prime's cultural preservation was not a passive effort; it was an active and dynamic process, deeply integrated into the daily life of its inhabitants. It was not merely a preservation of the past; it was a vibrant celebration of the present and a guiding principle for the future. The cultural preservation efforts on Eden Prime were not isolated initiatives; they were interwoven with their approach to environmental stewardship, reflecting a holistic worldview that connected human culture to the natural world in a harmonious and sustainable manner.

The ongoing dialogue between tradition and innovation, between technological advancements and cultural preservation, ensured the unique and valuable elements of Eden Prime's culture would thrive for generations to come. This holistic approach underscored the understanding that a healthy environment and a thriving culture were inseparable, mutually reinforcing elements of a sustainable and fulfilling society. The legacy of

Eden Prime demonstrated that true sustainability encompassed not only ecological balance but also the preservation and celebration of cultural diversity.

The vibrant tapestry of Eden Prime's culture was not woven solely from threads of tradition and ritual; it was richly embroidered with artistic expressions that mirrored the planet's unique ecosystem and its inhabitants' intimate relationship with it. These were not mere decorations or expressions of individual talent; they were powerful tools for cultural transmission, preserving knowledge, values, and a deep sense of connection to the land. The art of Eden Prime served as a living record of their journey, from the initial struggles of adaptation to the flourishing sustainable society they had built.

One particularly striking example was the widespread use of bioluminescent art. Given Eden Prime's unique flora, many plants possessed natural bioluminescence, a trait cleverly incorporated into various art forms. Artists cultivated specific species with varying luminescent properties, creating living canvases that shifted and changed with the seasons and the time of day. Entire buildings would transform at nightfall, their surfaces becoming living murals that depicted scenes from Eden Prime's history, its diverse ecosystems, or even abstract representations of ecological processes such as nutrient cycles or the flow of energy through the food web.

These were not static displays; they were dynamic works of art, constantly evolving and interacting with their environment, a testament to the living relationship between art and the natural world. Workshops taught techniques for cultivating and manipulating these bioluminescent plants, ensuring the continuation of this unique art form.

Beyond bioluminescent art, the landscape itself became a canvas. Land art, a prominent tradition on Eden Prime, involved manipulating natural elements to create large-scale installations that blended seamlessly with the surrounding environment. Using carefully selected plants, rocks, and water features, artists crafted intricate designs that echoed patterns found in nature, often focusing on themes of interconnectedness, sustainability, and ecological balance. These were not permanent installations; they were ephemeral creations that evolved with the seasons, reflecting the natural processes of growth and decay and reminding the inhabitants of the ever-changing nature of their world.

The creation of these installations often involved entire communities, transforming the artistic process into a collaborative celebration of creativity and shared responsibility. The placement of these installations often held symbolic significance, marking important historical sites or reflecting the natural rhythms of the planet.

Sculpture played a vital role in Eden Prime's artistic expression. Many sculptures were carved from sustainably harvested wood, meticulously shaped to represent the planet's diverse fauna, mythological figures, or scenes from their oral traditions. The artisans used traditional tools and techniques, ensuring the preservation of these skills while reflecting a profound respect for the natural materials.

The placement of the sculptures was also significant. Some were positioned in public squares and gardens, serving as focal points for community gatherings, while others were nestled within the natural landscape, blending seamlessly with their surroundings and often featuring carvings that reflected the local flora and fauna. The creation of these sculptures was often a multi-generational process, with younger generations learning from their elders and contributing their own unique perspectives.

Music and dance were integral to the daily life of Eden Prime, serving not only as forms of entertainment but also as powerful tools for cultural transmission and social cohesion. Traditional dances incorporated movements that mirrored the natural world, mimicking the swaying of trees in the wind, the flight of birds, or the flow of a river. The music accompanying these dances often utilized instruments crafted from natural materials, such as bamboo flutes, gourd rattles, and stringed instruments made from carefully harvested wood.

Musical compositions often recounted historical events, celebrated the changing seasons, or reinforced the values of community, respect for nature, and intergenerational learning. These musical performances were not confined to formal concerts; they were incorporated into daily life, from informal gatherings to ceremonies marking important milestones. Music competitions and festivals were held regularly, encouraging the evolution and preservation of these rich musical traditions while fostering a sense of shared identity and community pride.

Textile arts held a place of significant importance in the cultural heritage of Eden Prime. Using sustainably sourced fibers such as plant-based materials and recycled textiles, skilled artisans created intricate tapestries, clothing, and other decorative objects. These textiles frequently featured elaborate designs depicting flora, fauna, or scenes from their history and folklore. The colors were derived from natural pigments extracted from plants and minerals, reinforcing the connection between art and the environment.

Workshops and community centers ensured the continued learning of traditional textile-making techniques, fostering a sense of cultural preservation and pride. This ensured these skills were passed down through generations and that the cultural identity was represented in their clothing and other textiles.

The culinary arts of Eden Prime also served as a powerful form of artistic expression. The presentation of food was as important as its taste, with meals often being elaborate arrangements that highlighted the natural beauty and diversity of the ingredients. Seasonal ingredients were celebrated in intricate dishes and presentations, emphasizing the bounty of the ecosystems and highlighting their interconnectedness.

Cooking was not just a means of sustenance; it was a communal act that reinforced social bonds and cultural knowledge. The annual

Food Festival, where different communities showcased their culinary traditions, served as a powerful celebration of cultural diversity and intergenerational knowledge sharing. Culinary traditions were not merely passed down through families; they were carefully documented and shared through community cookbooks, online platforms, and educational programs, preserving the unique culinary identity of Eden Prime for future generations.

Literature played a crucial role in documenting and preserving the knowledge, beliefs, and cultural history of Eden Prime. Stories, poems, and plays were passed down orally for generations, but as technology evolved, they were also transcribed and preserved digitally. These literary works explored themes of environmental stewardship, community harmony, and the interconnectedness of life. They served as powerful educational tools, embedding ecological principles and cultural values into the heart of Eden Prime's society.

Emerging writers blended traditional storytelling with new technologies, creating interactive narratives and virtual reality experiences that engaged readers in a dynamic way, strengthening the relationship between literary traditions and technological progress. The literary arts of Eden Prime represented a dynamic exchange between tradition and innovation, sustaining the cultural heritage while adapting to the evolving landscape of their society.

The artistic expressions of Eden Prime were not isolated phenomena; they were deeply integrated into the fabric of their society, reflecting their close relationship with nature, their commitment to sustainability, and their belief in the power of cultural preservation. From bioluminescent murals to intricate textile designs and vibrant culinary creations, every artistic form served as a testament to the enduring legacy of Eden Prime, a living example of how art and culture can be powerful forces for environmental stewardship and social harmony.

The continuing dialogue between tradition and innovation ensured the vitality and relevance of their artistic expressions, creating a rich tapestry of culture that was both deeply rooted in the past and dynamically responsive to the challenges and opportunities of the future. This enduring legacy served as a beacon, highlighting the profound connection between human creativity and the well-being of the planet.

The vibrant artistic expressions of Eden Prime were not merely aesthetic pursuits; they were deeply intertwined with the planet's spiritual fabric. For the inhabitants, the natural world was not simply a resource to be exploited but a sacred entity, a living embodiment of a powerful interconnectedness that permeated every aspect of their lives. This was not a formalized religion in the traditional sense, but rather a profound spiritual connection woven into the very warp and weft of their daily existence, expressed through rituals, ceremonies, and a profound respect for the delicate balance of their ecosystem.

The concept of "The Great Web," a central tenet of their spiritual understanding, emphasized the intricate interconnectedness of all living things. They believed that every plant, animal, and even inanimate object held a vital role within this intricate web and that humanity was but one thread within this grand tapestry. Disrupting this balance through exploitation or disregard was considered not only ecologically damaging but also spiritually sacrilegious. This understanding fueled their commitment to sustainability and their unwavering respect for the planet's natural rhythms.

Their daily lives were infused with rituals that honored this connection. The "Morning Song," a communal chanting performed at dawn, expressed gratitude for the day's bounty and acknowledged their dependence on the natural world. This was not a rote recitation; it was a heartfelt expression of interdependence, where individuals voiced their hopes and anxieties, weaving them into a collective hymn of gratitude and reflection. Similarly, the "Evening Offering," performed at sunset, involved leaving small offerings of food and flowers at designated points within the landscape, a gesture of respect for the spirits believed to reside within the natural world. These offerings were not seen as appeasements to deities but rather as acts of reciprocity, acknowledging the planet's generosity and reinforcing their role as stewards of the land.

The annual "Harvest Festival," a significant event in Eden Prime's calendar, was a grand celebration of the planet's abundance and a reaffirmation of their spiritual connection. This was not just a time of feasting and merriment; it was a deeply spiritual occasion, incorporating elements of thanksgiving, reflection, and communal bonding. The festival involved elaborate ceremonies that integrated music, dance, and storytelling, all interwoven with symbolic representations of the harvest cycle and their deep respect for the planet's generosity. Participants engaged in ritualistic dances that mimicked the movements of plants growing toward the sun, the cycles of the seasons, or the journey of water from the mountains to the sea, visually representing their understanding of the interconnectedness of life.

Meditation played a significant role in their spiritual practice. Many Eden Primers spent time in quiet contemplation within the natural world, seeking to deepen their connection with the "Great Web." These were not structured meditation practices as understood by some other cultures; instead, they involved immersing themselves in the sensory richness of their environment listening to the rustling of leaves, feeling the warmth of the sun on their skin, observing the subtle movements of animals, and breathing in the fragrant air. This was a form of contemplative immersion in the natural world, allowing them to connect with the larger cycles of life and deepen their understanding of their place within it.

Spiritual guidance was not provided by a priestly class or religious hierarchy. Instead, wisdom was passed down through generations within families and communities, through storytelling, shared experiences, and observation of the natural world. Elders played a crucial role in this process, sharing their knowledge and insights, interpreting the signs and symbols found in nature, and guiding younger generations in their understanding of the "Great Web." These were not authoritarian figures; they were respected guides and mentors who helped individuals develop their own personal connection with the natural world.

Shamanistic practices, while not central to daily life, played a vital role in times of crisis or when seeking guidance on important community decisions. The "Vision Seekers," individuals with a heightened sensitivity to the natural world, undertook journeys into remote areas of the planet to seek guidance from the spirits. These journeys were not undertaken lightly; they required extensive preparation and a deep understanding of the environment.

The Vision Seekers were not seen as intermediaries between humanity and the divine but rather as individuals with a heightened ability to perceive and interpret the subtle messages embedded within the natural world. Their insights were valued but they were not treated as infallible authorities. Their findings were carefully considered within the community, with decisions made through collective deliberation and consensus building.

Their understanding of death also reflected their spiritual connection with nature. Death was not seen as an end but as a transition, a return to the "Great Web." Burial practices involved returning the body to the earth, allowing it to decompose and become part of the natural cycle. Mourning ceremonies focused on celebrating the life of the deceased and acknowledging their contribution to the community rather than dwelling on their absence. The emphasis was on the continuity of life, the constant cycle of birth, death, and regeneration, reflecting the natural processes they observed all around them.

The art of Eden Prime was not just an aesthetic expression; it was a visible manifestation of their spiritual understanding. The bioluminescent murals were not merely decorative; they were living representations of the "Great Web," depicting the intricate interconnectedness of life. Land art installations were not simply aesthetic creations; they were sacred spaces, embodying their reverence for the natural world. Even their everyday objects, from clothing to tools, were often adorned with symbolic representations of natural elements, reminding them of their profound connection with the environment.

The legacy of Eden Prime was not simply a technological marvel or an ecological success; it was a testament to the power of a profound spiritual connection with the natural world. It was a reminder that a truly sustainable society is not just built on scientific knowledge and technological innovation but also on a deep respect for the interconnectedness of all life, a profound appreciation for the natural world, and a commitment to living in harmony with the planet.

This spiritual understanding was not a set of rigid doctrines or beliefs but a living philosophy that permeated every aspect of their lives, shaping their values, their rituals, and their artistic expressions. It was a culture born not from a conquest of nature but from a deep and abiding reverence for it, a testament to the enduring power of human spirituality to shape a harmonious relationship between humankind and the environment. Their story served as a powerful reminder that true progress is not simply measured in technological advancement but in the depth and quality of our relationship with the planet that sustains us. The legacy of Eden Prime, therefore, transcended mere technological achievement; it was an enduring testament to the profound and transformative power of a truly spiritual connection with nature. Their harmonious existence was a beacon, illuminating a path toward a future where human ingenuity and spiritual awareness work in concert to create a sustainable and fulfilling future for all.

CHAPTER TEN

BEYOND EDEN

The shimmering bioluminescent cities of Eden Prime, nestled among the verdant, self-sustaining ecosystems, hummed with a quiet energy. The success of their harmonious existence, a testament to their deep-rooted spiritual connection with the planet, had bred cautious optimism. The population, while thriving, was growing, and the question of expansion loomed large. The concept of leaving Eden Prime, once unthinkable, was now a carefully considered necessity, a path toward ensuring the long-term survival and prosperity of their unique civilization.

The decision to embark on exploration missions was not taken lightly. Years of deliberation, community discussions, and consultations with Vision Seekers had culminated in a meticulously planned strategy that prioritized both expansion and the preservation of their ecological principles. The core tenet guiding these explorations was not the conquest of new territories but the careful assessment of their suitability for sustainable habitation, a continuation of their philosophy of living in harmony with the planet, not dominating it.

The first step involved advanced remote sensing technology. Utilizing a network of orbiting satellites equipped with sophisticated sensors, they meticulously scanned nearby star systems, mapping planetary compositions and atmospheric conditions and identifying potential sources of water and energy. This preliminary phase ruled out many candidates, eliminating planets with hostile atmospheres, insufficient resources, or signs of pre-existing life forms that could disrupt the delicate balance they strove to maintain.

The selected candidate planets, deemed promising after the initial scans, were then subjected to more detailed investigation. Specialized probes, equipped with advanced AI and capable of autonomous operation, were dispatched. These probes were not crude, resource-hungry machines; they were meticulously designed for minimal environmental impact, utilizing solar power and employing biodegradable materials wherever possible. Their mission was to collect detailed samples of soil, water, and atmosphere, analyze potential hazards, and assess the suitability of the environment for Eden Prime's unique bio-engineered ecosystems.

The data gathered by these probes was then meticulously analyzed by a team of scientists and Vision Seekers. The scientists applied rigorous methodology, examining the chemical composition of samples, modeling potential climate conditions, and assessing the geological stability of the planet. The Vision Seekers, on the other hand, brought their deep understanding of the interconnectedness of life, seeking subtle signs within the data that might reveal underlying patterns of energy flow, invisible connections, and the presence or absence of a vital "Great Web." Their insights, while not scientifically quantifiable, were considered an invaluable component of the decision-making process.

Only after both scientific and spiritual assessments yielded positive results was the next phase initiated: the deployment of manned expeditions. These were not large-scale colonization efforts; instead, they were carefully planned, small-scale missions designed to gather further data, establish basic research outposts, and test the feasibility of establishing sustainable settlements.

The spacecraft used for these expeditions were not conventional rockets that burned fossil fuels and left behind trails of pollution. Instead, they were bio-engineered vessels, utilizing innovative propulsion systems based on controlled fusion reactions, ensuring a minimal environmental footprint. The vessels were equipped with advanced life support systems that minimized waste and recycled resources, mirroring the principles of sustainability that guided Eden Prime's terrestrial existence. The crew, handpicked for their scientific expertise and spiritual understanding, underwent extensive training, simulating various scenarios and preparing for the challenges of establishing a new settlement while maintaining the ecological integrity of both their home planet and their new destination.

The first manned mission targeted a planet designated Kepler-186f, orbiting a red dwarf star. The planet boasted a relatively Earth-like atmosphere, although with lower gravity. The mission's primary objective was to establish a self-sufficient research outpost, capable of generating its own energy and producing food using bio-engineered techniques that mimicked Eden Prime's sustainable ecosystems. The crew carried with them a diverse array of plant and animal species, carefully selected to establish a balanced and resilient ecosystem, ensuring not only their own survival but the long-term viability of the outpost.

The outpost itself was designed as a symbiosis between technology and nature. It was constructed from biodegradable materials, interwoven with living organisms that helped to purify the air and water. Solar panels provided energy, while advanced water reclamation systems ensured efficient resource management. The outpost was not a sterile, technologically driven structure; it was designed to integrate seamlessly with the planet's environment, promoting a natural, harmonious relationship.

Throughout the mission, the crew meticulously documented their findings, sending regular reports back to Eden Prime. They conducted extensive research into the planet's geology, hydrology, and biodiversity. They also performed spiritual meditations, connecting with the planet's subtle energies and seeking to understand its unique spiritual essence. This integration of scientific and spiritual perspectives was crucial to their understanding of the planet and to their successful establishment of a sustainable presence.

Communication between the Kepler-186f outpost and Eden Prime was not instantaneous. The vast distances involved meant that messages traveled at the speed of light, resulting in considerable delays. However, this was not a hindrance. The community on Eden Prime had prepared for this, understanding that long-distance communication required patience and a deep sense of trust. They adapted their communication strategies, sending pre-recorded messages and receiving data in batches, managing their expectations and adjusting their timelines to the realities of interstellar travel.

The success of the Kepler-186f mission marked a significant milestone. It demonstrated not only the technological prowess of Eden Prime but also the resilience of their spiritual principles and their ability to adapt their way of life to a new environment. However, it also served as a reminder of the immense challenges involved in interstellar expansion, underscoring the need for careful planning, rigorous scientific research, and a deep respect for the delicate balance of life on other planets. The explorations were not simply about expanding their civilization; they were about carrying their unique blend of ecological harmony and spiritual wisdom to new worlds, ensuring a future where humanity and nature could flourish together, a testament to the enduring legacy of Eden Prime.

The journeys ahead were long and arduous, yet fueled by hope, guided by a deep respect for the cosmos and the interconnectedness of all things, the people of Eden Prime looked to the stars with a mixture of anticipation and reverence. Their future was not only in their hands but also in their ability to tread lightly and live in harmony with the universe itself.

The successful establishment of the Kepler-186f outpost was not just a victory for Eden Prime; it was a beacon, a testament to the possibility of sustainable interstellar expansion. News of their achievement, transmitted across the light-years, reached other nascent settlements scattered across the galaxy—settlements born from diverse origins, each with their own unique challenges and technological strengths. This sparked an era of unprecedented collaboration, a weaving together of knowledge and resources that transcended the limitations of distance and cultural differences.

One of the first partnerships forged was with a settlement known as Xylos, a community established on a planet orbiting a binary star system. Xylos possessed advanced expertise in energy generation, specifically in harnessing the power of stellar flares from their binary suns. Their technology, far more efficient than Eden Prime's controlled fusion reactors, offered the potential to drastically reduce energy consumption and minimize the environmental impact of interstellar travel. In exchange, Eden Prime shared their sophisticated bio-engineering techniques, enabling Xylos to develop self-sustaining ecosystems within their initially barren environment, transforming desolate landscapes into vibrant, life-supporting biomes.

This exchange was not a simple trade of technology; it was a collaborative process involving the sharing of knowledge and expertise. Teams of scientists and engineers from both settlements worked together, combining their unique perspectives and approaches. Xylos' engineers marveled at Eden Prime's intricate understanding of symbiotic relationships within ecosystems, while Eden Prime's scientists were captivated by Xylos' innovative approach to energy capture, a system that mimicked the planet's natural energy cycles. This fusion of ideas led to the development of a new generation of spacecraft, powered by a hybrid system that combined the efficiency of Xylos' stellar flare capture with the ecological consciousness of Eden Prime's bio-engineered propulsion systems.

Another significant partnership was formed with the inhabitants of Aethel, a settlement built upon a massive asteroid belt. Aethel possessed an unparalleled mastery of resource extraction and processing, utilizing advanced robotic mining operations that minimized environmental damage and maximized resource yield. Their expertise in refining rare minerals and developing sustainable materials was crucial to advancing both settlements' technological development. In return, Eden Prime shared their knowledge of bio-remediation, enabling Aethel to address the ecological impact of their mining operations and restore balance to their asteroid environment.

This collaborative approach extended beyond technology. The settlements also shared knowledge regarding social structures, governance models, and philosophical perspectives. Eden Prime's emphasis on spiritual harmony and ecological balance influenced Aethel's approach to resource management, while Aethel's experience with collaborative governance models inspired Eden Prime to refine their own decision-making processes. The exchange of ideas went beyond mere practicality; it fostered a deeper understanding between different cultures, challenging preconceived notions and paving the way for a more inclusive and cooperative future.

This interconnected network of settlements was not limited to just three; it gradually expanded to encompass many others. Each new partnership added another layer of complexity and diversity, enriching the overall technological and cultural tapestry. The sharing was not always equal; some settlements contributed more in certain areas than others. Yet the fundamental principle driving these partnerships was mutual benefit, a recognition that collaboration was essential for long-term survival and prosperity.

The development of a universal communication network was crucial to these partnerships. Although instantaneous communication remained a challenge, the settlements developed a sophisticated system of relay stations, using strategically placed orbital satellites and advanced signal amplification technology to minimize delays. This system, designed with redundancy and adaptability, ensured that communication remained reliable even in the face of unforeseen circumstances, such as stellar flares or asteroid impacts. This was more than just technological advancement;

it was the creation of a shared infrastructure, a physical manifestation of their interconnectedness.

Resource management became a shared responsibility. A central database, maintained collaboratively, tracked the availability and distribution of vital resources, ensuring efficient allocation and minimizing waste. This database did not dictate resource allocation; it empowered individual settlements to make informed decisions based on a comprehensive understanding of the overall situation. The system fostered transparency and accountability, promoting fairness and equitable access to resources. This advanced system went beyond simple data storage; it included sophisticated predictive models based on resource consumption and production rates and even factored in considerations such as the environmental impact of resource extraction and processing.

The success of these technological partnerships was not merely about technological advancement; it represented a profound shift in mindset. It marked a move away from a competitive, resource-hoarding mentality toward a collaborative, resource-sharing model, reflecting the ecological consciousness that guided Eden Prime's philosophy. It showcased the potential for humanity to transcend its limitations, to overcome the challenges of interstellar expansion through cooperation and mutual respect, building a future not of conquest and dominion but of collaboration and shared prosperity.

The long-term implications were far-reaching. The collective knowledge and resources pooled together had the potential to unlock breakthroughs in various fields, from medicine and genetic engineering to advanced robotics and artificial intelligence. These partnerships were laying the foundation for a new era of technological advancement, an era characterized by collective innovation and shared progress. The implications extended beyond the purely technological; it was a blueprint for a future where humanity transcended its tribalism and forged a new, unified identity grounded in shared purpose and collaboration.

The success of these partnerships also relied heavily on shared ethical considerations. A council of representatives from each participating settlement was formed to establish guidelines for responsible technology development and resource management. These guidelines, meticulously crafted, prioritized ecological sustainability and ethical considerations in all aspects of technological advancement and resource utilization.

The council acted as a safeguard, ensuring that the benefits of technological advancements were shared equitably and that potential risks were mitigated effectively. This was not merely a regulatory body; it fostered a sense of collective responsibility, ensuring that technological progress did not come at the expense of environmental integrity or social justice. It was a testament to the collective commitment to build a better future for all.

The story of Eden Prime's technological partnerships was not just about the exchange of technology; it was about the creation of a new paradigm, a paradigm built on cooperation, shared resources, and a collective commitment to a sustainable future. It was a story of hope, a testament to the power of collaboration and the potential of humanity to transcend its past limitations and forge a brighter, more sustainable future for all.

As they looked toward the stars, the settlements of Eden Prime and its partners were not just gazing into the vast unknown; they were looking into a future built on shared dreams and the unwavering belief in the power of unity. The universe, once a seemingly unyielding expanse, was now transforming into a network of interconnected civilizations, a collaborative effort to thrive amidst the cosmos.

The success of the Kepler-186f outpost spurred a wave of inter-settlement collaborations, extending far beyond simple technological exchanges. A crucial focus emerged: ecological restoration. While Eden Prime had mastered bio-engineering for creating self-sustaining ecosystems, many other settlements faced unique environmental challenges that demanded innovative solutions. This shared predicament became the catalyst for a new era of scientific cooperation, focusing on restoring damaged or barren worlds.

One particularly fruitful collaboration involved the settlement of Elysium, located on a planet with a severely depleted ozone layer. Elysium's atmosphere was thin, and radiation levels were dangerously high, making large-scale terraforming efforts prohibitively complex and resource-intensive. Eden Prime, with their expertise in atmospheric manipulation and bio-engineered radiation-resistant organisms, partnered with Elysium's scientists, who possessed advanced nanotechnology capable of precise atmospheric adjustments.

Together, they developed a phased approach. First, using Elysium's nanobots, they created a series of localized atmospheric shields to protect key areas from harmful radiation. These shields were not perfect, but they provided a crucial buffer zone that allowed Eden Prime's bio-engineered extremophile fungi to take root. These fungi, designed to absorb UV radiation and release oxygen, were deployed within the shielded areas, gradually beginning to thicken the atmosphere and reduce radiation levels.

The collaboration extended beyond the immediate project. Elysium's nanotechnology proved invaluable in developing advanced monitoring systems for tracking atmospheric changes and identifying areas requiring further intervention. Eden Prime's expertise in symbiotic relationships within ecosystems helped optimize the fungi's growth, enhancing their effectiveness. This synergy led to a rapid acceleration in the restoration process, bringing hope to a settlement previously facing a bleak future. The success of this joint venture demonstrated the power of combining different technological approaches and theoretical perspectives to tackle complex environmental challenges.

Another inspiring collaboration involved the settlement of Nova, a community established on a planet riddled with toxic waste left behind by a previous, unsustainable civilization. Nova's scientists had already developed some bio-remediation techniques, but their progress was slow and inefficient.

Eden Prime, along with Aethel, with their mastery of resource extraction and refinement, offered assistance. Aethel provided advanced robotic systems capable of precisely targeting and removing toxic substances from the soil, while Eden Prime contributed their knowledge of specialized bacteria and fungi engineered to break down complex pollutants. The collaboration saw Aethel's robots working in tandem with Eden Prime's bioengineered organisms, creating a sophisticated system that minimized energy consumption and maximized efficiency.

Nova, in turn, shared its knowledge of resilient plant species capable of thriving in harsh, contaminated environments, leading to the development of a rapid vegetation program. The barren, poisoned landscape began to transform, with new plant life gradually taking hold, effectively absorbing toxins and purifying the soil.

These collaborations extended beyond the purely technological. The scientists involved discovered new methods of collaborative research, which involved the regular exchange of data and expertise. This necessitated the development of sophisticated data-sharing protocols, ensuring the confidentiality and integrity of sensitive research information. Data security became paramount, particularly when dealing with experimental organisms or sensitive environmental data. Robust encryption and rigorous access control measures were put in place, safeguarding valuable data while simultaneously facilitating efficient collaborative research.

Moreover, the shared challenges and mutual successes fostered a strong sense of community among the participating scientists. Regular virtual conferences were held, allowing scientists from various settlements to share their findings, discuss obstacles, and brainstorm new solutions. These interactions fostered a culture of open communication, mutual respect, and shared responsibility for the well-being of the entire interstellar community. The collaborative spirit transcended scientific disciplines, with experts in fields such as social sciences and economics contributing to a holistic understanding of the challenges and opportunities involved in large-scale ecological restoration.

The shared database mentioned previously evolved into a crucial tool for managing and analyzing the vast quantities of data generated by these collaborative projects. It allowed scientists to track progress, identify emerging trends, and adapt their strategies accordingly. Predictive modeling software, incorporating data from various settlements, enabled researchers to anticipate potential problems and develop proactive solutions, significantly improving the efficiency and effectiveness of restoration efforts.

The focus was not solely on repairing damaged ecosystems; it also extended to preventing future environmental damage. The collaborative research led to the development of new sustainable technologies for resource extraction, energy generation, and waste management. The emphasis was on minimizing environmental impact and promoting long-term sustainability, a key element of the overarching philosophy that guided these collaborations. These were not merely technological improvements; they represented fundamental changes in how different communities approached resource utilization, ensuring that long-term ecological balance was prioritized over short-term gains.

The collective expertise led to breakthroughs in bio-remediation techniques. New species of organisms were engineered, specifically designed to tackle different types of pollution and environmental degradation. The scientists also developed methods for accelerating the natural processes of ecological succession, thereby speeding up the restoration of degraded environments. This research had implications far beyond planetary restoration, impacting the development of sustainable practices in space exploration and resource management.

The collaborative efforts yielded surprising benefits beyond ecological restoration. The knowledge exchange also spurred advancements in related fields such as medicine and materials science. For example, the development of radiation-resistant fungi led to breakthroughs in radiation therapy and cancer treatment. Similarly, the creation of new biomaterials for constructing sustainable habitats contributed to advancements in materials science and engineering. The synergies and unexpected discoveries that emerged highlighted the unforeseen potential of interdisciplinary collaborations.

Furthermore, the collaborative scientific approach fostered a deeper understanding of the interconnectedness of different ecosystems. Scientists learned that restoring a single element of an environment could have cascading effects throughout the entire system, highlighting the importance of a holistic approach to ecological restoration. This understanding promoted a more responsible and sustainable approach to resource management and technology development across the entire interstellar community.

The success of these collaborations was not just measured by the ecological restoration of various planets; it was equally measured by the development of a global scientific community, unified by a common goal and a shared sense of responsibility. The partnerships created a powerful model for future endeavors, demonstrating that even the most daunting environmental challenges could be overcome through cooperation, shared knowledge, and a commitment to a sustainable future for all.

This newly forged international scientific community became a powerful advocate for responsible space exploration and sustainable living, influencing policies and shaping the future of interstellar civilization. The collective success served as a testament to the enduring power of collaboration and the boundless potential of human ingenuity when focused on a shared vision. The universe, no longer perceived as a resource to be exploited, became a shared responsibility, a vast canvas upon which a thriving, interconnected civilization could paint its future.

The success of the inter-settlement collaborations in ecological restoration was not confined to the scientific realm. A parallel and equally important development was the blossoming of cultural exchange programs. Recognizing that technological solutions alone were insufficient to ensure long-term sustainability, Eden Prime initiated a comprehensive program to foster understanding and respect for the diverse approaches to living sustainably found across the various settlements. This was not simply an exchange of ideas; it was a deliberate effort to build bridges between cultures, sharing not only knowledge but also values, perspectives, and ways of life.

One of the most impactful initiatives was the *Symbiosis Symposium*, an annual gathering of representatives from different settlements. The symposium was not just a scientific conference; it was a cultural melting pot. Delegates from Elysium, known for their meticulous attention to detail and their mastery of nanotechnology, shared their traditional storytelling techniques, weaving narratives of resilience and adaptation in the face of environmental adversity.

These stories, often passed down through generations, served as powerful reminders of the importance of community and cooperation in overcoming challenges. Their artistic expressions, intricate sculptures made from recycled materials, and innovative music created using atmospheric soundscapes reflected the ingenuity and adaptability of their civilization.

In contrast, the representatives from Nova, a settlement forged from the ashes of a past civilization's environmental negligence, shared their unique perspective on resource management. Their emphasis on minimalism, deep understanding of cyclical processes in nature, and reverence for the planet's restorative power were striking. They shared their traditional farming practices, which combined advanced technology with ancient knowledge to create self-sufficient food systems that minimized environmental impact. Their art, stark and evocative, mirrored the harsh realities of their planet but also held a profound hope for the future. Nova's contribution extended to their innovative methods of conflict resolution, drawing upon their past mistakes to develop sophisticated and peaceful systems for resolving disputes.

The representatives from Aethel, a settlement renowned for its advanced resource extraction and refinement technologies, surprised many with their dedication to preserving biodiversity. While their technological prowess often generated awe, it was their profound respect for the natural world, commitment to sustainable resource management, and sophisticated understanding of intricate ecological systems that truly impressed.

They showcased their unique approach to architecture, creating habitats that seamlessly integrated with the surrounding environment, minimizing their ecological footprint. Their art, incorporating intricate geometric patterns inspired by the structures of natural systems, highlighted their approach to balancing technological advancement with ecological responsibility.

These cultural exchanges were not confined to formal events. Informal interactions, such as shared meals, recreational activities, and collaborative art projects, fostered a sense of camaraderie and mutual respect. Eden Prime's renowned culinary traditions, which combined advanced bio-engineered foods with traditional cooking methods, provided a culinary journey through diverse flavors, showcasing the ingenuity of their food scientists. Sharing food became a potent symbol of unity, celebrating the commonalities and differences between cultures. The collaborative art projects, combining different artistic techniques and styles, demonstrated the creative potential of cross-cultural collaboration.

The exchange was not a one-way street. Eden Prime actively shared its own cultural heritage. Their deep respect for nature, reflected in their holistic approach to ecological restoration and their profound understanding of symbiotic relationships within ecosystems, resonated deeply with the other settlements. Their history, which celebrated the power of collaboration and the enduring human spirit, inspired a sense of unity and common purpose. Their artistic expressions, characterized by vibrant colors, bold designs, and intricate details often depicting the interconnectedness of all living things, served as a source of inspiration and encouragement.

The impact of these cultural exchanges was far-reaching. It extended beyond the initial participants, spreading through the various settlements via virtual platforms, digital storytelling, and educational programs. The shared narratives, artistic expressions, and cultural values contributed to a sense of shared identity, strengthening the bonds between communities. The understanding of different cultural perspectives fostered tolerance, empathy, and respect for diversity.

The long-term impact of the cultural exchange program was undeniable. It fostered a deeper understanding of sustainable practices across the interstellar community, recognizing that solutions are not universally applicable but require adaptation to the unique characteristics of different environments and cultures. The shared experiences led to a profound shift in perspective, with the various settlements recognizing that long-term sustainability is not merely a technological or scientific challenge but a cultural imperative.

It also laid the foundation for a new era of collaboration, not just in science and technology but in all facets of life. The shared values of resilience, cooperation, and respect for diversity became cornerstones of interstellar governance, shaping policies on resource management, space exploration, and conflict resolution.

This shift in perspective had far-reaching consequences. It extended to the realm of conflict resolution, where previously conflicting interests were navigated through dialogue, understanding, and collaboration, leveraging the skills and wisdom gained through cultural exchanges. The lessons learned in inter-settlement relations significantly influenced the broader approach to interstellar diplomacy, fostering a more cooperative and peaceful interstellar community.

Moreover, the cross-cultural understanding fostered creativity and innovation. The exchange of ideas and perspectives challenged preconceived notions, breaking down barriers to creative problem-solving. This collaborative spirit led to advancements in many fields beyond ecological restoration, including medicine, agriculture, and resource management.

The cultural exchange program became more than just a set of activities. It became a living testament to the power of human connection, demonstrating that even in the vastness of space, shared values and cultural understanding can forge a sustainable and thriving interstellar civilization. It served as a reminder that the true measure of progress is not solely technological advancement but also the creation of a truly inclusive and harmonious community. The tapestry of human experience, woven from diverse threads of culture and knowledge, created a richer and more resilient future for all. The legacy of the program continues to shape the interstellar community, informing its policies and defining its future.

The interweaving of diverse cultures not only ensured ecological sustainability but also fostered a deeper sense of unity and shared purpose, a testament to the unifying power of human connection in the face of universal challenges. The universe, once viewed as an infinite source of resources, became a shared home, nurtured and protected by a community united by shared values and mutual respect.

The success of the cultural exchange programs laid the groundwork for a more profound and crucial collaboration: the sharing of resources. Eden Prime, with its advanced technology and relatively abundant resources, recognized that true sustainability could not be achieved in isolation. Their prosperity was inextricably linked to the well-being of the other settlements, a principle deeply embedded in their philosophy of symbiotic existence. This recognition fueled a massive initiative to share knowledge and resources, not as acts of charity, but as essential steps towards a shared future.

The first step involved a comprehensive assessment of the needs and capabilities of each settlement. Teams of experts from Eden Prime, working in collaboration with local representatives, conducted thorough surveys, analyzing environmental conditions, technological infrastructure, and resource availability. This involved detailed ecological mapping, analysis of soil composition, water quality assessments, and atmospheric surveys.

This meticulous approach ensured that the aid provided was targeted and effective, maximizing its impact and minimizing waste. The data gathered was meticulously compiled and analyzed, providing a clear picture of the resources each settlement possessed, the resources they lacked, and the unique challenges they faced.

This data-driven approach was crucial. It prevented the pitfalls of well-intentioned but ultimately ineffective interventions. For example, providing a settlement with advanced agricultural technology without considering their soil conditions or water resources would have been counterproductive. Instead, Eden Prime's approach involved a collaborative process, where local expertise and knowledge were integrated with advanced technology to develop tailored solutions. This ensured that the shared resources were not only utilized effectively but also empowered the receiving communities to become self-sufficient in the long term.

One of the most significant areas of resource sharing focused on advanced agricultural technology. Elysium, despite its technological prowess, faced challenges related to water scarcity. Eden Prime shared their advanced water purification and desalination technologies, along with drought-resistant crops that required minimal water consumption.

This involved not just the transfer of technology but also comprehensive training programs to ensure that the communities could effectively operate and maintain the new systems. The training incorporated both theoretical knowledge and hands-on experience, fostering a deeper understanding of the technology and its application in specific environmental contexts. The program also included long-term support and mentorship, ensuring continued success even after the initial training period.

Nova, with its deep understanding of cyclical processes in nature, received support in enhancing its self-sufficient food systems. Eden Prime provided them with advanced bio-engineered seeds specifically adapted to Nova's unique environmental conditions. These seeds exhibited enhanced resilience to pests and diseases, requiring minimal pesticide use and maximizing yield.

Moreover, Eden Prime shared its knowledge of sustainable farming techniques, such as permaculture and vertical farming, optimizing land use and minimizing environmental impact. This collaborative approach ensured that Nova's traditional practices were enhanced and not replaced, fostering a harmonious integration of ancient knowledge and advanced technology.

Aethel, known for its resource extraction expertise, received support in developing sustainable mining practices. Eden Prime shared its advanced technologies for mineral extraction and refinement, minimizing environmental damage and maximizing efficiency. This included environmentally friendly methods for waste disposal, ensuring that the planet's resources were used sustainably without compromising its ecological integrity. The partnership also involved comprehensive training on environmental monitoring and restoration techniques, empowering Aethel to manage its resources responsibly and minimize its ecological footprint.

The sharing of resources extended beyond technology and agriculture. Eden Prime generously shared its advanced medical technology, including disease prevention and treatment programs, contributing to improved healthcare across the interstellar community. They also provided advanced educational resources, including online courses and virtual libraries, to enhance educational opportunities and foster scientific and technological advancement in the other settlements. This included not only scientific disciplines but also the arts, humanities, and social sciences, recognizing that a holistic education was crucial for building resilient and sustainable communities. The curriculum was designed to be flexible and adaptable, catering to the specific needs and contexts of each community.

The sharing of resources was not simply a transaction; it was a collaborative endeavor. Eden Prime actively sought input and participation from the recipient settlements, recognizing that successful implementation required local understanding and involvement. This ensured that the shared resources were culturally appropriate and integrated effectively into the existing social and economic structures. The involvement of local communities in the decision-making process fostered ownership and responsibility, ensuring the long-term sustainability of the projects.

The collaborative nature of resource sharing fostered a strong sense of interdependence and mutual respect. The settlements, once isolated and struggling to survive, became interconnected partners, working together towards common goals. This sense of unity was reinforced through regular communication channels, collaborative projects, and joint decision-making processes. Regular virtual meetings, inter-settlement conferences, and collaborative research projects allowed for the free exchange of ideas, fostering a deep sense of partnership and mutual responsibility.

The success of the resource-sharing program was not just measured in technological advancements or economic growth; it was measured in improved quality of life, enhanced environmental sustainability, and the strengthening of community bonds. It demonstrated that true sustainability required a holistic approach, combining technological innovation with cultural understanding, environmental responsibility, and collaborative action. The interweaving of resources and knowledge fostered a deeper sense of interconnectedness, transforming the interstellar community from a collection of disparate settlements into a unified and resilient civilization.

The long-term impact of this resource sharing extended beyond the immediate beneficiaries. The collaborative approach fostered innovation and the development of new technologies and sustainable practices. The shared knowledge and expertise generated a multiplier effect, accelerating the progress of the entire interstellar community. The knowledge exchange not only improved the living standards of the settlements but also empowered them to become more self-sufficient and resilient to future challenges.

The process also established a new paradigm for interstellar cooperation. The experience of successfully sharing resources and building strong partnerships among settlements created a foundation for stronger alliances and broader collaborations. This experience would shape future interactions and lay the groundwork for addressing larger, more complex challenges, from climate change mitigation to asteroid defense.

Moreover, the resource-sharing program demonstrated the power of collaborative innovation. By sharing resources and expertise, the settlements were able to solve problems that they could not have solved alone. The combination of different perspectives, technologies, and approaches resulted in more efficient and effective solutions. This cross-pollination of ideas became a catalyst for further advancements, benefiting not only the participants in the program but also the entire interstellar community. This established a collaborative ecosystem where progress was not just the achievement of individual settlements but a collective effort with shared benefits and responsibility.

The program's success underscored a fundamental shift in perspective. The universe, once seen as an infinite source of resources for exploitation, was now viewed as a shared home, requiring collective stewardship and responsible management. The success of the resource-sharing program was a testament to the resilience and ingenuity of the interstellar community, demonstrating that through cooperation, collaboration, and a commitment to shared values, even the most daunting challenges can be overcome. The shared resources, both tangible and intangible, ultimately fostered not only ecological sustainability but also a deeper sense of unity, shared purpose, and global responsibility. The narrative of Eden Prime extended beyond a single planet, becoming a story of shared destiny and collective prosperity among the stars.

Chapter Eleven

A NEW DAWN

The success of the resource sharing initiative spurred a new wave of technological advancements on Eden Prime, advancements that were not merely focused on efficiency or profit, but on the interwoven goals of human well being and ecological restoration. This holistic approach, a hallmark of Eden Prime's philosophy, led to breakthroughs in several key areas.

One of the most significant advancements was in the field of vertical farming. Initially developed to maximize food production in limited spaces, the technology had evolved dramatically. The new generation of vertical farms were not just structures for growing food; they were self contained ecosystems, meticulously engineered to optimize resource utilization and minimize environmental impact. Sophisticated hydroponic systems powered by renewable energy provided nutrient rich water to the plants, while advanced LED lighting systems mimicked the natural sunlight spectrum, ensuring optimal photosynthesis.

These vertical farms not only produced a wider variety of crops than traditional methods, but also consumed significantly less water and land, reducing the ecological footprint of food production. The systems incorporated advanced sensors and AI driven algorithms to monitor plant health, optimize resource allocation, and predict potential problems, minimizing waste and maximizing yield. Furthermore, the farms were designed to integrate seamlessly with the existing urban landscape, often incorporated into building designs and creating green spaces within cities. This innovation was not merely about feeding a growing population; it was a demonstration of how technology could reshape our relationship with the environment, creating a harmonious coexistence between urban development and ecological sustainability.

Another crucial area of technological advancement was renewable energy. Eden Prime had long been a pioneer in solar and wind energy, but the new wave of innovation focused on energy storage and distribution. The development of advanced battery technology capable of storing vast amounts of renewable energy for extended periods solved one of the major challenges associated with intermittent sources such as solar and wind power. This meant that communities could rely on renewable energy sources even during periods of low solar irradiance or wind speeds.

The development of smart grids, utilizing sophisticated AI algorithms to optimize energy distribution and manage demand, further enhanced the efficiency and reliability of the system. These smart grids were able to predict energy demands and adjust accordingly, minimizing energy waste and ensuring a stable supply of clean energy.

This development extended beyond electricity generation. Eden Prime also invested heavily in wave energy converters, harnessing the power of the oceans for clean energy generation. The innovation in energy storage and distribution not only reduced reliance on fossil fuels, but also provided a resilient and sustainable energy infrastructure for the entire interstellar community. This technology was shared with other settlements, empowering them to achieve energy independence and reduce their carbon footprints.

The advancements in biotechnology were equally impressive. Eden Prime's scientists developed new bioremediation techniques to clean up polluted environments. These techniques involved using genetically modified microorganisms to break down pollutants in soil and water, significantly accelerating the natural remediation process. This was particularly important in addressing the legacy of past industrial activities.

Furthermore, breakthroughs in genetic engineering allowed for the creation of crops that were not only drought resistant and pest resistant but also significantly more nutritious. This technology was shared across the settlements, boosting food security and improving public health. The bioremediation techniques, coupled with advanced agricultural technologies, contributed to a larger effort in ecological restoration across the different settlements. The impact extended to repairing damaged ecosystems, restoring biodiversity, and improving overall planetary health.

Medical technology also saw significant advancements. Eden Prime developed advanced diagnostic tools capable of detecting diseases at very early stages, greatly improving the chances of successful treatment. New personalized medicine approaches, using genetic information to tailor treatment plans to individual patients, dramatically improved treatment outcomes. Significant progress was also made in regenerative medicine, with breakthroughs in tissue engineering and stem cell therapy.

This advanced medical technology was shared throughout the interstellar community, contributing to improvements in public health, reducing mortality rates, and enhancing overall quality of life. The sharing of these advancements demonstrated Eden Prime's commitment not only to its own well being, but also to the health and prosperity of the entire interstellar community.

The improvements in transportation technology were also noteworthy. Eden Prime developed advanced propulsion systems, reducing travel times and energy consumption. This included not only improvements to spacecraft, but also to ground based transportation systems. The development of high speed, sustainable transport networks ensured efficient and eco friendly movement of goods and people within the settlements, reducing reliance on private vehicles and minimizing traffic congestion. These advancements reduced the ecological footprint of transportation, leading to cleaner air and reduced greenhouse gas emissions.

All of these technological advancements were intertwined with a deep understanding of ecological principles. Every new technology was carefully assessed for its potential environmental impact, ensuring that progress did not come at the cost of planetary health. This holistic approach, combining technological innovation with environmental responsibility, was the key to Eden Prime's success.

The technology was not just about improving human life; it was about creating a sustainable future for all living beings. The development and dissemination of these technologies underscored a fundamental shift in how the settlements viewed their relationship with the environment. It was no longer about exploiting resources, but about nurturing and preserving the planet, fostering a symbiotic relationship between technology and nature.

The future was not just technologically advanced, but ecologically responsible, a harmonious blend of human ingenuity and planetary preservation. This new dawn was not only about technological progress; it was about the conscious co evolution of technology and nature, a testament to humanity's capacity for both innovation and stewardship.

The success of Eden Prime's integrated approach to development was not just about technological prowess; it was about achieving a delicate equilibrium, a harmonious dance between technological advancement and ecological preservation. This was not simply a matter of mitigating negative impacts; it was a conscious effort to weave technology into the fabric of the natural world, creating a symbiotic relationship in which both thrived.

The key was a profound shift in perspective, moving away from the exploitative model of resource extraction to one of stewardship and coexistence.

This new philosophy manifested in countless ways. Consider, for instance, the innovative approach to waste management. Eden Prime's cities were not simply disposing of waste; they were actively transforming it into valuable resources. Advanced recycling technologies, coupled with a robust composting system, ensured that virtually no waste ended up in landfills. Organic waste was processed in bioreactors, creating biogas for energy generation and nutrient rich compost for enriching the soil in vertical farms and urban green spaces.

Non organic waste was meticulously sorted and processed, with materials repurposed and reused whenever possible. This circular economy model, driven by automation and AI powered optimization, minimized waste and maximized resource efficiency. The system was not just efficient; it was elegant in its simplicity and effectiveness. It demonstrated how even the most mundane aspects of urban life could be re imagined to support ecological health.

The commitment to sustainability extended beyond waste management. The design of Eden Prime's cities reflected a deep understanding of ecological principles. Buildings were constructed using sustainable materials and incorporated passive design elements to maximize natural light and ventilation, minimizing the need for energy intensive climate control systems. Green roofs and vertical gardens were common features, providing habitats for wildlife and improving air quality.

Transportation infrastructure was carefully planned to minimize environmental impact, with pedestrian friendly designs and extensive networks of public transport, including electric buses and autonomous vehicles optimized for efficiency and low emissions. This was not just about creating aesthetically pleasing cities; it was about creating cities that were inherently ecologically sound, functioning as miniature ecosystems within the larger planetary ecosystem. The integration of green spaces, the use of permeable pavements to manage rainwater runoff, and the thoughtful placement of buildings to minimize disruption of natural water flow all contributed to a city that worked in harmony with, rather than against, nature.

Furthermore, the emphasis on sustainable development extended to the management of natural resources. Water conservation was a paramount concern. Advanced water treatment technologies, coupled with efficient irrigation systems in both vertical farms and traditional agriculture, minimized water consumption. Rainwater harvesting systems were integrated into buildings and urban infrastructure, supplementing municipal water supplies and reducing reliance on groundwater. The sustainable use of water was not simply a matter of efficiency; it was a recognition of water as a precious and finite resource that demanded responsible and careful management.

The success of Eden Prime's sustainable development was not just a matter of technological innovation; it was also the result of conscious social and cultural changes. A strong sense of community, coupled with a deep understanding of the interconnectedness of all living things, underpinned the commitment to ecological preservation. Education played a crucial role in fostering this understanding, with schools integrating ecological principles into their curricula and encouraging environmental stewardship from a young age. This collective understanding encouraged responsible behavior, leading to changes in consumption patterns, a reduction in waste, and an increased appreciation for the natural world.

The careful monitoring of ecosystems was vital to maintaining balance. Sophisticated sensor networks monitored various environmental parameters, providing real time data on air and water quality, biodiversity, and other key indicators of ecosystem health. This data informed decision making processes, allowing for prompt responses to environmental challenges and adjustments to development plans as needed. Continuous monitoring ensured that the delicate balance was not disrupted by unforeseen events or unintended consequences of technological advancements. The system demonstrated a proactive and adaptive approach to environmental management, highlighting the importance of continuous observation and adjustment in achieving sustainable development.

One of the most remarkable aspects of Eden Prime's success was its capacity for self correction and adaptation. The system was not static; it was dynamic, constantly evolving and adapting to new challenges and opportunities. This adaptability was built into its design, with feedback loops that allowed for continuous improvement and adjustments based on real time data and long term trends. This meant that the system was resilient and capable of responding effectively to unexpected events, whether natural or human caused. The capacity for self regulation and adaptation was crucial to maintaining the delicate balance between technological advancement and ecological preservation.

The spread of Eden Prime's sustainable development model to other settlements was not a simple transfer of technology; it was a transfer of knowledge, values, and a new paradigm of human environment interaction. It involved collaborative efforts, training programs, and the sharing of best practices. This collaborative approach ensured that the model was not just replicated but adapted to suit the specific contexts and needs of each settlement. It was not about exporting a ready made solution; it was about empowering communities to build their own sustainable futures.

The success of Eden Prime serves as a powerful example of how technological advancement and ecological preservation can coexist and even reinforce each other. It demonstrates the potential for human ingenuity to create a future in which both humanity and the planet thrive. This was not a utopian fantasy; it was a real world demonstration of the power of collaboration, innovation, and a fundamental shift in human values.

The Eden Prime model underscores a pivotal truth: a sustainable future is not just possible, it is achievable through a conscious and collaborative effort to integrate technological advancement with ecological responsibility. The future is not a choice between progress and preservation; it is a synthesis of the two, a harmonious blend that ensures the flourishing of both humanity and the planet.

This is not merely a technological achievement; it is a testament to the enduring power of human ingenuity when guided by wisdom and a deep respect for the natural world. The path to a sustainable future is not a straight line, but a continuous process of learning, adaptation, and a relentless pursuit of harmony between humanity and the planet. Eden Prime's story is not just a narrative of success; it is a roadmap for a future in which technological innovation and ecological responsibility work together to create a truly sustainable existence for all.

The success of Eden Prime's model did not remain confined to its borders. The principles of symbiotic coexistence, circular economies, and adaptive sustainability began to ripple outward, transcending geographical boundaries and political divisions. This was not merely the dissemination of technology; it was the sharing of a philosophy, a way of seeing the world and humanity's place within it. The initial hesitancy of other nations, clinging to outdated models of resource extraction and unchecked industrial growth, gradually gave way to a dawning realization. Eden Prime's prosperity was not an anomaly; it was a blueprint.

The Global Sustainability Initiative, born from the failures of countless international environmental accords, finally found fertile ground. This time, the focus was not on imposing restrictions or assigning blame. Instead, the initiative acted as a facilitator, a hub for knowledge exchange and collaborative problem solving. It was not a top down organization dictating policies, but a bottom up network empowering local communities to adapt Eden Prime's model to their unique circumstances. The initiative provided technological assistance, training programs, and access to a vast database of best practices. Experts from Eden Prime, alongside specialists from across the globe, worked tirelessly to customize solutions, ensuring that the principles of sustainability were translated into practical realities rather than theoretical aspirations.

One of the most striking examples of this collaborative approach was the transformation of the Amazon rainforest. For decades, the Amazon had faced the dual threats of deforestation and unsustainable agricultural practices. Working in close collaboration with indigenous communities and local governments, the initiative implemented a multifaceted strategy.

Advanced drone technology, initially developed for monitoring ecosystem health in Eden Prime, was deployed to detect illegal logging and forest fires in real time. This allowed for swift intervention, significantly reducing deforestation rates. Furthermore, the initiative facilitated the development of sustainable agricultural techniques, encouraging a shift from monoculture farming to agroforestry, a system that mimics the natural diversity of the rainforest while providing economic opportunities for local communities. This approach not only protected the forest but also improved local livelihoods, demonstrating a powerful synergy between environmental protection and economic development.

Similar collaborative efforts were undertaken in other ecologically sensitive regions across the globe. In the Arctic, where climate change rapidly altered the landscape, the initiative worked with local communities to develop climate resilient infrastructure and sustainable resource management strategies. In the Sahel region of Africa, where desertification posed a major threat, the initiative implemented innovative water harvesting techniques and drought resistant agricultural practices. These initiatives were not merely about mitigating damage; they were about building resilience and empowering communities to adapt to changing environmental conditions and create sustainable futures for themselves.

A crucial component of this global collaboration was the free and open sharing of knowledge and technology. The intellectual property rights associated with many of the technologies developed in Eden Prime were waived, enabling widespread adoption and adaptation. This was a deliberate decision, recognizing that the global environmental crisis required a collaborative rather than competitive response. The initiative established a global network of research and development centers, fostering innovation and ensuring that technological advancements were accessible to all.

This open source approach fostered a vibrant global community of innovators who constantly refined and improved existing technologies. New ideas emerged, adapting Eden Prime's strategies to address unique regional challenges. For example, coastal communities developed innovative methods for managing rising sea levels, combining traditional knowledge with cutting edge technologies. Mountainous regions created customized renewable energy systems to harness the power of water and wind. This global network of innovation transformed sustainability from a niche pursuit into a mainstream endeavor, demonstrating the power of collaborative problem solving.

The GSI also played a crucial role in promoting environmental education and awareness. Educational resources, developed in collaboration with leading institutions worldwide, were made freely available to help people understand the importance of environmental stewardship and sustainable living. These resources were not limited to formal educational settings. They were tailored for diverse audiences, including children, adults, and community leaders, and were delivered through a variety of mediums to reach the widest possible audience. The focus was on fostering a shared understanding of the interconnectedness of all living things and building a sense of global responsibility for the environment.

The success of this global collaboration was not simply about technological innovation or policy changes; it was fundamentally about a shift in human consciousness. It involved recognizing the inherent value of the natural world, not only for its economic utility but for its intrinsic worth. This shift was reflected in changing consumption patterns, a reduced reliance on fossil fuels, and a growing appreciation for biodiversity. It was not a top down imposition of values but a bottom up evolution of awareness, driven by a shared understanding of the need for collective action.

The collaborative spirit extended beyond environmental protection. The GSI facilitated knowledge sharing in other areas of global development, recognizing the interconnectedness of social, economic, and environmental challenges. Sustainable agriculture, affordable healthcare, and access to clean water and sanitation were all treated as integral components of a holistic approach to global development. This interconnected perspective challenged traditional siloed approaches and encouraged a more integrated strategy for global progress.

Moreover, the GSI's success was deeply intertwined with a renewed focus on international diplomacy and cooperation. The organization acted as a neutral platform that fostered dialogue and collaboration among nations, even those with historically strained relationships. This collaborative spirit extended beyond governments to include non governmental organizations, private sector companies, and individual citizens, creating a powerful global movement for sustainable development.

However, the path to a truly sustainable future was not without challenges. Geopolitical tensions, economic inequalities, and cultural differences continued to create obstacles to global collaboration. Yet the GSI's success in fostering dialogue and cooperation proved that these challenges could be overcome through persistent effort and a shared commitment to a common goal. The organization adapted its strategies to address these obstacles, employing innovative solutions to bridge divides and promote a more inclusive and equitable approach to global sustainability. This adaptability proved to be a crucial factor in its enduring success.

The story of the GSI was not simply about technological advancements; it was a testament to the human capacity for collaboration, resilience, and the transformative power of a shared vision. It demonstrated that even the most daunting global challenges could be addressed through concerted effort, a commitment to sustainability, and an unwavering belief in the possibility of a better future for all.

The journey toward a truly sustainable planet was ongoing, a continuous process of learning, adapting, and collaborating. But the success of the GSI offered a beacon of hope, a tangible proof that harmonious coexistence between humanity and nature was not just an aspiration but an evolving reality. The future, once a source of anxiety and uncertainty, now held the promise of a shared, sustainable, and prosperous world forged through global collaboration and a profound respect for the planet.

The shift toward sustainable practices was not a sudden revolution but a gradual evolution, a steady transformation of global consciousness. It began with individual choices, such as the decision to reduce, reuse, and recycle; the commitment to plant based diets; and the adoption of energy efficient technologies in homes and businesses. These individual actions, seemingly insignificant on their own, coalesced into a powerful collective force that reshaped consumer demand and influenced corporate behavior.

Corporations, once primary drivers of unsustainable practices, began to adapt as they recognized growing consumer preference for environmentally responsible products and services. Green initiatives, initially viewed as public relations strategies, became central to business models. Companies invested heavily in research and development of sustainable technologies, motivated by both ethical considerations and market demand. The development of biodegradable plastics, renewable energy sources, and sustainable supply chains became a race to the top, with companies striving for recognition as leaders in environmental stewardship.

This transformation was not limited to the private sector. Governments worldwide implemented policies that incentivized sustainable practices and discouraged unsustainable ones. Carbon taxes, subsidies for renewable energy, and stricter pollution regulations became increasingly common. These policies, though sometimes met with resistance, ultimately proved effective in accelerating the adoption of sustainable technologies and practices. The economic benefits of a green economy, including new job creation, reduced healthcare costs from cleaner air and water, and increased agricultural yields, outweighed the perceived costs of transition for many nations.

The educational system played a crucial role in this shift. Environmental literacy became a key component of curricula from primary school through university. Children learned about biodiversity, circular economies, and the impact of individual actions on the planet. This fostered environmental awareness from an early age and cultivated a generation of environmentally conscious citizens. Adult education programs focused on practical skills for sustainable living, empowering individuals to make informed choices about consumption and lifestyle.

The media also played a significant role, shifting its emphasis from sensationalizing environmental disasters to highlighting solutions and celebrating positive change. Documentaries showcasing the beauty and resilience of nature, along with success stories of sustainable communities, became immensely popular. News outlets reported on progress within the green economy, inspiring hope and encouraging collective action. The narrative shifted from one of impending catastrophe to one of possibility and empowerment.

The global adoption of sustainable practices was not without difficulties. Developing countries, often disproportionately affected by environmental degradation, required substantial financial and technological support to transition to sustainable models. The GSI played a critical role in bridging this gap, providing assistance and working closely with local communities to ensure that sustainable development projects were culturally appropriate and responsive to regional needs. This ensured that sustainability was not imposed from the outside but emerged organically from within each community.

One particularly successful initiative was the global campaign to restore degraded ecosystems. Through collaborative efforts among scientists, governments, and local communities, large scale reforestation projects were undertaken to restore forests lost to deforestation. Marine protected areas were expanded, helping to revive declining fish populations and protect endangered marine species. These initiatives not only reversed environmental damage but also created economic opportunities through ecotourism and sustainable resource management.

The transition to a sustainable world also required a significant shift in global trade practices. Fair trade principles became increasingly widespread, ensuring that producers in developing countries received fair compensation and were not exploited. Corporations adopted sustainable supply chains that emphasized transparency, traceability, and the elimination of harmful chemicals and unsustainable materials. The development of circular economies, in which waste is minimized and resources are continually reused, reduced the environmental impact of global trade and promoted greater resource efficiency.

Technology played a pivotal role in facilitating this transformation. Advanced monitoring systems allowed for real-time tracking of pollution levels, deforestation rates, and other environmental indicators. This information was then used to inform policy decisions and targeted interventions. Precision agriculture technologies helped farmers optimize water and fertilizer use, reducing their environmental impact while increasing yields. Renewable energy technologies became increasingly affordable and efficient, driving a shift away from fossil fuels.

The global community's commitment to sustainability extended beyond environmental protection to encompass social justice and economic equity. Recognizing the interconnectedness of environmental, social, and economic issues, the GSI integrated its efforts into a broader framework of sustainable development. This holistic approach addressed issues such as poverty, inequality, and lack of access to basic necessities, acknowledging that environmental sustainability could not be achieved without addressing these underlying social and economic challenges. This integrated approach fostered a more equitable and inclusive global community, ensuring that the benefits of sustainability were shared by all.

The success of the global transition to sustainable practices was ultimately a testament to the power of collective action. It demonstrated that even the most daunting global challenges could be overcome through collaboration, innovation, and a shared commitment to a sustainable future. While the journey was far from over, the progress made in the years following the establishment of the GSI offered a beacon of hope, a tangible proof that a harmonious coexistence between humanity and nature was not merely a distant dream, but a steadily evolving reality. The future, once painted with shades of dystopian uncertainty, now shimmered with the potential of a shared, sustainable, and prosperous world for all.

The Earth, once threatened, was slowly healing, a testament to humanity's capacity for collective action and transformative change. The journey continued, a constant process of learning, adapting, and collaborating, but the vision was clear: a planet thriving in harmony with its inhabitants, a testament to the enduring power of a shared, sustainable dream.

The air, once thick with the anxieties of impending ecological collapse, now carried a whisper of something different: hope. Not the naive, blind optimism of the past, but a hope tempered by experience, born from the tangible results of global cooperation. The shift was not instantaneous; the scars of past negligence remained etched upon the landscape, a constant reminder of the precariousness of the Earth's systems. Yet a palpable sense of progress permeated the atmosphere, a collective exhale after years of holding one's breath.

The revitalization of degraded ecosystems became a powerful symbol of this renewed hope. Reforestation projects, once seen as ambitious pipe dreams, yielded breathtaking results. Vast swathes of land, once barren and desolate, now teemed with life. The return of migratory birds, the rustling of leaves in newly planted forests, the joyous chirping of insects: these were not mere ecological metrics; they were affirmations of humanity's capacity for restoration.

Aerial photographs, presented at the annual GSI summit, showcased vibrant green patches spreading across continents, a living testament to the power of collaborative action. These images were not just data points; they were stories of resilience, woven from the threads of countless individual and collective efforts. Local communities, once marginalized and often bearing the brunt of environmental damage, were at the forefront of these efforts.

Their intimate knowledge of their land, coupled with the technological advancements provided by the GSI, resulted in innovative and culturally sensitive restoration methods. Indigenous knowledge, often overlooked in the past, was now recognized as a vital asset in the quest for sustainability. The elders, the keepers of traditional ecological practices, became invaluable partners, sharing their wisdom and expertise with scientists and policymakers.

The success of the ecosystem restoration projects was not limited to terrestrial environments. Marine ecosystems also showed signs of recovery. The establishment of marine protected areas, coupled with stricter regulations on fishing practices, led to a significant rebound in fish populations.

Coral reefs, once bleached and lifeless, began to regain their vibrancy, their colorful inhabitants returning to their once-deserted homes. The oceans, once viewed as limitless waste disposal sites, were slowly transforming into vibrant ecosystems once more. This recovery was not just an ecological success; it also had significant economic implications. Sustainable fisheries, eco-tourism, and the cultivation of marine resources provided livelihoods for coastal communities, creating a positive feedback loop that reinforced the commitment to conservation.

The transition to renewable energy sources continued to accelerate, driven by technological advancements and economic incentives. Solar and wind farms, once sparsely scattered across the landscape, now formed sprawling networks, powering cities and industries with clean energy.

The price of renewable energy technologies continued to fall, making them increasingly accessible to developing countries. This shift not only reduced greenhouse gas emissions but also created numerous new jobs in the renewable energy sector, contributing to economic growth and reducing energy poverty in many parts of the world. The development of smart grids, capable of integrating diverse energy sources and optimizing energy distribution, further enhanced the efficiency and reliability of renewable energy systems. The reliance on fossil fuels, once the backbone of the global economy, was gradually diminishing, replaced by a more sustainable and decentralized energy system.

The adoption of circular economy principles also played a pivotal role in the global transition to sustainability. Waste, once a problem to be disposed of, was now viewed as a resource to be recovered and reused. Innovative recycling technologies capable of processing complex waste streams emerged, transforming discarded materials into valuable resources. The design of products shifted from a linear model of take, make, and dispose to a circular one, prioritizing durability, repairability, and recyclability. This transition not only reduced waste but also created new economic opportunities in the recycling and remanufacturing industries.

The GSI, far from resting on its successes, continued to evolve, adapting to the ever-changing landscape of global challenges. The organization's focus shifted from crisis management to proactive planning, anticipating and mitigating future risks. The development of sophisticated climate models allowed for more accurate predictions of future climate scenarios, informing policy decisions and investments in climate adaptation measures. The GSI also played a vital role in promoting international cooperation on climate change, facilitating technology transfer and capacity building in developing countries.

The renewed hope was not confined solely to environmental restoration and technological advancements. It also manifested in a fundamental shift in human consciousness. A growing awareness of the interconnectedness of environmental, social, and economic issues spurred a wave of social activism.

The movement for social justice became inseparable from the movement for environmental sustainability, recognizing that environmental degradation often disproportionately affects vulnerable communities. The focus shifted from individual actions to systemic change, advocating for policies that promote equity and justice. This holistic approach recognized that environmental sustainability could not be achieved without addressing the root causes of poverty, inequality, and social injustice.

The arts also played a crucial role in this transformation. Artists, musicians, and writers used their creative talents to raise awareness about environmental issues, to inspire action, and to celebrate the beauty and resilience of nature. The narrative shifted from one of impending doom to one of hope and possibility, empowering individuals to take ownership of their actions and their impact on the planet. The stories of environmental heroes, the triumphs of community-based conservation initiatives, and the inspiring accounts of resilience became dominant themes in popular culture, shaping perceptions and inspiring action.

The progress made was undeniable, yet the journey toward a truly sustainable future remained long and complex. New challenges continued to emerge, demanding constant adaptation and innovation. But the sense of renewed hope, forged in the crucible of collective action, provided the necessary impetus to continue the fight, to overcome the obstacles, and to create a world where humanity and nature could thrive together in harmony.

The future was still being written, but the story now unfolded with a sense of optimism and purpose, guided by a shared vision of a sustainable and equitable planet for all. The Earth, scarred but healing, stood as a potent symbol of human potential, demonstrating that even in the face of seemingly insurmountable challenges, hope could bloom and a brighter dawn could break.

The path ahead remained challenging, demanding constant vigilance and innovative solutions, but the collective effort, the shared vision, and the palpable sense of renewed hope promised a future where humanity and nature coexisted not only in survival, but in a true and flourishing partnership.

CHAPTER TWELVE
THE LONG VIEW

The palpable sense of renewed hope, however, was not simply a matter of celebrating past successes. It demanded a profound shift in perspective, a move away from short-term gains toward a long-term vision of sustainability that encompassed not only environmental health, but also social equity and economic justice. This meant tackling the complex interplay of factors that had contributed to past environmental crises and developing strategies robust enough to withstand future shocks and stresses.

The Global Sustainability Initiative (GSI), now a truly global entity, recognized that its role had evolved. It was no longer sufficient to respond to immediate crises. Proactive planning and the anticipation of future challenges became paramount. This involved a massive investment in predictive modeling and scenario planning. Sophisticated climate models, integrating data from across the globe, were used to explore a wide range of potential futures, from optimistic scenarios of rapid decarbonization and ecosystem restoration to more pessimistic scenarios of continued environmental degradation and social unrest.

This foresight was not simply an academic exercise; it was crucial for informing policy decisions and investment strategies. Understanding potential risks allowed governments and businesses to make informed choices about infrastructure development, resource management, and disaster preparedness. For example, coastal communities, acutely aware of the risks associated with sea-level rise, were investing in resilient infrastructure and developing adaptation strategies informed by the GSI's projections. Similarly, agricultural practices were shifting toward drought-resistant crops and water-efficient irrigation techniques, mitigating the risks of future droughts and food shortages.

But anticipation was not enough. Ensuring long-term sustainability also demanded a fundamental rethinking of economic systems. The linear "take-make-dispose" model, which had driven much of the environmental damage of the past, was finally being replaced by a circular economy. This meant designing products for durability, repairability, and recyclability, minimizing waste and maximizing resource efficiency. Innovation played a pivotal role, with new technologies emerging to efficiently recycle complex waste streams and transform discarded materials into valuable resources. This transition was not merely environmentally beneficial; it created new economic opportunities, fostering the growth of industries focused on recycling, remanufacturing, and resource recovery.

The shift toward a circular economy also demanded a change in consumer behavior. A growing awareness of the environmental and social impacts of consumption drove a movement toward mindful purchasing, with consumers increasingly prioritizing products that were sustainably sourced, ethically produced, and designed for longevity. This shift was facilitated by transparent labeling schemes that provided consumers with clear information about the environmental footprint of products, allowing them to make informed choices. Businesses, recognizing the growing demand for sustainable products, responded by investing in sustainable practices and designing products that met the evolving needs of a more environmentally conscious consumer base.

Education played a crucial role in achieving long-term sustainability. Curricula were revised to incorporate environmental literacy and sustainability principles at all levels, from primary school to higher education. Children were taught about the interconnectedness of ecosystems, the importance of biodiversity, and the consequences of unsustainable practices. This investment in education ensured that future generations would have the knowledge and skills necessary to make informed choices and contribute to a sustainable future. Moreover, the education system emphasized critical thinking and problem-solving skills, empowering individuals to address the complex challenges of sustainability in creative and innovative ways.

Beyond formal education, public awareness campaigns played a crucial role in shaping attitudes and behavior. These campaigns, often using innovative and engaging communication strategies, fostered a greater understanding of environmental issues and the importance of individual actions. The use of storytelling, interactive media, and citizen science initiatives proved especially effective in motivating individuals to participate in sustainable practices and advocate for systemic change.

Equitable access to resources and opportunities was recognized as a critical component of long-term sustainability. The GSI played a vital role in facilitating technology transfer and capacity building in developing countries, ensuring that the benefits of sustainable development were shared globally. This involved providing access to clean energy technologies, promoting sustainable agricultural practices, and supporting the development of resilient infrastructure. Recognizing that environmental degradation disproportionately affects vulnerable communities, the GSI also prioritized projects that promoted social justice and empowered marginalized groups to participate in decision-making processes that affected their lives.

Financial mechanisms also underwent a significant transformation. Sustainable finance gained prominence, with investors increasingly prioritizing environmentally and socially responsible investments. Green bonds, impact investing, and other innovative financial instruments emerged, channeling investment toward sustainable projects and encouraging the transition to a low-carbon economy. This shift was crucial in mobilizing the capital necessary to fund large-scale sustainability initiatives, from renewable energy projects to ecosystem restoration efforts.

International cooperation remained essential, and the GSI continued to facilitate dialogue and collaboration among nations. Recognizing that environmental challenges transcend national boundaries, the GSI fostered the development of global agreements and frameworks that promoted shared responsibility and collective action. This involved strengthening international institutions, enhancing data-sharing mechanisms, and promoting the harmonization of environmental regulations. The emphasis shifted from unilateral action to collaborative efforts, recognizing that only through collective action could the global community achieve long-term sustainability.

The long view was not simply a matter of planning for the future; it was about fostering a culture of responsibility, resilience, and collective action. It demanded a fundamental shift in values, away from a materialist, consumption-driven mindset toward a more holistic perspective that valued the interconnectedness of all living things and the importance of preserving the planet's resources for future generations. This transformation was not merely a matter of technological innovation; it was a profound social and cultural shift, involving changes in attitudes, beliefs, and behaviors. The arts and humanities played a vital role in this transformation, using storytelling, music, and visual arts to convey the urgency of the situation and inspire hope and action.

The journey toward a truly sustainable future remains long and complex, and new challenges will undoubtedly emerge. But the progress made in recent years, fueled by a renewed sense of hope and collective purpose, offers reason for optimism. The long view, grounded in scientific understanding, social equity, and a commitment to collaboration, provides the framework for navigating the challenges ahead and creating a world where humanity and nature can thrive together in harmony. The path ahead requires constant vigilance, adaptation, and innovation, but the collective effort, guided by a shared vision of a sustainable future, promises a world where the Earth not only survives, but truly flourishes for generations to come.

The seeds of change have been sown. Nurturing their growth requires sustained commitment, ongoing innovation, and unwavering belief in the power of collective action to shape a brighter future. The long view necessitates a long-term commitment, a marathon rather than a sprint, to ensure the planet's sustainability and the well-being of its inhabitants.

The shift toward a truly sustainable future demanded more than policy changes and economic restructuring. It required a fundamental transformation in our capacity to understand and respond to the planet's complex systems. This necessitated the development of advanced environmental monitoring systems capable of tracking subtle changes across vast geographical scales and providing real-time data for informed decision-making. These systems represented a quantum leap beyond the rudimentary monitoring of the past, leveraging cutting-edge technologies and unprecedented levels of global collaboration.

One of the most significant advancements was the integration of satellite technology into environmental monitoring. High-resolution satellites, equipped with an array of sensors, provided a comprehensive view of the planet's surface, capturing data on deforestation rates, glacier melt, sea-level rise, and changes in land-use patterns. These data, combined with information gathered from airborne sensors and ground-based monitoring stations, provided a detailed picture of ecological changes occurring across the globe. No longer were scientists reliant on isolated data points or fragmented observations. They had access to a continuous stream of information, allowing them to track environmental trends with unprecedented accuracy and precision.

The sheer volume of data generated by these monitoring systems presented a significant challenge. Traditional data analysis techniques were simply inadequate for processing and interpreting this massive influx of information. This led to the development of sophisticated algorithms and artificial intelligence-powered analytical tools capable of identifying patterns, anomalies, and trends in complex datasets. Machine learning models were trained on vast quantities of historical data, enabling them to predict future environmental changes with a degree of accuracy previously unimaginable. These predictive models played a crucial role in informing policy decisions, guiding resource allocation, and enabling proactive interventions to mitigate environmental risks.

The integration of sensor networks across diverse ecosystems further enhanced the sophistication of environmental monitoring. These networks, comprising a multitude of interconnected sensors deployed across forests, oceans, and urban areas, provided real-time data on a range of environmental parameters, including air and water quality, soil moisture, temperature, and biodiversity. The data collected by these sensors were transmitted wirelessly to central databases, allowing scientists to monitor environmental conditions continuously and respond rapidly to any significant changes. For example, early warning systems were developed to detect the onset of wildfires or algal blooms, enabling prompt intervention and minimizing environmental damage.

The development of advanced environmental monitoring systems also necessitated a revolution in data sharing and collaboration. The Global Sustainability Initiative (GSI) played a pivotal role in establishing international standards for data collection, storage, and analysis. This involved developing common protocols for data exchange and creating secure platforms for sharing data across national borders. The free and open exchange of environmental data proved essential for fostering international collaboration and facilitating rapid responses to global environmental challenges. Scientists and policymakers around the world could access the same data, share insights, and collaborate on solutions to common problems.

Beyond the technological advancements, the success of these monitoring systems hinged on the development of robust data management and interpretation frameworks. This involved establishing clear data quality standards to ensure accuracy and reliability. Sophisticated data visualization tools were also developed, allowing scientists and policymakers to interpret complex datasets easily and make informed decisions. Interactive dashboards, geographical information systems, and virtual reality technologies were used to present environmental data in an accessible and engaging manner, facilitating communication and collaboration among stakeholders. The ability to present complex scientific findings in an understandable way was critical in informing public discourse and driving policy changes.

The applications of these advanced environmental monitoring systems extended far beyond simply tracking environmental changes. They played a crucial role in assessing the effectiveness of conservation efforts, monitoring the impact of pollution control measures, and evaluating the success of climate change mitigation and adaptation strategies. By providing objective and quantifiable data, these systems offered a means of assessing progress, identifying areas for improvement, and ensuring accountability. This data-driven approach to environmental management proved essential for fostering transparency and trust among stakeholders, ensuring that conservation and sustainability initiatives were both effective and accountable.

The accuracy and reliability of environmental monitoring systems depend not only on technological advancements, but also on the integration of traditional ecological knowledge and local expertise. In many parts of the world, Indigenous communities have accumulated centuries of knowledge about their local environments. Integrating this knowledge with advanced monitoring technologies provided a more holistic and nuanced understanding of ecological processes and changes. This collaborative approach ensured that environmental management strategies were culturally sensitive and aligned with the needs and priorities of local communities. It also helped bridge the gap between scientific data and community understanding, fostering greater engagement and participation in conservation efforts.

The economic implications of improved environmental monitoring are profound. Accurate and timely data on environmental conditions provide crucial information for investment decisions, risk assessment, and infrastructure planning. For example, data on climate change impacts, such as sea-level rise or increased frequency of extreme weather events, enable better planning for infrastructure development, minimizing risks and maximizing the longevity of investments. Similarly, real-time data on water quality and resource availability can inform agricultural practices and water management strategies, improving agricultural productivity and ensuring food security. The economic value of environmental monitoring is increasingly recognized, leading to greater investments in these technologies and systems.

Looking toward the future, the development of environmental monitoring systems will continue to be driven by technological innovation and scientific advancements. Advances in artificial intelligence, sensor technology, and data analytics will enable even more sophisticated and comprehensive monitoring of environmental change. The integration of drones, autonomous underwater vehicles, and other remotely operated platforms will provide access to previously inaccessible areas, expanding the reach and scope of environmental monitoring. Moreover, advancements in genetic sequencing and biodiversity analysis will provide a deeper understanding of ecosystem function and resilience.

However, the successful deployment of these advanced technologies relies on sustained investment in research and development, international collaboration, and effective data management practices. Ensuring that data are readily accessible to policymakers, researchers, and the public is crucial. Promoting open access to environmental data can facilitate scientific discovery, foster innovation, and enhance transparency and accountability. Addressing issues related to data security and privacy is also essential. Striking a balance between the need for open data and the protection of sensitive information is paramount.

Ultimately, the development and deployment of advanced environmental monitoring systems represent a critical step toward achieving a truly sustainable future. These systems provide the tools and information necessary for managing the planet's complex ecological systems, enabling proactive interventions to mitigate environmental risks, assess the effectiveness of conservation strategies, and build resilience to future challenges. The long-term success of these systems will depend on continuous innovation, international collaboration, and a collective commitment to sustainable practices. Monitoring is only the first step; the true value lies in using that data to inform, educate, and motivate us to act. The path to a sustainable future requires not only technological advancement, but also a fundamental shift in how we value and interact with the planet.

Predictive modeling, fueled by the unprecedented influx of data from advanced monitoring systems, has ushered in a new era of proactive environmental management. No longer are we reacting to environmental disasters; we are increasingly anticipating them. This shift from reactive to proactive management is a testament to the power of harnessing vast datasets and deploying sophisticated algorithms to forecast potential crises. These models do not simply predict; they offer a roadmap for preventative measures, allowing us to allocate resources efficiently and implement strategies to mitigate looming threats.

One of the most significant applications of predictive modeling lies in forecasting extreme weather events. By analyzing historical weather patterns, climate models, and real-time data from satellite imagery and ground-based sensors, scientists can now predict the likelihood, intensity, and location of hurricanes, droughts, floods, and heatwaves with increasing accuracy. This allows for timely evacuations, the pre-positioning of emergency supplies, and the implementation of early warning systems, minimizing the loss of life and property. Furthermore, these predictions are crucial for infrastructure planning, enabling the development of resilient infrastructure capable of withstanding the impacts of extreme weather. For example, coastal communities can use predictive models of sea-level rise to plan for coastal defenses, ensuring the long-term viability of their settlements. Similarly, agricultural communities can utilize drought predictions to implement water conservation measures and adjust planting schedules, ensuring food security.

Beyond extreme weather events, predictive modeling plays a crucial role in anticipating the spread of invasive species. By tracking the movement of invasive species and analyzing their ecological interactions with native flora and fauna, scientists can forecast potential outbreaks and implement proactive control measures. This includes targeted eradication efforts, habitat restoration, and the development of early warning systems to detect new invasions. Predictive models are also instrumental in managing the spread of diseases affecting both wildlife and humans. By analyzing disease transmission patterns and the environmental factors that influence disease spread, scientists can forecast potential outbreaks and develop strategies for prevention and control. This includes vaccination campaigns, targeted public health interventions, and the implementation of biosecurity measures.

The accurate prediction of deforestation rates is another critical application of predictive modeling. By analyzing satellite imagery, land use patterns, and socioeconomic factors, scientists can forecast deforestation hotspots and develop strategies for forest conservation. This includes implementing stricter regulations on logging, promoting sustainable forestry practices, and supporting reforestation efforts. Predictive modeling also enables the targeted allocation of resources to areas at highest risk of deforestation, ensuring that conservation efforts are effective and efficient. This capability is vital in mitigating the effects of deforestation on biodiversity, climate change, and human well-being.

Predictive models are not limited to large-scale environmental challenges. They also play a vital role in addressing local environmental issues. For instance, models can be used to forecast water quality changes in rivers and lakes, enabling the implementation of pollution control measures and the protection of aquatic ecosystems. Similarly, predictive models can be used to forecast air quality changes in urban areas, allowing for the implementation of air pollution control measures and the protection of public health. These models allow for the proactive identification of pollution sources and the implementation of targeted interventions that minimize environmental damage and improve public health.

However, the accuracy and reliability of predictive models depend on several factors. First, the quality and quantity of data are critical. The more comprehensive the data, the more accurate the predictions. Second, the sophistication of the algorithms used in the models is essential. Advances in artificial intelligence and machine learning are constantly improving the predictive capabilities of environmental models. Third, the ability to integrate data from diverse sources, including satellite imagery, ground-based sensors, and traditional ecological knowledge, is crucial for developing robust and accurate predictions. The integration of diverse data sources ensures a comprehensive understanding of the complex interplay of environmental factors that influence ecological processes.

The development and application of predictive modeling are not without challenges. One significant challenge is the complexity of environmental systems. Environmental systems are inherently complex, with numerous interacting factors that influence ecological processes. Accurately modeling these complex interactions is a significant undertaking and requires sophisticated algorithms and a deep understanding of ecological principles. Another challenge is the inherent uncertainty associated with environmental predictions. Environmental systems are dynamic and subject to unpredictable events, making precise predictions difficult. Therefore, it is crucial to recognize the uncertainties associated with predictive models and to consider a range of possible outcomes when making decisions.

Despite these challenges, the potential benefits of predictive modeling are substantial. By anticipating environmental crises, we can implement preventative measures that minimize the damage caused by environmental disasters. This proactive approach is more cost-effective and efficient than reactive management, leading to better environmental outcomes and improved human well-being. Moreover, predictive modeling provides crucial information for decision-making, enabling policymakers to allocate resources effectively and implement evidence-based policies. This data-driven approach to environmental management ensures that policies are effective and contribute to sustainable development goals.

The future of predictive modeling in environmental science is bright. Continued advancements in artificial intelligence, sensor technology, and data analytics will enable even more sophisticated and accurate predictions. The integration of drones, autonomous underwater vehicles, and other remotely operated platforms will provide access to previously inaccessible areas, expanding the scope of environmental monitoring and data collection. The development of more sophisticated algorithms and machine learning techniques will improve the accuracy and reliability of predictive models, further enhancing our ability to anticipate and mitigate environmental risks. The combination of advanced technologies and sophisticated algorithms will undoubtedly lead to more accurate and timely predictions, providing critical insights to inform effective environmental management strategies.

Ultimately, the success of predictive modeling depends not only on technological advancements, but also on the effective integration of scientific knowledge, policy, and community engagement. Sharing predictive model outputs with policymakers, local communities, and stakeholders is essential, as it allows for informed decision-making and effective resource allocation. Open access to data and model outputs promotes transparency and builds trust, fostering collaborative efforts to address environmental challenges.

Furthermore, engaging local communities in the development and implementation of predictive models ensures that these models are culturally sensitive and address the specific needs of local populations.

By bridging the gap between scientific knowledge and community understanding, we can ensure that predictive modeling contributes to sustainable development that benefits both the environment and the people who depend on it. The long view necessitates a unified approach that integrates scientific rigor with community involvement and clear, accessible communication, creating a holistic vision for a sustainable future.

The effectiveness of predictive modeling in environmental management depends significantly on the scale of its application. While national initiatives are crucial, tackling truly global environmental challenges requires a coordinated international effort. The magnitude of issues such as climate change, ocean acidification, and biodiversity loss transcends national borders and demands a unified, collaborative approach. This international cooperation takes many forms, from the sharing of data and resources to the establishment of binding international agreements and the fostering of collaborative research projects.

One of the most powerful instruments for international cooperation is the sharing of data. Environmental data, much like the weather, do not recognize national boundaries. Air pollution from one country can drift into another, affecting air quality across vast distances. Similarly, ocean currents transport pollutants and plastic debris across oceans, affecting marine ecosystems globally.

The sharing of real-time data from monitoring stations, satellite imagery, and other sources enables a comprehensive understanding of these transboundary environmental issues. International platforms and databases, accessible to scientists and policymakers worldwide, are essential for facilitating this data exchange. These platforms must adhere to strict data governance protocols to ensure data integrity, accessibility, and security. Open data initiatives further enhance transparency and foster collaboration, enabling researchers across the globe to contribute to a shared body of knowledge.

However, sharing data is not enough. International cooperation also requires the standardization of monitoring protocols and data formats. Inconsistencies in data collection methods can lead to difficulties in comparing data across different countries, hindering the development of accurate predictive models. The establishment of international standards, agreed upon by participating nations, is crucial for ensuring data comparability and facilitating effective cross-border analysis. This standardization extends beyond data collection to include the methodologies used for analyzing and interpreting environmental data.

Beyond data sharing, international cooperation also extends to the development and implementation of joint research projects. Tackling complex environmental challenges often requires the expertise of scientists from diverse disciplines and geographical locations. International collaborations allow researchers to pool their knowledge, resources, and expertise, leading to more comprehensive and innovative solutions. These collaborative research projects can range from studying the impacts of climate change on specific ecosystems to developing new technologies for pollution control. Joint research initiatives often involve the establishment of international research centers or consortia, providing a platform for scientists from different countries to collaborate effectively. The funding of these projects, often through multilateral organizations or international grants, is also a critical aspect of effective international cooperation.

International agreements and treaties play a crucial role in establishing binding commitments to protect the environment. These agreements, often negotiated under the auspices of the United Nations, establish common goals, targets, and timelines for reducing pollution, protecting biodiversity, and mitigating climate change.

The Paris Agreement on climate change, for example, is a landmark achievement in international cooperation, setting targets for greenhouse gas emissions reductions and promoting global efforts to combat climate change. However, the success of these agreements depends on the commitment and cooperation of all participating nations. Regular monitoring and reporting mechanisms, as well as enforcement measures, are essential for ensuring compliance and maximizing the effectiveness of these agreements.

Effective international cooperation also involves the transfer of technology and expertise. Developed nations often possess more advanced technologies and expertise in environmental monitoring, management, and remediation. The transfer of these technologies and expertise to developing nations is crucial for building capacity and enabling them to manage their own environmental resources effectively.

This transfer can take many forms, including providing training, technical assistance, and financial support for the implementation of environmentally sound technologies. International collaborations can also involve the establishment of joint ventures or partnerships between companies in developed and developing nations to promote the adoption of sustainable technologies.

Furthermore, capacity building in developing nations is vital. Many countries lack the infrastructure, technology, and skilled personnel to monitor and manage their environmental resources effectively. International cooperation can provide assistance in developing monitoring networks, training personnel, and transferring technology to build local capacity. This includes support for education and training programs, the establishment of research institutions, and the development of local expertise in environmental management.

Beyond these formal mechanisms, the informal exchange of information and best practices among scientists, policymakers, and environmental organizations plays a significant role in fostering international cooperation. Conferences, workshops, and online forums provide opportunities for experts from different countries to share knowledge, discuss challenges, and coordinate their efforts. The exchange of information and best practices can lead to the adoption of innovative solutions and the avoidance of costly mistakes. The sharing of lessons learned from past successes and failures is particularly valuable, enabling countries to benefit from each other's experiences.

Finally, the critical element of equitable resource allocation and financial mechanisms needs to be addressed. Many developing nations face severe financial constraints that limit their ability to participate fully in international environmental initiatives. International funding mechanisms, such as the Green Climate Fund, aim to provide financial support for developing countries to implement climate change mitigation and adaptation projects. However, ensuring equitable access to these funds and transparency in their distribution is essential for promoting fairness and inclusivity in international environmental cooperation. A fair system ensures that the burden of environmental protection is shared equitably, considering the historical contributions to environmental problems and the differing capacities of nations.

The path toward a sustainable future demands a collective, international commitment. The intricate web of environmental challenges transcends borders, requiring a collaborative global effort. By strengthening international cooperation through data sharing, joint research initiatives, binding agreements, technological transfer, and capacity building, we can enhance the effectiveness of predictive modeling and proactive environmental management. The long view demands not only technological advancement but also a commitment to equitable partnerships and a shared responsibility for the health of our planet. Only through united action can we hope to mitigate looming environmental threats and safeguard a sustainable future for all.

The preceding discussion highlighted the crucial role of international cooperation in addressing global environmental challenges. However, effective action requires not only collaborative mechanisms but also a fundamental shift in our ethical framework, a new global environmental ethic. This ethic moves beyond anthropocentric views that prioritize human needs above all else and embraces a more holistic perspective that recognizes the intrinsic value of nature and the interconnectedness of all living things. This shift is not merely philosophical; it represents a necessary paradigm adjustment for sustainable decision-making at every level, from individual choices to international policies.

This emerging global environmental ethic is not a monolithic entity, but rather a complex tapestry woven from diverse philosophical strands. Some perspectives emphasize the inherent worth of all living beings, arguing for a radical extension of moral consideration beyond the human species. Biocentrism, for instance, posits that life itself, in all its forms, is central to the universe's moral order. This viewpoint challenges the human-centric worldview that has historically contributed to environmental degradation, urging recognition of the rights and intrinsic value of all organisms, not just humans. Practical implications of biocentrism include reducing human impact on ecosystems, reforming industrial agriculture, and rejecting practices that cause unnecessary suffering to non-human life.

Ecocentrism offers another significant contribution to this evolving ethical framework. Unlike biocentrism, which focuses on individual organisms, ecocentrism prioritizes the well-being of entire ecosystems. It emphasizes the interconnectedness of life and the importance of maintaining ecological balance and integrity. From this perspective, the value of a species or habitat is not determined solely by its usefulness to humans, but by its role in the overall health and stability of the ecosystem. This leads to a focus on preserving biodiversity, protecting natural habitats, and promoting sustainable practices that minimize disruption to ecological processes. Implementing ecocentric principles would require significant changes in land-use planning, resource management, and the relationship between human societies and the natural world.

Other perspectives within this new global environmental ethic emphasize intergenerational equity. This principle stresses the moral obligation to future generations to leave them a planet that is healthy and capable of supporting human life. It compels consideration of the long-term consequences of human actions, recognizing that environmental degradation today will inevitably affect those who come after us.

This translates into sustainable resource management, climate change mitigation, and the protection of natural resources for future use. Failure to adhere to this principle could have catastrophic consequences, leaving future generations to struggle with a degraded environment and diminished quality of life.

Incorporating this ethic into decision-making requires a fundamental shift in how costs and benefits are evaluated. Traditional economic models often prioritize short-term gains over long-term sustainability, failing to account for environmental and social costs associated with unsustainable practices. The new global environmental ethic challenges this approach, advocating for a holistic economic framework that integrates environmental considerations into all aspects of decision-making. This involves developing more accurate methods for valuing ecosystem services, incorporating environmental externalities into cost-benefit analyses, and promoting sustainable consumption and production patterns.

A crucial aspect of this new ethic is environmental justice. This principle recognizes that the negative impacts of environmental degradation are often disproportionately borne by marginalized and vulnerable communities, which may lack the resources and political influence needed to protect themselves from hazards such as pollution, deforestation, and climate change. Environmental justice demands that these inequalities be addressed, ensuring that all people have the right to a healthy environment regardless of race, ethnicity, socioeconomic status, or geographic location. This requires participatory decision-making, equitable distribution of environmental benefits and burdens, and redress for past environmental injustices.

The implementation of this new global environmental ethic is a multifaceted endeavor, requiring action at multiple scales. International cooperation is crucial for addressing transboundary environmental challenges, developing common standards, and promoting global sustainability. National governments have the responsibility to implement policies that reflect this ethical framework, protect citizens' rights to a healthy environment, and promote sustainable practices within their borders. Businesses also play a critical role by adopting environmentally responsible practices, reducing their environmental footprint, and promoting sustainable consumption.

Individual actions, while seemingly small, are collectively significant in shaping environmental outcomes. Conscious consumption choices, support for environmentally friendly businesses and policies, and a commitment to reduce one's ecological footprint are all important contributions. Education and awareness play a key role in fostering a deeper understanding of environmental issues and promoting the adoption of responsible behaviors.

Through education, we can cultivate a greater appreciation for the intrinsic value of nature and a stronger commitment to protecting the planet for current and future generations. Public discourse should shift from a focus on economic growth at all costs to a balance between economic development and environmental protection.

The transition toward a society guided by this new global environmental ethic is a long and complex process. It will require overcoming entrenched interests, changing deeply ingrained values, and mobilizing collective action on an unprecedented scale. However, the urgency of the environmental crisis demands that we embark on this transformative journey without delay. Failure to do so risks irreversible environmental damage, jeopardizing the well-being of present and future generations.

The long view, as discussed earlier, demands a commitment not only to technological solutions but also to a fundamental shift in our ethical understanding of the relationship between humanity and the natural world. Only by embracing this new global environmental ethic can we hope to build a truly sustainable future for all. This ethic transcends national boundaries, uniting humanity in a shared responsibility for the well-being of the planet.

It is not merely a set of abstract principles, but a practical guide for navigating the complex challenges that lie ahead. It demands a radical shift in mindset, moving from a worldview of dominance over nature to one of stewardship and respect. The journey is challenging, but the stakes are too high to ignore the call for a fundamental change in our relationship with the environment.

It is a challenge that requires both collective and individual action. It is a call for global cooperation and a fundamental shift in our values. It is, ultimately, a race against time.

Chapter Thirteen

THE GUARDIANS

The urgency of the global environmental crisis demands more than just a shift in ethical frameworks; it necessitates the creation of a robust and globally interconnected system of training programs. These programs are not merely about imparting knowledge; they are about cultivating a generation of environmental stewards, equipped with the skills and understanding to navigate the complex challenges ahead. Their effectiveness hinges on a multi-pronged approach that blends scientific rigor with practical skills, ethical considerations, and collaborative spirit.

One crucial aspect of these programs is the integration of advanced scientific understanding. Future Guardians need a deep understanding of climate science, ecology, biodiversity, and environmental toxicology. This involves rigorous training in data analysis, modeling, and the interpretation of complex environmental datasets. The programs should incorporate hands-on experience through field research, lab work, and participation in citizen science projects. This practical application of theoretical knowledge is crucial for fostering critical thinking and problem-solving skills. For example, trainees might participate in biodiversity surveys, conduct water quality analysis, or contribute to climate change modeling projects. The focus should extend beyond mere technical skills, however, and include a nuanced comprehension of the social, political, and economic dimensions influencing environmental issues.

The training must also equip participants with the communication skills needed to convey complex scientific information to diverse audiences. Effective communication is vital for engaging the public, influencing policy, and fostering collaboration across different sectors. This necessitates training in public speaking, scientific writing, and digital media. Trainees should be proficient in communicating scientific findings in accessible and compelling ways, tailored to specific audiences, whether policymakers, the general public, or other scientists. Role-playing exercises, simulated press conferences, and opportunities to present research findings to diverse groups are valuable components of this training.

Moreover, the programs need to nurture a strong ethical compass. The Guardians of tomorrow must grapple with complex ethical dilemmas related to resource management, conservation, and environmental justice. The training should therefore incorporate ethical frameworks, discussions on environmental justice, and case studies examining the ethical implications of specific environmental challenges. This requires incorporating philosophers, ethicists, and legal experts into the curriculum to provide a nuanced understanding of the ethical complexities involved. Interactive workshops exploring real-world ethical dilemmas can also aid in developing ethical reasoning skills. For example, a scenario-based exercise could involve participants debating the ethical considerations surrounding the construction of a dam that might displace indigenous communities while providing crucial energy resources.

Collaboration is not just a desirable outcome of the training; it is a fundamental element woven throughout the curriculum. The global nature of environmental challenges necessitates a collaborative, interconnected approach to solutions. The programs should foster collaboration among trainees from diverse backgrounds, perspectives, and geographical locations. Team-based projects, international exchanges, and collaborative research initiatives should be central components of the training. This cross-cultural exchange is critical for building relationships, sharing knowledge, and fostering a sense of global citizenship. Furthermore, collaborative projects will emphasize the importance of consensus building, negotiation, and compromise in tackling shared environmental concerns.

In addition to the core curriculum, specialized training pathways should be available, catering to the unique skills needed in various fields. These might include specialized training in renewable energy technologies, sustainable agriculture practices, environmental law, conservation biology, and environmental engineering. This modular approach allows trainees to specialize in areas that align with their interests and career aspirations, ensuring that they gain the specific expertise required to effectively tackle diverse environmental problems. For example, a specialized track in sustainable agriculture might involve practical training in organic farming, permaculture design, and agroforestry techniques.

The success of these training programs relies heavily on strong partnerships between academic institutions, research organizations, government agencies, and private sector companies. Collaboration will ensure access to cutting-edge research, state-of-the-art facilities, and real-world experience. It also creates pathways for future employment, fostering a community of practice among graduates. This networking aspect is crucial for the sustainability of the programs and for ensuring that trained professionals find meaningful employment in the environmental field. It is important to support research collaborations to ensure the programs remain relevant and responsive to emerging environmental challenges.

Furthermore, these training programs should foster a commitment to lifelong learning. The environmental field is constantly evolving, with new scientific discoveries, technological advances, and policy changes emerging regularly. Therefore, the programs should equip trainees with the skills and mindset needed to continue their learning long after they have completed their formal education. Access to online resources, professional development opportunities, and networks for continuing education should be provided. This approach ensures that the Guardians of the planet remain at the forefront of environmental knowledge and innovation throughout their careers.

Funding for these comprehensive training programs is a critical consideration. A mix of public and private funding mechanisms is needed to ensure the long-term sustainability of these crucial initiatives. Governments have a responsibility to invest in the education of their future environmental stewards. Private sector organizations can also play a significant role through corporate sponsorships, scholarships, and the creation of internship and apprenticeship programs. International collaborations will ensure a larger pool of resources and an emphasis on tackling global environmental concerns collaboratively. Secure funding models are essential to maintain the quality and accessibility of these programs, making them inclusive and accessible to individuals from diverse socioeconomic backgrounds.

Finally, a crucial aspect of success is the assessment and evaluation of the effectiveness of these training programs. Regular evaluation ensures that the programs remain relevant, up-to-date, and effective in achieving their goals. This evaluation should include gathering data on the career paths of graduates, their impact on environmental protection efforts, and feedback on the curriculum itself. This data-driven approach is vital to ensure continuous improvement and better alignment with the evolving needs of the environmental field. Regular audits and peer reviews are needed to maintain high standards and improve the effectiveness of the training provided.

The creation of comprehensive and globally connected training programs is not merely an investment in education; it is an investment in the future of our planet. By fostering a new generation of environmental stewards equipped with the knowledge, skills, and ethical commitment to tackle global environmental challenges, we can hope to build a sustainable future for generations to come. This is not simply a matter of training; it is a fundamental transformation in how we educate future leaders in environmental protection. This represents a collective responsibility, a global commitment to safeguarding the planet's future.

The culmination of rigorous training and unwavering dedication manifested in the emergence of a new breed of environmental leaders. These were not simply individuals with advanced degrees; they were passionate advocates, skilled strategists, and tireless workers, united by a common goal: the preservation of the planet. Their stories, woven together, formed a tapestry of commitment, innovation, and unwavering hope for a sustainable future.

Dr. Anya Sharma, a leading climate scientist and former trainee in one of the pioneering global environmental programs, exemplified the transformative power of education. Her research on mitigating the effects of ocean acidification had earned her international recognition, but more importantly, it had spurred real-world change. She was not confined to the ivory tower of academia; she was a vocal advocate for policy reform, working tirelessly with governments and corporations to implement sustainable practices. Her impact was not limited to scientific publications; she used accessible language and engaging visuals to communicate the urgency of the crisis to the general public, inspiring a wave of grassroots environmental activism. Her work showcased the crucial role of scientific literacy in driving meaningful change, proving that scientific expertise could be a powerful tool for advocacy and societal impact.

In stark contrast to Dr. Sharma's academic background, Mateo Rodriguez's journey began in the heart of the Amazon rainforest. Growing up among indigenous communities, he witnessed firsthand the devastating effects of deforestation and unsustainable resource extraction. His training within the global network had equipped him with the skills to translate his indigenous knowledge into modern scientific understanding, creating a unique approach to conservation. He spearheaded community-based projects that combined traditional practices with cutting-edge technology to protect biodiversity and promote sustainable livelihoods.

His work demonstrated the critical importance of integrating indigenous knowledge into modern environmental management strategies, showcasing the power of collaboration and mutual respect. Mateo's success lay not only in his technical expertise but also in his ability to build bridges between diverse cultures and perspectives, effectively navigating the complexities of local politics and international conservation initiatives.

The contributions of these leaders extended far beyond individual accomplishments. They formed a global network, sharing knowledge, resources, and strategies. This collaborative approach proved crucial in tackling transboundary environmental issues, such as the management of shared water resources or the protection of migratory species. The network facilitated the exchange of best practices, the development of joint research projects, and the coordination of international advocacy campaigns. This interconnectedness amplified their individual impacts, creating a powerful force for global environmental protection. Regular virtual conferences, facilitated by advanced communication technologies, became a crucial hub for knowledge sharing and collaborative problem-solving, allowing for real-time responses to environmental emergencies.

One remarkable example of this collaborative spirit was their response to a major coral bleaching event in the Great Barrier Reef. Dr. Sharma, leveraging her expertise in ocean acidification, contributed vital data on water chemistry. Mateo, drawing on his experience with community-based conservation, coordinated efforts with local fishing communities to implement immediate protective measures. Other members of the network provided technical support, financial resources, and logistical assistance. This coordinated, multi-faceted response showcased the effectiveness of a global, interconnected network in tackling large-scale environmental crises. Their rapid and effective response prevented further damage and served as a model for future collaborations.

The training programs themselves were not static; they continuously adapted to emerging challenges. As new technologies and scientific discoveries emerged, the curriculum evolved, ensuring that the next generation of environmental leaders was equipped with the most up-to-date knowledge and skills. This dynamism, a commitment to lifelong learning, was a hallmark of the program's success. Regular reviews of curriculum and feedback mechanisms ensured responsiveness to changing environmental realities. The integration of virtual reality simulations provided immersive training experiences, allowing future leaders to practice complex decision-making scenarios in realistic settings without the risks associated with real-world application.

The global network of leaders also played a significant role in shaping environmental policy. Their expertise was invaluable in informing international agreements and national legislation, ensuring that policy decisions were grounded in sound science and ethical considerations. Their advocacy efforts, often coordinated through the network, led to significant policy changes in various countries, including the establishment of new protected areas, the implementation of stricter environmental regulations, and the investment in renewable energy sources. Their involvement in policy-making was not confined to high-level negotiations; they also worked to ensure that policies were implemented effectively at the local level, reaching out to communities and incorporating their voices into the decision-making process.

Furthermore, these leaders recognized the importance of fostering a new generation of environmental stewards. They actively mentored young people, sharing their knowledge and experience, and inspiring them to pursue careers in environmental protection. They established educational programs, workshops, and internships, providing opportunities for young people to learn from the best and contribute to real-world environmental initiatives. This mentorship program, organically grown within the network, ensured the continuity of their work, building a lasting legacy for future generations. The emphasis on mentorship nurtured not just technical expertise but also a sense of community and shared purpose, creating a strong, supportive network that extended beyond the formal training programs.

The stories of these leaders were not just about individual success; they represented a collective shift in consciousness, a global awakening to the urgency of the environmental crisis. They demonstrated the power of education, collaboration, and unwavering commitment in creating a more sustainable future. Their dedication serves as an inspiration for future generations, a testament to the transformative potential of human action when guided by a shared vision of a healthy planet. The work continues, and the challenges remain immense, but their success offers a beacon of hope, a powerful demonstration that even the most daunting environmental challenges can be tackled with determination, innovation, and a global commitment to protecting our shared home.

Their legacy is not simply their individual accomplishments but the ripple effect of their influence, the inspiration they provide, and the movement they represent: a global community dedicated to safeguarding the planet. Their stories are a reminder that leadership is not about titles or positions, but about the courage to act, the dedication to persevere, and the vision to build a better future for all.

The success of the environmental leaders was not solely due to their individual expertise; it stemmed from their ability to mobilize global advocacy. They understood that effective environmental protection necessitates a shift in global consciousness, a widespread understanding of the environmental crisis, and a collective commitment to action. This realization led to the formation of powerful advocacy groups, acting as the megaphone for their crucial message.

These were not merely lobbying groups focused on influencing policy; they were sophisticated organizations employing a multifaceted approach. They combined scientific rigor with compelling storytelling, using data-driven analyses to highlight the severity of environmental challenges while also framing the narrative in a way that resonated emotionally with a global audience. Their campaigns were not confined to academic journals or government reports; they utilized social media, documentaries, public forums, and art installations to reach a broad spectrum of people, transcending geographical and cultural barriers.

One prominent example was the "Guardians of the Reef" campaign, launched in response to the devastating coral bleaching events. The campaign utilized breathtaking underwater footage combined with clear and concise scientific explanations to showcase the fragility of coral reefs and the dire consequences of climate change.

The campaign did not just highlight the problem; it offered solutions, presenting examples of sustainable practices and encouraging individuals to adopt eco-friendly lifestyles. The campaign went viral, garnering millions of views and sparking a wave of global support for coral reef conservation. The impact was not limited to raising awareness; the campaign directly resulted in increased funding for research and conservation efforts, showcasing the power of global advocacy in driving concrete change.

Another critical aspect of their advocacy work was the development of impactful educational materials. They created easily accessible resources, from interactive websites and mobile apps to engaging educational videos and informative infographics. These tools provided individuals with the knowledge and tools needed to make informed decisions and participate actively in environmental protection. They did not just provide information; they empowered people to become agents of change.

The groups also prioritized collaboration with diverse stakeholders. They fostered partnerships with governments, corporations, non-governmental organizations, and community groups, creating a powerful coalition dedicated to environmental protection. This collaborative approach proved instrumental in achieving significant policy changes. For example, their advocacy played a vital role in the successful negotiation of the "Global Ocean Treaty," which established comprehensive protections for the high seas. This treaty, a landmark achievement in international environmental law, would not have been possible without the coordinated efforts of the global advocacy network.

The advocacy groups were not static entities; they continually adapted their strategies based on emerging challenges and technological advancements. They effectively leveraged social media to mobilize rapid responses to environmental emergencies, coordinating global efforts to address issues such as oil spills, deforestation, and extreme weather events. Their use of social media was not simply for information dissemination; they utilized it to build communities, fostering a sense of shared responsibility and collective action. They organized virtual campaigns, online petitions, and crowdfunding initiatives, empowering individuals to contribute to global environmental efforts irrespective of their geographical location.

A key success factor was their ability to translate complex scientific data into accessible narratives. They understood that environmental issues were not merely scientific problems; they were human problems, deeply intertwined with social, economic, and political realities. Their advocacy campaigns, therefore, included compelling human stories that resonated with people on an emotional level, making abstract concepts like climate change and biodiversity loss more tangible and relatable. They showcased the human impact of environmental degradation, giving a face to the crisis and compelling a more emotional and resonant response.

Beyond awareness campaigns, the advocacy groups focused on fostering a sense of collective responsibility. They promoted sustainable lifestyles, encouraging individuals to reduce their environmental footprint through conscious consumption choices, responsible waste management, and support for renewable energy sources. Their message was not about guilt or shame; it was about empowerment and positive action. They presented sustainable living as a pathway toward a healthier and more fulfilling life, emphasizing the interconnectedness between environmental well-being and human well-being.

The impact of their work extended beyond individual behavioral changes. They successfully advocated for policy reforms at the local, national, and international levels. They worked closely with governments to implement stringent environmental regulations, promote sustainable development goals, and invest in green technologies. They were not content with just influencing policy; they also actively monitored its implementation, ensuring that environmental regulations were enforced effectively and that environmental commitments were upheld.

Moreover, the advocacy groups recognized the critical role of education in driving long-term change. They established educational programs for children and adults, providing opportunities for learning about environmental issues and developing the skills necessary to address them. These programs did not just focus on imparting information; they encouraged critical thinking, problem-solving, and civic engagement. They aimed to nurture a generation of informed and empowered citizens capable of contributing meaningfully to environmental protection.

Their advocacy was not limited to specific environmental issues; they championed a holistic approach, recognizing the interconnectedness of various ecological challenges. They addressed issues such as climate change, biodiversity loss, pollution, and resource depletion simultaneously, emphasizing the need for integrated solutions. They also recognized the importance of social justice in environmental protection, highlighting the disproportionate impact of environmental degradation on vulnerable communities and advocating for equitable solutions.

The global advocacy groups, therefore, emerged as powerful instruments of change. Their success was not only about raising awareness or influencing policy; it was about fostering a global movement of environmental stewardship, a collective commitment to safeguarding the planet for present and future generations. Their work demonstrated the transformative potential of collaborative action, showcasing the ability of diverse individuals and organizations to unite around a common goal and achieve extraordinary results. Their continuous efforts represent not only a response to the environmental crisis but also a testament to the enduring power of hope, collaboration, and human determination. The future remains uncertain, but the legacy of these groups—their dedication, their innovation, and their tireless advocacy—shines as a beacon of hope in the ongoing struggle for a sustainable future. Their success is a testament to the power of collective action and a powerful example for future generations of environmental advocates. The fight for a healthy planet continues, but the groundwork laid by these pioneers offers a foundation for a more sustainable and equitable future.

The legacy of the global advocacy groups extended far beyond raising awareness and influencing policy. A crucial element of their success was their unwavering commitment to environmental justice. They recognized that environmental degradation disproportionately affects vulnerable communities, often exacerbating existing social and economic inequalities. This understanding fueled a significant portion of their work, leading them to champion policies and initiatives that addressed these disparities directly.

Their approach to environmental justice was not simply about adding a social justice lens to their environmental work; it was deeply integrated into the core of their strategies. They understood that a healthy environment and a just society are intrinsically linked. They did not view environmental protection as a separate issue from social justice; rather, they saw them as two sides of the same coin, mutually reinforcing and dependent on each other.

One of their key strategies involved conducting thorough environmental impact assessments, meticulously examining the potential consequences of industrial projects and development initiatives on various communities. These assessments were not merely bureaucratic exercises; they incorporated community voices and perspectives, ensuring that the concerns and needs of vulnerable populations were prioritized. They went beyond typical assessments by examining not just the immediate ecological impact but also the long-term social and economic consequences, including impacts on health, access to resources, and economic opportunity. This participatory approach ensured that the voices of marginalized communities were not silenced, and their concerns were addressed proactively.

Furthermore, they actively engaged in community-based initiatives, working directly with residents of vulnerable communities to address localized environmental challenges. This involved organizing clean-up drives, planting trees, and creating green spaces in areas lacking access to natural resources. These grassroots initiatives were not simply symbolic gestures; they fostered a sense of ownership and empowerment within the communities, transforming them into active participants in the environmental protection process. They supported local initiatives that promoted sustainable livelihoods, helping communities transition to environmentally friendly practices that would also benefit their economic well-being.

The advocacy groups also played a critical role in advocating for policy reforms that advanced environmental justice. They worked tirelessly to ensure that environmental regulations were equitably applied, preventing industries from disproportionately burdening vulnerable communities. They lobbied for stricter enforcement of environmental laws, ensuring that polluters were held accountable for their actions and that communities were compensated for damages caused by environmental pollution. This included advocating for stricter environmental standards in historically disadvantaged communities, often bearing the brunt of industrial pollution.

A significant achievement was their successful advocacy for the "Environmental Equity Act," a landmark piece of legislation that mandated the consideration of environmental justice in all government policies and projects. This Act was not just about incorporating environmental justice into existing frameworks; it mandated a paradigm shift, requiring government agencies to actively seek out and address environmental disparities. The Act was the culmination of years of advocacy, lobbying, and grassroots mobilization, a testament to their persistent commitment to achieving equitable outcomes.

They also prioritized the development of educational resources that promoted environmental literacy and awareness within vulnerable communities. They created accessible materials explaining environmental issues in clear, concise language, avoiding jargon and technical terminology. They used culturally relevant approaches to ensure the information was understood and readily adopted by the targeted communities. These educational efforts were not merely about conveying information; they sought to empower communities to advocate for their own rights and participate meaningfully in environmental decision-making processes. This involved training residents in the skills necessary to monitor environmental conditions, participate in public hearings, and engage in advocacy efforts.

Beyond their direct actions, the advocacy groups played a critical role in raising global awareness about environmental justice issues. They created impactful campaigns that highlighted the inequities faced by vulnerable communities, showcasing the human consequences of environmental degradation. These campaigns went beyond typical statistics and graphs, instead relying on compelling narratives and personal stories to highlight the human impact of environmental injustice. They humanized the issue, allowing individuals from all walks of life to connect with the suffering of communities affected by environmental hazards. They used a range of media, including documentaries, social media campaigns, and artistic collaborations, to reach a broad audience.

The groups also collaborated extensively with other organizations, forging strong alliances with community-based groups, academic institutions, and international organizations to amplify their efforts. This collaborative network provided access to a wealth of expertise and resources, strengthening their ability to advocate effectively for environmental justice. It ensured that their work was not siloed but rather part of a broader movement for social and environmental justice.

A crucial aspect of their success was their ability to build trust with vulnerable communities. This involved establishing long-term relationships based on mutual respect, transparency, and genuine commitment to empowering these communities. They listened to their concerns, valuing their local knowledge and expertise, and worked side by side with them to find solutions. This genuine engagement was essential in fostering collaboration and ensuring that their initiatives were truly community-driven.

The fight for environmental justice is an ongoing struggle, but the legacy of these global advocacy groups serves as a powerful example of the transformative potential of collective action. Their work demonstrated that environmental protection and social justice are inextricably linked and that a sustainable future can only be achieved through equitable solutions that address the needs of all communities.

Their tireless efforts laid the groundwork for a more just and sustainable world, inspiring future generations of environmental advocates to continue the fight for a healthier and more equitable planet for all. Their work underscored that environmental justice is not just a worthy goal; it is a fundamental prerequisite for a truly sustainable future. The success of their efforts highlights the importance of inclusivity, collaboration, and a deep understanding of the complex interplay between environmental issues and social realities.

The challenges remain significant, but the path they forged offers a powerful roadmap for future generations of environmental stewards. The future of environmental justice hinges on continued commitment to equitable solutions, collaborative efforts, and the empowerment of marginalized communities.

The success of the global advocacy groups was not solely due to their impressive policy influence or extensive awareness campaigns. A deeper analysis reveals a profound understanding of interconnectedness as the bedrock of their approach. They recognized that environmental issues are not isolated incidents; they are intricately woven into the fabric of social, economic, and political systems. This holistic perspective allowed them to develop strategies that addressed the root causes of environmental degradation rather than simply treating the symptoms.

This understanding manifested in several key ways. Firstly, their environmental impact assessments were not confined to the purely ecological. They delved into the intricate web of social and economic consequences, considering the impact on vulnerable communities with meticulous detail. For example, the proposed construction of a hydroelectric dam in a remote region would not just be assessed for its impact on fish populations and water flow; it would also scrutinize its effects on indigenous communities' access to traditional lands, their livelihoods, and their cultural heritage.

The assessments incorporated traditional ecological knowledge alongside scientific data, recognizing the invaluable insights of communities who have lived in harmony with their environment for generations. This holistic approach ensured that the project's overall impact, encompassing both ecological and social dimensions, was thoroughly evaluated before proceeding.

Furthermore, their advocacy extended beyond specific projects. They worked tirelessly to promote systemic change, recognizing that lasting solutions required a fundamental shift in how we interact with the environment. This involved advocating for policies that incentivized sustainable practices and penalized environmentally damaging ones. For instance, they spearheaded campaigns for carbon pricing mechanisms, not simply as a means of reducing greenhouse gas emissions, but also as a way to promote investment in renewable energy and create new economic opportunities in green technologies. They understood that economic growth and environmental sustainability are not mutually exclusive; they can be mutually reinforcing. Their work highlighted the potential for a green economy to create jobs, reduce poverty, and improve public health, demonstrating the interconnectedness of environmental and economic well-being.

The advocacy groups also championed the concept of ecosystem services, recognizing the immense value of natural resources and the crucial role they play in supporting human life. They emphasized the importance of preserving biodiversity not just for its intrinsic value but also for the vital services it provides, such as clean air and water, pollination, and climate regulation.

This understanding led them to advocate for policies that protected ecosystems and promoted sustainable resource management, highlighting the economic benefits of preserving natural capital. For example, they successfully lobbied for the establishment of protected areas that provided vital ecosystem services while also boosting local economies through ecotourism and sustainable harvesting. This approach demonstrated the interconnectedness between environmental protection and economic prosperity.

Another crucial aspect of their approach was their focus on building strong partnerships and collaborations. They worked closely with community groups, scientists, policymakers, and businesses to create a powerful network of support. This collaborative approach allowed them to leverage diverse expertise and resources, maximizing their impact. For instance, their partnership with local communities in the Amazon rainforest led to the development of sustainable agriculture practices that both protected biodiversity and improved the livelihoods of indigenous populations. The collaboration resulted in innovative solutions tailored to the specific needs and circumstances of the region, highlighting the importance of local knowledge and participation in conservation efforts.

The groups recognized that environmental challenges are global in scope and require international cooperation. They actively participated in global forums and collaborations, advocating for international agreements and treaties that addressed transboundary environmental issues.

They emphasized the interconnectedness of the global environment, highlighting the fact that environmental problems in one region can have significant repercussions in others. For example, their efforts to address climate change involved collaborating with international organizations to promote emission reduction targets, technology transfer, and financial support for developing countries. This global approach highlighted the importance of collective action and international collaboration in addressing environmental challenges that transcend national boundaries.

Their educational initiatives played a vital role in fostering a deeper understanding of interconnectedness. They created engaging and accessible materials that explained complex environmental issues in a way that everyone could understand. They went beyond simply presenting facts and figures; they emphasized the human dimension of environmental problems, highlighting the social and economic consequences of environmental degradation.

For instance, they developed educational programs that explained the link between deforestation and climate change, illustrating how the loss of forests contributes to extreme weather events that disproportionately affect vulnerable populations. This holistic approach to education enabled people to see the interconnectedness of environmental issues and their impact on their lives.

The success of these advocacy groups is a testament to the power of collaboration, the importance of understanding interconnectedness, and the transformative potential of collective action. Their work highlights that environmental protection is not a separate issue but rather an integral part of a broader movement for social and economic justice.

Their legacy extends beyond specific achievements; it is a paradigm shift in how we approach environmental challenges, encouraging us to move away from fragmented, siloed approaches and toward a more integrated and holistic understanding of the world. The path they paved demonstrates that the most effective solutions to environmental problems are those that consider their intricate connections with social, economic, and political systems. Their work is a powerful reminder that a sustainable future is achievable only through a commitment to equity, collaboration, and a deep understanding of the interconnected web of life.

The fight for environmental justice, therefore, is not just about protecting the environment; it is about creating a more just and equitable world for all. The legacy of these advocacy groups serves as a blueprint for future generations of environmental stewards, demonstrating the importance of holistic approaches, collaborative partnerships, and a deep understanding of interconnectedness. Their work underscores that environmental protection is not a luxury but a necessity, a prerequisite for a sustainable and flourishing future for all. The challenges remain substantial, requiring continued commitment, innovation, and collective action.

But the vision they established, a world where environmental sustainability and social justice are inextricably linked, provides a beacon of hope and inspiration for the years to come. The work continues, driven by the profound understanding that our fate is intertwined with the fate of the planet. The more we understand the complex web of interconnectedness, the more effectively we can address the urgent challenges before us and build a more sustainable and equitable future for generations to come. This understanding, born from years of struggle and achievement, forms the cornerstone of a more hopeful future, a future built on the principles of interconnectedness and collective responsibility. The legacy of these groups, therefore, is not just a narrative of past successes but a guiding light for the future, illuminating the path toward a more just and sustainable world.

Chapter Fourteen
A New Harmony

The shift toward a sustainable future was not solely dependent on policy changes and public awareness. A critical component was the development and implementation of technologies that actively promoted harmony between human activities and the natural world. This was not just about reducing environmental impact; it was about creating a symbiotic relationship, where technological advancements actively enhanced ecological health and biodiversity.

One striking example is the widespread adoption of vertical farming techniques. These were not merely about increasing agricultural yields in urban settings; they were meticulously designed to minimize resource consumption. Sophisticated sensors monitored environmental conditions within the farms, optimizing water usage, nutrient delivery, and light exposure.

Artificial intelligence played a crucial role in analyzing this data, predicting potential issues, and automatically adjusting parameters for optimal growth. The farms themselves were often integrated into existing buildings, repurposing underutilized spaces and reducing the need for land conversion. The excess heat generated by the lighting systems was even captured and used to heat adjacent structures, creating a truly closed-loop system. This was not merely efficient agriculture; it was urban ecosystem engineering. The vertical farms, strategically placed, became micro-ecosystems within the city, providing habitats for beneficial insects and offering spaces for urban biodiversity initiatives such as rooftop gardens.

Beyond agriculture, advancements in renewable energy sources were not just about replacing fossil fuels; they were designed to actively enhance ecosystems. For example, offshore wind farms, while generating clean energy, were carefully planned to provide habitats for marine life. The structures themselves, designed with biodiversity in mind, created artificial reefs, attracting fish and other organisms. The careful placement of turbines minimized disruption to migratory patterns and protected sensitive marine areas. This integration of energy production with marine conservation demonstrated a paradigm shift from extractive practices to a co-existent model. Similar innovations were seen in solar energy, with solar farms integrated into landscapes in ways that complemented existing ecosystems, often incorporating native plants and creating habitats for pollinators and other wildlife.

Waste management underwent a radical transformation. The linear "take-make-dispose" model was replaced by circular economy principles. Smart waste management systems, employing AI and sensor networks, optimized waste collection routes, reducing fuel consumption and emissions. Advanced sorting facilities separated materials with incredible precision, maximizing recycling rates and minimizing landfill waste. Innovative technologies converted organic waste into biogas and compost, providing renewable energy and enriching soil fertility. This was not just waste reduction; it was a transformation of waste into a valuable resource, closing the loop and minimizing the environmental footprint of human consumption.

The concept of biomimicry, drawing inspiration from nature to design innovative solutions, experienced a surge in popularity. Architects and engineers increasingly looked to natural systems for design cues. Buildings were designed to passively regulate temperature, mimicking the insulation properties of animal fur or the ventilation systems of termite mounds.

Materials were derived from sustainable sources, such as bioplastics made from algae or mycelium, minimizing reliance on fossil fuels and reducing the carbon footprint of construction. This approach demonstrated a profound shift in thinking, from imposing human-centric designs onto the environment to collaborating with nature to create sustainable and resilient structures.

Transportation also underwent a significant overhaul. Reliance on individual vehicles was reduced through the development of efficient public transport systems, coupled with the rise of electric and autonomous vehicles. Smart traffic management systems, utilizing real-time data and AI algorithms, optimized traffic flow, reducing congestion and fuel consumption. The development of high-speed rail networks and integrated transportation hubs facilitated efficient and sustainable travel, connecting urban and rural areas. The shift toward electric vehicles was not just about reducing emissions; it was about creating cleaner and quieter urban environments, enhancing public health, and improving quality of life. The charging infrastructure was carefully integrated into urban planning, often incorporating solar panels and other renewable energy sources.

Water management underwent a similarly profound transformation. Smart water grids, using sensor networks and AI, monitored water usage in real-time, identifying leaks and optimizing distribution. Water purification technologies, drawing inspiration from natural processes, reduced the environmental impact of wastewater treatment. Water-sensitive urban design incorporated green infrastructure, such as rain gardens and permeable pavements, reducing stormwater runoff and improving water quality. These advancements were not merely about supplying water; they were about creating resilient water systems that were both efficient and environmentally responsible.

The development and integration of these technologies were not isolated events; they were part of a broader systemic shift. This shift involved close collaboration between scientists, engineers, policymakers, and the public.

The technologies were designed not only to be environmentally friendly but also socially equitable and economically viable. This meant ensuring that the benefits of these technological advancements were shared widely and that they did not exacerbate existing social inequalities.

Furthermore, educational systems were redesigned to foster a deeper understanding of the interconnectedness of technology and nature. Students were taught not only about the technical aspects of these innovations but also about the ecological, social, and economic implications. This understanding was crucial in ensuring the responsible development and deployment of these technologies.

The success of this technological harmony was not solely due to technological advancements. It was also the result of a fundamental shift in human values and priorities. It required a collective commitment to sustainability, a willingness to embrace innovative solutions, and a deep understanding of the interconnectedness of human society and the natural world. The integration of technology and nature was not about dominating nature; it was about cooperating with it, building a future where both thrive together. The path forward continues to evolve, with ongoing research and innovation driving the creation of even more harmonious technologies that enhance both human well-being and environmental health.

This continuing evolution is not just about maintaining the present harmony but about proactively anticipating and addressing future challenges, ensuring that technological progress remains a force for positive change on the planet. The journey toward a technologically harmonious future is an ongoing process of learning, adaptation, and collaboration, reflecting a profound understanding that our destiny is inextricably linked to the health of the planet. The ongoing commitment to research and development, alongside responsible implementation and public education, ensures this symbiotic relationship will continue to flourish, creating a more sustainable and prosperous future for generations to come. The very fabric of our future depends on this ongoing balance, a testament to the power of human ingenuity when channeled toward a harmonious coexistence with the natural world.

The vision of sustainable cities was not merely a utopian dream; it was a meticulously crafted reality, a testament to humanity's capacity for innovative adaptation. These were not simply cities with green spaces; they were intricate ecosystems, meticulously designed to minimize their environmental footprint and maximize the well-being of their inhabitants. The core principle was symbiosis, a harmonious coexistence between human infrastructure and the natural world.

Imagine a city where buildings were not just static structures but active participants in the urban ecosystem. Rooftops transformed into vibrant gardens, providing habitats for pollinators, absorbing rainwater, and mitigating the urban heat island effect. Building facades, clad in living walls of vegetation, purified the air, reduced noise pollution, and offered aesthetic beauty. These were not mere cosmetic additions; they were integral parts of a carefully designed system, enhancing the city's resilience and ecological health.

Transportation within these sustainable cities was revolutionized. High-speed rail networks connected urban centers with outlying areas, reducing reliance on individual vehicles and promoting efficient, low-carbon travel. Autonomous electric vehicles navigated streets, optimized for minimal congestion and fuel consumption, while dedicated bike lanes and pedestrian walkways encouraged active transportation. The cityscape itself became a seamless network for movement, prioritizing human well-being over vehicular dominance. The integration of charging stations, powered by renewable energy sources, eliminated range anxiety and further promoted the adoption of electric vehicles.

Water management was a critical aspect of these cities' sustainability. Smart water grids, equipped with advanced sensors and AI algorithms, monitored water usage in real time, detecting leaks and optimizing distribution. Water-sensitive urban design incorporated permeable pavements and rain gardens, minimizing stormwater runoff and reducing the burden on conventional drainage systems. Greywater recycling systems repurposed wastewater for non-potable uses, such as irrigation, significantly reducing water consumption. These cities were not just consuming water; they were learning to manage and conserve it, creating a resilient water cycle within the urban environment.

Waste management in these cities was a model of circular economy principles. Advanced sorting facilities separated waste with unparalleled precision, maximizing recycling rates and minimizing landfill waste. Organic waste was transformed into biogas and compost, providing renewable energy and enriching soil fertility. The "take-make-dispose" model was replaced by a closed-loop system, where waste was viewed not as a burden but as a valuable resource. This approach was not simply about reducing waste; it was about transforming it into a positive contribution to the urban ecosystem.

The design and construction of buildings themselves reflected a commitment to sustainability. Biomimicry, the practice of drawing inspiration from nature, guided architectural and engineering decisions. Buildings were designed to passively regulate temperature, harnessing natural ventilation and sunlight. Sustainable materials, such as bioplastics and mycelium composites, replaced traditional, energy-intensive materials, reducing the carbon footprint of construction. These were not simply buildings; they were symbiotic structures, seamlessly integrated into the urban environment.

The energy needs of these cities were met through a diversified portfolio of renewable energy sources. Solar panels integrated into building facades and rooftops harnessed the sun's energy, while wind turbines, strategically positioned to minimize environmental impact, harnessed the power of the wind. Geothermal energy tapped into the earth's heat, providing a reliable and sustainable source of energy. These cities were not reliant on fossil fuels; they were self-sufficient, generating their own clean energy.

Food production within these sustainable cities was not confined to distant farms. Vertical farms, integrated into buildings and repurposing underutilized spaces, provided fresh produce locally. These farms employed advanced technologies, optimizing water usage, nutrient delivery, and light exposure, maximizing yields while minimizing resource consumption. The farms themselves became micro-ecosystems within the city, providing habitats for beneficial insects and creating opportunities for urban agriculture initiatives. This localized food production reduced the environmental impact of transportation and strengthened the city's food security.

Beyond the physical infrastructure, the social fabric of these sustainable cities was equally critical. Community engagement was a cornerstone of their success. Citizens were not merely residents; they were active participants in shaping the city's sustainable future. Education programs fostered a deep understanding of environmental issues and promoted responsible consumption patterns. Green initiatives and community gardens connected residents with the natural world, nurturing a sense of stewardship and responsibility.

The economic model of these cities was inherently sustainable. Green jobs created a thriving economy, fostering innovation and supporting local businesses. Circular economy principles minimized waste and maximized resource utilization, creating economic opportunities while protecting the environment. These cities were not just environmentally sustainable; they were economically vibrant and socially equitable.

The transition to sustainable cities was not a sudden transformation but a gradual evolution, driven by a collective commitment to sustainability. Policy changes, technological innovations, and community engagement all played a crucial role. This transformation was not just about environmental protection; it was about creating healthier, more resilient, and more equitable urban environments. It was a paradigm shift, moving from a human-centric approach to a holistic, symbiotic relationship between humanity and the natural world.

These sustainable cities, functioning as vibrant ecosystems, represented a significant step toward a more harmonious future. They demonstrated that urban development and environmental protection were not mutually exclusive; they were inextricably linked. The success of these cities serves as a powerful inspiration, showing that a sustainable future is not merely a possibility but a tangible reality achievable through collective effort, innovative solutions, and a fundamental shift in human values and priorities. The lessons learned from their design and implementation can guide the development of future urban environments, ensuring that cities continue to be spaces of human flourishing while minimizing their environmental impact and maximizing their contribution to a healthy planet.

The integration of technology, nature, and community spirit showcased in these thriving urban hubs provides a model for a future where sustainability is not merely a goal but an integral and celebrated aspect of human civilization. The ongoing evolution of sustainable city design promises even greater advancements, leading to a future where urbanization and ecological health coexist in perfect harmony, shaping a truly resilient and thriving world for generations to come. This harmony extends beyond the immediate urban environment, demonstrating the interconnectedness of ecosystems and the ripple effects of sustainable practices on a global scale.

The model of the sustainable city extends beyond mere urban planning; it represents a shift in societal values, prioritizing long-term environmental stewardship and the well-being of future generations over short-term economic gains. The success of these cities underscores the potential for humanity to coexist harmoniously with the natural world, demonstrating that a sustainable future is not just a possibility but an achievable reality, born from collective commitment, innovation, and a profound respect for the planet.

The success of these sustainable cities hinges not only on their innovative infrastructure but also on the resilience of their integrated ecosystems.

These were not simply green spaces interspersed within concrete jungles; they were meticulously designed ecological systems, robust enough to withstand and even thrive in the face of environmental challenges. The design principles behind these resilient ecosystems were multifaceted, drawing inspiration from both natural processes and cutting-edge technology.

One key aspect is biodiversity. Instead of relying on monocultures, these urban ecosystems embraced a wide array of plant and animal species. Rooftop gardens were not simply filled with aesthetically pleasing flowers; they were carefully curated habitats, supporting pollinators like bees and butterflies, which in turn contributed to the overall health of the urban environment. Native plant species were favored, as they were better adapted to local conditions and required less maintenance.

Green walls, carefully chosen for their varied textures and abilities to attract beneficial insects, provided a vital layer of biodiversity, improving air quality, regulating temperatures, and creating havens for wildlife. The presence of diverse plant life also enhanced the ecosystem's resilience to pests and diseases, preventing widespread damage.

The water systems within these cities were designed to be exceptionally resilient. Rather than relying solely on traditional drainage systems, the urban landscape itself acted as a sponge, absorbing rainwater through permeable pavements and rain gardens. This approach reduced the risk of flooding during heavy rainfall and replenished groundwater supplies. Furthermore, these systems were equipped with advanced sensors and AI-driven algorithms, allowing for real-time monitoring of water levels and early detection of leaks, minimizing water waste. Greywater recycling systems played a crucial role, reusing wastewater for non-potable purposes such as irrigation, reducing pressure on municipal water supplies. This integrated approach to water management enhanced the resilience of the urban ecosystem to drought and other water-related stresses.

Waste management within these resilient ecosystems was based on the principles of circularity. Waste was not seen as a disposal problem but as a valuable resource. Advanced sorting facilities separated waste with high precision, maximizing recycling rates and minimizing landfill waste. Organic waste was composted and used to enrich the soil of urban farms and green spaces, completing the nutrient cycle. Biogas was produced from organic waste and used to power parts of the city's infrastructure, reducing reliance on fossil fuels. This cyclical approach not only reduced environmental impact but also created valuable resources, bolstering the city's resilience and sustainability.

Energy resilience is another crucial aspect. These cities rely on a diverse mix of renewable energy sources, including solar, wind, and geothermal. Solar panels are seamlessly integrated into building designs, while wind turbines are strategically located to minimize noise and visual impact. Geothermal energy taps into the Earth's stable temperature, providing a consistent source of energy. Furthermore, smart grids efficiently distribute energy, optimizing consumption and minimizing waste. Energy storage systems, such as advanced battery technologies, ensure a reliable energy supply even during periods of low renewable energy generation. This diversified and intelligent energy system enhances the cities' resilience to power outages and fluctuating energy sources.

The food systems in these resilient cities are designed for localized production and security. Vertical farms, integrated into buildings and other underutilized spaces, provide fresh produce locally. Hydroponics and aeroponics technologies minimize water usage and maximize yield, ensuring food security even in challenging environmental conditions. These urban farms are not isolated systems; they are integrated into the wider urban ecosystem, interacting with surrounding green spaces and contributing to overall biodiversity. The reduced reliance on long-distance transportation lowers the carbon footprint and enhances the city's resilience to supply chain disruptions.

Social resilience is just as important as ecological resilience. These cities promote community engagement and education, empowering residents to participate actively in shaping their sustainable future. Community gardens, green initiatives, and educational programs foster a sense of ownership and responsibility toward the environment. This strong social fabric enhances the city's resilience to external shocks and stresses, as collective effort can better manage and overcome challenges. The emphasis on green jobs creates a thriving economy and reinforces the city's commitment to sustainability.

The resilient ecosystems within these sustainable cities are not static entities; they are dynamic systems that adapt and evolve over time. Monitoring and data analysis allow for continuous improvement, identifying areas for optimization and adaptation to changing environmental conditions. Climate change modeling plays a crucial role, predicting potential future stresses and informing the design of resilient infrastructure. This adaptive management approach enhances the long-term sustainability and resilience of the entire urban ecosystem.

The integration of nature-based solutions is another cornerstone of these resilient ecosystems. Instead of fighting against natural processes, the cities work with them, using natural elements to mitigate environmental risks. For instance, green infrastructure, such as wetlands and urban forests, helps manage stormwater runoff and reduces the urban heat island effect. These natural features not only improve the ecological health of the city but also provide aesthetic value and enhance the quality of life for residents.

The design of resilient ecosystems involves a holistic approach, considering not only environmental factors but also social and economic considerations. The creation of these resilient ecosystems is an ongoing process, requiring constant monitoring, adaptation, and innovation. It is a testament to the potential of human ingenuity to create cities that are both vibrant and ecologically sound, fostering a harmonious relationship between urban development and environmental sustainability. The success of these integrated ecosystems represents a paradigm shift in urban planning, moving away from a purely human-centric approach toward a symbiotic relationship between humanity and the natural world.

The long-term success of these resilient ecosystems relies on continuous monitoring and adaptation. Advanced sensor networks, coupled with sophisticated data analysis tools, provide real-time insights into the health and functioning of the urban ecosystems. This constant feedback loop allows city planners and managers to make informed decisions, adapting strategies as needed. For example, if a particular plant species is struggling to thrive in a rooftop garden, the data can be used to identify the problem, such as insufficient sunlight or poor soil drainage, and implement corrective measures. This adaptive management approach ensures that the urban ecosystems remain resilient in the face of unexpected challenges, such as extreme weather events, pest infestations, or evolving environmental conditions.

Furthermore, community engagement remains critical to the long-term sustainability of these ecosystems. Citizen scientists contribute to data collection and monitoring efforts, enriching the understanding of the urban ecosystems and fostering a sense of ownership and responsibility. Participatory planning processes ensure that residents have a voice in shaping the development of their neighborhoods and green spaces.

This collaborative approach not only strengthens the social fabric of the community but also improves the effectiveness of urban ecosystem management. It transforms residents into active participants in ensuring the long-term health and resilience of their shared environment. Community-based monitoring initiatives can also provide early warnings of potential problems, allowing for timely interventions and minimizing potential damage.

Beyond specific technological and managerial solutions, the success of these resilient urban ecosystems depends on a fundamental shift in societal values. This requires a long-term perspective, prioritizing the well-being of future generations over short-term economic gains. It necessitates a profound understanding of ecological principles and the interconnectedness of all living things. It fosters a sense of stewardship, recognizing the responsibility humans have to protect and enhance the natural world. The transition toward resilient urban ecosystems is not merely a technological challenge but a cultural and societal transformation.

This transformation is driven by a collective commitment to sustainability, encompassing policy changes, technological innovations, and a widespread shift in public awareness and engagement. Education plays a vital role, fostering a deep understanding of environmental issues and promoting responsible consumption patterns. The integration of sustainable practices into everyday life becomes a norm, creating a feedback loop that reinforces ecological consciousness and strengthens the resilience of the entire urban environment.

This long-term commitment to sustainability is essential for ensuring that these vibrant, resilient urban ecosystems continue to thrive for generations to come. The legacy of these sustainable cities will extend far beyond their immediate boundaries, serving as models for urban development globally. The integration of technology, nature, and community spirit showcases a future where urbanization and ecological health are not mutually exclusive, but rather complementary aspects of a thriving, sustainable world.

The transition toward sustainable cities necessitates a fundamental shift in our relationship with the natural world, and at the heart of this transformation lies biodiversity conservation. No longer a niche concern of environmentalists, biodiversity conservation has become a global priority, recognized as essential for the health and well-being of the planet and its inhabitants. The interconnectedness of ecosystems means that the loss of even a single species can trigger a cascade of unforeseen consequences, impacting the stability and resilience of entire systems. The intricate web of life, where species interact in complex and often unpredictable ways, underscores the importance of preserving the full spectrum of biodiversity.

This global recognition is reflected in numerous international agreements, conventions, and initiatives aimed at protecting biodiversity. The Convention on Biological Diversity (CBD), for instance, provides a framework for national action and international cooperation, setting ambitious targets for biodiversity conservation. These targets often focus on protecting specific habitats, such as forests, wetlands, and coral reefs, recognizing their crucial role in maintaining biodiversity. The establishment of protected areas, national parks, and wildlife sanctuaries are key strategies in safeguarding biodiversity hotspots and preserving the genetic diversity of plant and animal species.

However, the challenge extends beyond simply establishing protected areas. Effective biodiversity conservation requires a multifaceted approach that addresses the underlying drivers of biodiversity loss. Habitat destruction, driven by urbanization, agriculture, and deforestation, remains the primary threat.

Sustainable land management practices, such as agroforestry and reforestation, are crucial in mitigating habitat loss and restoring degraded ecosystems. This includes promoting sustainable agriculture techniques that minimize the use of pesticides and herbicides, thereby reducing their impact on non-target species. Sustainable forestry practices, which emphasize selective logging and replanting, can minimize the impact on forest ecosystems and maintain biodiversity.

The illegal wildlife trade poses another significant threat, driving many species toward extinction. Combating this illegal trade requires international cooperation, stricter law enforcement, and increased public awareness. Education campaigns highlighting the devastating consequences of illegal wildlife trade are essential in changing consumer behavior and reducing demand. Furthermore, strengthening border controls and improving traceability mechanisms can help disrupt the networks that facilitate this illegal activity.

Climate change exacerbates the threat to biodiversity, creating new challenges for conservation efforts. Rising temperatures, altered precipitation patterns, and increased frequency of extreme weather events can disrupt ecosystems, pushing many species beyond their adaptive capacity. Conservation strategies must incorporate climate change adaptation and mitigation measures, such as assisting species to migrate to more suitable habitats or protecting critical habitats from the impacts of climate change. Investing in climate-resilient infrastructure and supporting the development of climate-smart agriculture practices are equally crucial.

The integration of biodiversity conservation into urban planning is another critical aspect. Sustainable urban development must prioritize the creation of green spaces, urban parks, and green corridors that connect fragmented habitats. Rooftop gardens, green walls, and permeable pavements can enhance urban biodiversity, improving air quality, reducing the urban heat island effect, and providing habitats for a range of species. These urban green spaces also offer significant social and recreational benefits, improving the quality of life for urban dwellers.

Citizen science initiatives play an increasingly important role in biodiversity conservation. Through community-based monitoring programs, volunteers can contribute to data collection, species identification, and habitat assessment. This participatory approach not only enhances the effectiveness of conservation efforts but also fosters a sense of ownership and responsibility among citizens. The involvement of local communities is crucial, as they possess invaluable knowledge about local ecosystems and species.

Technology is also revolutionizing biodiversity conservation efforts. Remote sensing technologies, such as satellite imagery and drones, allow for large-scale monitoring of habitats and species populations. Genetic analysis techniques enable researchers to identify and track threatened species, assess genetic diversity, and monitor the impact of conservation interventions. These technological advancements enhance the efficiency and effectiveness of conservation programs, providing crucial data for informed decision-making.

Beyond technological innovations, effective biodiversity conservation requires a fundamental shift in societal values and priorities. A holistic approach that considers the interconnectedness of ecosystems, acknowledges the intrinsic value of biodiversity, and understands its contribution to human well-being is essential. Integrating biodiversity conservation into economic development strategies, valuing ecosystem services, and promoting sustainable consumption patterns are all crucial steps toward achieving this goal.

The economic benefits derived from biodiversity, such as ecosystem services like pollination, clean water provision, and carbon sequestration, are often overlooked. Putting a monetary value on these services can help illustrate the economic importance of biodiversity conservation and incentivize action. Furthermore, promoting sustainable tourism that respects local ecosystems and communities can generate economic benefits while simultaneously supporting conservation efforts.

Finally, effective biodiversity conservation requires strong governance structures and robust policy frameworks. International cooperation is crucial, with countries working collaboratively to implement conservation strategies and enforce environmental regulations. National governments need to develop and implement effective legislation that protects threatened species and habitats, promotes sustainable land management practices, and addresses the drivers of biodiversity loss. This requires a multi-sectoral approach, engaging government agencies, businesses, NGOs, and local communities. Transparency and accountability are essential to ensure the effective implementation of conservation policies.

The challenge of biodiversity conservation is immense, but it is not insurmountable. By adopting a comprehensive and integrated approach that combines scientific knowledge, technological advancements, community engagement, and robust policy frameworks, we can safeguard biodiversity for future generations. The success of our efforts will not only ensure the health of the planet but will also contribute to human well-being and sustainable development for years to come. This global commitment is not simply an environmental imperative; it is a matter of our collective survival and prosperity. The future of our cities, our economies, and our planet itself hinges on our ability to protect and cherish the incredible diversity of life that surrounds us. The interconnectedness of life demands a unified, global response.

The vision of global sustainability, once a distant aspiration, is gradually taking shape, a testament to humanity's growing understanding of our interconnectedness with the natural world. It is a story not of singular triumphs but of countless small victories, of shifts in policy, technological innovations, and a profound change in collective consciousness. The success we are witnessing is not just environmental; it represents a paradigm shift in how we view our place in the world, a recognition that our well-being is inextricably linked to the health of the planet.

The transition has not been easy. Decades of unsustainable practices have left their mark: depleted resources, degraded ecosystems, and a climate system teetering on the brink. Yet the collective response has been remarkable, fueled by a growing awareness of the urgency of the situation and a shared recognition of the shared fate of humanity and the environment.

International cooperation, once a slow and cumbersome process, has gained momentum, with nations working together to address shared environmental challenges. The Paris Agreement on climate change, for example, represents a landmark achievement, demonstrating a global commitment to mitigating climate change and adapting to its impacts. This collaborative spirit extends beyond climate change, encompassing efforts to protect biodiversity, manage water resources sustainably, and transition toward renewable energy sources.

A crucial aspect of this global shift is the increasing emphasis on sustainable development. This holistic approach integrates economic, social, and environmental considerations, acknowledging that genuine progress cannot be achieved at the expense of environmental sustainability. The Sustainable Development Goals (SDGs), adopted by the United Nations in 2015, provide a comprehensive framework for achieving sustainable development by 2030. These goals address a wide range of issues, from poverty and hunger to climate action and life below water, recognizing their interconnectedness and the need for integrated solutions. The SDGs serve as a blueprint for global action, guiding policies and investments toward a more sustainable future.

Technological advancements have played a pivotal role in achieving global sustainability. Renewable energy technologies, such as solar and wind power, are rapidly becoming more efficient and cost-effective, offering a viable alternative to fossil fuels. Improvements in energy storage technology are addressing the intermittency of renewable sources, making them a more reliable energy supply. In agriculture, precision farming techniques, leveraging satellite imagery and sensor data, are optimizing resource use, reducing waste, and increasing yields while minimizing environmental impact. Similarly, advancements in water management technologies are enhancing water use efficiency in agriculture and industry, helping to address water scarcity.

Beyond technological solutions, a critical element of global sustainability is the empowerment of local communities. Indigenous and local communities hold invaluable knowledge and traditional practices that can contribute to sustainable resource management and environmental conservation. Their participation is not merely beneficial; it is essential for ensuring that sustainability initiatives are culturally appropriate and environmentally sound.

Empowering these communities often involves securing land rights, providing access to education and training, and ensuring their voices are heard in decision-making processes. This participatory approach recognizes the importance of community-based conservation, acknowledging that effective environmental management must be rooted in local contexts and involve those who are most directly affected.

Education and public awareness campaigns are instrumental in fostering a global culture of sustainability. By raising awareness of environmental issues and promoting sustainable lifestyles, we can encourage individuals to make conscious choices that benefit the planet. From reducing our carbon footprint to embracing sustainable consumption patterns, individual actions can collectively contribute to a more sustainable future.

This change in mindset is not simply about individual responsibility; it reflects a broader shift in values, a growing understanding of our interconnectedness with the natural world, and a commitment to intergenerational equity.

The financial sector has also begun to play a significant role in driving global sustainability. The growing recognition of environmental, social, and governance (ESG) factors in investment decisions is leading to increased investment in sustainable businesses and projects. Sustainable finance initiatives are mobilizing capital toward renewable energy, sustainable agriculture, and other environmentally friendly ventures. This influx of capital is not just beneficial for the environment; it creates economic opportunities, stimulates innovation, and promotes sustainable economic growth. The integration of ESG factors into investment strategies is transforming the financial landscape, aligning financial incentives with environmental goals.

The journey toward global sustainability is far from over. Challenges remain, including the need to address inequalities, enhance global cooperation, and implement effective policies to curb environmental degradation. However, the progress made so far demonstrates the power of collective action, the potential of technological innovation, and the importance of a shift in societal values. Global sustainability is not merely an environmental goal; it is a pathway toward a more equitable, prosperous, and resilient future for all.

The interconnectedness of global challenges necessitates a global response, one that transcends national boundaries and fosters collaborative efforts toward a common goal. This journey requires a sustained commitment, continuous innovation, and unwavering dedication from individuals, communities, businesses, and governments alike. Only through a united global effort can we achieve a future where both humanity and the planet thrive. The vision is clear; the path is challenging, yet the destination a sustainable and thriving planet is worth the collective effort.

CHAPTER FIFTEEN
THE FUTURE OF EDEN

Eden Prime, once a desolate wasteland ravaged by decades of unsustainable practices, now stands as a beacon of hope, a testament to the transformative power of human ingenuity and collective will. Its resurrection is not a mere environmental success story; it is a societal and economic revolution, a living laboratory demonstrating the feasibility and desirability of a truly sustainable future. The principles guiding Eden Prime's transformation are now being emulated globally, inspiring communities to embrace eco-conscious lifestyles and contributing to a burgeoning global movement toward environmental stewardship.

The heart of Eden Prime's success lies in its holistic approach, seamlessly integrating economic prosperity, social equity, and environmental protection. This was not achieved overnight; it was a gradual, iterative process shaped by trial and error, adaptation, and continuous learning. Early efforts focused on remediation – cleaning up the polluted soil and water, restoring degraded ecosystems, and mitigating the effects of past environmental damage.

This involved innovative technologies, including bioremediation techniques to detoxify contaminated land, advanced water purification systems, and the development of resilient agricultural practices adapted to the region's unique challenges. The community actively involved itself in the cleanup, transforming the initial burden of remediation into a shared endeavor that fostered community cohesion and instilled a sense of collective responsibility.

Simultaneously, Eden Prime prioritized the development of renewable energy sources. Harnessing the region's abundant solar and wind resources, it established a robust, decentralized energy grid, eliminating dependence on fossil fuels and significantly reducing the community's carbon footprint. This transition was not solely about technological advancement; it also involved significant changes in energy consumption patterns. Education campaigns promoted energy efficiency, responsible consumption, and a shift toward a more sustainable lifestyle. The community embraced a circular economy model, minimizing waste through recycling, composting, and upcycling initiatives. This focus on resource efficiency was not just about reducing environmental impact; it also boosted the local economy, creating new jobs and opportunities in recycling, waste management, and renewable energy sectors.

Agriculture in Eden Prime has been completely revolutionized. Traditional, resource-intensive farming practices have been replaced by regenerative agriculture techniques. These methods focus on soil health, biodiversity, and minimizing environmental impact. Permaculture principles are widely adopted, creating resilient and productive food systems that require minimal external inputs.

The emphasis on local and sustainable food production has strengthened food security, reduced reliance on long-distance transportation, and supported local farmers and businesses. The community gardens, collectively managed and providing fresh produce to residents, have become integral parts of the social fabric, fostering community interaction and a sense of shared ownership.

Beyond the environmental and economic achievements, Eden Prime showcases the importance of social equity and inclusion in building a sustainable society. The community has actively involved marginalized groups in the planning and implementation of sustainability initiatives, ensuring that the benefits of the transition are shared equitably among all residents.

This has involved creating opportunities for education and training, supporting local businesses owned by underrepresented groups, and addressing historical injustices that have contributed to environmental and social inequalities. The community also emphasized the importance of preserving indigenous knowledge and traditional ecological practices, recognizing their value in creating sustainable and resilient communities. The integration of traditional practices with modern technology has created a unique and effective approach to sustainable living.

Eden Prime's success is not solely attributed to technological advancements; it is equally, if not more, a product of a significant shift in societal values and consciousness. The community embraced a culture of cooperation, shared responsibility, and collective action. Decision-making processes are inclusive and participatory, ensuring that all voices are heard and considered. This fosters a strong sense of community ownership and responsibility for the shared environment.

Educational programs and awareness campaigns have played a vital role in shaping this cultural transformation. These initiatives aimed not only to impart knowledge but also to inspire action and foster a sense of collective responsibility. The focus on long-term sustainability, rather than immediate gains, has fostered a mindset of intergenerational equity, recognizing the responsibility to leave a healthy planet for future generations.

The transformative journey of Eden Prime provides a compelling case study for other communities striving to achieve sustainability. Its success demonstrates that sustainability is not an unattainable utopia; it is a viable and desirable path toward a more equitable, prosperous, and resilient future. The community's holistic approach, integrating environmental, economic, and social considerations, provides a valuable blueprint for other communities to follow. Eden Prime's model showcases the importance of community participation, collaborative governance, and a long-term perspective in achieving sustainability goals.

The lessons learned in Eden Prime have spurred a global movement toward sustainable living. Communities around the world are drawing inspiration from Eden Prime's success, adapting its principles and practices to their own unique contexts. The sharing of knowledge, technologies, and best practices has created a collaborative network of sustainable communities, fostering a global conversation about environmental stewardship and the creation of more sustainable and equitable societies. This global network has not only facilitated the dissemination of successful strategies but has also enabled collaborative problem-solving, leveraging collective intelligence to address shared challenges.

Moreover, Eden Prime has attracted significant attention from researchers, policymakers, and international organizations. The community serves as a living laboratory for sustainable development, providing valuable data and insights that are informing global sustainability initiatives. Studies conducted in Eden Prime are providing crucial evidence of the effectiveness of various sustainability strategies, contributing to the development of evidence-based policies and guidelines. International collaborations have emerged, with Eden Prime serving as a model for sustainable urban planning, renewable energy deployment, and community-based resource management.

Beyond its practical contributions, Eden Prime's story holds deep symbolic value. It represents a shift from a paradigm of environmental degradation to one of environmental restoration and renewal. It is a powerful narrative of hope, demonstrating that even in the face of seemingly insurmountable environmental challenges, human ingenuity and collective action can bring about positive transformation.

This narrative resonates globally, inspiring individuals and communities to believe in the possibility of a sustainable future and encouraging them to actively participate in building a more environmentally conscious world.

The story of Eden Prime's rebirth is a potent antidote to environmental despair, fostering a sense of agency and empowering people to become active agents of change.

The legacy of Eden Prime extends far beyond its geographical boundaries. It is a powerful symbol of hope, demonstrating that sustainable living is not merely a theoretical aspiration but a tangible reality. Its success is a testament to the power of human collaboration, innovation, and a shared commitment to a better future for all. The principles and practices developed in Eden Prime continue to inspire communities worldwide, providing a blueprint for a more sustainable and just world. The journey toward global sustainability remains ongoing, but Eden Prime stands as a beacon of what is possible, illuminating the path toward a future where humanity and nature can coexist in harmony. It is a future worth striving for, a future where the lessons learned in Eden Prime become the guiding principles for a world striving for balance and lasting prosperity. The impact of Eden Prime's example will undoubtedly continue to reshape our understanding of what is possible, inspiring generations to come to embrace a more sustainable and equitable way of life.

The blueprint for Eden Prime's success was not solely technological; it was woven into the very fabric of its community. It was a societal shift, a conscious uncoupling from the relentless pursuit of material wealth and a re-engagement with the intrinsic value of the natural world. This transition was not imposed from above; it was organically grown from the grassroots, a testament to the power of collective action and shared vision. The community embraced a philosophy of *slow living*, prioritizing quality of life over the relentless accumulation of possessions.

This involved a conscious reduction in consumerism, a shift toward locally sourced goods and services, and a renewed emphasis on community-building activities. Local markets thrived, showcasing the bounty of the region's regenerated agricultural systems and fostering direct connections between producers and consumers. This shift not only reduced environmental impact but also bolstered the local economy, creating a virtuous cycle of sustainability and prosperity.

Education played a pivotal role in shaping this new societal consciousness. From early childhood, residents were immersed in environmental literacy programs, learning about the intricate interconnectedness of ecosystems and the vital role humans play in maintaining ecological balance. These programs were not just about imparting facts and figures; they focused on fostering a deep appreciation for nature, instilling a sense of responsibility, and cultivating a mindful approach to consumption. Adult education programs continued this effort, offering workshops on sustainable living, permaculture, renewable energy technologies, and community-based resource management. This continuous learning process ensured that the community remained adaptable and innovative, constantly refining its approaches to sustainability. The emphasis on lifelong learning fostered a culture of continuous improvement, ensuring that Eden Prime remained at the forefront of sustainable practices.

The governance structure of Eden Prime mirrored its commitment to participatory democracy. Decision-making processes were decentralized and inclusive, ensuring that all voices were heard and considered. Community councils, comprised of elected representatives from various sectors of society, oversaw the planning and implementation of sustainability initiatives. These councils fostered open dialogue and collaboration, ensuring that policies reflected the needs and priorities of the entire community. This participatory approach not only enhanced the effectiveness of sustainability efforts but also strengthened the social fabric, fostering a sense of shared ownership and responsibility. Transparency and accountability were paramount, ensuring that community members had access to information and could hold their leaders accountable for their actions.

The economic model of Eden Prime fundamentally departed from the traditional growth-oriented paradigm. The community prioritized quality of life over economic growth, focusing on creating a stable and equitable economy that met the needs of all residents while minimizing environmental impact. This involved the development of a circular economy, minimizing waste and maximizing resource efficiency. Recycling and composting programs were highly effective, diverting significant amounts of waste from landfills. Upcycling initiatives transformed discarded materials into new products, extending the lifespan of resources and reducing the demand for virgin materials. This approach not only minimized environmental impact but also created new economic opportunities in the recycling, waste management, and upcycling industries.

Furthermore, the community actively cultivated a diverse range of economic activities. Beyond agriculture and renewable energy, Eden Prime supported a vibrant ecosystem of local businesses, promoting entrepreneurship and innovation in sustainable sectors. These businesses not only contributed to the local economy but also provided valuable employment opportunities, empowering residents and fostering economic independence. The emphasis on local production and consumption strengthened the community's resilience, reducing its dependence on external factors and enhancing its ability to withstand economic shocks. This approach fostered a sense of economic security and stability, allowing residents to focus on enhancing their quality of life rather than chasing fleeting material gains.

Beyond the tangible achievements, Eden Prime's success lies in its intangible assets: its strong sense of community, its shared values, and its collective commitment to sustainability. The community's social fabric is richly woven, characterized by mutual respect, trust, and collaboration. Residents actively participate in community events, volunteering their time and skills to support various initiatives. This sense of collective identity and purpose fosters resilience, enabling the community to overcome challenges and adapt to changing circumstances. The community's commitment to social equity and inclusion ensures that the benefits of sustainability are shared equitably among all residents.

The remarkable transformation of Eden Prime offers a potent counter-narrative to the prevailing narrative of environmental doom and gloom. It demonstrates that a sustainable future is not merely a utopian ideal but a tangible possibility, attainable through human ingenuity, collective action, and a profound shift in societal values. The journey was not without its obstacles; the community faced challenges related to technological limitations, economic constraints, and social resistance to change. However, through perseverance, adaptation, and continuous learning, Eden Prime overcame these challenges and emerged as a beacon of hope for a more sustainable world.

The lessons learned in Eden Prime are invaluable, offering a roadmap for other communities striving to achieve sustainability. It is a testament to the power of human agency, showcasing what is possible when individuals, communities, and governments work together toward a common goal. The community's holistic approach, integrating environmental, economic, and social considerations, provides a valuable framework for other communities to adapt and implement. Eden Prime's success is not just about environmental protection; it is about creating a more just, equitable, and resilient society, where humans and nature coexist in harmony.

The impact of Eden Prime extends far beyond its geographical boundaries, inspiring communities worldwide to embrace sustainable practices. Its success serves as a potent catalyst for global change, demonstrating the viability of a sustainable future and providing a blueprint for others to follow. The story of Eden Prime is not just a story of environmental success; it is a story of human resilience, innovation, and the transformative power of collective action. It is a narrative that offers hope and inspiration, reminding us that even in the face of seemingly insurmountable challenges, a sustainable future is within our reach. Eden Prime's legacy is one of hope, resilience, and the unwavering belief in the power of human collaboration to build a better world for present and future generations. It stands as a testament to the extraordinary potential of human ingenuity when harnessed for the common good. The world watches, learns, and adapts, drawing strength and guidance from Eden Prime's enduring example.

The success of Eden Prime did not remain confined to its verdant domes and meticulously managed ecosystems. News of its thriving, sustainable society spread like wildfire across the solar system, initially met with skepticism and then with growing fascination. The initial wave of disbelief, understandable given the prevailing narratives of resource depletion and environmental collapse on Earth and other colonized planets, gradually gave way to cautious optimism.

Scientists, initially driven by curiosity, began conducting rigorous studies of Eden Prime's unique model. Their findings, meticulously documented and widely disseminated, confirmed the feasibility of Eden Prime's approach. The data painted a compelling picture of a society that not only survived but thrived in harmony with its environment, achieving a level of sustainability previously thought impossible.

This burgeoning interest ignited a wave of interplanetary dialogue. Representatives from various colonies and space stations, facing their own environmental challenges, reached out to Eden Prime, seeking guidance and collaboration. Initially, these interactions were tentative, characterized by cautious exchanges of information and technological know-how.

However, as the evidence of Eden Prime's success mounted, these exchanges evolved into a more formal, structured collaboration. An Interplanetary Sustainability Council was formed, comprising representatives from Eden Prime and various other spacefaring communities. This council served as a platform for sharing best practices, coordinating research efforts, and addressing common environmental challenges on a cosmic scale.

One of the first collaborative initiatives undertaken by the council involved the development of advanced, self-regulating agricultural systems. Eden Prime's success in regenerating depleted soils and developing highly efficient hydroponic systems inspired other colonies to adopt similar technologies. The council facilitated the sharing of genetic material and agricultural techniques, accelerating the adoption of sustainable farming practices across the solar system. This collaborative effort led to a significant reduction in the ecological footprint of various colonies, mitigating the strain on local resources and lessening the environmental impact of food production.

Another area of significant collaboration was in the realm of renewable energy. Eden Prime's pioneering work in harnessing solar, wind, and geothermal energy served as a model for other communities seeking to transition away from fossil fuels. The council facilitated the transfer of technological expertise and the sharing of blueprints for advanced energy systems. This collaboration accelerated the adoption of renewable energy technologies across the solar system, contributing significantly to the reduction of greenhouse gas emissions and the mitigation of climate change.

Beyond the technical aspects, the council also addressed social and governance issues. Eden Prime's commitment to participatory democracy and its emphasis on social equity served as an inspiration for other communities seeking to improve their governance structures. The council organized workshops and training sessions on participatory decision-making, conflict resolution, and community-building techniques. This exchange of ideas and experiences helped foster a more collaborative and inclusive approach to governance in various colonies, promoting social harmony and strengthening community resilience.

The collaborative efforts extended beyond specific projects and initiatives. The council fostered a culture of mutual learning and support, encouraging communities to share their experiences, challenges, and successes. This open exchange of information facilitated innovation and accelerated the adoption of sustainable practices. It also fostered a sense of shared responsibility and collective action, underscoring the importance of working together to address environmental challenges on a cosmic scale.

The council became a vital platform for networking and collaboration, connecting scientists, engineers, policymakers, and community leaders from across the solar system. This network of experts worked together to develop solutions to complex environmental problems, promoting innovation and fostering a global understanding of sustainable development.

The success of the Interplanetary Sustainability Council stemmed from a fundamental shift in perspective. Rather than viewing other communities as competitors, the members embraced a spirit of cooperation and mutual benefit. They recognized that environmental challenges transcended geographical boundaries and that a collaborative approach was essential for addressing them effectively. This spirit of cooperation led to the creation of a powerful network that amplified the collective impact of individual communities. The shared understanding of the interconnectedness of planetary systems fostered a collective responsibility to protect and preserve the environment. This approach went beyond simply sharing technologies and expertise; it fostered a deeper understanding of the interconnectedness of human society and the environment.

One striking example of this cooperation was the joint effort to restore the damaged atmosphere of Mars. This ambitious project, involving scientists and engineers from multiple colonies, utilized advanced technologies developed in Eden Prime and other communities to introduce oxygen-producing microorganisms into the Martian atmosphere. While the project was still in its early stages, the collective effort and shared commitment demonstrated the transformative power of interplanetary cooperation. This initiative highlighted humanity's capacity to undertake ambitious, large-scale projects when working collaboratively, transcending national and even planetary boundaries.

The creation of an interplanetary archive of environmental data was another significant achievement. This centralized database, accessible to all participating communities, collated information on diverse ecosystems, climate patterns, and environmental challenges. It served as a valuable resource for researchers and policymakers, allowing them to analyze global trends, identify potential problems, and develop comprehensive solutions. The open sharing of this data underscored the importance of transparency and collective action in addressing global challenges.

As the years passed, the influence of the council extended beyond environmental issues. It became a forum for discussing and addressing social and economic inequalities across the solar system. This holistic approach to sustainability recognized that environmental health was inextricably linked to social justice and economic stability. The council fostered initiatives to promote equitable access to resources, opportunities, and technologies, striving to create a more just and sustainable future for all inhabitants of the solar system.

The council facilitated programs aimed at educating the public about the importance of sustainability, emphasizing the interconnectedness of all planetary systems and the need for collective action. These programs helped raise awareness and encourage participation in various sustainability initiatives.

The legacy of the Interplanetary Cooperation was not just about technological advancements or policy changes. It was about fostering a new paradigm of human interaction, one characterized by collaboration, shared responsibility, and a profound respect for the environment. It was a testament to humanity's ability to learn from its past mistakes and build a more sustainable and equitable future for generations to come, transcending the limitations of individual planets and embracing a shared destiny among the stars.

The story of Eden Prime became a symbol of this new era, a beacon of hope demonstrating that unity and cooperation can overcome seemingly insurmountable challenges. The lessons learned, shared, and implemented across the cosmos created a legacy far exceeding the bounds of any single planet, leaving an indelible mark on the future of human civilization. The interconnectedness of humanity, once a concept relegated to philosophical discussions, had become a tangible reality, forged in the fires of necessity and cemented by the enduring power of shared purpose.

The success of Eden Prime, however, was not solely reliant on its initial technological breakthroughs or its meticulously planned ecosystems. Its enduring prosperity hinged on a commitment to continuous learning and adaptation. The Eden Prime model was not static; it was a dynamic system constantly evolving and refining itself in response to new challenges and emerging opportunities. This commitment to lifelong learning permeated every aspect of Eden Prime society, from its educational institutions to its governance structures.

The educational system of Eden Prime was not merely focused on imparting knowledge; it emphasized critical thinking, problem-solving, and adaptability. Students were encouraged to question established norms, explore innovative solutions, and embrace lifelong learning as a fundamental aspect of their lives.

The curriculum included a strong emphasis on environmental science, sustainable technologies, and collaborative problem-solving, preparing students for the challenges and opportunities of a rapidly changing world. This was not a theoretical exercise; practical application was at the heart of their education. Students were actively involved in research projects, contributing to ongoing initiatives and helping to shape the future of Eden Prime.

Beyond formal education, continuous learning was woven into the fabric of daily life on Eden Prime. The community embraced a culture of experimentation and innovation, encouraging citizens to share their knowledge and experiences. Regular workshops, seminars, and community forums provided opportunities for ongoing learning and collaboration. Experts from diverse fields shared their knowledge, sparking new ideas and collaborative ventures. This constant exchange of ideas fostered a dynamic and adaptable society, capable of responding effectively to unexpected challenges.

This commitment to continuous learning extended to the governance structures of Eden Prime. The council, far from being a static body, evolved in response to the changing needs of the community. Regular reviews of policies and practices ensured that the system remained adaptable and responsive to emerging challenges. The council actively sought feedback from the community, incorporating citizen input into its decision-making process. This participatory approach fostered a sense of ownership and responsibility, promoting a more resilient and adaptable governance system.

One significant area where continuous learning proved crucial was in the management of Eden Prime's ecosystems. The initial success of the meticulously planned environments did not guarantee their long-term stability. The team of ecologists and environmental scientists continuously monitored the ecosystems, analyzing data and adjusting their management strategies as needed. Unexpected weather patterns, unforeseen interactions between species, and changes in resource availability required ongoing adjustments. This necessitated a flexible and adaptive approach, with a willingness to experiment and learn from both successes and failures.

The development of new technologies was also intrinsically linked to continuous learning. Eden Prime's scientists and engineers did not simply develop and deploy technologies; they continually refined and improved them based on ongoing feedback and new discoveries. This iterative process ensured that the technologies remained effective and efficient, adapting to changing conditions and technological advancements. The open-source nature of many of Eden Prime's technologies further encouraged this cycle of continuous improvement, fostering collaboration and accelerating innovation.

The sharing of knowledge and expertise was not limited to Eden Prime. The Interplanetary Sustainability Council played a crucial role in facilitating continuous learning across the solar system. Regular conferences, workshops, and collaborative research projects encouraged the exchange of ideas and the development of best practices. This facilitated the rapid adoption of new technologies and management strategies, accelerating the progress toward sustainability across various communities.

The council also played a vital role in adapting to unforeseen challenges. For example, when a previously unknown pathogen threatened agricultural production on several colonies, the council coordinated a rapid response. Scientists from across the solar system collaborated to identify the pathogen, develop treatments, and implement preventive measures. The shared knowledge and collaborative effort ensured a swift and effective response, preventing a major agricultural crisis.

The emphasis on continuous learning was not just confined to technological or scientific domains. It extended to the social and cultural aspects of life on Eden Prime and across the collaborating communities. As societies adapted to sustainable living, social structures evolved. The importance of community cohesion, conflict resolution, and equitable resource distribution was continually revisited and refined, ensuring social harmony alongside environmental sustainability. Cultural exchanges also played a crucial role. Different communities shared their knowledge of resource management, conflict resolution, and social structures, fostering a deeper understanding of the challenges and opportunities involved in building sustainable and equitable societies.

The Interplanetary Sustainability Council actively promoted lifelong learning through various initiatives. It established a vast online library of resources, including scientific papers, educational materials, and best practices from across the solar system. This readily accessible information fostered collaborative research and accelerated the adoption of innovative solutions. The council also funded research projects focused on sustainable technologies, resource management, and social equity, driving innovation and accelerating progress toward a sustainable future. Regular workshops and training sessions were held, covering diverse topics from sustainable agriculture to conflict resolution and intercultural communication.

Furthermore, the council facilitated the development of virtual reality and augmented reality training programs, providing immersive and engaging learning experiences. These programs simulated various environmental challenges and allowed participants to practice applying sustainable practices in realistic scenarios. They fostered critical thinking, problem-solving skills, and collaborative learning in an accessible and engaging way. The result was a highly trained workforce across the participating communities, equipped with the skills needed to address the challenges of a sustainable future.

The ongoing monitoring and evaluation of the effectiveness of different sustainability initiatives were integral to the continuous learning process. The Interplanetary Sustainability Council established rigorous data collection and analysis protocols to track the impact of various programs and initiatives. This data-driven approach enabled the identification of best practices, the refinement of existing strategies, and the development of more effective approaches. This cyclical process of evaluation, adaptation, and improvement ensured that the efforts toward sustainability remained dynamic and responsive to changing circumstances.

The long-term success of Eden Prime and the broader interplanetary collaboration rested on the unwavering commitment to continuous learning and adaptation. It demonstrated that a truly sustainable future required not just innovative technologies and effective governance, but also a culture of lifelong learning, collaboration, and a willingness to embrace change. The shared understanding and collective effort in addressing environmental challenges established a new paradigm for human civilization, one where continuous learning became not just a desirable trait, but a prerequisite for survival and prosperity. The legacy of this collective endeavor extended far beyond individual colonies and planets, shaping a future where adaptation and ongoing learning were the cornerstones of a truly sustainable existence. This interplanetary cooperation, fueled by a shared thirst for knowledge and a commitment to progress, represented a powerful testament to humanity's capacity for growth, collaboration, and the enduring pursuit of a sustainable future among the stars.

The very air we breathe, the water we drink, and the soil that nourishes our food are all testaments to this profound interconnectedness. The health of the planet is inextricably linked to the well-being of humanity. This understanding, once a philosophical notion, has become the cornerstone of Eden Prime's enduring success and the foundation of the broader interplanetary collaboration. The shared destiny is not just a concept; it is a lived reality, a fundamental principle guiding every decision, every action, and every innovation on Eden Prime and beyond.

The initial success of terraforming was not simply a technological triumph; it was a profound recognition of our symbiotic relationship with the environment. Eden Prime was not merely constructed; it was meticulously cultivated, a delicate balance between human ambition and environmental stewardship. The ecosystems were not treated as passive resources to be exploited; they were active participants in a vibrant, self-regulating system. The understanding that our survival depended on the health of the planet permeated every aspect of life on Eden Prime.

This understanding extended beyond the purely scientific realm. It transformed the social fabric of Eden Prime, shaping its cultural values and ethical framework. The economic systems were designed not to maximize profit at the expense of the environment, but to promote sustainable growth and equitable resource distribution. A deep respect for nature was ingrained in the cultural ethos, reflected in art, literature, and daily life. Children were raised with a profound understanding of their place within the larger ecosystem, learning to appreciate the delicate balance of nature and their role in maintaining it.

The educational system, as mentioned before, went beyond mere textbook learning. It fostered a deep appreciation for the interconnectedness of all living things, encouraging students to view themselves not as separate from nature, but as integral parts of it. Practical experience was emphasized, with students actively involved in environmental monitoring, restoration projects, and sustainable agricultural practices. They learned not just about the science of ecology, but the art of living in harmony with the planet.

This holistic approach to education extended into the broader community. Citizens were encouraged to participate in citizen science initiatives, contributing to ongoing research and monitoring efforts. Community gardens and urban farms thrived, fostering a sense of connection to the food system and promoting sustainable agricultural practices. Regular community events celebrated the achievements of environmental stewardship and highlighted the importance of preserving the planet's biodiversity.

The Interplanetary Sustainability Council played a pivotal role in disseminating this ethos of shared destiny across the solar system. The council did not merely focus on technological solutions; it emphasized the crucial role of cultural exchange and the adoption of sustainable practices across diverse communities. The sharing of knowledge and experiences was not limited to scientific breakthroughs; it extended to traditional ecological knowledge, indigenous wisdom, and diverse cultural perspectives on environmental stewardship.

One striking example of this cultural exchange was the adoption of permaculture techniques developed by a community on Kepler-186f. These techniques, adapted to the specific conditions of each planet, revolutionized agricultural practices, dramatically increasing crop yields while minimizing environmental impact. The sharing of this knowledge sparked a wave of innovation and adaptation across various colonies, demonstrating the power of cross-cultural collaboration in addressing environmental challenges.

Another significant contribution of the council was the development of virtual reality simulations that allowed people to experience the impact of different environmental policies and actions. These simulations were not just educational tools; they fostered empathy and understanding, allowing people to visualize the consequences of their actions on the environment and on future generations. These immersive experiences profoundly impacted decision-making processes, leading to more informed and responsible choices.

The council also established a comprehensive system for monitoring and evaluating the effectiveness of sustainable practices across the solar system. This data-driven approach enabled continuous improvement, allowing communities to adapt their strategies in response to changing conditions and new challenges. The sharing of this data fostered a culture of transparency and accountability, promoting a sense of shared responsibility for the planet's well-being.

The concept of a shared destiny was not simply about environmental stewardship; it encompassed the social and economic dimensions of sustainability as well. The council actively promoted equitable resource distribution, ensuring that the benefits of sustainable development were shared fairly across all communities. This commitment to social justice was an integral part of the broader sustainability agenda, recognizing that environmental degradation and social inequality were deeply intertwined.

The council's initiatives extended beyond the realm of formal policy and governance. It fostered a culture of environmental activism and citizen engagement, empowering individuals to become agents of change. Community-led initiatives thrived, with citizens actively involved in environmental restoration projects, waste reduction programs, and the promotion of sustainable lifestyles. This grassroots movement amplified the impact of the council's efforts, creating a powerful force for positive change across the solar system.

The journey toward a shared destiny was not without its challenges. Technological setbacks, unforeseen environmental changes, and social conflicts tested the resilience of the interplanetary collaboration. However, the commitment to continuous learning, adaptation, and collaborative problem-solving allowed the communities to navigate these obstacles, emerging stronger and more united.

The shared destiny of humanity and the planet is not a utopian ideal; it is a challenging but achievable goal. It demands a fundamental shift in our mindset, a transition from a worldview that prioritizes individual gain at the expense of the environment to one that recognizes the inherent interconnectedness of all living things. It requires a commitment to continuous learning, adaptation, and collaboration, a willingness to embrace change, and the courage to confront the challenges of a rapidly changing world.

The legacy of Eden Prime and the broader interplanetary collaboration is a testament to the power of shared purpose and collective action. It is a beacon of hope, demonstrating that a sustainable future is not merely a possibility, but a tangible reality. It showcases the transformative potential of human ingenuity, collaboration, and a deep respect for the planet we call home. The shared destiny is not just a narrative; it is a living testament to our capacity for resilience, innovation, and the unwavering pursuit of a future where humanity and the planet thrive together. It is a future where the stars themselves bear witness to a symbiotic relationship, a harmonious dance between humanity and the cosmos, a future built not on exploitation but on understanding, cooperation, and the enduring power of a shared destiny.

AUTHOR'S NOTE

*T**he Legacy of Eden* was born from a deep reverence for our planet and a conviction that storytelling can be a powerful force for change.

As I wrote this book, I found myself thinking often of the real-world individuals who quietly and tirelessly dedicate themselves to healing the Earth—scientists, activists, Indigenous leaders, educators, and everyday citizens who plant seeds of renewal in a world too often focused on extraction. This story is my tribute to them and to you, the reader, who dares to imagine a future shaped not by fear but by care.

The journey of Eden Prime reflects more than a fictional path forward. It is a meditation on resilience, cooperation, and the possibility of harmony between technology and nature. I hope it sparks questions, conversation, and courage.

If you felt moved by this book, I invite you to learn more about environmental stewardship in your own community. Every small act, every seed planted, every species protected, every voice raised, contributes to a legacy worth leaving behind.

Thank you for reading. May you walk gently and boldly on this Earth.

Diane Kann

ABOUT THE AUTHOR

Diane Kann writes eco-speculative science fiction and fantasy that blends wonder with urgency, exploring the edges of technology, memory, and planetary healing. Their novels invite readers to imagine a world where hope isn't naïve; it's revolutionary.

When not writing, they can be found spending time with family, their pet dogs, and dreaming of futures worth fighting for.

EXPLORE THE ECHO LEGACY UNIVERSE

The Echo Legacy Universe

The Legacy of Eden is Book 4 in the Echo Legacy Universe. Explore the full journey:

The Aquatica Chronicles

    1. Beneath the Triangle

    2. Shattered Resonance

    3. The Convergence Protocol

The Eden Sequence

4. The Legacy of Eden

5. The Orchard of Reverence

And the stories continue...

For bonus stories, reading guides, and timeline maps, visit [dmvolans.com].

DISCUSSION & REFLECTION GUIDE

Perfect for book clubs, classrooms, or individual reflection.

Reflection Questions

1. What does Eden Prime symbolize in today's world?

2. How did the integration of traditional knowledge and AI challenge your understanding of progress?

3. Were there moments that made you feel hopeful or uneasy about our own environmental future? Why?

4. Which character's journey resonated most with you?

5. If you could design your own *Eden*, what would it look like?

ACKNOWLEDGMENTS

T hank those who supported the writing journey: editors, beta readers, family, researchers, and others. A special thanks to my family, who encouraged and supported me during the long hours of research, writing, editing, and promotion.

www.ingramcontent.com/pod-product-compliance
Lightning Source LLC
Chambersburg PA
CBHW020129310726
48970CB00006B/1788